I0452698

THE EMPTY SPACES
a concept novel

BRIAN S HALL

First Edition: November 2011
ISBN: 978-0615551333

The Empty Spaces is a novel about chocolate, marijuana, smartphones, working for a living, outer space and the space between us all. It was inspired by The Beatles.

This is a work of fiction.

Synopsis

Jackie Paper is a hot shot coder who hopes to strike it rich when he creates a smartphone app that determines each user's mood, exactly, then plays a song to match their mood.
It is never wrong.
The app, which Jackie christens Empty Spaces, even seeks out others nearby that feel and hear exactly the same.
Empty Spaces becomes wildly popular, spurring both investor interest and new forms of social contact. What Jackie can't share is that his app is also a secret method of contacting extraterrestrials.
For he is certain they are out there.

[EMPTY SPACE]

To A & P
"You can go your own way.
Don't go away."

"Reaching out. Touching me. Touching you."
Neil Diamond

Playlist

Pipes of Peace

Imagine

Walls and Bridges

Venus and Mars

Sentimental Journey

Blast From Your Past

Band on the Run

All Things Must Pass

Cloud Nine

The Band

Jackie Paper, it's a steady job but

JaDe Shockwatel, taking the easy way out

Prudence Skiffle, see the world spinning round

Pamela Ann Drogeny, how does it feel to be

Reginald Kenneth Orville (RKO) Nutt Barr, see how they run

Francis Howerd Mustard, and nobody seems to like him

Session Players

Sickspack Shankar, I need to make you see

Michelle Maybelle, everybody's got something to hide

Geraldine (nee Nutt) Barr, they have taken her away

Theo Preston, move over once move over twice

Maxwell Edison, hey bulldog

Cyn Skiffle, for no one

Gong Shwo, you don't know what you're missing

Honah Lee, getting better all the time

Ganja Patois, it couldn't get much worse

TRACK ONE
Pipes of Peace

Paperback Writer

"Tell me. I want to know everything."

"What else to say? They passed."

"Completely?"

"No interest. Fuckers."

"Damn. None?"

"Sky Saxon Ltd declined to invest in our technology. The search for life continues. Plus they hated the name. "

"Name could be better. Empty Spaces?"

"A technology that can predict what song a person wants to hear even before they know they want to hear it. That learns its user's mood. Soon, I can make it hop from smartphone to smartphone like magic. Fucking magic."

"Agreed."

"Leaving now. For good."

"Did they choke on the dollars?"

"Just a million five is all I asked for."

"Just?"

"Should have asked for more. I talked big then asked small. Lesson learned. Not like they're hurting. Bet they spent more than a million on this crappy hotel chain carpet and these god awful cubicles. Good riddance."

"Wait. Leaving for good? Not just the day? You said fund my idea or I quit?"

"Heat of the moment. Wise, no?"

"No. But, you're smart. You'll get another job."

"Don't want another job. That's why I created this."

"We always have my diversion."

"Selling pot? Does selling pot scale?"

"Shit. Ask fucking Saskatchewan if pot scales. Hold on. Gotta take this call."

"Later."

"Nevermind. False alarm."

"Taking the Seabus back to the apartment. Pick up some dinner?"

"Sushi."

"Again? Had that the other night. Thai?"

"Iron Butterfly?"

"That works."

"You buying?"

"Always do. Any changes in the numbers?"

"Numbers look good. I think you have a winner, my friend. Sending now."

[Empty Spaces downloads: 37,3xx]

"Almost 40,000. seems like a lot. Up from just this morning."

"Yes, it does. Plus, I know a guy willing to trade a couple used cable TV servers for some well-tended BC bud."

"This is why we're partners. That should carry us through till we can get real funding."

"Funding may require a business model. Revenues. Isn't that what investors want?"

"Business plan. Next on the list. Hold on. Getting on the Seabus. Off grid for a couple minutes."

"Revenues maybe not so much of an issue. Investors primarily want users. We have users. They want recurrent usage. Done. Business model flows from that."

"What's that? Didn't catch it?"

"Lots of business model options, I expect."

"Now you have plenty of time to write them down. Shit. Now you're gonna be in the apartment all the time."

"Funny. First and foremost, it's a music recommendation service. I think that's our entry point. Music is universal. It's easy to lock in on a person's feelings with music. Everyone's focused on location, on identity. Wrong. Feelings are the undiscovered market."

"I got none of that. You on the water?"

"Fuck. Yes on the water."

"Ok. No job, plenty of time to finalize a business plan."

"Works better if I can show people. Like magic."

"Better for you, maybe. This is business, right? Seems to me if you want their money they will demand a actual business plan."

"Agreed. There in an hour."

"Sushi?"

"Thai. Already settled."

"Out."

Get Back

Having reviewed thousands of texts, calls, blog entries, social profiles, status updates, comments, user playlists, emails, check-ins and other documents, I am confident that this work provides a truthful telling of the continuing story of Empty Spaces.

Jackie Paper, age 29, resident of Vancouver, British Columbia, created a free mobile phone program which he christened 'Empty Spaces.' Empty Spaces could recognize a user's mood, in real-time, and select songs to perfectly match their mood. The chosen song would play in the user's ear piece, phone or speaker, as selected. Empty Spaces succeeded beyond even Jackie's own lofty expectations. At its peak, Empty Spaces reached approximately 40 million active users.

Many users, in fact, considered Empty Spaces magical. It was that good at understanding the user's emotional state. All thanks to its uncanny ability to not merely access but to intuit the meaning and significance of the legion of real-time and archival data contained within a user's smartphone. This included but was not limited to the user's music preferences, calendar, personal and professional interactions, texts, emails, status updates, location, movements, contacts, conversations, purchases, photos, aural and visual media habits and any tags or incidental information associated with each of these.

When Empty Spaces reached nearly 50,000 active users, and certain of his creation's potential, Jackie Paper abruptly ended his work contract with mobile security firm, Sky Saxon Ltd. He hoped the company, as they previously had with other staff, would offer him start-up capital and the necessary expertise to help turn Empty Spaces into a functioning business. They declined. He resigned.

Jackie then began searching for investors, firm in his belief that Empty Spaces, once linked with a capable business model, could make himself, his roommate and partner, JaDe Shockwatel, and any backers exceedingly rich. With his limited connections to money and no experience starting or running a business, this proved more difficult than Jackie initially suspected.

Though listed as a partner, JaDe (pronounced like the singer, Sade), age 32, a former pro football player and part-time marijuana grower, in fact offered more encouragement than expertise. Along with a great apartment, nearly rent free. JaDe assisted Jackie wherever possible in network maintenance, provided insight that made Empty Spaces easier for users to download, proved an effective sounding board for Jackie's ideas and, most importantly, helped Jackie remain focused even as the business side of Empty Spaces sputtered, at least initially. To his credit, not once did Jackie seek to limit JaDe's minor ownership claims on Empty Spaces.

Complex in design, Empty Spaces was remarkable both for its simplicity of purpose and capacity to truly understand its users. Empty Spaces instantly detected if a user's mood was, say, glum, and automatically selected the exact right song(s) to mirror their mood; all in real-time, all processing managed in the background, and without any user involvement. Next, and this directly led to its viral-like growth, Empty Spaces would seek out and 'hop' to all nearby smartphones [optimally within a 25-feet radius]. Empty Spaces could even determine if a proximate individual(s) was in a similar mood. If so, the song from the originating device would play in the new user's phone (or ear bud) and the originating user's contact information would appear, depending upon pre-approved settings. Though not its original intent, Empty Spaces quickly became a sort of real-time, location-based social network and dating service centered around mood and music. This dramatically expanded the user base. Empty Spaces soon grew from thousands of users to the millions.

In researching this story I have reviewed numerous primary source materials. Discrepancies in statements or disputes of facts are the result of multiple, opposing views, or conflicts within the documents themselves. Where appropriate, I have attempted to provide clarification. Sources included but were not limited to:

PERSONAL INTERVIEWS
- Jackie Paper
- Michelle Maybelle
- Honah Lee
- Theo Preston
- Sickspack Shankar
- Anonymous sources from the offices of Representative RKO Barr, Moon Unit Investment and the woman's business group, Party Line

SOURCE MATERIALS
- Blog posts (Daytripper by JaDe Shockwatel)
- Blog posts (Bitter Water by Prudence Skiffle)

- Text and call transcripts of public officials (including Congressman RKO Barr, Francis H. Mustard, Pamela Drogeny, Prudence Skiffle and Theo Preston)
- Empty Spaces server logs
- 'Mixin Up the Medicine', self published manuscript by Jackie Paper
- "Must Go Free", the website of Maxwell Edison

One After 909

The first thing you notice about Jackie Paper is the hair. Thick brown hair that grows down towards his face, covers his ears and if not for a fierce part, which takes the hair on a sudden turn toward the right, would fall well below his eyes. Jackie cannot remember when his hair was not like this.

After the hair would be the nose. Straight, broad, surprisingly so. The bright crooked smile, the light blue eyes, which if they were wide might light up a room. Considering he lived in the habitual rain of Vancouver his skin was not terribly pale. Next, the blue Michigan hoodie, which he wore almost always and everywhere. Jackie looked like everyone's best friend. When properly incentivized, he was also an A+ coder specializing in narrow bandwidth wireless communications.

Jackie's business partner for Empty Spaces was, in fact, his roommate, JaDe Shockwatel. While it is verifiable that Jackie created the bulk of Empty Spaces, its features and algorithms, JaDe provided emotional support, inspiration and proved a reliable sounding board.

JaDe and Jackie lived in a 1200sf two-bedroom condo that JaDe had purchased shortly before the Vancouver real estate market unshackled itself from all known economic forces. Along with his real estate riches, which were difficult to tap, JaDe lived off the small player pension he received as a 7-year veteran linebacker with the BC Lions of the Canadian Football League (CFL). That, and he periodically sold the marijuana which he grew but did not personally consume; this produced in a small grow-op he maintained inside the very large walk-in closet attached to his bedroom.

JaDe had one sibling, a sister, Feuillete, who was two years older. He grew up in western Michigan. Like his father, JaDe played high school football. Only, JaDe displayed enough promise that he was awarded an athletic scholarship to the University of Michigan. In his senior season, JaDe was the second leading tackler on the team and earned the nickname Blunt Force. A series of bone-jarring hits on his final game, against archrival Ohio State, garnered him the moniker "The Shock!"

Several NFL scouts suggested the possibility that JaDe could be a 3rd to 5th round draft pick. Three days after the Ohio State game, however, the coach tossed JaDe off the team following his second failed drug test of the year. This was a marijuana test. A minor marijuana habit, which JaDe attributed to equal parts college student, sore football player, and personal crusade, blossomed during his final year of college. JaDe was not drafted by the NFL.

Physically, JaDe was distinguished by his long dreadlocks, his wide, effervescent smile, his very black skin, which seemed to glisten on those rare days of Vancouver sunshine, and by the fact that he was a hair under 6' tall, and weighed over 250 pounds; all muscle. In an interview with the Vancouver City Paper, soon after he retired from the CFL, JaDe remarked: "Marijuana is my physical therapy, my psychotherapy and, since I grow the stuff, the diversion that keeps me out of trouble."

According to his parents, JaDe likely suffered from mild depression. Two years after his retirement from football, JaDe was diagnosed with social anxiety disorder. Also following retirement, he learned yoga, Ayurveda, the ancient system of holistic medicine, and repeatedly failed at vegetarianism.

Extracted from JaDe's social profile:
- Jackie paid nominal rent though did pay for utilities, most of the food, and sundry other items.
- Raising marijuana consumed more of JaDe's time than any other single activity. He consumed a good deal of what he grew. Most of it, in fact.
- Both JaDe and Jackie attended University of Michigan; they never met in college.
- JaDe and Jackie were both US citizens and held permanent resident status in Canada.
- Though invited to try out at the NFL football draft combine, JaDe never attended. He subsequently claimed the NFL's policy against marijuana was the reason for his decision.
- JaDe repeatedly considered becoming a Hindu.
- JaDe posted frequently to his blog, Daytripper. Posts typically discussed marijuana, marijuana growing and related concerns.

Day Tripper
Blog: Daytripper
Hydroponics

Greetings, dear readers. I know I promised to post more regularly but this time I have an excuse. I've been helping my partner slash roommate get his business off the ground. Anybody have a few million dollars? $1 million? Not too much to start a new music revolution, right?

Jackie, my roomie, calls his creation Empty Spaces. A name I hate. Basically, it's a program inside your phone that understands how you are feeling. Yes, feeling. Feeling is the final commercial frontier of the planetary data grid. The missing link, if you will.

Empty Spaces understands how you feel and plays music to match your feeling.

How? Magic! And numbers! Mostly, by accessing your texts and location and your calendar and your likes (or dislikes) that week, that day, that very moment. Basically, all the stuff you are doing and thinking and saying and working on, and all the other data contained within your phone.

But wait, there's more! Empty Spaces can actually seek out and find others nearby that feel just like you. The program jumps to other devices, literally, looks for a compatible match, and shares your song and your information with them.

Cool, eh?

No I am not high. It really does all this!

Okay, fine. I am high. But the shit works. Download it yourself. It's free.

Back to my day job. I just updated the FAQ on hydroponics since that's something readers often ask me about. Before you dig in, I must remind everyone once more: growing marijuana, even for your own adult use in your own adult home with your own adult hands, is probably illegal where you live. Even here in Vancouver I have to watch my back. But I promise. I only grow what I consume. Most of the time.

FAQ

What is hydroponics?
Hydroponics is the science of gardening without soil.
Was hydroponics invented to support marijuana growing?

No! Ancient Egyptians grew fruits and vegetables using hydroponics. The hanging gardens of Babylon, one of the seven wonders of the world, my friends, was a giant hydroponic garden! And probably one cool ass place.

Is hydroponics green?

Is walrus, gumboot? Hydroponics uses less water than conventional gardening. Oh, and no run-off of fertilizers and pesticides. In fact, in British Columbia, 90% of the greenhouse industry is now hydroponic. (Confession: I don't actually know this for a fact, but saw it in the paper a few years ago, so there you go.)

Is hydroponics hard?

Hard? I'm an ex-jock. If I can do it you can do it. Unless, of course, you went to (the) Ohio State University. In which case you'll have to get your fat mom or your ugly sister that I probably nailed to help you out.

Does having your own hydroponics set-up make people think you are just growing marijuana?

Not just. I grow other things. Peppers, for example. Herbs. Fuck what people think.

Author's Note:

JaDe's blog post continues on this topic. It contains no additional information relevant to Empty Spaces. What's most noteworthy here is that this post was the first public mention that Empty Spaces could 'hop' from one user (or device) to the next. It is also the first time there is any public mention from either man seeking external investment for their technology.

JaDe's post leaves out some of Jackie's more inventive coding. Quite possibly, this was a subject he did not fully understand. It deserves recognition, however. Empty Spaces would uncover holes, or gaps, in an individual's smartphone processor, seize any available computing resources and generate a proprietary data packet. This packet contained the user's approved contact information, their mood, as determined by Empty Spaces, and the current song being played, along with a compacted version of the Empty Spaces software itself. The packet was then transmitted from the originating user's device (phone) to a nearby device via a series of short, intensive bursts of radio energy over unlicensed wireless spectrum.

It should be noted. That Empty Spaces was able to spread 'virally' was not the primary reason for its popularity. First and foremost, Empty Spaces fully succeeded at understanding its users, matching the exact right song to the user's exact mood with uncanny accuracy. More than one user described Empty Spaces as "magical." One of the earliest users, in fact, a cautious believer in magic and a passionate lover of all things chocolate, was Prudence Skiffle, age 31, of Arlington, Virginia.

As much as Prudence loved Empty Spaces, however, she was probably most responsible for its demise.

Dear Prudence

Wednesday morning, at five o'clock, and Prudence Skiffle pushed aside her mother's breaching line of products; acutely powerful medications, several containers of lotions, tonics, chewable vitamins. The two women, mother and daughter, shared one bathroom, and one bedroom, in a cramped but comfortable and well-located Arlington, Virginia apartment. There was in fact a second bedroom, though this was filled with boxed belongings that neither ever managed to sell or trash. Should they ever have guests, he or she could have been accommodated with some effort.

When her father died, 15 years ago, there was far less money, far less of everything, than either Prudence or her mother had long assumed -- and grown accustomed to possessing. The smallish apartment was a necessary downsizing. The second bedroom, along with the space above the kitchen cabinets, behind the living room couch, every empty space, in fact, was filled with books, boxes, pictures and the flotsam of a life accumulated from earlier days.

Her mother, Cyn Skiffle, 74, Prudence had come to acknowledge, was not merely old, older than she ever told anyone outside immediate family, which was now just the two of them, but lately seemed to be aging at an accelerated rate. It was as if suddenly one day were two. What once took two pills to relieve now took four. More and more prescriptions were necessary. Add to that numerous over-the-counter drugs, pads, applicators, a footstool for when she sat on the toilet. Cumulatively, these were not cheap. Symbolically, their cost was even greater.

Prudence was readying herself for work and taking longer than normal. A particularly troubling new blemish had suddenly appeared, like magic, on the bottom left corner of her chin. It refused to be concealed.

"Prudence. Prudence! Take that thing out of your ear, please."

Prudence complied, removing the stylish earpiece that played her music; often much too loud. The device, synched to her phone, was one of the few purchases where Prudence spent more than she knew was reasonable. Still, it was attractive, fit well, offered great sound quality. Riding the subway every work day, and the fact that her work cubicle was positioned along a well-traveled corridor, were justification enough for the purchase, she felt. Though most in neighboring Washington, DC sported such earpieces to signal to the world that they made and received calls, as if this were some badge of distinction, with the exception of calls to and from her mother, Prudence used her earpiece almost exclusively for listening to music. Which was now exclusively served by Empty Spaces.

"That pimple. On your chin. That you are trying to cover up. It's all that chocolate. Men don't like so much make-up on a woman. Not these days." Her mother looked at Prudence through the mirror.

"Yes, mother." Prudence responded.

"Too much chocolate. That's why you need all that make-up."

"Mother, that's simply not so. In fact, a recent study at the University of Missouri exonerated chocolate -- "

"I don't need to hear any study. I see!"

Prudence knew otherwise. It wasn't the chocolate. Even if it was, which it was not, it was not as her mother assumed. Rather, something much deeper; holy, even. Prudence chose to believe that God, who had after all blessed this world with chocolate, the world's most faultless food, had demanded of its true believers, such as herself, to offer some form of penitence. In her case, the tithe for chocolate was bad skin. Such a small price to pay, she thought.

"Your lunch is on the counter. Have you had all the coffee you want? I don't like to throw anything out."

"I'll drink it on the way." Prudence was no more than about a 10 minute walk from the Metro train but if she left any later, and was forced to take the next train, she would not get a seat.

"Will you be home by 6? I can make us that chicken."

"Yes, as always."

"No other plans?"

"No, mother. Same as every other day."

"Good. No one likes dry chicken. What are you listening to, anyway?"

"Not sure of the song, but I love it. Just what I need to get me going this morning. It's from a service I overheard Pam mention, called Empty Spaces. It plays music to match my mood."

"Careful of that bitch." Prudence's mother put her finger to her lips and silently asked for forgiveness.

"Yes, I know."

"I don't trust her. She doesn't recommend something to you cause she likes you. She's there for only one person. That's herself."

"I overheard. She didn't recommend it to me. Probably doesn't even know I know about it. Somehow it analyzes what's on my phone and figures out my mood. Then plays a song to match it. Magic."

"I'm telling you. She knows you should have her job. She shakes her ass that's how she got it."

"She's actually pretty smart."

"She's a bitch. I don't trust her. And I don't like all that make-up you're putting on."

"It's just for these blemishes."

"It's all that chocolate! Your skin is telling you."

"We've already discussed this, mother. Chocolate doesn't cause acne."

"It causes those!"

"I'm not going to give up chocolate."

"Not give up. Just not so much."

"I've been eating a lot less recently, in fact."

"At your age you want your skin to be perfect. Love is a battlefield."

There was a brief silence as Prudence completed her morning ritual.

"I need to use the bathroom, dear."

"Just another minute."

"Fine. No more. I can't hold it."

Prudence would preferred to have slept in, or just not go in to work at all, truth be told. However, she never liked being rushed, never liked veering from routine. She could not understand those people that simply jumped out of bed and raced to work. She needed time to embrace the day, embrace her reality; or at minimum bend her will toward acceptance. And, yes, make herself as attractive as possible.

"Now?"

"Yes, but I need to get back in."

If I ever get to G-14 pay grade, Prudence thought, I swear we sell this place and get an apartment with two full-size bathrooms. Plus, a real kitchen. She stole a quick glance in the mirror.

At 31, Prudence could still pull off 28, when necessary. She had long, jet black hair, full and pretty, which she curled along the front of her face. Her face was round but cute, with big eyes, proportionate nose, a full mouth with dimples on either side. This helped her look younger, when necessary. She had a 36D chest, nearly perfect, she told herself. And, yes, she would often confess, only to herself, her hips, her thighs, her butt were all too large, by today's standards, but only slightly. She was not overweight. Pretty, curvy, bright, with a good job. Repeat that to yourself, she thought.

If Prudence was an ordinary beauty, her days were more so. Home. Metro. Work. Metro. Home. Five days a week. Forty-eight weeks a year. Errands on the weekend. Church on Saturday afternoons with mother. Even at work Prudence texted or video called her mother at least once a day, without fail. Prudence could not help but wonder on occasion how living with her mother, caring for her, fashioning her life around her, in fact, was extorting its toll. Still, she at least ventured out into the world each day. There were people and places and change; life. Her mother, on the other hand, was truly all alone. Of which Prudence was acutely aware.

Prudence dashed to the small, cramped kitchen. She carefully spooned two tablespoons of high-quality chocolate powder into her coffee mug, poured out the rest of the coffee, and added one tablespoon of full cream, all under her mother's watchful eye. "Thought you needed to get into the bathroom."

"Never you mind."

Prudence grabbed her bag, kissed her mother, headed out the door, rode down the elevator and walked the precisely 12 minutes it took for her to arrive at the nearby Metro train station. Soon enough, she would be at work, at the FCC, seated at her cubicle, for a minimum eight hours. None of this was particularly joyful, nor did Prudence expect it to be otherwise. Her new boss, Pam Drogeny, made it less so.

Pamela Ann Drogeny, who arrived in Washington, DC from Vancouver, was the former girlfriend of Jackie Paper, creator of Empty Spaces. Prudence did not know of this relationship. Likewise, Prudence could not know of course, none of them could, in fact, that Empty Spaces would soon bring all three together. And change their lives forever.

"Have a good day, dear. Call me."

"I will."

A Day in the Life

It's just another day, Prudence reminded herself. She walked unhurriedly to the Metro, which would take her into the city, followed by a short walk to her office – cubicle -- at the FCC. Prudence was typical of the area's professional grunt class. Government employee. Long-timer. Decent salary, though nothing special. Great benefits. Although lately benefit cuts meant more of her mother's necessities came directly out of pocket. All in all, Prudence knew, better than most.

Her boss, Pam Drogeny, was in stark contrast to the workaday Prudence. Pam was one of Washington's beautiful people. Or soon would be, Prudence suspected. Too young, too thin, too smart, and all too easy. Pam was in a serious relationship with a Congressman's aide, one Francis H. Mustard, who, along with being ten years Pam's senior, according to Prudence's mother, recently received a glowing write-up on a popular political website, naming him one of ten rising Beltway stars. Everything exactly as it should be, per the well-constructed story of her life, no doubt. Whereas Prudence still sought a narrative.

Prudence had been with the FCC almost a decade. She was a graduate of nearby TC Williams High School. At her mother's insistence, Prudence participated in the drama club, which she enjoyed, though rarely had a speaking part. Prudence had the grades to attend a well-ranked university, although with little money and her mother alone, she chose instead to matriculate nearby at commuter-friendly George Mason University. While a part-time student, she was offered a job at the National Institutes of Health (NIH). Barely two years later she jumped to a better-paying position with the FCC. Where she remained.

Despite having grown up around Washington, DC, politics were of minor concern to Prudence. Years ago, she had two dates with a handsome man who worked on several Republican campaigns. Or so he claimed. Notwithstanding a goodbye kiss the morning after, she never heard from him again. Only rarely did she think this her fault.

As Prudence approached the cavernous Metro entrance, she manually checked in via her smartphone, at her mother's insistence, letting her know all was well. Aggressive, more determined riders rushed passed, taking the down escalator two and three steps at a time. Soon all were deep underground, waiting for the Orange Line; nearly all with their heads buried in their phones, listening or reading or watching or communicating, isolated from the influences around him. Thanks to her sleek new earpiece, and Empty Spaces channeling music to match her mood precisely, Prudence was happily afforded a larger cognitive sphere. If lucky, which she was about eight times out of ten at this early hour, Prudence would score a seat. A seat being hard orange, brown and milk colored plastic, not terribly wide, yet a reward nonetheless.

The walk from the Metro station to her office, as with the walk from her apartment to that nearby Metro station, was barely over ten minutes. The ride itself no more than twenty. A far better commute than most, Prudence reminded herself. Enough time, as well, especially when seated, to write a new post for her blog, Bitter Water, a moderately popular site on the boundless glories of chocolate.

Blog: Bitter Water
Check-in. Ballston. Metro.

Good morning, readers! I got a seat on the Metro! You know what that means -- time for a new blog post. Sorry for not having posted in several days. Between work and mother it seems like I haven't had a moment to think about chocolate. Well, that's not true, of course. I've thought a great deal about it. Certainly, I've eaten my fair share, even if less than normal – and certainly far less than my mother would tell complete strangers.

Most of the chocolate I've sampled these past few weeks has, regrettably, not been as satisfying as I should expect. Therefore, instead of a review, since I don't like to give bad reviews, I thought a quick summary of the history of chocolate might be of interest to my newer readers. If you want to be a regular contributor to the site you should know at least these important date and facts. As always, comments are welcome!

- Chocolate comes from the fermented, roasted, and ground beans (aka nibs or pods) of the cacao tree (Theobroma cacao).
- Chocolate, in various forms, has been consumed by humans for over 3000 years.
- Among the very first to cultivate cacao were the Aztecs and Mayans. They did not typically eat chocolate. Rather, they ground the cacao beans for use in a bitter hot drink. This drink typically contained chilis, achiote and other peppers and spices.
- The cacao pod was often represented in religious rituals. Mayan texts refer to cacao as god's food.

- The Aztecs attributed the creation of the cacao plant to their god Quetzalcoatl who descended from heaven carrying a cacao tree stolen from paradise.
- When the Aztecs conquered a village, they ordered 'tribute' in the form of cacao beans.
- In 1519 Spanish explorer Cortes sent cacao beans back to King Charles V, along with recipes and tools on how to transform cacao to chocolate. Soon, the Spanish were mixing cacao beans with sugar, vanilla, nutmeg, cloves and cinnamon. From Spain, chocolate quickly spread to the rest of Europe.
- Though not native to the region, today almost two-thirds of the world's cacao comes from West Africa, primarily from the nation of Côte d'Ivoire. Most African cacao plantations are owned by giant multi-national corporations.
- The first chocolate house opened in London in 1657. Chocolate houses were popular alternatives to the pub.
- By the 1700s, mechanical mills were used to squeeze cacao butter from the cacao beans. This helped to create hard, durable chocolate, which in turn led to more widespread sale of chocolates throughout western Europe.
- In 1765, the first chocolate factory in the US opened.
- In 1828, Coenraad Johannes van Houten patented a method for extracting the fat from cacao beans and making powdered cacao (cocoa). This reduced the price and improved the quality of chocolate, particularly common drinking chocolate.
- Soon after, J.S. Fry and Sons, a British chocolatier, begins making commercially available eating chocolate (no longer just drinking chocolate).
- In 1867, Daniel Peter, a Swiss candle maker, began experimenting with milk as an ingredient in chocolate. He brought his new product, milk chocolate, to market in 1875.
- Next, Rodolphe Lindt invented a process called conching. Conching involves heating and cooling chocolate solids under very specific temperatures and methods to ensure that the liquid is evenly blended, giving chocolate its luxurious mouth feel. This further increases chocolate's popularity.
- In the late 1800s in America, Milton Hershey develops a means for mass producing milk chocolate, resulting in extremely affordable chocolate bars that could also withstand long distribution routes.

Note how many of these names are still with us today: Hershey, Cadbury, Fry, Van Houten, Lindt.

I promise to post again before the end of the week. I was able to procure some organic chocolate bars made by a small company from Portland, including one with ginger. Can't let mother find out how much they cost. I'll be sure to review each one.

COMMENTS:

Before I forget, I'm drowning out the noise of my morning commute thanks to a clever music program called Empty Spaces. It's free! Once it's downloaded onto your smartphone, it plays music to match how you feel. I'm hearing songs I've not listened to in years, some I've never heard before, but I promise you they perfectly match my mood. Even the lyrics match what I'm thinking! It's magic. I know! You heard it here first.

-PS

TRACK TWO
Imagine

A Taste of Honey

The taxi skirted about a maze of soft boys, tech toys and white noise. The streets of downtown Vancouver smelled of popcorn and urine.

Red light.

The cab stopped short. A homeless man sprung to life, walked up to the taxi window, mumbled something indecipherable.

Green light.

The driver pulled out too quickly for me to hand the haggard looking man a dollar. Moving faster now, the cityscape appeared more like a failed collage, with too much material forced inside too small a frame.

Jackie wanted to document this, his first cab ride to his first meeting with a potential investor in Empty Spaces. He wanted to recall every moment, every detail. Only, it was much too early, and he was much too groggy to think clearly. He pulled out his smartphone and, losing himself amongst the glass towers, posted to his wall:

"I'm so tired. I haven't slept a wink."

A few moments later, he exited the vehicle and stood not ten feet from the entrance of one of numerous semi-attractive and fully interchangeable bluish-green glass and steel office towers that dotted Vancouver and its surrounding suburbs. He checked his phone. Twenty minutes till his meeting. He hated arriving anywhere early. Once more he posted to his wall:

"Waitin' for the man."

In fact, Jackie was waiting for his meeting with Sickspack Shankar, founder of a Vancouver-based business incubator. Sickspack's specialty, he reminded Jackie more than once, was connecting those who created high-potential high-growth high-tech products and platforms, with real people who possessed very real money, and lots of it. After weeks of unemployment, and no venture capitalists banging down his door, the calm, discerning Sickspack was salvation.

Portions of his semi-rehearsed elevator pitch bubbled inside Jackie's brain, if periodically in the wrong order: "A technology for turning a person's smartphone, a device everyone on the planet carries with them, into a way of magically unlocking and even sharing their feelings, yes, feelings, with those around them, seems impossible in both conception and design. Not so. Not any longer. Not with Empty

Spaces. Empty Spaces opens up untold opportunities for connecting people, places and content."

How could this Sickspack person not want in?

Jackie continued honing his pitch as he waited. "Everyone listens to and enjoys music -- from birth to death – almost instinctively, and acknowledges its ability to nourish the heart, the soul and to banish demons. It is to music we dance, shout, study, meditate and share. Music is our magic christian. Empty Spaces its organized religion."

Jackie smiled. Despite his best efforts, despite being so early into the process, he could not prevent himself from thinking, once again, what his world might be like if Empty Spaces succeeded – as per his dreams. Though the full meaning of success remained not entirely defined, the expected riches were quite easy to imagine. Tangible. Indeed, Jackie had already pegged a figure -- $100 million -- and had already spent precious dream time on how he would allocate such earthly treasure.

$100 million after taxes by Jackie Paper…

- $15 million would be spent on three properties; a West Coast designed home in North Vancouver, a sleek, steel and glass condo in Vancouver, perfect for guests, parties and creativity spikes, and a traditional family home in Ann Arbor, Michigan for when he cared to return to his place of birth.
- $5 million would be allocated for upkeep and taxes on the properties, in perpetuity.
- A gift of $25 million, to be provided in $1 million installments over a twenty-five year period, to his alma mater, University of Michigan. Which would name something after him, certainly. A building, most likely. An entire school, possibly.
- He would give his parents $10 million. Knowing his parents, they would probably put it all in a passbook savings account.
- Saving himself the aggravation, he would place his parents in charge of a $10 million fund to disburse undetermined amounts to relatives. He would oversee a similar $5 million fund directed toward long-time friends.
- $10 million would be earmarked for first class travel all around the world, forever.
- The remainder would be provided to him as an annuity. Jackie assumed he would live a good fifty or more years. With interest and investment returns, he should easily have $10,000 placed into his wallet at the start of each month. Every month. Forever. Fuck yeah, he thought.

At the moment, however, Jackie's reality was starkly different than his dreams. Despite the growing popularity of Empty Spaces, already with 400,000 users, of which each paid nothing, there was still no real money coming in. Worse, Jackie wasn't terribly sure, nor 100% interested, truth be told, in his abilities or his desire to unlock, unleash and manage the actual revenue generating business potential of Empty Spaces.

This was not, however, his primary concern. Weeks after abruptly leaving his contract job, Jackie had yet to receive any unemployment compensation There was no other job, good or bad, waiting for him. Both credit cards were nearing their breaking point. Despite his certainty in the potential of his creation, and the assumed financial return, given its growing user base, there had been no call backs, no leads, no investors, no partners. Nothing. Not one. Until two days ago, when he received a call from Sickspack Shankar. Sickspack made no promises, but from how he talked, Jackie was certain he understood the dream.

Jackie entered the building. He strode past the receptionist guard, pretended as if he belonged, walked across the atrium, the sun sneaking through, and entered the elevator. All by himself. He pressed 4. The doors closed. For the next three seconds Jackie watched the news and entertainment video feed on the screen above. He exited the elevator, took less than a second to determine if he should go left or right, and spotted Sickspack's office.

MOON UNIT INVESTMENTS

As he entered, Jackie reminded himself: "make sure to mention the sensors algorithm." Along with all the other smartphone data it accessed, his latest build of Empty Spaces now utilized real-time feedback from the array of sensors incorporated within a typical user's phone. Empty Spaces could thus determine if the user was inside, outside, up, such as on the fourth floor of an office building, down, like in a basement, if it was wet or dry, hot or cold, how far the person was from another person (or device), and if those persons (or devices) were already known to the user (or user's device), and if the person were moving, and whether fast or slow. This improved music selection by nearly 6%.

Despite the perfunctory design of most modern office towers that populated downtown Vancouver, the interior of Sickspack's office was striking. Brightly lit, with colorful plants and flowers on nearly every flat surface. On a table sat a small statue, about 3 feet high, that Jackie assumed was an Indian god, both owing to Sickspack's name and since it was unlike any statue of Buddha he had ever seen.

Wait. Fuck. Is Sickspack Indian, Jackie asked himself, suddenly panic stricken? Did he mention something? Was Sickspack a Punjabi, he wondered? Does it matter? Would there be time to re-check the man's profile? Jackie reached for his phone just as he approached the receptionist.

"Hello. I have an 8am meeting with Mr. Shankar," Jackie said to the young woman.

"Yes. You are Mr. Paper, correct? Mr. Shankar will be with you in a few moments. Won't you have a seat. Yes, right there next to the garden Buddha."

Jackie took a seat. The chair was made of cloth, but firm. It had an attractive orange swirl pattern on both the seat back and cushion and upon that rested two small pillows, one orange, of a different hue then the chair, the other brown. Neither of which Jackie knew what to do with so he shoved them, uncomfortably, to his sides. The small dark brown wooden end table across from the chair held a small vase with attractive purple flowers, a plant that may have been a common aloe vera, a candle, and a tablet. Jackie reached for the tablet, which turned itself on.

Click [here] for our list of our ROUND A investments.
Click [here] for a list of Sickspack's rules.

Jackie clicked on the rules link:
1) Technology never dies, ever. We merely cease to distinguish it.
2) All our actions liberate or incarcerate our true selves.
3) There are negative consequences to everything we do, regardless of intentions.
4) The smartphone is the computer. A node in the singular, it exudes humanity's values in the aggregate.
5) Our connected world has rendered space and time irrelevant. Counter-intuitively, this makes nothing more important as right here right now.
6) We are what we share.
7) Money is understood by all. It is humanity's counter to God's destruction of the tower of Babel.

8) You can radiate everything you are. You can celebrate anything you want.
9) Magic lives. Boring is death. In today's brave new world, if it is boring, it will not survive. If it is magical, it can never die.
10) Think locally scale globally. Without this, your business model cannot succeed.

What is this shit, Jackie thought? He assuaged himself by noting that people who make themselves into successful angel investors, who oversee a small business incubator, were almost certainly inclined to believe all their passing thoughts were pools of wisdom.

"Fuck it," he told himself. "This guy can say whatever the hell he wants." Jackie needed backing. He was not going to live 9-5, not going back to contract work, not again. Empty Spaces was magical. He was going to make sure that Empty Spaces was also a success; the carrier of his dreams. Sickspack was his ticket to ride.

"I hope we passed the audition."
Jackie was grateful for the intrusion of JaDe's text message.
"Still waiting. You should be here."
"This is your dream."
"No. You helped. Partners."
"Thanks. But you don't need me there. Besides -- "

"Mr. Paper?"
"Yes?" Jackie quickly stood up and reached out his hand.
"Mr. Paper. Hello. My name is Sickspack Shankar. Please, follow me."

Baby, You're a Rich Man

Author's Note: The following is excerpted from *Mixin' Up the Medicine by Jackie Paper*

"Jackie, welcome, please, sit down, sit down."

Sickspack Shankar, casually dressed, rich brown skin, dark hair, surprisingly thin, probably vegetarian. Noticeably long fingers and pointed nails. He motioned me to a chair not quite at the center of the conference table, across from himself and his three associates. He spoke with a perfect Canadian accent, if such a thing exists. I guessed his age to be that of a man in his 50s who looked like he was in his late 30s.

"Please. Let me introduce to you my associates."

This was of no value. I instantly forgot their names as soon as I was told them. A failing I had long ago accepted as irreversible. One that is mitigated, however, by my uncanny ability to remember those I meet via their obvious, if banal, personal characteristics. For Sickspack's associates, highlights included:

- We are cool men with our cool men hand shakes.
- "Excuse me, I have to take this."
- Yeah. I'm a VC but my real passion is heliboarding.
- I'm Asian. I'm smart. I wear glasses. But I'm special. You can tell that from my wicked hair style.
- Texting. Looks up. Nods. Texting. Looks up. Nods. Texts. Asks question with incredulous tone while looking up. Head back down. Texts some more. He's the really smart one.
- "Take us over that last point one more time, Jackie."

"Jackie, instead of reading resumes, which are nearly all identical and similarly duplicitous, I prefer to go right to the bottom. Where people list their interests."

"Yes, well I -- "

"Your interests impressed me. Radio signal propagation. Mountain biking. Hydroponics. That's an uncommon set of avocations."

"My partner, JaDe Shockwatel, he's the hydroponics expert. You saw both resumes."

"Oh, yes. The football player."

I sneak in a quick view of Vancouver's north shore, its water and mountains, from the conference room window; happy to call this place home.

Still more small talk.

"Jackie, if you don't mind. Before we get started, I'd like to present a few slides on the role of an angel investor."

"Oh, fuck," I thought. "Slides = Death."

"Brett. Lights please."

"First slide"

- Angel investors are typically but not always successful entrepreneurs in their own right.
- Angel investors provide $20 billion dollars per year to Canadian entrepreneurs.
- More than three quarters of proposals reviewed by angel investors are rejected outright.
- Angel investors help transition the business from the self-funded phase to formal commercial development to the venture capital stage to public offering.

"Jackie. I'm sorry. Can we get you something? Brett, can you bring us some tea? Thanks."

"Second slide"

What do angel investors want?

- For every one dollar of investment, the angel wants seven dollars returned, after taxes, within no more than 5 years.
- The thrill of building a successful business.
- First right of refusal for subsequent funding rounds.
- Protective provisions

I have no idea what that last bullet even means.

"Third slide"

Business Plan

At which point, the following words were spoken, in no uncertain order:

- Pro forma
- Taxes
- Profit and loss
- Market research
- Customers
- Competition
- Replacements
- Facilities

- Geography/Location
- Platforms
- API

A solid, seasoned management team with proven leadership is a must!

"Jackie? Any questions so far?"
"No. I'm good."
"Oh, thank you, Brett. Jackie, tea?"

"Fourth slide"
- Equity
- Securitization
- Five-year projections
- Cash flow
- Vesting schedule
- Valuation

"We'll also go into this a bit more later."

"Slide five"
"Jackie? Just so you know, my policy is to never give a presentation with more than five slides. Bad form. No one that's good will need more than five slides. Understand? For our purposes here, however, I wanted to provide you with a comprehensive review."
"Thank you."

- Active involvement in the company by the angel investor
- Mentor relationship
- Founder and angel will communicate regularly.

"Founders. Not founder. There's two of us. JaDe and myself."
"Oh, yes. Understood."

"Slide six"
Exit strategy

END
"Lights, please, Brett."

"I've got big plans for Empty Spaces, Jackie. Very big."

"I'm happy to hear that. I know it has the potential you are looking for."

"First, tell me. Do you want to build a business?"

"Yes."

"Do you want to grow it, manage it, nurture it, watch it take over the world?"

"Yes."

"Bullshit! Do you know how many people I interview in a week? Everyone says they want to build a company and grow it. Bullshit. They want to sell it. Sell big. Sell for millions. Billions. Every single one, Jackie."

"Okay -- "

"No. Don't react. This is not a bad thing, my friend. No. For here we traffic in ideas. Brilliant ideas. Innovative ideas. New business models. New ways to destroy the old. New tools to enhance our daily lives. And, if we are keen, make us rich along the way."

"I –"

"I've helped raise seed capital for several companies, Jackie. All right here in Vancouver. From the moment I read a business plan, I'm assessing it, nearly always, based on what I think I can sell it for -- quickly. I finally have your attention."

"I've been paying attention this entire time. Want me to recite your slides?"

"Not necessary. I do not mean your attention per se. More, your eagerness, your aspiration. I believe that in Empty Spaces we have a potential winner. I truly believe that, Jackie. The missing piece, as always, is the right investor -- with the right amount of money."

"I was expecting up to $5 million – "

"That will not be an issue."

"Oh? That's good."

"I have a 10:5:2 rule, Jackie. I am always working with at least ten investors. For any potential business I am shopping, such as Empty Spaces, of these 10 investors, 5 will be very eager. Of these five, perhaps 2 will commit to an offer sheet. Empty Spaces is magic, no question. But this, connecting the idea with the money, is my magic. I, with my associates here, have the connections not simply to money, you must understand. But to the right money. The money that will take your creation, structure it, nurture it, and give it life."

"That is why I focused on your firm."

"Indeed. Naturally, we will need to work on your business plan. Yours was a solid first draft -- "

"I assumed there would be some gaps -- "

"We vet not only the technology, Jackie, but the business plan, the business model, obviously, the potential market. Each is critical. Funding is not the same as succeeding. Remember that. Funding is merely a single step toward success. Your plan was not only short on costs and earnings details, but missed obvious opportunities for monetization. Not to worry. Empty Spaces is, essentially, an algorithm. A number. In this next phase, we will focus on another number. Several, in fact. Costs. Investment dollars. Monetization. Earn outs."

I look around. Sickspack's associates are unreadable. Bored? Covetous? I could not tell.

"At Moon Unit we think in terms of love and rockets. Due diligence of the technology, yes, but also of the idea itself, the power of that idea, and the person from whence it came. The dream, if you will. We make dreams happen, yes. That is our role. Dream maker."

I started to speak, but Sickspack continued.

"Dreams are what reshape the world, after all. Tell me, Jackie. What is your dream?"

"Jackie?"

Run For Your Life

"Pam, love, you there?"

"Here. Where are you taking me to lunch? All I've had today is coffee."

"I'll think of something. Running a bit late. Usual fires."

It was only noon and Pam, Pam Drogeny, was hungry. She had been in the office five hours already and would be there at least seven more. The long hours were less a reflection of how much she cared for the FCC, her employer, or the small department within it that she oversaw. Rather, as JaDe Shockwatel once told her, Pam's belief in herself, in her future, was so fervent, so intense, that it often manifested itself in ways not always positive. Right or not, Pam was hungry and not a little bored. Lunch out was exactly what she needed.

Her lunch companion this afternoon was her fiancé, Francis Mustard, Chief of Staff to Congressman RKO Barr. Francis had similarly been at work for over five hours. Longer, in fact. He, however, never felt the need to leave everything behind. Nor ever leave the office. Today was a rare exception.

"Need a favor, sugar sugar. Remember we discussed Empty Spaces?"

"I do. Remember that I told you paperwork was submitted weeks ago? Any mobile phone service that runs over unlicensed radio spectrum has to file with the FCC."

"I'm going to convince the congressman to invest in the technology. That's confidential. Between us, only. I'll be part of the investment group. Wheels already in motion."

"That's great –"

"It is. For the both of us, in fact. I need two things. One, the congressman has to work up the courage to pull the trigger. That's the difficult job. I'll take care of that. What I need from you is –. Shit. Entering the tunnel. I may –"

[Call terminated]

"You there?"

"Here. You are aware that I know the founder, right? Jackie Paper. He's – "

"No. No I did not know that."

"We used to date. I told you that ages ago."

"I do not believe you did, love. That I would remember."

"No. I'm pretty sure…"

"Mother Fuck. Was it serious?"

"Stop it. Too young to be serious. We met in college."

"Goddamit. Why would you not tell me this when I mentioned Empty Spaces the first time? You know how I feel about secrets."

"I didn't make the connection."

"You made a fucking connection, all right."

"Francis, stop. It was a long time ago. How was I supposed to know he was involved? His name was not attached to any paperwork. I don't see all the filings that come in here, obviously…"

"Fuck."

"Besides, he was never the type to, you know, follow through and build something. Pretty impressive, actually."

"I wish I had known of this earlier."

"It's over. Been over. You know I only have eyes for you. And any black man."

"That's not funny."

"Fine. You were saying? Empty Spaces. Outstanding issues. Are you sure this is where you want to invest? A shared music service?"

"One second. I need to take this."

[Call transcript not available.]

"Shared music service? Surprised at you, Pam, dear. That's exactly what the congressman said. Think bigger. Think of how powerful something like this could be if directed properly."

"Or you could just tell me."

"Deconstructed, Empty Spaces is not a music recommendation service or a music sharing service. It is a messaging platform. Advertising is a form of messaging. Think of that. All advertising is a call to action. As is politics. We send out messages; an infinite number of them. Most are forgotten, ignored. Not so with Empty Spaces. It understands the exact right message you need to hear right this moment. Even better, people welcome it! Because the music – the message – is exactly what they want to hear. Empty Spaces flips the entire messaging ecosystem on its head. Yes, now its emphasis is on music. Fine. Probably the easy route for its inventor. Everyone listens to music."

"Not you."

"Not me, correct. That's probably why I understand that music is simply a type of message, nothing more. That's the primary source code; messaging. Empty Spaces offers the potential to understand the user's state of mind, their emotional state, exactly as it is, in real time. Armed with that knowledge, it then delivers a message, a song in this instance, targeted specifically to that individual. Fucking brilliant."

"And?"

"Pam, love, I know how smart you are. Empty Spaces is the perfect platform for persuasion, which is the crux of every single political campaign. People stick a tiny speaker inside their ears and listen, voluntarily choose to listen, to whatever Empty Spaces offers them. Think about that. Music, now, but that's the narrow view. Music is the carrier, nothing more. Sad, bittersweet, happy, angry, rage-filled. Each song, each message, is targeted for each individual user, constructed to match exactly with the person's emotional state. Even better, each user is convinced that Empty Spaces is performing just for them. It's not. It's a message in a bottle, only to everyone. One that each person hears differently."

"It sounds more like you're convincing yourself."

"I'm already sold, love. Imagine how this can be used for a political campaign! Why do you think some voters have a visceral dislike of one party or one candidate? Or fall in love and volunteer their time to help another? They have internalized various messages. Including the ones they're not aware of; especially those. Empty Spaces is a tool that understands what each user's emotional state is, serves up exactly the message they need to hear at that exact moment. That's power. Because the owner of the platform can direct those feelings."

"Thing is, Francis, I know Jackie. As we've already discussed. I have my doubts that's what Empty Spaces does, or how he intends to use it. I just don't think he sees the world that way."

"You let me worry about that."

"Don't dismiss what I have to say. You know I hate that."

"Pam, love. Empty Spaces works. Trust me on this. I've had my eye on it for weeks now. Empty Spaces, whether your boyfriend meant it to or not, understands its users. Like nothing else before. One program on one device, a smartphone, that links our calls, our chats, our messages, our appointments, our likes, dislikes, what we play, what we watch, where we are, where we are going. Who we are with, or if we're alone. Fuck. People hand over all that data about themselves. Empty Spaces dissects that mass of information, data that otherwise just floats off into space, and responds. It knows each user to the point that it can intuit their mood. That is powerful. Jesus Christ, so powerful. On an emotional level, it distills everything around us into one singular powerful message. In this case a song. But it doesn't have to be a song! As I said, the song is a carrier, carrying a message. And messages can be shaped, directed."

"Are you sure it can do all this now? That you're not imprinting your hopes onto it?"

"Nothing like this exists, love. Nothing like Empty Spaces has ever existed. But it is real. To have this technology be nothing more than a music service would be criminal. A waste. In the right hands…"

"I know one of my staffers uses it. She probably heard me mention it when we were discussing their filing. She's always looking over my shoulder. Maybe I should move her desk."

"Who?"

"Prudence. Prudence Skiffle. G-11. Smart. Pretty. Not terribly ambitious. Why?"

"Just curious. Let's not mention this to anyone else. Deal, love? Not now, not with the congressman's involvement. That would complicate matters. Our little secret."

"I suppose."

"But I still need that favor."

"You're asking a lot."

"It will be worth it. That's my promise. I want you, in your official capacity – and this is all above board, completely – to research Empty Spaces. Something official, coming out of the FCC, so it's legit. Focus on who might be impacted by it, who might appeal to the FCC to shut down unlicensed radio services, any possible enemies of the service. The entrenched interests have never liked that we helped open up unlicensed radio spectrum. Is there any way for them to slow us down? I have my doubts but if we can get FCC validation, we're home free."

"I suppose. We are being tasked to validate the potential benefits of any new wireless services. This would fall under that."

"This works, then you and I – and, yes, your college boyfriend – just might be rich."

"I'll ask Prudence to look into it, since I'm swamped. Plus, I'm not as comfortable as you obviously are with secrets."

"That's all we need."

"I haven't spoken to Jackie in over a year. Maybe I should call him? How far away are you, by the way? I'm starving."

"No. Don't call. Not yet. Promise me that. Like I said, that would spook the congressman and everything would fall through."

"No, he deserves a call, at least. I'm now involved."

"Just sit on this a bit longer. For me, love. Only because we can't let anyone suspect the congressman is involved. Not at this stage. Promise me."

"Okay, for now."

"Thanks, love. I owe you. Five minutes away. "

"I'm leaving my office. See you at the west entrance."

"Buckle up, love."

Pam got into the car, buckled herself in, reached over and kissed Francis.

"Not so fast."

"How'd some fucking Canadian figure this out? A technology that can essentially understand us. I mean, he got everything right. Something like this has to originate from the smartphone, right? We all have one. We carry it with us everywhere. It's what knows us probably better than just about anything else – anyone else."

"Jackie's not Canadian. American, remember. I dated him. Are we still talking about this?"

"Fair enough, love. Sushi?"

"Fish again?" No. Take me to Lychee instead.

"Lychee? Needlessly expensive."

"Don't be cheap, Francis. I like that place. Besides, this is supposed to make us all rich, right?"

"Where'd he get his money?"

"Who? Jackie? We're talking about him again? But I can't call him? I don't think he has any money. Did this cost a lot to build? Jackie's sharp when he puts his mind to something. Plus he was always working on one side project or another. Just let me call him."

"You know what the congressman is like. Man's got no balls. You call your ex, he tells someone, word gets out and the congressman backs off. That kills it for all of us. Listen, promise you won't call, not until the deal is signed, sealed, delivered. That way, everyone wins."

"Maybe."

"He doesn't have a record, right? Nothing that might prevent a deal from going through?

"I don't think so. Jackie can be a slacker but he doesn't do anything illegal. JaDe, his roommate, used to grow pot. Small time stuff. What? Don't look at me like that. It's Canada."

"Just promise me you won't call him. Not till after we finalize everything."

"I won't call. Promise. But I can't help it if he calls me. I'm hard to forget. He could be thinking about me right this second."

[Empty Spaces downloads: 738,3xx]

I'm Looking Through You

"Fuck me."

Jackie sat in front of his computer screen, speaking mostly to himself. JaDe was tending to his plants.

"We're closing in on a million users."

Despite repeated boasts that he was finished working for someone else, finding himself unemployed, still with no backers for Empty Spaces, this despite the many and fanciful words of Mr. Shankar, Jackie spent an increasing amount of time fixated on the tedious minutiae of his creation. If merely to remain in close contact with the dream.

The more Jackie tinkered with the inner workings of Empty Spaces, the more he sought to optimize server downloads, deconstruct user reviews, teach himself marketing, the more he became convinced that, if only he could score a significant investment, or catch a break, Empty Spaces possessed lotto-level potential

This fervent belief manifested itself, however, given the quantity of free time on his hands, in obsessing over the very details he had least control over. Although Empty Spaces could run without his persistent oversight, Jackie nonetheless decided to take still one more look at the server download process.

The instructions flashed on his screen.

Hello!

You have submitted your identification [xxx.xxx] to emptyspaces.net. Empty Spaces is a user-specific music recommendation engine. By accessing the data within your phone, Empty Spaces quickly learns to understand your mood. The program then instructs your mobile device to play music personalized for you, in real-time.

Empty Spaces can even seek out and find people who feel just like you, wherever you are, with no work required on your part. When Empty Spaces discovers a match, select contact information is shared. Only information you choose to share is provided.

Goodbye!

Personal invite code:
http://www.es.net/start?I3c7b70c849ae7079d15d26a0

DIG IT!

Once on your phone, Empty Spaces will immediately analyze your music selections, along with your location, preferences, habits, messages, calls, calendar, requests, status updates, relationships, tweets, texts, wall posts, voice call transcripts, recent transactions, search history and other digital fingerprints. Based upon the information contained within, Empty Spaces will soon understand how you feel That's right, Empty Spaces understands how you feel.

You can opt out of the service, or any of its individual reference points, at any time.

JaDe n JacKie

Jackie leaned forward in his chair. "JaDe, shit. I hate it when you spell my name like that!."

JaDe stepped out of his room. "What's that, mate? Didn't hear you."

"Never mind. I'll change it. We need to make sure we stay professional."

"Since when? Smoke?"

"No. Thank you. I'm gonna check out some of the latest reviews."

Chains

REVIEWS AND FEEDBACK

5 star	73647
4 star	28569
3 star	16632
2 star	7397
1 star	139

"Wait! JaDe? Have you been going through any of the feedback?"
"Some."
"Is this low? Should we expect more users to post a review? I don't know."
"Not sure. Most like it, though."
"There's one here about interference. That's absolute bullshit. Signed anonymous. Probably think I can't pinpoint their exact fucking location."
"I think I'll leave you alone with your mistress."

MP Rhodes (Middleton, WI)
Why is this necessary? What are the ramifications?
0 people found this review helpful.

"Shades of mediocrity. Create something yourself, dick..."

J. Hawl (Wales)
Love it most when I'm on the train. Sometimes, you see people's faces and know that they are listening to the same music and feeling the same way you do. Even when it's bad. Especially when it's bad.

Beta Tester Alpha (parts unknown)
This app is double the size of what it should be. The code's proprietary. I hear he's peddling this to VCs. I haven't run actual tests yet but it appears to be using up too much power. Anyone done battery tests?

"You got it for free. Ass. And no one is forcing you to use it."

Prudence Skiffle (Arlington, VA)
With Empty Spaces, I can go into my own world on the Metro. Or, when I want, connect with those around me who feel just like I do. I just think it's so clever. It truly brightens my day. Even if I've had a

fight with my mother, Empty Spaces seems to know somehow and plays exactly what I want/need to hear.

It's my psyche, put to music.

"Nice profile. Cute."

ATESIN0324 (Allen Park, MI)
This program understands us. It knows that we are all very much alike. It offers each of us a chance to reveal our true selves, even to strangers. There is music all around us. It is best shared. Empty Spaces makes that happen. Thank you!

"All that and only 4 stars?"

JB (Boston, MA)
If you were to trace the arc of popular music from the past three generations, at least based on what gets promoted, you would have to assume that in about 20 years or so popular music would be nothing more than a series of punctuated non-rhythmic sonic booms, designed to be felt rather than heard. Empty Spaces proves this is not so -- and that there are many who have similar tastes that mainstream outlets refuse to acknowledge.

ABH (West Vancouver, BC)
Is this the best thing since sliced bread? Yes, it is. I don't even bother with playlists or downloads or radio anymore. This program is uncanny in knowing exactly what I want to hear. Get this now! FIVE STARS!!

"JaDe? Do you know an ABH? In West Van?"
"Don't think so. Why?"
"No reason. Some pretty nice reviews. I have to make sure to forward some of these to Sickspack. I think he mentioned Asia in his presentation. Wish we had more users in Asia."
"Thoughts on lunch?"
"No. Not hungry. Wait. One of our users just sent me an email. Prudence Skiffle. Checked out her profile on the comments board. Not bad."
"That's why we did this, right? To get laid."
"She's in Arlington, Virginia."
"Near Washington? Pam?"
"Absolute coincidence."

"Always are."
"Let's see what she has to say. I'll just make a sandwich later."
"Shit. That's no fun."

From: Prudence Skiffle
To: Empty Spaces team
Subj   I can't feel anymore than I'm singing!.

Empty Spaces is this sort of magical computerized hyper-aware being that knows me, understands me. When I need it, it reaches out, with music, or with someone that feels like me. Only, it's not creepy. It's liberating. I want to share it but don't want to share it. I almost fear it will become diluted the more people begin to use it, like one more thing to be commercialized, then discarded. I would hate that.

Can you tell me if you are planning to enable this for more than music? What if I'm reading on my phone and someone nearby is reading the same book? Would that work?

Sincerely,

Prudence Skiffle

PS. If you're interested. I am passionate about chocolate. Check out my site [link]. Companies often send me samples to review. I'm happy to send you a thank you box. Consider it payment for Empty Spaces.

"An entire site about chocolate," Jackie marveled? He had little interest. He was, however, bored and unemployed, and aware that distraction offers its own reward. Besides, she's attractive, he thought. He clicked the link.

Forget what you read about the health benefits of chocolate. This is not what chocolate is about! Rather, it is the joy, the pleasure, the longing, and satisfaction. For every study touting the health benefits of chocolate, there is far more evidence of chocolate's nourishing impact upon our soul.

"Click."

"I decided to make a quick stir fry. Try some." JaDe re-entered the inner sanctum and passed the plate to Jackie.

"Thanks."

"When do you expect to hear back from our friend, Mr. Shankar?"

"Fuck if I know. Not true. Actually, no later than Thursday."

What're you reading?"

"Website. About chocolate."
"Really? Not porn?"
"Funny. Her site gets 40,000 readers a month."
"Everyone loves chocolate I guess."
"I never cared for it."

The Fool on the Hill

That not everyone liked chocolate was less important to Congressman Reginald Kenneth Orville (RKO) Nutt Barr, heir to the Nutt Barr fortune and acting President of the failing Nutt Barr Co., than the fact that those who once seemed to love this most common of indulgences were suddenly finding their pleasures elsewhere. Sales at the private company were down, again. Only, for this most recent quarter the drop was precipitous. Even a sizable increase in advertising had failed to alter the company's fortunes. That other, larger chocolate companies were experiencing a similar painful shift in consumer behavior was of little comfort to the congressman, or to anyone associated with Nutt Barr Co., in fact. Save one. This most disturbing of business calamities proved rather fortuitous for Francis Howerd Mustard, Congressman Barr's Chief of Staff and Chief Legislative Director.

Norwegian, in the strictest sense of the word, Francis Howerd Mustard returned from a rare lunch outside the controlling confines of Capitol Hill more resolute than ever. The congressman must invest in Empty Spaces. Barr's money and access were essential for Francis to achieve his dream. Once in physical, legal possession of the service, and all its wonderful ethereal code, able to hone in on exactly what each user felt, Francis knew he would then possess a sort of holy grail of political messaging and thus, political power.

Francis likewise knew, in a way that its creator, Jackie Paper, had never considered, that inside Empty Spaces, amongst its colliding ones and zeros, stirred a magic potion. Because knowing beget controlling. Empty Spaces knew a person's emotions, therefore it offered a means to control a person's emotions. Or, if not control, a way at least to link, perhaps permanently, a person's feelings, any person's, at any moment, at any place, with exactly the right message; one explicitly designed to implant doubt or faith or joy or hate or adulation or derision. For his gain.

Empty Spaces was his opening; his path to a much larger goal, one far greater than money. Only, to reach that goal, he required Barr's money, Barr' access to power and, for the moment, his collection of fears and weaknesses, each ready to be manipulated.

After multiple face-to-face exchanges, Congressman Barr, weak, rich and ever fearful of anything that smacked of a fight, was at last close to signing off on the Empty Spaces investment. Their little secret. It was Francis that persuaded him of the need to diversify his assets, even if the congressman was convinced it was his own idea. Likewise, Francis illustrated to the congressman how Empty Spaces would promote his failing candy business – through improved, personalized advertising. Neither of these were a lie, Francis knew. That Congressman Barr, like everyone else, failed to grasp the limitless potential of the service, however, was not his fault.

Had he believed in fate, Francis would no doubt have felt touched by the divine. Which is why he could not hide his shock when he walked into the congressman's office, unannounced, as always. There the Congressman sat, interacting with a young staffer, Theo Preston, discussing Empty Spaces.

"Francis, join us. Theo and I were just talking."

Theo Preston, the sharp, young, legislative aide hired by Francis, truth be told, because he was obviously qualified and just as obviously black, and less obviously, but no less important, not to newer arriving constituents, he was part Mexican, and from the congressman's district, nodded perceptibly. The Congressman, never above reminding even his most valued aid who was in charge, held a smile in check. Barely.

Francis and Congressman Barr were nothing at all alike; neither in appearance, demeanor, background, upbringing or stature. Not surprisingly, there was little about Francis that the congressman liked. Not his overbearing personality, the manner and certainty with which he stated everything, the reflexive drive to aggressively oppose any and every view any other member of his staff volunteered, merely to show he was smarter or more perceptive, or boss, which he was not. Barr did not care for the man's religiosity, his insincere sycophancy, and, frankly, he wasn't all too sure Francis washed his hands after going to the bathroom, which, in the Congressman's mind, spoke volumes. That Francis possessed a herculean work ethic, that he never shied from the hard decisions, especially with staff and lobbyists, was why Barr relied upon him. Nonetheless, if a moment presented itself to remind everyone, or even just himself, who was truly in charge, the congressman not-so-graciously embraced it.

Reminding everyone was indeed necessary. The patriarch of the Nutt Barr chocolate empire still cleared important business decisions with his mother, just as he did political ones with Francis. Only in this instance, however, the Congressman was truly eager to speak with the young Theo Preston. Not merely for effect; to remind Francis that he did not get to control even his conversations. Barr was genuinely piqued with his handsome staffer. The slight, bright, cocoa-skinned Mr.

Preston, the congressman learned, after Theo mentioned it to him, was of Mayan descent, on his grandmother's side. He had actually enjoyed traditional chocolate beverages as a child. Asking the smart, eager, young man to sit with him, privately, in his office, on the one occasion when Francis was out, was as much coincidental as deliberate.

"Please, Francis, take your seat."

"It can wait, congressman. I would hate to interrupt any fun you two must be having." The pause was for Theo's benefit. "Whenever you can make the time, we should discuss the campaign, media invites for the party at the Barr estate. Both are critical, I'm sure you understand. I also have news about Project L." Project L being what Francis decided they would call the congressman's investment in Empty Spaces.

"Of course. Theo. Thanks for coming in. If you could excuse us."

Francis stood silent and erect, watching Theo walk across the office and out the door. He watched the door close behind the gunning young staffer. Then quickly moved to take his seat directly across from the Congressman.

"Congressman, I have been conducting additional research into Project L -- Empty Spaces. We need to act before someone seizes this opportunity. I have shown, congressman, that this technology will not only support your asset diversification goals, as we have discussed, and have a indirect but appreciable benefit on Nutt Barr sales, as we also previously discussed. I am now convinced that Empty Spaces presents an opportunity for significantly improving your re-election efforts. And, of course, sir, any larger political goals you might entertain going forward."

The Congressman tried to hide the red in his sallow cheeks. He knew as Francis knew, as it seemed everyone knew, that Nutt Barr Co. was losing market share, almost uninterrupted, for five consecutive quarters. Vultures, ready to pick over a corpse, as well as the fervent believers in the financial benefits of corporate consolidation, circled above the company. As is the way of bad news, Barr thought, business worries now coincided with his most difficult re-election campaign ever. Politics, like business, was nothing if not personal, he knew. Fair or not, the blame for falling sales, along with falling voter approval ratings, was laid squarely upon Barr's narrow shoulders.

Barr was no fool, however. Despite any help Empty Spaces -- Project L -- might bequeath him, Barr knew his chief of staff stood to benefit. More troublesome, Barr was not especially pleased with the notion that the man who this moment sat across from him; a man who did all the dirty work, loved it, in fact, might soon transition from direct report to equal. Partners, Barr knew, automatically meant Francis would take a fundamentally different role in his political life and, with Empty Spaces, possess a connection to the family business. This was problematic, to say the least. Francis already wielded as much power as any congressional aide in any congressional office. Barr, however, had long mollified himself with the thought that he could always get rid of Francis. Not so if the pair were actual partners, he knew.

"You are proposing?" Barr asked.

"Thank you, congressman."

Francis, always ready to tell that portion of the truth the other person most needed to hear, again sold the congressman on Empty Spaces. "We both know that politics and business, at their core, are about selling. To succeed, both demand an effective message, a message that resonates -- emotionally. The great messages, the powerful ones, the messages that drive action, that either lead to a sale – or a vote – are the gold standard, of course. Many such messages, congressman, are reliant on a song; a tune that everyone remembers. Just like a favorite song deeply touches a person, an advertising jingle is similarly powerful. It leads to an emotional state, which drives the person to action. More than that, congressman, the song, or jingle, becomes a part of them; a memory, more so if shared. It's impact permanently imprinted."

"And you believe Project L does all these things? Like some magic music box?"

"Yes." Francis smiled, knowing the congressman had hoped for anything other than a simple, definitive answer.

"Think about it, congressman. People carry this magic box as you call it with them everyday, everywhere they go. It's their phone. Only the phone can deliver both personalization and scalability -- nothing else does quite like it. Everyone uses their phone not just to call or to text but to stay in constant contact with friends, with family, with everyone and everything -- from the status of the moisture in their house, to the inane behavior of their favorite sports star. They make friends, build businesses, play games, compete against other users, other devices, anywhere in the world, They use their phone to watch videos, listen to music, organize their life, increase their productivity, improve their health. All of this, and more. From childhood to adulthood to senior.

"The problem, of course, is that this knowledge, this mirror of the person, is buried, inaccessible. How does the person truly feel, what is truly motivating them? What are their fears, hopes, concerns? Some of this information is captured, of course, but most floats off into space, unmoored from the outside world. Until now."

Francis paused, assuming, incorrectly, that the congressman had a question. He continued.

"That is why I've urged you to act decisively on this, congressman. Empty Spaces is a platform that touches all of these bits of information, liberating the user's true self. The ability to understand the person, truly understand them, their emotions, their feelings, even as these change, especially as they change, from moment to moment, is unprecedented."

The congressman motioned to speak, paused, hoping to make Francis think he followed along, but only needed a moment to think through his concerns. "I appreciate your passion, Francis, though I'm just not convinced this technology is as robust as you suggest."

This was a lie. Francis knew. The congressman, ever fearful, was merely hoping for time; hoping that time would pass and no decision on his part would be required.

"Congressman, with Empty Spaces, we have a means to deliver our message -- exactly what and exactly where and when we want. To anyone, to everyone, and in a manner where the message will most deeply and permanently resonate with the individual."

The congressman arched his brow. Francis knew he had won.

"How? Exactly. Project L -- Empty Spaces -- may indeed understand how a person feels if I understand this correctly. Then it plays music that mirrors that feeling. Clever. And for people that love music, I suppose it is quite powerful. But it's music. Not a political advertisement."

Francis breathed in. "Remember the original Nutt Barr jingle, congressman? Well, of course you do. It worked -- people loved the jingle, loved the Nutt Barr, loved the company – and all they thought it represented. That jingle was a call to action, congressman, residing just below the surface; dormant but easy to reawaken. The jingle no longer works, sir. Not because it's lost its power. Rather, it's lost its carrier. There is no means for the Nutt Barr jingle to be transmitted. Radio, television, these have all become marginalized. Think of Empty Spaces as a tool that delivers the jingle to everyone, everywhere. On a device they refuse to ever turn off."

"Possibly. I see where you're going with this. I'm still not sure this helps us in crafting –"

"Congressman, as an individual calls and texts and send messages or updates their personal status, completes their to do list, changes their calendar, everything, really, Empty Spaces begins to understand them. It's so good it essentially anticipates the person's needs. No, not needs, excuse me, that's the wrong word. Anticipates what the user wants, at any particular moment, no matter where they are, no matter who they are with, no matter what they are doing, even when they themselves are not fully aware of their feelings. That's power! As the person continues these activities, goes about their business, listens to music, reads a book on their phone, watches a film, sends out an angry email, for example, posts a negative review on something, Empty Spaces understands them, profoundly. Stressed, sad, angry, aggressive, joyful, whatever. That's critical, congressman. Understands– exactly – how the individual feels. The music, what everyone appears to focus on, is merely the reflection of that understanding; a instrument if you will that merely affirms the person's emotion. Which is what everyone, secretly, wants."

"I'm not entirely certain..." Barr's voice trailed off as he shifted uncomfortably in his chair. It now seemed as if Francis was trying to force him into something; agreement, perhaps.

"With Empty Spaces, we get both the understanding of the person and the vehicle to deliver our message."

"Perhaps if we tested –"

"Congressman, if I may, just a bit longer. These days, everyone pre-selects their own content; music, video, websites, whatever. We can't craft an effective jingle, if you will, not because people's tastes have changed, but because there is no shared comprehension, no message that can effectively reach out to everyone. Not so with Empty Spaces. Jingles fail today, for example, because people have the ability to tune them out. With Empty Spaces, there is no escape. Why? Because this technology knows how the person feels, and knows what the person needs, because of how they feel. They make Empty Spaces a part of themselves. There is no sell required."

No sale required. This thought pleased the Congressman. "Back up. It seems like what you're saying is that a user feels a certain way, then they hear a song, thanks to Empty Spaces, and that solidifies their feeling. And feeling leads to action. Correct?"

"Correct. Only, it gets better. With additional funding and oversight, congressman, I am convinced that we can transform Empty Spaces into much more than a means of merely understanding how a person feels. I believe we can begin to weld feelings to messages for our unique benefit. If they are frustrated, we tell them why. Angry, happy, sad, bitter, vengeful; we tell them why. We, alone, understand them. And in our messages, they find comfort, solace, affirmation and take action, just as we suggest. For now, we start with music, yes. A solid business in its own right. That is how Empty Spaces was originally constructed, after all, as a music recommendation service. Of all forms of communications, music is the most universal, the most elemental."

"You don't even like music, Francis. I've never even heard you whistle."

"I'm the exception. And the best part congressman, the user believes that the very message we have directed at them was constructed of their own unique set of insights and emotions. You know what voters are like, congressman. Just like consumers. There's nothing you can make them do. Nothing. Except, feel. Feel angry, feel happy, sad, nostalgic, frustrated, morally superior. With Empty Spaces, I believe we have a means of connecting the right message, our message, with each person's feelings, whatever they may be. That's a tool that will sell a lot of Nutt Barrs, congressman. I can promise you that. Nutt Barrs and votes."

Francis leaned back in his chair, seated behind his desk, in his rather stately office. His office was smaller than the congressman's, true, though better positioned. He knew he had sold the congressman. Better, only he still appreciated the full power of what Empty Spaces could offer its holder. Which is not to suggest that Francis Howerd Mustard was power mad. More like, power destined, is how he viewed himself. One of the good guys; only with balls. A modern-day Dick Tracy. Indeed, with his fedora hat, thick suit coat, broad power tie, along with his hard good looks, square jaw and fearlessness; the resemblance, Francis knew, was uncanny.

Like Dick Tracy, Francis was of his time, he knew. And his time needed him. The nation had grown soft and scared, like Barr. It was no longer willing to accept its earned role of alpha dog in a large, leaderless world. Francis understood, in a way the effete congressman did not, that at times the alpha dog may seem harsh, severe, may be required to make examples of others to insure order. In the end, of course, even if so many refused to acknowledge this harsh truth, the group as a whole was stronger, more prosperous under such an arrangement.

Trouble was, the noise of everyday living now prevented even the alpha dog's bark from penetrating the weak's disconnected aural flotsam. There were simply too many messages, too much distraction. Except -- he had found a way. Through some music program created by some unemployed hack in fucking Canada brought to him by some fucking Indian venture capitalist thinking he could score with the biggest market in the world, the US fucking government. Francis was determined to take possession of Empty Spaces, and everything he knew it could achieve. Fuck the congressman and his god damn jingles, he thought. Barr was merely one more stepping stone.

Francis suddenly had a powerful urge to tear at Pam's thin, soft limbs. That will come. He texted her a picture of himself, shirt undone, then returned his focus to the work of the office. His first constituent group meeting of the afternoon was scheduled in twenty minutes. Two women and a man seeking support for a simpler form of gluten-free labeling. God damn these small people, Francis thought. Every fucking one of them. The Congressman, included.

Money (that's what I want)

I am a Nutt Barr!
We are all Nutt Barrs!
Get yourself a Nutt Barr!
Chew chew cha-chew!

A jingle is a short musical hook designed explicitly for commercial purposes. Intended to promote a product or brand, a jingle implants a sentiment inside each person that hears it, with the purpose of inducing them to buy and consume a specific product.

A jingle helped build the regionally popular Nutt Barr, a gooey milk chocolate and Virginia peanut confection, into one of southern America's favorite chocolate bars, from the late 1940s to the turn of the century. For people of a certain age, particularly in America's southeast, the happy silly catchy Nutt Barr jingle, ever present on radio and television, was a shared part of their life.

Only, nobody listened to radio anymore. And everyone paid for their television programming, which now came without jingles. No one hears the Nutt Barr jingle anymore, no one sings it, few recall it. The death of the jingle and the long, progressive decline in sales of the Nutt Barr were almost certainly related, Congressman Barr realized. Although that failed to explain the recent significant drops in sales, which seemed to defy explanation. He had no answers.

Derisively labeled the Candy Man by friends and foes alike, erroneously, Barr assumed, because of his family ties, Barr was nonetheless not self unaware. Business was simply not his strongest suit, he knew that much. Perhaps, Francis was right. Even if he was a prick. Find a way to get your message into people's heads, wherever and whenever, through music at first, and you have their hearts and their minds. Soon, their wallets. Maybe their votes. What was it Francis said? The only thing you can make someone do is feel. That seemed correct.

Barr leaned forward in his snug black leather chair, hands upon his fine brown-red shagbark hickory desk; made in Virginia, not far from the Barr family estate. There was a matching bookcase back and to the left of the congressman, both having relocated from his father's office after the old man passed away. He scanned the papers on his desk. Polling data. Recent sales figures his mother had sent over. A calendar that notified him of an endless series of meetings, lunches, votes, receptions, lobbyist dinners and periodic trips back to the district office.

None of which, at this moment, rarely, in fact, appealed to him in the slightest.

Take away the old desk, the bookshelf, the congressional seal, the flags, USofA and Virginia, and there sat a slight, pale, wisp of a man, 5'8" at most, and topping out at 150 pounds, with a soft belly and thinning hair. Not terribly athletic, seemingly impervious to change, yet uncomfortably fitted inside the uniform he had worn yesterday and nearly every other day since taking office: dark navy blue blazer, red tie, crisp white shirt, cufflinks, suit pants, leather belt, as he hated braces, pen in his left hand ready to sign...something.

No one knew for sure, possibly not even Barr himself, that he was gay. This was of little consequence to almost no one, save some voters and the more uncouth members of the media. In his fifty-odd years on this planet, few had as impressive a resume as Congressman RKO Nutt Barr, even if it contained a dearth of actual accomplishments. He had won election to Virginia's 14th district some fifteen years ago. He was the scion of Mendips Barr, the much beloved president of Nutt Barr Co. A southern gentleman who, as the story is often told, had taken extra special care of the very region of Virginia he grew up in and who, through force of will, a number of long-held favors, and a sizable amount of cash got his son elected to Congress of the United States. By the time the old man was dead, Reginald had been safely re-elected twice. Most years now, there was no challenger. Rarely was any real legislative achievement required.

This was not the case for the upcoming election. This time, there was a legitimate challenger. A man with fewer connections, far less money, no name recognition. But, Barr had to admit, the man had resilience; which contrasted starkly with the incumbent Barr. Nonetheless, despite having no actual legislative record to stand on, Barr had learned much on the Hill. He would not go down, not without a fight. Trouble was, of course, he never learned how to fight. That's what Francis was good at.

Barr could now admit to himself the truth of what Francis told him. Empty Spaces was a sound, low-risk, high-reward investment. It could, at least in theory, reinvigorate Nutt Barr fortunes and, more importantly, Barr's listless re-election campaign. Of all the things Barr hated most about the job, even more than the lying, the required and unceasing duplicitousness of life on the Hill, it was campaigning. Even with his campaign money, his seniority, his name, Barr still was forced to go out periodically and meet people and tell them why they should like him; like him enough to vote for him. For a man whose entire life was a legacy, this was cruel, indeed. Thank God, he thought, that he did not have to beg for donations. The thought sickened him, literally.

A legacy, indeed, Barr, like his father, graduated from Virginia Commonwealth University; somewhere in the lower middle. He was a member in good standing of Lambda Chi Alpha fraternity, though these many years later kept in touch with only two men from the house. Not wanting, at that time, to enter into the family business, Barr chose instead to study History in college. Upon his father's wishes, however, he soon switched to Packaging. At his mother's urging, upon graduation he began working in the tiny marketing office of what was then Nutt Barr Candies. He followed this with a position in the equally small research and development office. There, he learned of the many ways of incorporating proteins, how corn was turned into sugar, popular flavors, coatings and sizings that encouraged people to eat more than they wanted.

This led to a series of positions, not unlike his current role, where he met many people, held a number of meetings and signed a wealth of documents. Upon his father's death and his mother's very public transition to the chairmanship role, Barr was named President of Nutt Barr Co. The chief difference between his role at Nutt Barr and his work on Capitol Hill being that, on the Hill, he answered to many. As President, he answered only to his mother. Which was worse was difficult to say.

His various congressional committee and sub-committee assignments, even after seven terms, offered little glamor, and limited options for any major accomplishments. Nonetheless, businesses and lobbyists never stopped coming, never stopped requesting. At least, in that there was some joy Barr could extract. The supplicating stream of very well dressed, very smart, eager, well-paid men and women, prototypically attractive, that sought his input, sought his buy-in, desired his stamp of approval, his vote, his ability to promote or block something, anything, that would have caused joy or pain to those who paid the high salaries of these men and women, was a perverse thrill. Francis had no vote. His mother had no vote. Barr had a vote. These people wanted his vote. Barr savored that. Capitol Hill was preferable, he decided.

Nonetheless, Barr knew, of course, that if he failed to win re-election, which was for once a very real possibility, the meetings would cease. The supplicants would vanish. He would return, as a child, to being invisible.

He would as Francis advocated. As usual, that seemed the best course of action.

Twist and Shout

Barr's decision, unfairly, he thought, did not ease his immediate burdens. Sales at Nutt Barr Co. were falling, quickly, and there seemed nothing he nor anyone else could do about that. The drop was unprecedented. Other chocolate companies, even the larger ones, were experiencing similar declines, Barr reminded himself, even if most of his competitors had long since diversified. Chocolates, candies, cakes, even pet food were part of their product mix. Not so Nutt Barr Co. Nearly every penny came from the eponymous product, as it had for decades.

He surveyed again the mass of papers before him. Tables, numbers, charts. What, exactly, was he supposed to do with all their information? Glean some sort of insight, he wondered? While publicly recognized as the President of Nutt Barr Co, and certainly this was repeated to all during his re-election bid, the Congressman and those inside the halls of the aging Nutt Barr offices knew the truth. Barr had little say, little influence and possibly less interest in actually running the company. Even the title, president, was a misnomer. All major decisions, and most of the smaller ones, were made by Mother and a coterie of staff.

Mother, however, was in decline. Everyone knew. At the very least, it was presumed that should the congressman not be prepared to make real decisions, he would prevent his mother from making foolish ones. So far, blessedly, this had not been necessary. That day of reckoning, however, might be nearing.

Dammit, Barr thought. He was a Congressman; one of the most senior. He was in a re-election fight. He never once was given any real responsibilities with the company. Now he was supposed to divine some decision, some strategy, by reviewing a report with its numbers and colored charts and warnings set before him? It simply wasn't fair.

NUTT BARR CO.

Nutt Barr Co. is a manufacturer of chocolates and confectionery with $1.2 billion in annual sales. Headquartered in Glockenspiel (unincorporated) Virginia, the company has factories and distribution facilities in Roswell, GA; Taylor, MI; and Rappahannock, Virginia. The company holds 9% of ChocHealth, a Vermont-based health foods and granola bar company, and 12% of HappyHappyFroth, a maker of soda pop in Shenzhen, China.

Nutt Barr Co.'s eponymous Nutt Barr comprises 88% of annual sales. Other confections include:

- Cracker Barr
- Lemon Pipers
- Fruitgum
- Sugar Sugar
- Yummy Yummy Yummy

The Nutt Barr was created by Mendips Barr as a gift to his new wife, Geraldine Nutt. The Nutt Barr is a mixture of milk chocolate, Virginia peanuts, Virginia honey and Virginia butter. Each has a white 'G' stamped on it. The Nutt Barr has been the company's best selling candy since its debut.

Nutt Barr family net worth:
$489 million
17 million Class B shares Nutt Barr Co.
- 15 million Class B shares held by G. Nutt Barr
- 5 million Class B shares held by RKO Barr
- 1 million Class B shares held by Glockenspiel Farm Trust

According to "The Commonwealth" magazine, G. Nutt Barr is the 19th and RKO Barr the 47th richest persons in Virginia.

None of this was helping, Barr thought. The nearly 100-year-old firm was not doing well, that was clear. Sales were down, again. Margins were down. The new ad campaign was obviously not working. Product complaints were rising. The recipe hadn't changed in generations and product complaints were rising, he thought, incredulously. How could he possibly amend such reality?

Despite recent minor improvements to the quality of the chocolate, customers were now insisting that the taste of the famous Nutt Barrs had changed, its joy diminished as much as sales had fallen. Worse, Barr knew, the complainers now possessed the tools to state their message, loudly, and to have it magnified, intensified, echoed, seemingly instantly into a welcoming digital universe as vast as outer space. That was the problem. A few complainers were able to spread their message, unchecked. To hell with them Barr thought. To hell with these numbers. Then out loud, "it's not like people are going to stop eating chocolate." The problem would resolve itself, he thought.

Barr did not notice Francis standing in the doorway. He jumped.

"Francis, I did not hear you come in."

"My apologies, congressman." I just had a videoconference with our liaison for Empty Spaces."

Barr still had not collected himself.

"I'm sure I mentioned it earlier, congressman."

"Yes. Of course. With the inventor?"

"No. A videoconference." Francis pulled out his phone and gestured to the congressman. "I spoke with Mr. Shankar, in Vancouver. He is the individual who brought Empty Spaces to our attention. We're commissioning him to bring us opportunities."

"Yes. And?"

"Let me beam you my notes, congressman."

"More God damn data," the congressman told himself. "Charts, probably."

"Not to worry, I've summarized everything, including the video call. I realize how busy you are. You should have it now."

"Thank you, Francis. Please close the door on the way out."

Barr opened up the latest attachment.

NOTES FROM FRANCIS HOWERD MUSTARD ON BEHALF OF MAMACOCO VENTURES

Attendees
Francis Mustard, Chief of Staff
Maxwell Edison, research (video)
S. Shankar, Moon Unit Investments (video)

Equity
- Proposed investment: $15m - $27.5m
- Equity percentages: tbd

Discussion highlights
- People are increasingly interacting in physical space using digital channels
- New social norms
- Regulatory concerns re unlicensed "white space" radio spectrum (none expected; Barr to support)
- One-to-many messaging
- Proprietary algorithm = IP protection
- Shankar: "a transformation in how people tangibly interact with their emotions and one other"
- "ability to *track* and *shift* personal intent
- "mass communications -- individualized" (advertisement potential)

- Shankar: "we are approaching a state of being where our own choices can be reviewed in real-time, deconstructed, modified, improved, and returned to us in more useful ways. A wave that crashes upon us all yet perceived as uniquely personalized by the individual."

This Shankar fellow seems like a piece of work, Barr thought. Looks Indian. Wonder how Francis found him? Less than an hour later, Barr received a follow-up message from Francis:

"I hope you had a chance to review my call notes, congressman. Questions? Diversification of assets and IPO-level returns are nearly guaranteed. The *potential* of Empty Spaces both to support Nutt Barr Co. and your re-election bid should likewise be apparent. Empty Spaces leads us to the holy grail: connecting directly with an individual at an inflection point of time, place and need, when people make decisions on what they buy, what they reject, who they vote for. Once formed, such bonds are nearly unshakeable!

"I strongly suggest we meet personally with the Empty Spaces team* at your earliest convenience, congressman. There will be other serious investors and the founders are inexperienced in these matters. Without Shankar's guardianship, they probably would have already taken someone else's money."

*I need to discuss with you in real-time some of Shankar's concern re one of the two Empty Spaces founders. Neither should be regarded as conventional entrepreneurs.

You Like Me Too Much

"Follow-up meeting with Sickspack was good. You should have come."

"I intimidate people. This the last one?"

"Not sure."

"Another meeting? Third meeting like third date. Time to consummate."

"He bought me lunch. His driver bringing me back to the apartment. That's like second base."

"Not the same. Where you at?"

"Georgia and Cardero."

"Can you pick up some supplies for me?"

"What? Seeds?"

"Relax. Lights. I'm going to see if more lights will help. Smoke not so good, lately. Take hard left onto Denman. Store's right next to Kingyo."

"Time for new vocation? We need to be respectable now."

"Respectable? I'm part of a long and celebrated tradition. Sending my latest post.."

Blog: Daytripper
In the year 2525, if man is still alive…

Cannabis, commonly if erroneously referred to as marijuana, has been used for five thousand years. Then, as now, marijuana was used for medicinal, spiritual and (of course) recreational purposes.

Evidence of charred cannabis seeds has been found in in a ritual brazier from circa 3000 B.C. in the area now known as Romania. Cannabis was used by the ancient Hindus and Nihang Sikhs of India, and the Assyrians, who used it in religious ceremonies. In fact, the Assyrian word for smoke, 'qunubu' is likely the origin for the word 'cannabis'.

The Aryans introduced cannabis to the Scythians and Thracians, whose shamans, the kapnobatai--"those who walk on clouds" – burned cannabis flowers to induce a state of trance. A leather basket filled with cannabis leaf fragments and seeds was found next to a nearly three thousand year-old mummified shaman in the northwestern Xinjiang Uygur Region of China. Pipes dug up from the garden of Shakespeare's home contained traces of cannabis. Shakespeare's "noted weed" mentioned in Sonnet 76 and the "journey in my head" from Sonnet 27 are commonly viewed as references to cannabis use.

From the ancients to shamans to Shakespeare to now... This, my friends, is the issue. The union of the natural, the communal, with the spiritual, is as it always has been, catalyst for change, for questioning, searching. Marijuana is the leading cause of the machine breaking down. Let everyone have access to it, then what happens? We create our own sonnets, liberate our own magic.

JaDe out.

That JaDe declined to attend luncheon with their potential benefactor was, in retrospect, Jackie thought, probably a good thing.

"Although, had JaDe attended, he probably would have stopped me from talking so damn much."

The Inner Light

Every word Sickspack spoke was a clue. It all sounded so engaging, so limitless. Yet upon reflection, even when that reflection arrived in the back of a limo, the clues led not to more certainty, but less. Was this a unique quality of Sickspack's, Jackie wondered? Part of some mysterious process known only to the gatekeepers of venture capital? Or a con? That seemed unlikely, Jackie thought. Sickspack achieved some measure of success launching Vancouver-area start-ups. That much, at least, Jackie had verified.

Empty Spaces continued to grow, received good reviews. The potential was evident. Where was the money? Fuck it, Jackie thought. JaDe was right. Third meeting, third date, consummate. If there was nothing certain, not just whispers, something with real numbers attached, a letter of intent, say, within the next forty-eight hours, he would walk. Jackie's options were, he knew, limited, particularly in a poor economy and 1,000 miles from the heart of venture capital, but he had Empty Spaces. That mattered. Jackie was certain of this, even if investors were not clamoring to give him their money. From the start, he had played the amateur, behaved as though he needed their money, their approval, more than they needed Empty Spaces. Too acquiescent, too patient, too willing to please. No more, he thought.

"Yes, turn here driver. Thank you."

He was going to give Sickspack an ultimatum. One short and simple. For God's sake, Jackie told himself, stop talking so damn much.

In fact, all Sickspack asked was, 'tell me about yourself, Jackie. The real you. The man who created Empty Spaces.'

Sickspack's voice, like his words, were comforting, pleasing. "Tell me about yourself…" And with his belly full, his hopes high, Jackie complied, if haltingly at the start.

"Not sure what to tell, really. I went to college. University of Michigan. The States. Graduated. Decent grades, nothing spectacular. Met this woman my senior year. Pam. Followed her out here to Vancouver."

"Was she Canadian?"

"No. Neither of us were, just young. We thought Vancouver was exciting. We'd make it, somehow."

"And you are no longer with her, yes?"

"We had different expectations. I think, for her, she was very smart, very attractive, but also very determined, always looking for the right platform that would, I don't know, establish her identity."

"And where is she now?"

"She moved. To Washington, DC. I stayed, obviously. I like Vancouver. Even the rain. And the people and the food. The public transportation. All of it. Plus, JaDe couldn't survive outside of Vancouver. Ha."

"Yes, Jade. Your silent partner."

"JaDe. Capital J, capital D. Correct, we're partners."

"Yes. Indeed. Would you like another drink?"

"No thank you."

"Good. I need to respond to this text. Can you forgive me a moment?"

Jackie picked at the plate of berries while he waited for Sickspack. Reviewed his messages. Checked the latest download numbers.

[Empty Spaces downloads: 2,227,7xx]

Sickspack returned shortly. He poured himself a club soda and added a lemon from the fruit tray. "My apologies. Where were we? Oh, yes. My goal here, Jackie, please understand, is not to build businesses. No, anyone can do that. Rather, to make dreams come true. Tell me, what are your dreams?"

After all the mental and emotional preparation necessary for this meeting, which Jackie hoped would culminate, frankly, in at least a check and possibly a sheaf of papers to sign, a press announcement, perhaps, and a guaranteed future, this was not a question he had remotely expected. Which is probably why, eager to reveal as much as to please, he said far more than necessary.

"My dreams? I want Empty Spaces to be huge. Historic. I want it to make me rich, honestly."

"Of course you do. Only, those are dreams like everyone has, my friend. What dream defines you?"

The biggest surprise to Jackie, more even than the question itself, more than his willingness to share something so personal with this semi-stranger, was just how near the surface his dream lingered. Like time in a bottle.

"It was the first time my dad took me to a baseball game."

Jackie recalled the scene vividly. The entirety of that memory situated itself at the fore of his brain.

"Please. I am eager to hear."

Jackie filled his cup.

"One day my father took me to a baseball game. I was ten. It was hot, late summer. The team, the Detroit Tigers, wasn't doing so well. I probably had unreasonably high expectations, as boys typically do.

We parked about a mile from the stadium, on a street that sided an abandoned lot. Probably just a grass field now. My dad would never pay for parking. Never. Or hot dogs either -- he could see no justification for those prices. Though he did buy me a lemonade and a bag of chips. He had a beer, one beer, which he grumbled about, because of the price, and we split a bag of peanuts.

"I loved that day. The faultless dimensions of the field. The peculiar overhang of the wall in right field. The deep chasm in center, the hard plastic seats, the meticulousness of the grounds, the blare of the organ player, the smell of hot dogs and beer; all the shiny happy people. I loved the way the players ran onto the field at the start of the game, unable to contain their excitement; grown men on a losing team in the dead of summer in a rundown city yet fully aware they had the best job in the world.

"The Tigers won, too. At least I think they did. I romanticize the day. That part may not be true."

"I suspect much of that day is romanticized."

"We stayed till the final out. My dad knew I didn't want it to end. We walked back to the car, my dad and I. It was dark, warm, humid. I sat in the front seat."

"Memories reside in the details."

"The game is over, we are back in the car, driving out from the city. Each mile or so I would turn back to see the lights of the stadium. I suppose they clean the stands right after the game, so the lights are kept on. They were still on as we drove home. Another mile, another look back. Another mile, another look back. I did this for several miles. Pause, look back. Turn and face the front. Pause, look back, see the lights.

"'Why do you keep looking back?' my dad finally asked.

"'To see the lights,' I said, too excitedly. 'I can still see the lights above the stadium. Even though we're so far away..'

"My dad smiled. 'Just look up. You can see the stars.'"

Jackie paused, briefly.

"Wonderful. Truly magical are the memories which shape us."

"A thought struck me, like lightning, one which I blurted out, and which dad had no answer. 'If we can see the stars, they can see us!'"

"And that is your dream, then? To see the stars? With a giant telescope, perhaps?" Sickspack was not entirely sure if this was the end of Jackie's tale.

"No. Not to see them. To reach them. At least, reach out to them."

From Sickspack's reaction, Jackie wondered if he told his story properly. The remainder of the meeting focused less on Jackie's past and more on the specifics of investing, of building a business, earnest promises of things like term sheets, review process and everything that, to Jackie's ears, sounded full of promise. Still, with no payoff.

As Sickspack escorted him out of the Moon Unit offices and toward the elevator, Jackie's mind was filled with competing emotions. A dream had been unleashed, one alive since childhood, and demanded to be expressed. Waiting for the elevator, Jackie could not resist. "Have you ever heard of the Wow signal?"

"The wow signal? No. I do not believe so. The car will be waiting for you downstairs."

"The Wow signal was a radio signal detected by Dr. Jerry Ehman on August 15, 1977. He was working on the SETI project. Do you know what SETI is? SETI stands for Search for Extra Terrestrial Intelligence. It's an abandoned project that sought to capture and decode radio signals from space. You know, signals that might provide evidence of alien life."

"Yes, I believe I have heard of SETI, in fact." Sickspack pushed the 'down' button again out of habit.

"The Wow signal, and most people actually write it with an exclamation point -- W-O-W-! -- lasted for 72 seconds. Its length and type was such a shocking event, it was so unlike all other radio signals, that Dr. Ehman literally wrote 'Wow!' on the accompanying computer printout."

"Marvelous." Sickspack pushed the button.

"The frequency of the Wow signal was at 1420MHz. Hydrogen, the most common known element in the universe, resonates at 1420MHz. Very possibly, this has been alleged, extraterrestrials use this universally common frequency to send out messages."

Jackie could tell Sickspack was tuning off just as he was turning on.

"It's just something people enjoy contemplating."

"Fascinating. Looks like it will be the middle elevator here."

"The Wow! signal originated from the constellation Sagittarius. It was never recorded again. Only that once"

The elevator doors opened.

"Hold, please!" A middle aged woman from a nearby office, fit but unattractive, ran towards the elevator. Sickspack pleasantly held the door open. The woman stopped running and transitioned to a brisk walking pace.

"The SETI project was cancelled. Did you know? Sad, really. If an intended signal were to reach Earth, we would never hear it. Nor they us."

"Terrible. So many great ideas, so little funding."

The doors closed and he went down.

Jackie walked across the ground floor, exited the building, and stepped into the waiting car. He was not fully certain of what was going to happen next or when. But he remained more convinced than ever that Empty Spaces held limitless potential. WOW! potential. Despite himself, he wondered what Pam, fresh again in his mind, despite having not seen her in over a year, would think of him right this moment; on the cusp of realizing his dreams.

Eleanor Rigby

Prudence didn't care what anyone else thought, she hated the perfect Pam Drogeny. Perhaps hate was too strong a word; dislike, disdain, distrust. Those all worked, she thought. Since Pam arrived, Prudence had been coerced, shamed, pressured and guilted into working longer hours, arriving at the office much earlier than she could ever get used to, and was expected to produce far more than she believed was fair.

Worse, Pam, that bitch, mother was right, was one of those women that kept Prudence constantly ill at ease, somehow made her question everything about herself. Cutting remarks, sneering glances, senses that culled out any change, any deviation, every new outfit, old outfit, how often it was worn, her shoes, god that woman had a shoe fetish, every tiny mistake on every meaningless report, every bite of chocolate she took. Everything. Prudence stopped. "Is there anybody going to listen to my story...?" she wondered.

Thus, on this bright, sunshiny day, instead of walking through the big glass doors at the FCC HQ, and taking the elevator up to her cubicle, she chose instead, at this moment, despite already being late, to walk to the nearby coffee shop and treat herself to a full fat mocha. She earned the right to continue humming her sad song.

Technically, Prudence did not work for Pam Drogeny but for the Wireless Telecommunications Bureau in the Department of Communications Business Opportunities of the Federal Communications Commission (FCC). The FCC was housed in a monstrously large squarish ten-story faux stone, glass and steel structure with just enough detail to assure all who entered that it was good enough for government work. It was also designed, explicitly so, to keep out those who had no professional reason for being there. And, it seemed to Prudence, as if by some black magic, designed to not let her forget that she had to spend 300 days inside its hulking, impressive facade, every year, for a good twenty plus more years, before she could dare dream of escape.

She grabbed her special cup and swallowed the final swig of her mocha; hot, filling, though far less blissful than she craved on this dreary morning. Clearly, the local coffee shop had switched to lesser chocolate. She would remember that.

Work could not be put off any longer. Prudence's phone identified her as she walked through the front glass doors of the FCC then to the elevator which similarly accessed her credentials before hurrying her to the fifth floor. Pam Drogeny, who always took the stairs, never the elevator, because she was perfect, was already in her office. There as well, not surprisingly, were her stupid, evil blonde minions, which is how Prudence referred to the three sycophant co-workers that could feel no greater joy, apparently, than when permitted inside Pam's radiant orbit.

Prudence sat on her chair, leaned forward against her desk, inside the three walls of her cubicle, turned on her computer, and asked the good Lord for strength. She secured the expensive earbud in her right ear, and let Empty Spaces transport her, magically, anywhere from here, she hoped. Anywhere. Whether anyone else was hearing the same song or not.

"It's getting better all the time," she reminded herself.

TRACK THREE
Walls and Bridges

Here, There, and Everywhere

One woman's magic is another man's code. Or path to riches, perhaps. For Sickspack Shankar, conveniently, Empty Spaces was both. He well knew that investing in start-ups was fraught with uncertainty. In his field, high failure rates were not simply the norm, they were a badge of honor. He also knew that the costs to guide, build out and fully secure the promise of Empty Spaces, a one of a kind idea aching to be enjoined to a one of a kind business opportunity, and to fight the unquestionable battles with entrenched industries, including music, radio, communications, and to fend off competitors, especially those more than willing to funnel profits from an established venture into a copycat of Empty Spaces, choking off any profit potential, would require far more resources then his small Vancouver incubator could ever dare risk. His golden ticket carried a high price.

Sickspack truly believed in the potential of Empty Spaces. More so, he thought, than anything else he had ever been involved in. Which was why, in this instance, he was, not without regret, ready to take a much smaller cut in exchange for a long-term deal with Francis Mustard and Congressman Barr. Neither of whom, it was obvious, he could trust by word alone. No matter, trust was not important. Money, access to Washington, the US Government, and still part of Empty Spaces; these were worth the price, he knew. It was also why, and this was perhaps hardest of all, he was prepared to kill the dreams of a young man who was clearly full of them.

Government is a growth industry, Sickspack reminded himself; steadying his doubts. Francis Mustard was a prick, no doubt. Barr was an effete, weak fool, near as he could tell. But together, the pair had access to tens of millions of investment dollars, at least, all gathering dust, and what's more, access to the true levers of power – not least of which included a congressional committee seat that oversaw America's FCC and its multi-trillion-dollar communications industry. That, Sickspack knew, was his end of the rainbow.

Barr's money. Mustard's sword. If Francis Mustard had a long game, and he must, so too did Sickspack Shankar. The Canadian immigrant with the funny voice, who always knew he was special, and just always found himself on the outside looking in. His parents sacrificed much for him. He would repay their sacrifice. The phone rang.

No Reply

"Sickspack. Say the word."

"Mr. Howerd, yes. Review my last correspondence. Empty Spaces certainly meets your baseline. It's a fully functional semantic discovery engine that leverages real-time proximity-based..."

"Sickspack, stop. You are not speaking English. Talk to me like a person."

"The engine can drive how people connect -- "

"Good. Just needed reassurance. And what about pushing out our own message?"

"Per our assessment, I believe yes. Not how it's designed, you must understand, though I expect with minor -- "

"It can, right?"

"Yes. Definitely. I can begin working on this at the appropriate time."

"Excellent. Ever hear of the phrase 'all politics is local'? We get our hands on Empty Spaces and we can craft highly personal hyperlocal messages. Only, for the first time ever, scale them to everyone, everywhere."

"Yes, my team are reviewing any possible scalability concerns. I expect that Empty Spaces could -- "

"Think local scale global. That's what led me to you, Sickspack. That insight is gold."

"Thank you, my view is that -- "

"Hold that thought. Any concerns with the founder? Nothing to scare off the congressman?"

"There's two inventors."

"Don't you give me that shit. We both know Mr. Paper's carrying his friend".

"It would appear so, yes. Mr. Paper nonetheless insists his friend, Jade Shockwatel, be part of the process."

"What the fuck kind of stupid name is Jade Shockwatel?"

"He is a former football -- "

"Not important. We're too close."

"I envision a number of business models, from content purchase, to advertising, corporate branding."

"Agreed."

"I will send you a summary of my recent meeting notes with Mr. Paper, as well as any audio recordings. Perhaps the congressman would like to review them. Attached."

"Not necessary. Time to pull the trigger. Though take care of the jock if you can. He'll only complicate matters."

"Thank you. Bye."

Glass Onion

    FROM: Sickspack Shankar
    TO: Jackie Paper
    SUBJ: Dream on!

Congratulations! As promised I have secured investment for Empty Spaces. A few questions. You may have previously answered these but to proceed we will now require any additional information such as it exists. Please respond via this email:

- A list of all filings you have made with respect to patent and trademarks, in Canada, the US or elsewhere.
- All current known methods of tracking both downloads and users.
- We will require all code (even extraneous) related to the function, maintenance and development of Empty Spaces.
- You must confirm your exclusive ownership to Empty Spaces and all its components. Any open source code or other intellectual property, licensed or unlicensed, must be acknowledged in full detail.

Questions related to carrier control, radio signal interference, and user privacy must be addressed at the appropriate time.

I envision multiple paths to revenues. Empty Spaces can deliver not only music but other messages, targeted for an individual or a group based on their location, their preferences, habits, activities -- and intent. ADVERTISING IS INTENT MONETIZED. INTENT IS SHAPED BY EMOTION. EMPTY SPACES CAPTURES EMOTION. This is potentially revolutionary! By coupling intent with emotion, in real-time, we may have the most powerful platform for advertising yet designed.

A meeting between you and the investors, in person, will almost certainly be required.

This is great news! I told you this would happen soon!

I'll call tomorrow morning.

Truly,

Sickspack

Fixing A Hole

"Advertising." The disdain in his voice was unmistakable. Jackie read Sickspack's message as he walked down a crowded Vancouver street, on a clear afternoon, filled with people. He wasn't exactly certain why he felt such mixed emotions. "It's the beginning of a new age," he told himself, forcing a smile. The realization of a dream, close enough, at least, if only with the requirement of even more grunt work, at someone else's demand, because they manned the gates, they held the money. Jackie felt as if buried inside Sickspack's message, he was being praised for a job well done while being positioned to jump through still more hoops, perform one more trick for his masters.

"How am I supposed to provide every note and code compile?" he asked himself.

Jackie re-read Sickspack's email. He was reading too much into it, he decided, or perhaps simply not being fully honest with himself. Until this moment, a moment he had long hoped for, dreamt for, Empty Spaces, no matter what anyone else thought of it, whether they had money or without, was his creation, his dream – the carrier of all his dreams, quite possibly. Now it would become, Jackie wasn't sure, exactly, something else entirely. Not fully his. Owned, at least in part, probably large part, by people he had yet to meet, might never like, and who already envisioned it, quite unambiguously, as a means to a quick buck at its most base level. How would this change his own dream? He could not help but wonder. And, clearly, these fuckers were already determined to not include JaDe.

"Watch what you're doing!"

With Empty Spaces blaring out a rage-fueled tune into his ear, his eyes buried deep into his phone, his thoughts oblivious to those around him, Jackie stepped on a young woman's foot. She was not pleased. She was, however, quite pretty, he thought. Asian. Early 30s, maybe, wearing tight fitting athletic pants and top. She stared back at him. That meant something, he knew. A call from Sickspack halted his advance. His prey blended back into her surroundings; lost forever.

"Jackie. Hello. Listen. Everything's moving fast. Which is good. That's why I am calling now. I want you to make yourself available tomorrow morning, even if you've not prepared everything. There is much to finalize. Can you give me access to your calendar?"

"Yes."

"Great. Tomorrow morning, 9am. That looks like it works for both of us. Have a good day."

"Thanks, see you tomorrow."

"Fuck," Jackie thought to himself. "Everybody's trying to be my baby."

He stood against the outside of a bus terminal and began to type out a text to JaDe. They were about to be shipped off to the big leagues. He was stopped cold, however, by an email from a Mr. Gong Shwo. An email that should not have gotten through, nor one he ever expected to read:

"Mr. Paper. This is my second inquiry. I do hope you are able to respond. Please refer to my specifications from earlier correspondence. My tests have confirmed the presence of a non-random power surge each time Empty Space [sic] initiates a search for nearby devices. This should be unnecessary. I very much look forward to sharing with you my thoughts regarding your program. You may reach me at 8675309."

Gong Shwo,

Shenzhen, China

"All I fucking need," Jackie thought. "It's a free music service. Not like we're 'fixing a hole in the ocean'.. Fuck. Fuck. Fuck."

Jackie was not about to allow some semi-anonymous Chinese hacker, apparently, derail his dreams. Not now, especially. He decided to ignore the man and his claims. Nonetheless, he felt it prudent to at least review the man's public profile. Jackie focused at the man's picture, searching for clues:

- Thin
- Chinese
- Possibly tall, Jackie couldn't be certain from the profile. The picture was only from the chest up and Mr. Shwo, whom Jackie guessed was in his late twenties, give or take, could stand anywhere from 5'6" or closer to six feet tall.
- Straight black hair and glasses. Good, lord, he thought. A walking stereotype. The man even wore what appeared to be a free company branded t-shirt. The kind handed out at trade shows.
- Graduate of Shanghai Jiaotong University. "Never heard of it."
- PhD in Micro-Electronics, two years ago. Probably correct about his age, Jackie thought.
- Few friends on his profile.
- Works for Jai Guru, electronics displays facility.

"Fuck it. Delete."

I Saw Her Standing There

Jackie breathed in the moist, clean air. The news was good, great even, he reminded himself. The Chinese coder was an annoyance; just. Advertising was an obvious target market. He stepped into a nearby house of noodles for a celebratory bowl of Udon, and texted JaDe.

"We have liftoff!."

"Never doubted it."

"Video call with investors tomorrow. 9."

"Nothing's gonna change my world."

"On the Seabus right now. Need to do some bullshit grunt work for Sickspack and team."

"NDA?"

"No. That's not done, apparently. We should probably be on the call together, you think?"

"Maybe. I'm the silent partner, remember? My presence probably won't help."

"When we sign for a check you have to attend."

"Sign for a check, then I'll be there."

"Okay. See you in 30."

"Later."

"Maybe not. Might get lucky."

"You? Unemployed engineer with too much hair? Send me a picture."

"Sending."

"Well, she was just 17..."

"I know what you mean. Looks French Canadian."

"Then she might even fuck you."

"Vouz le vou que she..."

"Avec mois?"

"Indeed. A little biscuit with honey."

"Just how you like them."

"Score one for Empty Spaces. Jumped from her to me. Ironic, no? Strangers. On the Seabus. Brought together. That's so much bigger than using Empty Spaces for fucking advertising."

"People with money don't see clearly."

"Not sure why we should both be hearing the same song right now?"

"What is it?"

"Loud. Angry. Never heard of them."

"Can't hide horny. Empty Spaces will out."

"Suppose. Surprised I'm not the only one here. Who else beside me would be going to the North Shore in the middle of the afternoon?"

"Tourists."

"Confirmed: her travelling companions, male and female, are together. This shit works. I'm a fucking genius."

"Your woman definitely dressed to be noticed. I'm sure you will blow it, of course. So on the way home stop and pick up a couple tins of sardines and some crackers. And hot sauce. And beer. We are low. Cookies too. Maybe pick up some broth from Pho Nam Enol."

"Tuna. Alcohol. Junk food. Same as always. That 3000 calorie a day diet treating you well?"

I'm 6'1" and an athlete."

"5'11" and former athlete."

"Fine. Skip the crackers."

"Just gave me the look. Knows we are listening to the same music. Must feel the same. Shit, all I'm feeling is like getting laid so that's got to be a good sign, right? She's standing up. Mountains in view. Later."

"Hi. I think we're hearing the same song" The young woman pointed toward her tiny white earbuds; a song, angry and poignant, was pounding in her ear. She sat down next to him.

"Guilty."

"You visiting?"

"No. I live here."

"Oh. The three of us are visiting. We have a hotel on the north shore."

"Nice. This is a great place."

"You listen to the Head Lice a lot?"

"First time. Empty Spaces decided it's what I needed to hear."

"I love them. The band. Controlled aggression. Like 70s Detroit punk. Hard and fast. Just slightly professional."

"I'm from Detroit. And just slightly professional."

"Hard and fast? Funny. Seriously, from Detroit?"

"But momma, that's where the fun is."

"What?"

"Nothing. So, what other music do you like?"

"Whatever stays inside my head. Retro-punk, mostly. Never expected to meet someone needing to hear my music, not here, middle of the day."

"Been a weird day."

"Weird good or weird bad?"

"Good. I think."

"We're changing at the hotel. Then gonna do some mountain biking. Interested?"

"First tell me your name."

"Alanis."

"I would love to go mountain biking with you, Alanis."

"Great. That's at least two things we have in common."

'Hello, Goodbye

"You're back!"

"She's a woman who loves her man. From Quebec City. And, fuck. She's definitely here for a good time."

"Gets it while she can?"

"No doubt. Remind me to support bilingualism if it ever comes up for a vote."

"You can't vote. So you showed her a good time, I hope?"

"I've got nothing to say but it's okay."

"Excellent. Help clear your head. You needed that, I imagine, what with your big call tomorrow morning."

"Shit. I got work to do."

"Speaking of clear heads, there's a message for us on my computer."

"For us? I get anything?"

"Maybe they weren't sure you wanted to see it. From Andre."

"Andre? Pam's friend? Haven't seen him in a while."

"Our friend, but yes. Pam's engaged."

Jackie re-read the message. For a third time Pam was engaged. It was official. She would be married. Later this year. In Washington, DC.

The relationship between him and Pam was finished, long ago, Jackie knew, even if he allowed himself to periodically entertain the alternative. However, its painfully clear demarcated finality was not something he had been expecting to contemplate. Not so soon. Not today, certainly; not when so much else had gone right.

Not thinking, he scanned his phone for a picture of Pam; pulled up one of his favorites. Taken no more than a few weeks before their final break. At Sunset Beach. The twilight upon the water highlighting Pam's seashell eyes, her windy smile.

"What the fuck kind of name is Francis Howerd Mustard?"

Hours later, away from JaDe, Jackie learned exactly what kind of name Francis Howerd Mustard was, and what the man did for a living. Chief of Staff and Chief Legislative Director for Congressman RKO Barr. The very same RKO Barr that Sickspack previously disclosed, in strictest confidence, after Jackie hinted he might walk, that was considering investing in Empty Spaces. A confidence Jackie had not revealed to anyone, not even to his roommate and partner. At the time, of course, Jackie assumed it was all just more Sickspack bullshit. He wondered now if Sickspack, whom always seemed to talk little and say less, had perhaps said too much?

The connections seemed too improbable. Pam. Mustard. Barr. Sickspack. Empty Spaces?

Just how much does she know, Jackie wondered? About Empty Spaces? About the congressman's interest? Did she know before he knew? More than he knew? Might she have pushed her fiancé to push his boss to invest in Empty Spaces. Was she secretly trying to help him, reach out to him? Pam had not called him, not once, nor Jackie knew, even texted him so much as a single time in over a year. Now this? Engaged. Second hand news.

Back when he was still working at Sky Saxon, Jackie felt it best that JaDe file the paperwork with the FCC, lest prying eyes within the company attempt to make a claim on his invention. He naturally assumed any forms, all filed online, would never be seen by anyone that mattered amongst the hundreds of FCC employees. Certainly not Pam. Was he wrong? Did she know? And when?

At the time, it had taken all his powers to not call her, to tell her what he made, how he made it, what he thought of its potential, to hear what she thought about it, about him. He knew how weak that would make him sound. When Pam wanted to, she could make him feel like he'd never been born.   If he was wrong about everything, or right, or somewhere in between, that was still no excuse for her not to reach out to him.

Pam told him once that women thought looking forward, men thought looking backward. If this meant she could force herself to forget him, forget her past…Jackie let his mind drift. Then harden. The next time he spoke with Pam, saw her, he decided, would be on his terms. Yes, presently he was unemployed -- of his own volition. Yes, he was living with JaDe, still. And a casual afternoon romp with a young woman that, unlike Pam, was slightly overweight and, yes, a college dropout, was possibly the highlight of his month.

No. He corrected himself. The second highlight of his month. Things had changed. He built something, something successful. Tomorrow morning he would hear from investors, possibly this Congressman Barr, himself. His creation would touch millions and millions of people. Making him, he was sure, very rich. Legitimately successful. Connected. What would Pam say to all that?

TRACK FOUR
Venus and Mars

Devil in Her Heart

"This is all wrong."

Prudence glanced at the text message from Pam with a smack of bitterness. There was little joy working for someone that was younger, yes, prettier, and in all likelihood smarter, particularly when despite these gifts, everything that Pam had still seemed greater than the sum of her parts. Pam was not someone that bad things, thought Prudence, like the sudden loss of a father, or struggles with money, or a bad job or a shitty boss or small apartment or blemishes would ever apply. Only the good stuff.

Prudence placed her phone on vibrate, pushed herself away from the report she was reviewing, which, if anyone noticed, was about chocolate and the industry's growing concerns over recent declining sales, not at all work related, and walked the few steps from her cubicle into Pam's office.

"Well, of course, I know platinum is more precious that gold. I didn't know everyone else did."

"Oh, it's so beautiful, Pam. And, big."

"Yes, that's Francis."

"Never could be any other one."

"You wanted to see me?" Prudence was happy to interrupt.

Pam and her three assistants, FCC staffers who happily volunteered their souls to spin round her sun, instantly turned to face Prudence. She tried but failed to stand noble under their critical stare.

"One second." Pam never had issues with making others wait for her, Prudence knew.

"Tell us, Pam. How does it feel to be one of the beautiful people?"

Wonderful, Prudence thought. Yet another mindless conversation between the devil woman Pam and her stupid minions. The minions, as Prudence labeled them, were three women, two older than Prudence, one younger, two, the younger and one of the older, were heavy set, and all three disgracefully enraptured by being not Pam's friend, not really more like her treasured pet.

In the eternity of that moment, standing there silently as Pam finished her meaningless conversation with her meaningless sycophants, Prudence did what she always did, despite, she knew, its damaging imprint upon her spirit. She assessed the woman seated before her, hoping, this time, to uncover any flaws.

1)   Gorgeous long hair, blonde.

2) Dyed. Obviously.
3) Big eyes, green, tastefully accentuated.
4) Pretty face, albeit pretty in a contemporary sense, not classically pretty.
5) Perfect nose.
6) Pouty lips. Her two front top teeth just touching up against the lip, almost aggressively. Men find this erotic, inexplicably.
7) A little too thin, could have used a few pounds.
8) Long limbs, small bottom, pretty, narrow size 6 feet, though not really, compounded by an obvious shoe fetish, and complimented by narrow, almost other-worldly ankles. Having ankles that were slightly too large and therefore made her legs appear thicker than they really were, this last trait was a tender spot for Prudence.

And the worst part, Prudence thought? Pam's breasts. Which, in His inexplicable way, He had made as full and round and pert and perfect to such a degree that Prudence assumed there simply had to be other reasons for their very existence; reasons beyond mere physical appeal. He had endowed Pam with what was clearly planet-spanning man kryptonite for reasons no mortal could fathom.

Prudence's mother always reminded her what a pretty face she had. That much was true. But Prudence also knew that men, those that might lust for her, more often than not focused their longings upon her chest. Even still, and though larger, it was not in Pam's league.

Physical assessment notwithstanding, Prudence was, to be sure, more thorough than catty. And before Pam's very first day on the job, Prudence had already memorized the highlights of Ms. Drogeny's resume. Looks were but one arrow in the her quiver.

- Graduate of the University of Michigan, Honors Program
- Received MBA in Telematics Engineering from the University of British Columbia while concurrently employed with mobile security firm, Sky Saxon. She received several promotions while in the company's employ.
- Presented at numerous conferences on mobile device security.
- At least three interviews on Canadian business news programs regarding the smartphone industry.
- Holds patent with three others at Sky Saxon on methods for securely routing data via temporary mobile networks.
- Classical violinist training.
- Raised outside Cleveland, Ohio.

- Single, no children.
- Sleeping with, now apparently engaged to, Francis Mustard, Chief of Staff for Representative RKO Barr and rising Beltway star.
- Bitch

And with no problems wielding the power of her office, Prudence reminded herself. Which, truth be told, wasn't all that much power, even if it most definitely did include the power of this very office, which meant power over Prudence. Prudence edged closer to Pam's desk, revealing her impatience.

"Lunch," Pam asked her three minions? "1:30?"

It was 1:25. Prudence took this not as a slight but a blessing. The three minions picked themselves up and walked out, feeling privileged. Pam did not ask Prudence to have a seat. As Pam shifted her focus to her monitor, Prudence decided to sit, nonetheless.

In the several months since Pam arrived, she had, Prudence realized for the first time, done an excellent job redecorating the office. No doubt at taxpayer expense. Still, it was tasteful, functional, she thought. Instead of a traditional desk, Pam had a large white table, upon which rested several well arranged folders and papers, a monitor, a white vase with a single flower, and a small box of chocolates, which, judging from the packaging were of rather pedestrian quality attempting to appear, falsely, as if they were the work of some local craft boutique. Marketing masquerading as quality, Prudence thought derisively.

Directly above the desk hung two lamps, each with white shades. Her chair was modern and appeared quite comfortable, though Prudence did not like that it had no arm rests. There was a large black bookshelf, which from floor to ceiling, possibly built specifically for this office, Prudence thought, wondering again how much something like that might cost. Upon its two highest shelves were several photos, what appeared to be at least one of her degrees and various tastefully accentuated memorabilia.

There was a small adjoining dresser-like piece. Atop the dresser stood three small white vases, of varying sizes, all filled with flowers, and a green bowl with no apparent purpose. There was a second chair, which Prudence sat on, a bit uncomfortably due in part to it also possessing no arm rests. Obviously a thing with her, she decided. Finally, there was a couch, white, with a low back and a sort of industrial metal frame meant to serve as part of the design, rather than merely functional. Otherwise, the walls were bare.

"You wanted to see me?"

"One second -- "

"Congratulations, by the way."

"Thank you."

"Here it is. Thank you for waiting. I'm going to forward you several documents. Go over them. I want you to compile a report on a mobile service, obviously, called Empty Spaces. How it operates, any competing services, any possible concerns raised over its use of unlicensed radio spectrum, including by FCC-like agencies outside the US. Related issues. It's a – "

"Yes, I've heard of Empty Spaces," said Prudence, cutting Pam off. "It's a music recommendation service. I use it, myself," she noted, proudly.

Pam considered this for a moment.

"Very nice for you. I had sex with its maker." This elicited a cacophony of affirmative merriment and much high praise from her minions, all of whom apparently had little to do but stand outside Pam's door, waiting.

Prudence had no idea how to respond. Thus, she sat there, mute.

"In particular, I need authoritative information on the service and any pending issues related to the means which the technology utilizes radio spectrum, licensed or not. Plus anything else you --"

Prudence couldn't help herself. Finally an assignment that wasn't merely killing time. "Is there an issue? Privacy? Because that's quite easily managed, if you'd like me to explain it to you. Possible interference?"

"No. No issues. Just assimilate the information that's available. This will simply be part of a larger report on the value of these services and their compatibility with existing mobile technologies and regulations. I don't expect any issues. I expect there will be no privacy concerns. No interference concerns. That is important. You don't need to be reminded that the FCC wants to encourage use of open spectrum. Services like this will help. Anything else you wish to add."

"It's 1:35!" Two of Pam's minions, the two chubby blondes, appeared at the door."

"One moment. Prudence, do you think you can handle this?"

"Of course."

"Excellent. And make sure there is an executive summary. Those I circulate this to won't read the entire thing."

Pam stood up, which meant Prudence had to stand up. "Oh, one more thing. You like chocolates, correct?"

Prudence nodded perceptibly, not sure why Pam was asking.

"Francis gave me these. He knows I don't eat them. Fattening." Pam handed the small, nicely decorated box to Prudence and motioned her out of the office.

"Thank you. Are you sure you don't want them?"

"Certain. You take them. I know how much you like them."

Pam stood at the door, shielded by her toadies. Prudence clearly not a member of the club. She searched for something to say. "Oh. Dark chocolates. Most people don't realize that these contain more polyphenols than green tea."

Pam looked at her minions incredulously. "Yes, but that's not really the point, is it? They make you fat." Prudence, who was not fat, indeed, was at most ten or so pounds over her absolute optimum weight, felt as if she had just been branded. One of the minions giggled and she went red.

She recovered, faked a smile. "True. Even good chocolates do have a lot of sugar and fat. Probably why everyone enjoys them so much."

"We're done here."

As Pam left, Prudence, alone, inexplicably humiliated, returned to her desk and did her best to disappear inside the three low walls of her cubicle. She placed the earbud inside her right ear, hoping Empty Spaces would help her escape from everything, and everyone. The music, she realized, its solace, its softness, exactly as she needed, was more comforting, even, than her beloved chocolate. She could not recall if that had ever happened before. Before she could stop herself, she quickly consumed four pieces of Pam's cheaply made confections. Each of which tasted worse than the one before. Only Pam, Prudence thought, could take away the pleasure from chocolate.

The thought of which was so disconcerting that as Prudence clicked through the various links embedded within the many documents that Pam sent her, all connected to Empty Spaces or related unlicensed services, she could no longer be certain how exactly she arrived upon on a trove of reports, seemingly unconnected, that linked her beloved chocolate with marijuana.

Prudence skimmed the material she found of interest:

"Researchers reported in the 8.22 issue of the journal Pharmaco-Nature that chocolate contains substances that mimic the effects of marijuana.

"Chocolate, dark chocolate in particular, contains small quantities of *anandamide*. Anandamide, also known as N-arachidonoylethanolamine or AEA, is an endogenous cannabinoid neurotransmitter. The name is derived from the Sanskrit word ananda, which means "bliss."

"Anandamide appears to play a critical role in mood, and to a lesser extent in pain, depression, fertility and even memory."

"Researchers speculate that anandamide helps account for the brief feelings of 'high' that chocolate provides, similar to marijuana, albeit in a much milder form. 'Both THC, the principal active chemical in marijuana, and anandamide stimulate the very same neural receptors,' remarked one of the researchers."

"Additionally, we discovered two ingredients contained in chocolate that actually inhibit the breakdown of anandamide, and thus, in effect, extend and even increase the feelings of 'bliss' within the brain."

Did this matter, Prudence wondered? Chocolate and chemicals and cannabinoids and brain receptors? Right now she felt, even if she dare not verbalize it, almost mad with chocolate. She continued reading. At very least, there might be enough material for several blog posts, she decided; all researched on work time.

1.) Chocolate triggers feelings of bliss.
2.) Chemicals within chocolate are able to make these blissful feelings last.

Both points were obvious; certainly not worthy of government or university research dollars. That something in chocolate, anandamide, mimics marijuana and, more importantly, bonds with the very same receptors in the brain as marijuana, however, was both new and exciting. It had been a long time since Prudence learned something new about chocolate.

How many others know of this, she wondered? There can't possibly be many readers of Pharmaco-Nature. Intrigued, though not wanting anyone at the FCC, or elsewhere within the government to think she was searching for anything related to marijuana, Prudence thought it best to link her research with her work.

Search: anandamide and wireless communications

She was shocked that a relevant result popped up instantly:
"The NIH has conducted a series of studies on wireless/mobile phone radiation and human health. The NIH classifies mobile phone

radiation on the IARC scale into Group 2B - possibly carcinogenic. Research is inconclusive and ongoing."

The NIH, or National Institutes of Health, was one of the largest, most influential bureaus within the government. Prudence was not at all surprised, given the agency's scope, that someone at sometime researched mobile phones and cancer, or possibly radio wave propagation and cancer. Or, possibly, smartphones and hearing damage. She wasn't terribly interested, truth be told. That there was, in some way, a link with chocolate, however, compelled her to continue.

"Recent tests associate a positive correlation between mobile phone usage and a heightened production of enzymes which convert anandamide into arachidonic acid."

"Wait." Prudence realized the word escaped her mouth. She looked around. Saw no one. "Probably still at lunch," she thought. Mobile phone usage and anandamide? She repeated the terms to herself, silently. She typed in a new search, starting her focus on what she knew she did not know:

Search: anandamide and mobile phone radiation

"Prudence!"
"Oh, sorry. I was listening to my music. Empty Spaces, actually."
"Great. So you already got started on the report, then?"
"Yes. It's my priority, just as you requested."
"Good. I expect you should be able to complete it soon. Oh, you liked the chocolates, I see."
The half eaten box was clearly visible.
"Yes, well -- "
Pam's phone buzzed. "Have to take this. I'll want a solid draft by the end of next week" she demanded walking quickly into her office.
"Bitch."
Prudence managed to keep the thought to herself. Her phone's screen lit up. Empty Spaces beamed a song into her earbud, one she had not heard probably in years. It was exactly what she needed. Prudence marveled. "How does it do that?"
"End of next week? Then I have plenty of time," she thought." Prudence was eager to tell her readers of her latest discovery. Chocolate. Marijuana. Something called anandamide. "Definitely I

should get several posts out of this." She placed the half-eaten box of chocolates in a drawer, texted her mother, and settled in.

"Chocolate and anandamide. Mobile phones and chocolate," she repeated to herself. "What isn't our government involved in?"

Good Day, Sunshine

"Michelle? It's Prudence. Prudence Skiffle. How are you doing?"

Prudence hated calling people. She carried her phone with her everywhere, true, but rarely for talking to a live human being.

"Dear Prudence! Come out to play?" Michelle always put Prudence at ease and simultaneously on edge.

"Work, I'm afraid."

"How is the FCC these days?"

"Fine, considering. I now report to the future Mrs. Francis Howerd."

"And how is Ms. All Tomorrow's Parties?"

"Devil spawn."

"Prudence. You know my policy. Sister power."

"I know. She's not really so bad, I suppose. Anyway, she asked me to do some research on a mobile service called Empty Spaces. It's out of Canada. Pretty clever, actually. They originally submitted a filing because it uses unlicensed radio spectrum."

"White spaces radio band, yes. And?"

"One of the documents in my research contained a link which included a reference to a very curious NIH study on mobile phone radiation. Not sure why, exactly. There's no other reference to this study and I'm not having any luck here finding a copy of the results. It specifically mentioned chocolate, oddly enough. Can't imagine why. Would you be a dear and see if you might be able to get a copy of the report? I'll send you the information I have."

"Empty Spaces. FCC. NIH study. Chocolate. And people wonder where the money goes."

"Probably it's nothing, I know, but I wanted to find out more. There may be some connection, I'm not sure how. Only, no one's bothered to respond to me. And none of the materials are accessible through normal channels."

If Prudence aspired to more, much more, than her current station, she would no doubt look to Michelle Maybelle for guidance. Michelle was, and all who knew her agreed, respected, vital, accomplished, and still only in her mid 30s. Super fit if not justly attractive. Whip smart, fearless, utterly capable, blessed with boundless energy, sharp wit. No one forgot her. Everyone admired her, it seemed.

Michelle spent eight years advancing through the manifold levels and competing offices within the NIH, where she developed a wealth of contacts and maximized opportunity at every turn. The NIH was where

Prudence first met Michelle, having spent a brief period with the institute before taking her current job at the FCC. The two quickly became friends, although Prudence rightly suspected that Michelle was friends with everyone.

If Pam seemed to achieve a level of success that Prudence knew she might never match, through looks and guile, Michelle would achieve far more, Prudence believed, owing instead to a combustible mix of intelligence, perception, a knack for taking the right risk at the right time, and a near-religious commitment to improving the lot of all the women she worked with. That, and Prudence realized, results. Michelle always got the job done. Better, faster; often with a solution a magnitude greater than the original problem ever indicated. Taught to jump from rock to rock merely to stay afloat, this last talent was always the subject of both deep admiration and inexplicable misapprehension by Prudence.

"I've not been with the NIH for nearly four years, remember."

"I know. I also know you always leave on good terms -- with many doors welcoming you back."

"I assume this won't be a problem. Will let you know if otherwise. Lunch this week?"

Prudence was flattered, if fearful. "That would be great."

"Phone shows we both have Thursday open. I know a great place. Time and directions are now on your calendar. All my best to your mother."

Realizing that was not so much a question, and that Michelle was about to hang up, Prudence agreed.

"Just the two of us, correct?" Michelle was gone.

Prudence feared more than just Michelle might attend. Michelle was the center of an informal women's networking group she called Party Line. All women either employed in government or for a private firm that made its living off government contracts. Prudence, in fact, had started out in the club, thanks to Michelle's personal request. Only, intimidated by the sharply confident nature of the women, Prudence attended just two of their after work drinking sessions. Though she could never admit this to Michelle, Prudence was happy living with her mother and, all things considered, happy working at a job that rarely demanded more than she could deliver.

I'll Follow the Sun

JaDe sat on the couch, passed his cigarette to Jackie, seated in the chair nearby. Jackie took a short puff, inhaled deeply, exhaled slowly. He was unaware that he was shaking his head, slightly, as if responding negatively to some unstated question.

"I just never wanted to believe that people who could get up every day to go to work, day after day, year after year, till they were almost dead, well, they couldn't feel about things, like music, for example, the way I do. Not true. Empty Spaces was my way of reaching out."

"Some choose not to be reached."

"Music matters to me. I listen to a song and I am released, transported; a part of something else. I am a child again, or with friends from school, or it takes me to how I felt, exactly how I felt, I don't know, two weeks after I broke up with Pam, say, or my first girlfriend in high school." He handed JaDe the cigarette.

"People think memory is a chain. It's not. It's individual pieces, scattered."

"Empty Spaces has to work."

"It will. Shit. It does. You know the numbers. People about to hand you over real money."

"I can still recall where the original idea came from. I'm on the Skytrain. A woman takes her place near me, and she's humming this song. And I start to sing that song, too, in my head. And I realize, it's exactly the right song for how I felt. No. For how I needed to feel. Exactly. That could not be a coincidence, I think. There must be some connection between us, unearthly perhaps, channeled through the music. I got off at the next stop. Never saw her again. But for that one moment, the empty space between us disappeared."

JaDe took another drag. "Here I am. This is me. I am ready to hear from you. That's what we have. Empty Spaces is a signal to those around us that we are here and we seek to close the gap."

Jackie sat up. "Right. And Empty Spaces does that. Through music."

"Music is our mood ring. Our social profile, only on a different plane."

"Here I am. This is me."

"Moving at the speed of sound."

Jackie got up, walked into the kitchen, searching for food. He passed on the chocolate cookies, preferring instead a plate of cold chicken. He also grabbed some pickles. "Anything," he asked JaDe?

"I'm good."

Jackie returned, sat back down. JaDe handed him another cigarette but Jackie brushed him off.

"Did you know that on the 30th anniversary of the launch of Pioneer, when it was more than 7 billion miles away from Earth --"

"Billion?"

"Right. Billion, not million. 7 billion miles away, it was still able to send radio signals back to Earth?"

"No shit?"

"Traveling at 30,000 mph, headed straight toward the constellation Taurus."

"Sure you don't want a smoke? Tell me the truth. This weed sucks, right? I did not grow this. Got it from some Indo Canadian. Ought to wring his neck for this shit."

"Always wise to anger drug dealers."

"I just want some good weed? Fuck."

"When Pioneer was launched, in 1972, NASA put this gold plated plaque inside it that contained information about Earth. You know, information about people, how we evolved, lived; in case there was life out there and they happened upon the craft. I've always thought that was a great idea. Only, poorly executed. A golden disc with imprinted pictograms? It's too limiting, static."

"What would you prefer?"

"Real voices."

"Whose?"

"Everyone's."

JaDe now stood up. He put on a thin yellow rain slicker, one Jackie purchased for himself but gave to JaDe after discovering, too late, that it had no pockets.

"You're going out?"

"I have to find me some decent weed. Come along?"

"Pass. Speaking with Sickspack and our investors tomorrow morning. Probably ought to finish preparing."

I Call Your Name

The alarm on his phone blared. Jackie knew he slept too late; cursed himself appropriately. His head was pounding, his mouth dry, stomach rumbling. At least he could stay in his room and conference with Sickspack and all others, he reminded himself. He quickly washed up, brushed his hair, to little avail, and prepared himself for the big moment.

His phone trembled. Sickspack flashed onto the screen. Jackie recognized the framed posters with their hollow inspirational messages on the walls of Sickspack's office.

"Jackie. Good morning. Good morning. I am conferencing in Maxwell Edison. He will serve as our technical advisor on this project and coordinate between my office and our investors. Tell us about yourself and Empty Spaces."

Fuck, Jackie thought, forcing himself awake. What is this bullshit? Invest or not, goddamit.

"Jackie?"

"Yes. You want me to go over Empty Spaces, right? Haven't we covered everything?"

"Jackie, Maxwell, here. I need to make our investors comfortable with both you and the service. We need to put our people at ease." Despite himself, Jackie regarded Maxwell's position as reasonable, even if not favorable to his own situation. He would let Sickspack know offline that no delays, no bullshit would be accepted.

Avowals notwithstanding, Jackie acknowledged to himself that he was awake, he was on the phone, and, at the moment, had no other prospects; least not ones that were willing to put up the millions Sickspack dangled before him. So, once more he told of the inspiration that led to Empty Spaces, his decision to focus on music, the way the service understood a person and their mood, his clever coding that allowed the service to hop from one device to another, over unlicensed spectrum. The way it could bring strangers together. And, since Maxwell requested, all the details surrounding certification of the service with the FCC, which was simple enough, and construction of the data packets that were transmitted as Empty Spaces jumped from phone to phone, which was quite complex.

The call went on far longer than Jackie had anticipated. He tried hard to keep still, to simply stare into the screen and speak. He was much more comfortable while moving, however. "And I realized that there was nothing else like this. Music connects us on some deep level with our emotions." Shit. Selling it, he thought. There better be a damn check waiting for me before this call is over.

"We have many selves, all of which we avail to those around us. In due time, of course."

Jackie was certain that Sickspack was attempting to coax him into something more than simple agreement but unsure what, exactly. Maybe Sickspack just couldn't put the brakes on his bullshit, he thought. Jackie appreciated his skill in observing a person's physical traits and habits. Sickspack was tall and trim and fit with nice brown skin. Owing to his ethnicity, his immigrant parents, and that he spent his formative years in the middle of Canada, he spoke with an oddly comforting accent. Like the manager of an Indian outsourcing operation, Jackie imagined, there to put frustrated Americans at ease. Only now, staring at Sickspack on the small screen, Jackie noticed that the man rarely seemed to blink. Odd that he hadn't spotted that before, he thought.

Jackie continued, employing his most professional voice, fully aware that he was inching closer to a funding milestone. "I had been working on building various services for other companies, all of which were limited in scope. I wanted to take full advantage of the power of music, of smartphones, and all the personal data locked inside them. My thought was that identity and location were overvalued and that –"

"Jackie. This is Maxwell. Were you under contract with any of these companies at the time you created this service?"

"I worked as a contractor, so not really. It was mostly one company, and their clients, and none of them were even contemplating anything like Empty Spaces. I spent most of the past three years with -- "

"Very good. Thank you. Please, continue."

"As I began looking at the multiple data streams people present via their phones, everything from location to who they are communicating with to what about, it became fairly easy, if time consuming, to develop an algorithm to rapidly scan all that information, in real-time. The result, obviously, is understanding a user's emotional state then instantly finding and playing music to match that state."

"Maxwell, again. I can't tell you that I like the name Empty Spaces. But that's for later. Tell me, how could the service know what a song's emotional intent is, for example?"

Maxwell Edison was a large man, such that his physical presence was fully framed within Jackie's small smartphone screen. He was round, thick, very pale, fish like, with short black hair that was precipitously graying. He was speaking from a monitor in what Jackie assumed was his office, possibly even his home; wherever that was. He spoke with what Jackie assumed was an Australian accent, possibly South African. And, Jackie realized, his very large hands were balanced against very thick, stubby fingers.

"How does the service know the song's intent? Yes. That's actually easy to answer. Nearly every commercially available song is tagged and indexed, meaning it contains highly reliable crowdsourced information regarding form, genre, artist, musical type, lyrics, articles associated with the song, such as a review; lots more, in fact. And all available to be streamed to any device. Plus, there are large scale computer-generated linguistic studies that mathematically score a song's placement within various genres, count the use of pronouns, for example, repetitive words, tense, connotation. We're awash in this kind of detail, actually. Intent can be decrypted just as an emotion can be categorized."

"Yes. Or branded."

"Jackie. Maxwell again. Thank you for that. I'm curious. There appears to be a larger than necessary burst of radio energy from Empty Spaces each time it prepares itself to jump to another device. Why is that? Is it analyzing each user, finding a match before the jump? What, exactly?"

"Partly correct. The radio burst is to ensure all necessary information, which is contained in the data packet, is effectively transmitted and that no security – "

"That was my assumption. It was obviously a non-random event. More important, what does that mean as far as scalability is concerned?"

"There are no limits to scaling the service. In theory, of course. Admittedly, there are some necessary limitations with distribution of Empty Spaces by viral means. The data packet contains an abridged version of the service. The full capabilities of Empty Spaces are only available once the entire package is downloaded from our servers. That's why the program, once installed, knows to call our servers, pending the user's acceptance, obviously, and download the complete application. I'm working on streamlining this but presently it's not practical to transmit the full software embed from phone to phone. The user would perceive a lag."

"Indeed, perception is a quagmire. I find it fascinating how the various emotional and intellectual, even physical cues that Empty Spaces captures provides a sort of subconscious stamp if you will; validation of the person's public psyche. It opens up a deep dark truthful mirror onto who we really are."

"Yes. That is why I realized the value of having Empty Spaces hop from user to user. It's not simply to grow the service virally, nor even to improve the recommendation algorithm – which it does by the way – but because the song a user is hearing reflects exactly who they are at that point in time and space. If that song also plays for someone else, someone nearby, who thus feels like they do, than this creates a potentially very powerful connection between two persons."

"Powerful, indeed. It exposes our true self, even to a stranger."

"Jackie, does the additional overhead when hopping impact battery life?"

"Technically, yes. Everything does, really. We are working on optimizing that."

"We?"

"Yes. JaDe Shockwatel. My partner. I can try and reach him now if you like."

"Oh, yes. Sickspack mentioned him. Thanks, no need."

"And how often is Empty Spaces wrong?"

"Well. Never."

"Never?"

"I mean, it's constantly improving itself. Learning the user with each data point. If the user believes Empty Spaces is incorrect, they can always move to a new song."

"Certainty is illusory, Jackie. Don't you agree, Maxwell? But I do think you make a valid point about music and emotional states, Jackie. I just remembered that they call those songs that get into your head, the ones you can't get rid of, earworms. Marvelous word. It points to the elemental origins of music, don't you think?"

"In fact, our brains use up more processing power, if you will, for sound than for vision." Jackie instantly regretted saying this. Though he wanted to make sure he fully conveyed the potential value of Empty Spaces, he was not at all interested in a cordial discussion with Sickspack, nor Maxwell. Funding, now, was all that mattered.

"More processing power for sound than vision? That is surprising."

"I have something on my phone. I'll forward the link. The thalamus, that's the part of our brain that gets input from our ear, can identify pitch and loudness. The secondary cortex, which is located in the center of the brain, detects the melody and rhythm. The tertiary auditory cortex of the brain then pieces all these inputs together."

"Wonderful. Just one piece of one song impacts so many parts of our brain."

"Jackie? Maxwell. I do think we should quickly explore methods to route around those increases in processing power and signal propagation when the service hops from user to user. I'm sure you did your best, though they do appear to be unnecessarily demanding. We can bring in additional coders for support."

"I suppose." Rather than feeling slighted, Jackie assumed that Maxwell had just tipped his hand. Despite any criticisms, the man was already planning on okaying the investment, he thought. "It's only a very brief uptick in processing power, and it serves a useful purpose. JaDe and I –"

"Jade Shockwatel, yes? Maxwell was writing something down.

"Yes. It's two syllables. Ja-De."

"Ja-De. Thank you. More details on the hop, if you would."

"That's my area of expertise. And it's something I continue to improve upon, in fact. As you know, Empty Spaces experiences a brief surge when hopping from user to user. This takes place in an approved band of unlicensed radio spectrum, in the 900MHz region. The unlicensed spectrum is the best, cheapest means of using available bandwidth to enable Empty Spaces to jump from one person, or one device, to the next. There are no fees, no licensing requirements – other than certification paperwork. This same spectrum, in fact, is already used by communications carriers to off-load traffic from their network. It's highly reliable."

"Understood. Continue."

"Hopping from device to device creates an instant connection, physically between devices and psychologically, we hope, between users. Empty Spaces seeks out nearby devices approximately 30 times per second. If a device is detected, a data packet is prepared and this burst of information is exchanged in real-time, via the aforementioned unlicensed spectrum. The packet then installs a customized version of Empty Spaces, along with information about the originating user, header and security information, extraneous data and so forth onto the receiving device. If Empty Spaces detects a match between the persons who feel the same, hear the same song if you will, then both users are notified."

"Amazing potential, don't you agree Maxwell? We never put a horse in a race to the bottom, Jackie."

"I have another meeting, Jackie, Sickspack. Let's end this now, shall we? I will follow up with you directly, Sickspack, soon. Good day, all."

"Thank you."

"Bye."

Jackie and Sickspack stayed on the call a few moments longer.

"What we have here," said Sickspack, talking more to himself than to Jackie, "is a recommendation engine for living. Truly. This is life altering. I believe that. Forget about the music. This small amount of code understands both our self and the world around us. That is powerful. Insanely powerful. Imagine this running some plastic female robot. Every fucking Japanese man will want two and buy four. Every company wants to get inside peoples heads, especially at the right time, the time the user is most open to their message. Such potential…

"With Empty Spaces and our smartphone we now possess a tool, one we all carry around with us every day, everywhere we go, that understands each of us better than our own mother, perhaps. Better than our spouse, better than our best friend. Everything is linked together by simple code. Empty Spaces is more than just a means of uncovering how someone feels. It provides something tangible that reflects those feelings! Something actionable. In this case music, but why stop there? Do you have any idea of how fucking much coffee and fast food can be sold using this?"

Jackie really had no idea.

"…No, the real money is in knowing how people feel. That's the missing piece of the puzzle. Anyone can sell or market; can seek to dissect and determine what people want, and when, and why and where. But Empty Spaces has cracked the DNA on how people feel. In real-time. At the point of presence. What we have in Empty Spaces is an engine that spits out how someone is feeling, right now, right where they are standing. The possibilities are endless. Absolutely fucking infinite…"

The call over, and with concrete assurances from Sickspack that investors would sign off soon, Jackie texted JaDe.

"Gone? You never leave the place."

"4/20. Acquisitioning provisions for the block party."

"Finished call with Sickspack. Investors loved it! All systems go."

"Sure? This just arrived. I was copied.

Jackie scanned his messages. "Son of a bitch."

Message from Gong Shwo, Shenzhen, China

Dear Mr. Paper, this is Professor Shwo. You have misunderstood my previous message. I believe that Empty Spaces may be in violation of ITU guidelines. For approved spectrum, even unlicensed radio spectrum, the standard range for services such as Empty Spaces is commonly no more than 4 meters square and relegated to line of sight. When Empty Spaces calls out to a nearby device, I have confirmed that the signal waves are measurably more powerful then necessary for the applicable distances required of such a proximity-based service. Indeed, the signal propagation burst appears to mimic a limited sky wave. As well, there appears little need for the service to scan for other devices at its current rate of 35 times per second. Can you please clarify?

I have verified that Empty Spaces establishes a temporary synchronized authToken to ensure the originating user's personal information is transmitted only to an appropriate receiving user. These actions then are not necessary for security purposes. I would also very much like to know how you are able to achieve such signal power considering the limited computing resources available within a user's smartphone."

"Professor?" Jackie thought. "Well, professor, I know all this. Dick."

Jackie stared at his phone for several seconds. How the fuck did this fellow in China even learn of Empty Spaces and why was he texting him? Why was he trying to tear apart the service, literally? Empty Spaces was free. It worked. People enjoyed it, it made them happy. They were calling out to strangers, to those within reach, to those just like them, in fact. No one and no thing was harmed.

Fuck you, he thought. He paused, then messaged the man back, accepting there was a small chance this would only complicate matters.

Professor Shwo:

Empty Spaces meets FCC guidelines in the United State and likewise holds CRCC certification in Canada. It is expected that there will be no issues with ongoing approvals in other countries as necessary. In the past 18 months the FCC has approved additional white space bandwidth for unlicensed use, provided the device satisfies applicable non-interference guidelines with commercially regulated spectrum. Empty Spaces satisfies all such guidelines. Most countries are expected to follow the FCC standard.

[Author's note: Jackie did not know if this last point was true.]

I will review the service for any bugs. Thank you for using Empty Spaces.

P.S. "Professor. Go fucking build something on your own and stop trying to reverse engineer my stuff."

This last Jackie said to no one but himself.

Till There Was You

The upside to anger, Jackie thought, was adrenaline. Only, he realized in this case, and this was doubly frustrating, he had nothing to do. He only now realized there were no follow-ups from his call with Sickspack, which seemed surprising. Action items, to do's, reports; business lived on that shit, he thought. He had no job. JaDe was still out. Outside, it was drizzling. He could go for a run later. He was in no mood to do any work on Empty Spaces, not that it required anything of him. The service, in fact, now seemed strangely, for the moment at least, out of his hands and, also for the moment, just as strangely, he was happy about this. Nonetheless bored, he strode to the apartment's front room window. Perhaps it was no longer raining.

It was. "Who loves the sun?" he asked himself.

Jackie stared out into the sky, a touch of grey. The windows along the north facing side of the apartment were regrettably small. Tilting his head just so, however, and looking up, he could see Grouse Mountain. Directly below him was a small urban park. Neither beckoned.

He and JaDe lived in a pleasant condo tower, one of many on the North Shore; theirs favored with a view to the north and east. The building was about 20 years old, tall, rectangular, non-descript, thoroughly common, and probably worth, given its location, 1100 plus square feet, two bedrooms and two bathrooms and functioning kitchen, well in excess of $1 million. All JaDe's. He purchased it for significantly less during his days with the BC Lions.

In the front room was a television, couch, recliner, two tables, one long, one short, a gas fireplace which they never used. Also, JaDe's guitar, rarely used, a functioning server Jackie promised to eventually move, a large number of well-concealed cables, an ancient eReader.

He walked over to the couch and lay down, struggling to get comfortable. One of the early users of Empty Spaces, Prudence Skiffle, had told him of her blog. It was about chocolate. This topic was of nominal consequence to him; probably less. Surprisingly, however, several of the articles she linked to or forwarded directly to him, he found quite interesting. Jackie reached for his phone, went to her site, and clicked on one of the links.

Blog: Bitter Water
The Impetus for Cacao Cultivation was an Alcoholic Beverage not a Chocolate Drink!

The earliest known use of cacao, the source of our modern day chocolate, has been pushed back more than 500 years to somewhere between 1400 and 1100 B.C.E.. More than three thousand years ago! This was confirmed thanks to a new chemical analysis of residues extracted from pottery excavated at an archaeological site at Puerto Escondido in Honduras.

Strikingly, the new evidence also indicates that for these earliest users, it was the fruit pulp of the cacao plant, not the pods where chocolate comes from, that was so important. The pulp was used to make a fermented beverage, containing about 5% alcohol. According to archaeochemist Dr. Patrick McGovern, Senior Research Scientist with the University of Pennsylvania Museum of Archaeology and Anthropology, and one of the paper's five authors...

Jackie had briefly fallen asleep. Only a few minutes, apparently; his phone remained at the article where he had drifted off. He looked about, cleared his eyes and continued reading.

...carrying on this ancient tradition, an alcoholic beverage from the pulp continues to be made in parts of Latin America. The famous chocolate beverage of the Mayan and Aztec kings, originally served at special ceremonies and feasts, came later.

Dr. McGovern has found that alcoholic beverages go hand in hand with the earliest development of human cultures. As with the cacao fruit in Central America, high-sugar fruits were similarly used to produce alcoholic beverages in other parts of the world, including in Neolithic China and the Near East, two regions where...

Again, Jackie drifted off, this time awakened by JaDe.

"Going back out. I got to find me some decent smoke. Want anything?"

Jackie was startled by JaDe's entrance. "What? Sure. Who'll stop the rain?"

"Rain stopped 20 minutes ago. What've you been smoking?"

Jackie sat up, looked through the window.

"Just sittin here ya ya…"

Revolution I

"News. Nothing major. See you at lunch tomorrow."

Prudence was only mildly surprised when she received a text from Michelle late afternoon, the day before their scheduled lunch date. Her first reaction, nonetheless, was fear. Michelle Maybelle had never, not once, been anything but supportive. Still, Prudence found her utterly intimidating. Not once could she recall a single instance when Michelle did not appear completely in command of herself, her situation and those around her. Prudence could not quite comprehend how she managed such a trick.

Likewise, for all her professional accomplishments, Michelle personally never looked anything other than her best, Prudence knew. Michelle's long dark brown hair was inviting and perfect. Always. Her breezily confident smile, lightly bronzed perfect skin, twinkling eyes, straight nose, perfect white teeth, full, glossy lips, long, feminine neck, athletic physique and a body that while not killer, which maybe would have detracted from strangers grasping how smart she was, was certainly better than most. Much better, in fact. Michelle was current and topical and witty and fun to be with; well read, well connected, justly admired. Prudence was hopelessly intimidated.

It was the middle of the day, Thursday, and Bourgeois Tagg on Massachusetts Ave., Michelle's choice, was well occupied but tranquil. Michelle, not surprisingly, looked especially lovely, Prudence thought, in a black blouse; loose, comfortable, expensive, fully complimenting her curves. Her skirt was equally fitting; conservative, certainly, though still revealing enough of Michelle's shapely legs and backside to elicit the occasional leer. All of which made Prudence feel doubly uneasy in her standard workaday attire. This was compounded by the fact that the restaurant, though quite nice, was far more expensive than Prudence had expected.

"Prudence! You look beautiful."

"Thank you. You are gorgeous as ever."

"Always nice to hear."

"Tell me. Seeing anyone?" Michelle asked. A rather handsome man obviously bored with his lunch date was seated no more than ten feet away. Michelle quickly spun her gaze, hoping to catch him staring at her.

Prudence seized upon the moment to dodge the question. She renewed her focus on the menu. Michelle already knew what she would order. Prudence required a few more minutes, mindful that she not eat anything that would be too messy, or too fattening, or looked like she was trying to lose weight, or needed to lose weight, or that she had to consider how much something might cost. When the waiter listed the day's special, she chose that, with water, reminding all she had to return to work. Michelle's white wine would have definitely put her to sleep, Prudence feared, so she resisted her friend's appeals to join her.

Owing to Michelle's busy schedule, small talk was otherwise kept to a minimum. Michelle revealed that she would be launching her own business, within the year; a start-up that utilized mobile devices and location tracking data to improve health outcomes. She mentioned a few of the women in Party Line that Prudence still remembered. They discussed her work at the FCC over salad.

"Tell me, then. Why the interest in Empty Spaces?"

The restaurant was less noisy than Prudence expected and she felt as if she were talking too loud. "Well, Pam asked me to look into it." Prudence immediately realized this made her sound less significant than necessary. "Plus, I'm a user. I think it's great. I expect it to be pretty big, actually. When it IPOs."

"Wasn't my cup of tea."

"Well, Lisa Mayers, not sure if you know her, one of Pam's toadies, don't frown, I know. Anyway, she mentioned to me that Pam's fiancé, along with Congressman Barr, plan on investing in it." This bit of knowledge helped Prudence feel as though she were an insider. If not in the same league as Michelle, she was at least now playing the same game.

"That is interesting," Michelle responded, taking a sip from her wine. "The Congressman launched a small investment fund recently. Probably wants to prove he can do something on his own. I hear business has not been so good lately."

"I read that. The entire industry, in fact. Fascinating stuff."

Michelle looked as if she did not think it fascinating.

"Anyway, while researching Empty Spaces, since I think it's an important technology, I noticed a citation referencing a recent NIH study on mobile devices and electromagnetic radiation. There was a particular focus on mobile services over selected wireless bands, which would include Empty Spaces, obviously. The study mentioned the 'enzymatic breakdown' of certain chemicals in the brain, including chemicals found in chocolate. Only, I couldn't locate the actual study or any materials directly related. No one at the NIH could provide me any feedback. Partly I was curious. You know, it's chocolate."

"Interesting. Though I suspect it's nothing. Oh, before I forget, let me take a picture of the two of us. There."

"Not fair. I didn't dress for this."

"You look as adorable as ever."

Prudence smiled. She took a bite of salad.

"Well, I have the report."

"I knew you would."

"Not a problem, honestly. A friend of a friend involved with one of the leads emailed me a copy shortly after I made the request. It was a small study. Very limited funding, which is a bit atypical since teams at the NIH don't like to move on anything unless they're certain they have some long-term funding source to tap. I'm not sure what you were hoping to find. The NIH found nothing out of the ordinary; everything within acceptable ranges. From my contact, who understand had limited involvement on this project, there was apparently a minor albeit measurable increase in electromagnetic radiation found on devices that used Empty Spaces. It is expected, she told me, that the same results would apply to any similar service that travels over the same designated higher frequency radio spectrum. Nothing bad, nothing terribly revealing, not very interesting, I'm afraid."

"At least it did specify Empty Spaces. I would hate for all this to turn out to be non-work related."

"From what was explained to me, a measurable increase in radiation is caused when Empty Spaces prepares to hop to another device. But, again, it was nothing out of bounds. No issues. No connection with cancer, far as they could tell. I doubt the project will resurrected from what I've been told. Funding cut combined with pedestrian outcomes. That sort of thing"

Pam beamed the documents to Prudence's smartphone.

"Thank you so much. I didn't know what I wanted to find, truthfully. I'll make sure to include, of course, it since you went through all the trouble. I'm glad we could get together, even if this didn't turn out to be much."

"No trouble, dear. Besides, Party Line. Every other Tuesday. 6-9pm. You're always welcome."

"I know. But with work and mom."

"Just a suggestion. Of course, from what I understand of Empty Spaces, its best suited for helping singles find their potential mate. Keep using it and maybe you'll have more than work and mom." Michelle winked, asked the waiter for another glass of wine and the check.

"I'm not really looking. Though I do expect Empty Spaces to be huge. Maybe Congressman Barr has some inside info?"

"Not likely. He's usually the last to know anything. Though his Chief of Staff might. I suspect Mr. Howerd is the one pushing the investment. Looking for a quick score, no doubt. Might as well make some money. No one will ever elect him to office. You can't hide being a dick."

"Michelle!" Prudence did not have to fake being startled. "I'm sure you're right, of course. Pam's fiancé, after all. She's not going to end up with someone who doesn't have a lot of money."

"Pam will be fine, no matter who she chooses. Excuse me, I have to take this." Michelle reached for her phone and Prudence realized lunch was over.

Everyone seemed to have something to do; something that pulled them away, Prudence thought. On the way back to her office she stopped and treated herself to a dark chocolate covered strawberry. The indulgence was not terribly satisfying, unfortunately, despite the price. As with most chocolate she consumed lately, the delight was short-lived, or else it never showed up at all. Prudence worried that the little voice inside her head was beginning to sound too much like her mother's.

Chocolate has not changed, Prudence thought. I have.

.

What Goes On

Blog: Bitter Water

What goes on in our chocolate

Dear readers,

I recently tried an expensive line of craft chocolates from a large company that shall not be named. Sadly, I was unimpressed. The chocolates were strikingly packaged, in a thick square brown box with gold lettering. Each chocolate wrapped in gold foil. Signifying…disappointment.

I have read several reports over the past few months that sales of chocolates, both craft and mass produced, have declined significantly. The entire industry is facing an unprecedented retrenchment. We should not be surprised. Do not cut back! Do not offer nicely packaged chocolates that are of pedestrian quality.

In their greed, their incessant drive to increase margins, create new markets, the industry has not only disappointed us true believers, but they have ultimately harmed themselves. It is no wonder that sales are down. Clearly, the quality is not there. We can taste the difference!

Without something sublimely delightful to review, I thought that for today's post -- get your pencils ready -- a brief review of the chemical composition of chocolate!

Chocolate is derived from the cacao bean. Cacao is comprised of numerous chemicals, including:

- Serotonin
- Histamine
- Salsolinol
- Methyltetrahydroisoquinoline
- Phenethylamine
- Spermidine
- Tryptamine
- Spermine

Interesting, no? No, I suppose not. Perhaps this will change your mind? Several of the chemicals found in chocolate have psychoactive properties. It's true. Chemicals in cacao beans with potential psychoactive effects include theobromine (which comprises approximately 1-3% of the bean's weight) and trimethylxanthine, also known as…caffeine.

Caffeine, as you doubtless already know, produces a stimulating effect on the body. Not much of one in this case, given that there is so little caffeine in chocolate. For example, an 8 oz. cup of coffee typically contains in excess of 100mg of caffeine, while a 1 oz. milk chocolate bar contains only 6mg.

Theobromine, a similarly well-researched stimulant, and the chemical responsible for the bitter taste of chocolate, also produces a caffeine-like effect on the body. Too much theobromine, just like drinking too much coffee, can cause nausea, insomnia and restlessness. Theobromine levels are higher in dark chocolate (approximately 10 g/kg) than in milk chocolate (1-5 g/kg). In addition, higher quality chocolate tends to contain more theobromine than lower quality chocolate.

This next I did not know, however. Chocolate contains anandamide, a *cannabinoid*. Cannabinoids are substances that act like cannabis -- marijuana. In fact, the name 'anandamide' comes from *ananda*, the Sanskrit word for "bliss". Scientists are only just beginning to understand anandamide. What they have discovered so far is that it plays a role in pain, depression, appetite, memory, even fertility. Perhaps chocolate is an aphrodisiac after all!

As a cannabinoid, anandamide's effects upon the brain behave similarly to marijuana. How, you ask? By reaching out and connecting with specific protein receptors in the brain. The very same receptors that tetrahydrocannabinol (THC), the active chemical in marijuana, binds with!

When THC binds to specific brain receptors, the person feels "high." Anandamide binds to these same receptors and thus produces a similar effect to "being high." Only better. Because it lasts longer! Anandamide naturally breaks down in the body rather quickly. However, chocolate contains two other substances, N-oleoylethanolamine and N-linoleoylethaolamine, which inhibits this breakdown process, thus extending the high.

Hungry for more?

Anandamide acts as a chemical messenger between the embryo and uterus during implantation of the embryo in the uterine wall. In a sense, the very first call from mother to child happens due to anandamide.

Remarkable. Perhaps one day we might be able to purchase drugs, pain killers, say, the kind you get from the apothecary, that are made from chocolate! Just like hundreds and possibly thousands of years ago. No worries about legalizing marijuana then.

We Can Work it Out

Pleased with her latest post, Prudence acknowledged that work summoned. Seated at her desk, in her cubicle, Prudence sought to achieve, if not bliss, at least a well-earned truce. She leaned back in her perfectly acceptable reasonably comfortable office chair. She took her eyes off her screen, nicer and larger than most due to the number of years she had been with the FCC, and glanced at the pictures, papers and memorabilia scattered about the industrial wood-plastic top of the 'desk' that nearly encircled her. Her cubicle was four-sided, technically, which meant it had three and a half walls and an opening, on the right. The walls were beige colored, with the highest of the walls, to her left, rising only 5 feet. Enough to afford her privacy from those stationed to her immediate left, as seated, facing the screen, though not from anyone, most especially her boss, that might walk along the corridor to her right.

Had Prudence been at all inclined to investigate what terms the sellers of cubicles such as hers used in their marketing literature, she would have learned that those who profited from their sale were rather unabashed in their praise. Common terms included, but were not limited to:

- Office of the millennium
- Functional
- Practical
- Modular
- High tech
- Simplistic
- Semi-private
- Personal expression
- Efficient
- Comfort
- Business solution
- Adaptable

None of which were terms Prudence would have considered.

Along with her desk, monitor and the cubicle walls, there was a multi-buttoned, wired telephone that she used solely when calling someone else within the government. Black wire shelves sat on the desk and held several reports, folders and a thick blue binder that once meant something. Under the desk, to the left of her chair, were two large gray metal filing cabinets. Above the desk, to the right, were two gray metal covered shelves, filled with various materials she rarely needed. Atop one of the shelves was a medium-sized aloe plant in a white pot. Fortunately, again owing to her relative seniority in the department, Prudence was stationed very close to a large window. True, from her vantage point she could not actually see out the window, not while seated, but it did brighten her day and helped keep her plant alive. The only other distinctive feature of her space was a small, modern-looking tan colored chair for guests. Of which there were none.

Prudence reached into the top drawer of the nearest filing cabinet and took out a small piece of white chocolate. This was not terribly satisfying. Which was partly deliberate. Prudence reminded herself that if she kept something better in there, it would be much too easy to over-indulge.

She rolled her chair closer to her monitor and re-read a portion of the draft report on Empty Spaces she was finalizing for Pam. Or, that devil woman, as her mother had called her, again, just this morning. Mostly to make Prudence feel better. Which it did, fair or not. She needed to revise a section on something called cognitive radio, only, truthfully, she found it all rather boring.

Cognitive radio and non-licensed wireless spectrum
Empty Spaces enables rich, personalized and automated communications between mobile devices via a solution commonly referenced as cognitive radio. Data, texts, voice and select bandwidth-limited applications may be transferred utilizing non-licensed, unrestricted 900-megahertz band spectrum. This is the same band utilized for baby monitors, cordless phones, security cameras and a variety of approved and non-approved short-range wireless devices.

The FCC actively supports cognitive radio as a means of encouraging device innovation, open airwaves competition and as a reliable method for enabling communications carriers to temporarily offload traffic bursts from increasingly congested licensed wireless networks.

Prudence stopped there. Fact was, she had a good job, that much she knew. Decent pay, decent benefits. Still, the work was oftentimes tedious. Needing a break from the report she opened a link that Jackie Paper had recently sent her.

Following her initial contact with Jackie -- strictly as a user of the Empty Spaces service – and after several subsequent emails she sent to him, the two had since periodically exchanged articles they hoped the other would find interesting. To date, Jackie's responses to her had been depressingly judicious. Prudence wasn't certain if this meant anything or not.

She accessed his online profile, again decided that he was cute, despite the broad nose, which she did not much care for. Maybe he had a girlfriend, she wondered, more than once. Or was gay. Or the obvious, he lives thousands of miles away, she reminded herself.

Luckily for Prudence, much of what Jackie sent her could, in theory, pass for research should anyone decide to review where she spent her time online during work hours. Jackie's latest was an article about something called 'backmasking'.

Backmasking, also known as backward masking, is a recording technique in which a sound or message is deliberately recorded backwards onto a track that is meant to be played forward. Backmasked words are unintelligible noise when played forward, but when played backwards they are revealed.

Backmasking was popularized by The Beatles, who used backward vocals and instrumentation on their 1966 album Revolver. Singer John Lennon and producer George Martin both claimed they discovered the backward recording technique during the recording of the album tracks "Tomorrow Never Knows" and "I'm Only Sleeping," and the single "Rain". Lennon stated that, while under the influence of marijuana, he accidentally played the tapes for "Rain" in reverse, and enjoyed the sound. The following day he shared the results with the other Beatles.

Artists have since used backmasking for artistic, comedic, and satiric effect.

"What are you reading?"

One of Pam's minions had stopped by on her way to touch the hem, Prudence suspected, startling her. Probably wants a cookie for reporting on my every move. "Oh, research. For Pam." Prudence clicked once and the screen jumped to her official report. "Nothing terribly exciting." She shifted her focus back to her monitor, hoping the acolyte would leave her. Which she did.

With Empty Spaces, a smartphone's antenna scans for a clear channel in the 900-megahertz range 35 times per second. Once detected, the device 'claims' the unused spectrum and then transmits data to other nearby devices. The typical range is 25-50 feet. Due to the ad-hoc nature and availability of unlicensed spectrum, communications must be kept short; a single burst of data from one device to the next is often all that can reliably occur.

Prudence wasn't sure whether cognitive radio was more interesting than backmasking, or the reverse, but she was tired of work and chose accordingly.

"Accusations have been made by various groups that backmasking can be used to create subliminal messages. In the late 1970s, fundamentalist Christian groups claimed that backmasked messages could bypass the conscious mind and reach the subconscious, where they would be unknowingly accepted by the listener. Allegations of demonic backmasking were likewise made by social psychologists, parents, and critics of rock music.

With the advent of compact discs in the 1980s, it became more difficult to listen to recordings backwards, and the controversy faded.

Prudence thought she heard someone walk towards her cubicle and switched screens.

The commercial potential for cognitive radio to increase spectrum has spurred many companies and investment groups to develop new products and services. Several entrepreneurs use cognitive radio to create temporary wireless networks in select physical locations, such as an urban park, a shopping mall or stadium. This reduces the burden on existing infrastructure and supports real-time, low-cost hyperlocal messaging.

Prudence wasn't too sure about that last sentence. Though she was sure that she was not interested in writing any more about cognitive radio. She again returned to Jackie's article.

Pink Floyd incorporated a backmasked message into "Empty Spaces", from 1979's The Wall, which stated: 'Congratulations. You have just discovered the secret message'

"Oh. Is that how he got the name," she wondered?

Her phone vibrated. "Quitting time," she said out loud, though unintentionally. She emailed her draft report to Pam, put her monitor to sleep, and texted her mother that she was leaving.

Not a Second Time

Typical of these government lifers, Pam thought. Prudence forwards her a draft of the Empty Spaces report promptly at 5pm, probably after screwing around, then leaves for the day.

Pam shook her head disapprovingly, and decided to think no more of it. She had a dinner date with Francis and would review the draft later. She finalized a summary of the action items from an earlier inter-departmental meeting, grabbed her phone and left for her apartment.

Long-term living arrangements for the future Mrs. Mustard had not yet been finalized. Probably, Pam told herself, she and Francis would buy a house together, possibly in McLean, since Francis favored Virginia, or, as she hoped, in Potomac, Maryland, where women much like herself happened to congregate. For now, Pam lived in a new, sparse, luxury condo development on L Street, NW, in Washington, DC. A series of four ten-story towers, connected with one another on the ground floor, on which was located a variety of amenities, including a boutique grocery store, wine shop, a gym with an indoor pool, a large "Club Room" for residents and their guests and other shops, providing everything she needed, for the time being.

Pam lived on the 8th floor of tower 1. The building itself was an impressive mix of glass, metal and concrete. Each apartment facing east, of which Pam's was one, enjoyed ten-foot floor-to-ceiling windows, and a small outdoor balcony. Pam rarely ventured onto the terrace, which subsequently held nothing but a plant that had long since died.

Inside was just as nice. Tasteful, surprisingly comfortable chairs. Two small tables. Two large mounted television screens; one in the bedroom, one in the living room, which also included a gas fireplace. The smartly arranged modern kitchen included several shiny new silver and black appliances, with the area bounded by an island bar. Three metal chairs sided the bar. Pam typically ate out, although she periodically made her own coffee or prepared herself a raw smoothie. These were enjoyed while standing along the island.

Francis would arrive in a couple hours. Pam decided it best to feed and walk Levon, her over-sized terrier, sooner than later. Although advanced in years, Levon remained as loyal and vigilant as ever. His legs could no longer carry him as quickly. His black coat, once off-set only by a small tuft of white on his snout, now sported gray patches throughout. If he chased a ball, Pam feared he might go into cardiac arrest.

Levon had no known issues with Francis, though Francis was never terribly approving, claiming the dog made unnecessary demands on Pam's time. A quick feeding, a short walk and Levon would be satisfied, Pam knew. She also knew it probably for the best if he stayed locked inside the spare bedroom. Following that, she would shower, then review the report Prudence forwarded to her.

The walk took longer than expected. Pam also stopped to speak with several building residents, all of whom found her radiant, and were each dearly pleased with the news of her engagement. On the slim chance Francis showed up on time, which was unlikely, Pam thought it best to browse the draft from Prudence. She was not expecting any surprises.

Executive Summary

Pam skipped over the first part of the summary which included a history of the FCC's support of unlicensed spectrum and the economic and end user benefits it generated.

Empty Spaces employs a short-range high frequency wireless communications technology based on the ISO 14443G standard which enables devices to exchange a series of files about both the device and user at a rate of 848gbps. Open source geolocation data and 'angle of arrival' signal propagation measurements are used by Empty Spaces to determine the position and availability of other mobile phones. Once a phone is located, Empty Spaces 'jumps' from the originating (active) device to the receiving (passive) device where it unpacks a truncated version of the software. The software algorithms then determine the new user's mood. If Empty Spaces finds a compatible match amongst proximal users, a variety of information is shared; typically text, photograph(s), mapping data, personal contact information and a song. This entire process takes less than one second and all occurs over unlicensed spectrum via a temporary secure channel. Note: It is technically possible to share video, however, the temporal reliability of unlicensed spectrum makes such attempts dubious.

"How the hell did Jackie pull that off on his own?" Pam was impressed. "Temporal reliability? So Prudence can use a thesaurus."

Uses and applications

Pam skipped this section.

Standards
Pam skipped this section.

Privacy concerns
Pam earmarked this section, with the intent of reading it later that night.

Mobile cryptographic protocols
Pam skipped this section.

Anandamide and Smartphone Radiation
Pam stopped here. "Anandamide? What the hell is that?" There seemed to be no rationale for this section, or the study it referenced.

In a study using artificially high doses of smartphone radiation, NIH researchers discovered a way to minimize and even eliminate the high produced by THC, the active ingredient in marijuana, by neutralizing the brain's cannabinoid receptors...

Pam continued, wondering again what possible rational Prudence would have for including such information. Smartphone radiation was not a concern, and if it was, it was certainly not appropriately addressed in this report. She most definitely would have Prudence expunge this nonsense.

Researchers posited that a similar neutralizing effect could occur with anandamide, a cannabinoid found in chocolate. Anandamide impacts the brain in a similar manner as THC in marijuana. As with receptors in the brain that bind with THC, these receptors likewise bind with anandamide.

How is it possible, Pam wondered, that Prudence could possibly work chocolate into this report? Is this a goddamn joke, she thought? "Is she trying to get back at me for something?" Pam swiped the page and skimmed additional portions of the cited NIH study, finding it increasingly difficult to concentrate.

The specific absorption rate (SAR) levels of smartphone radiation varies...
..though none attained the artificially high levels reached in the study sample.

...researchers looked at Empty Spaces as one example of smartphone-based services for possible high electromagnetic radiation outputs...

"What the fuck is she doing?" Pam spoke out loud. "I damn well guarantee there's no correlation between Empty Spaces and radiation, nor cancer, nor any such thing. Why would she put this in an FCC report? A report for mother fucking political appointees?"

Initial findings disprove effects of above-normal SAR levels based on cumulative use. Contraindications suggest peak bursts represent far greater impact than long-term exposure at standard levels...
...the delta between average SAR level and peak SAR level is most critical in deducing causal relationship...

Pam paused. Her brain idling rapidly. "Wait. What is this saying? Have they come to any actual conclusions?" Some minor NIH study, already concluded, and with inconclusive results on a problem, a potential problem, already researched, and whose impact has long since been dismissed. If there is a link between smartphones and cancer, people have decided that is an acceptable risk. Goddamit. I'll want this entire section taken out" she told herself. "Francis would goddam flip if he ever saw this. From now on, I'll have to make sure Prudence understands the importance of what to include and what not include in a report that might become public." She took a deep breath. "Marijuana and chocolate?." Pam couldn't hide her resentment at such careless work. Her phone rang. Levon barked. Francis was down below, waiting for her.

"Chocolate, again! Jesus fucking christ."

Two of Us

Whatever others might think of her, if they thought of her, Prudence felt most assured, most pleased with herself and her station, when writing about chocolate. Which she did often. This was both joy and sanctuary.

Her mother had gone to bed early, which, truthfully, had become her new normal time. Prudence sat on the couch in the living room, staring into her computer, a half-eaten, mostly forgotten piece of an expensive chocolate confection from Denmark on the end table beside her. Empty Spaces was streaming from a nearby speaker. Time to answer reader questions, she thought.

Blog: Bitter Water
Questions! Cacao vs Cocoa

Dear Prudence, can you help us decide, once and for all, the issue that divides families, nations, peoples, generations. Do we say cacao or cocoa?
The answer: yes. To both questions.

Chocolate comes from cacao, specifically the cacao pods (or nibs or beans, if you will), of the *Theobroma cacao* tree. The scientific name Theobroma comes to us from the Greek θεοβρῶμα which means "food of the gods".

Not surprisingly, professionals in the chocolate industry, including growers, scientists, makers and others, typically refer to the "cacao tree" as such. Unfortunately, they just as often refer to the seeds of the tree -- and the chocolate powder made from these seeds -- as "cocoa." Puzzling, to be sure.

Why such confusion?

The Theobroma cacao tree soon came to be called simply the cacao tree (no theobroma) and this word, cacao, become Anglicized, and morphed into the term most people now use, cocoa. This is exacerbated by the fact that cacao can refer to the tree itself, to the beans, the resultant cacao butter, or the ground cacao powder. Both are accepted, though I prefer cacao.

Dear Prudence, what is most important when determining the quality of a chocolate?
Taste. Nothing is more important than taste! Lately, I've noticed an increasing number of chocolates that simply fail to deliver the joy to my palette or my soul, that their cost – and ingredients – would

otherwise indicate. Clearly, chocolate makers large and small are doing something wrong. For truly magical chocolate, sublime mouthfeel and rich, deep, satisfying flavor, each of these are essential:

- The quality and age of the cacao beans
- How the beans are roasted, and when
- Grinding, blending, and conching all require special care
- The quality and amounts of other ingredients used (for example, vanilla; condensed milk; and spices, such as ginger or chilis)
- Special care in the handling, packaging and distribution are undervalued but crucial
- The chocolate maker's skill and experience

What does the percentage of cacao listed on a chocolate bar's packaging actually represent?
This is simply the percentage of the bar that is derived from all the various components of the cacao bean: chocolate liquor, cacao butter and cacao powder.

Is a bean blend or single origin chocolate better?
This is usually a personal preference. Most artisanal makers source from a single region and believe this makes for a higher quality chocolate. Companies that sell millions of pounds of chocolate typically source from very specific growers under specific conditions using pre-specified bean types.

How much caffeine is in chocolate?
Very little. A standard 4-ounce bar of milk chocolate contains about 6mg of caffeine; about the same as a cup of decaffeinated coffee. Regular coffee contains closer to 100mg of caffeine per cup.

Does chocolate liquor contain alcohol?
No. Chocolate liquor is the smooth, liquid paste made by grinding up the center of the cacao bean (or nib, as some call it).

Keep your questions coming! My next post will focus on the history of chocolate in America.

It's All Too Much

Francis drove fast, unable to move at the pace of regular people. His BMW M3 skirted through traffic and around the Capitol Building, past the city's many chokepoints, and was now headed, faster than the speed limit permitted, into Northern Virginia. From there, it was south and west, leading, ultimately, to the Barr family estate; the venerated Glockenspiel.

Every other week, on Wednesday morning, the chief of staff for Congressman Barr would have tea and biscuits, literally, with the congressman's mother; one of the few persons who cherished becoming meaner with age. These meetings were the highlight of Mother Barr's week, invariably. For Francis, the path to his vision lay as much with the elderly Barr, whom any fool could tell ruled the Barr empire, so-called, than it did with the congressman.

Francis arrived at the office at 6am, which was not uncommon for him. He left for Mother Barr's at 9:30am. Tea would consume at least an hour or more of his time. That, along with at least three hours required for the full circuit, no matter the traffic, which was always bad, would still afford him several hours back at the office. For now, however, all he could do was make phone calls.

"Pam. Voice mail? Shit. Any news on the Empty Spaces front? I'm expecting clear skies. Remember, we can't let anyone know the Congressman is about to invest in it. Top secret. Sorry about tonight. Reception on the Hill for some for-profit schools group. Influential group. Can't miss. Trust me, you would not enjoy the crowd. Boring as shit. I'm driving now to Glockenspiel for tea with mother Barr. Love."

"Maxwell Edison here. Speak to me."
"Maxwell. Francis. Got your email re Empty Spaces. No changes?"
"No. It's solid. Sickspack's team was reasonably thorough. The service was coded a bit sloppy, you ask me. Which you have."
"What did you think of the founder?"
"Cookie cutter, mostly. Decent skills. Had the big idea, lucky or not. Tries a little too hard to please."
"The Congressman will like that."
"I did discover --"
"One second, Maxwell. My apologies. I have to take this."

"Francis Mustard speaking."

"Mr. Mustard? Oh, good. This is Ganja Patois. Mrs. asked I check up on you."

Ganja Patois was one of two full-time nurses that cared for the elderly Mrs. Barr. Jamaican, she had brought her two children, no husband, from her homeland to Washington, DC. Through a variety of circumstances and odd jobs, Ganja ultimately landed in the employ of the Barr family. At mother Barr's request, the help referred to the elderly woman simply as Mrs.

"I should be there in 1 hour, Ganja. Please be sure to tell Mrs. Barr that I am looking forward to tea, as always."

"Thank you, sir."

"Maxwell. Francis, again. I plan to bring out this Mr. Paper soon. Make the Congressman feel better about what I'm trying to do here. Can't let him wimp out now. Though damn if he's not trying. Scared of his own fucking shadow. You were saying? No issues?"

"No. He looks and acts the part. He's American, by the way. I vetted him as well as Empty Spaces itself."

"Good. Intellectual property issues? Scale? Costs?"

"You will have my full report by the end of the week. Expect no surprises. The service does appear to work better when an individual user downloads the application directly from a server, rather than through an exchange of user devices. That impacts scale, somewhat. Which impacts costs, obviously. Tighten up the application itself, I'd say, but nothing you weren't expecting."

"Understood. Anything else?"

"The issue you raised regarding ownership is valid. Mr. Paper created this while at the same time he was a contractor for a company called Sky Saxon. They make mobile device security tools for medium-sized businesses, primarily in Canada. I'm guessing you know that. Per Mr. Paper, no company resources were used and he built the service on his own time. I can show otherwise. Good enough for a lawyer, at least."

"Send me the report by Friday. Will you look at this cocksucker sitting in the left lane. Thanks again, Maxwell."

"Out."

"Theo."

"Good morning, Congressman Barr's Office. Mr. Mustard? Yes, this is Theo."

"Theo. I'm in my car. Can you forward the number to the CEO of Sky Saxon. I believe they are located in Vancouver, British Columbia.

ASAP. Also, remind the congressman and staff that we have a all-hands meeting promptly at 3pm. These will continue each Wednesday until election day."

"Got it."

"Good day. This is Francis Mustard, Chief of Staff for US Congressman RKO Barr. Is this Charles Hawtrey, CEO of Sky Saxon?"

"Mr. Mustard. Yes, this is Mr. Jones. Your office said to expect your call. I'm not completely sure why."

"I would like to talk to you about a mobile service that the Congressman and I are about to acquire. I assume you know he sits on the Telecommunications Oversight committee."

"Yes. I saw that."

"Excellent."

[Redacted]

"Pam, love. That was fast."

"I was finishing up a meeting. I saw that you called."

"Plans for tonight without me?"

"Stay at home and sulk, naturally."

"Not funny."

"It's a little funny. Off to old lady Barr's?"

"Yes. She loves her tea."

"She'd rather have you as a son."

"In this case, that says more about the congressman than me. That report you were preparing, for Empty Spaces?"

"Ongoing. Had one of the lifers put together a report."

"Who?"

"Prudence Skiffle. I'm sure I've mentioned her before. Not sure I can trust her judgment. Her draft included references to a study at the NIH over smartphone radiation. I took it out. It was nonsense."

"That's bullshit. Radiation from mobile devices -- "

"I said I had her remove it. Not to worry."

"No, wait. Sorry, love. Maybe you're thinking too small. Here's a thought. Keep it in."

"What? So we're saying it does emit harmful radiation?"

"No. Keep the reference in, is all I'm saying. The study is inconclusive, correct?"

"Correct. I spent almost an entire day looking into it. Not terribly happy about that. But yes, inconclusive."

"Inconclusive. May or may not be harmful; no conclusive link to cancer. You follow? Uncertainty from the top minds in the US government. If they can't be sure, no person or private company can be certain, right? That provides cover. Don't cut it, let's embrace it."

"Possibly. I suppose. But --"

"No buts. Leave it in. Trust me. I know how these things work."

"I'll have to reverse myself. I already told her to remove it. I can't say I like this person. Seems like she's always judging me."

"Not judging, jealous."

"Maybe. I won't be seeing you at all tonight, then?"

"No. I expect this reception to go late. I'll be wiped out. I'll take you out somewhere nice, tomorrow. I know a great place for cod. Have to go. Bye."

"Sickspack. Francis. I'm pulling into a meeting so not much time. Few more concerns on Empty Spaces."

"Yes. Your associate, Mr. Edison, has already sent me a list of concerns."

"I'm aware of what Maxwell has sent you. Firstly, I am going to make sure our hands are clean with respect to ownership. Mr. Paper, of course, insists there are no actionable claims on Empty Spaces from his former employer."

"That is correct."

"As expected. Though false. That's leverage. Second. The congressman will have to meet Mr. Paper in person. It's the only way I can push him over the line. I assume that will not be an issue."

"Mr. Paper will likely request that his partner be part of such a meeting."

"Christ. I was afraid of that. Acceptable. As for you, I had the congressman place a call personally to immigration. You'll be a fully fledged US-based venture capitalist soon enough. Get you out of fucking Canada."

"Canada is fine, but thank you. Anything more for Empty Spaces, then?"

"I'll set it up for when we bring out Mr. Paper. Again, we don't want this played out real-time until we're ready to pounce."

"Yes. I will again impress upon Mr. Paper --"

"At my target now."

And Your Bird Can Sing

About an hour and ten minutes southwest by car, from Washington, DC, at the speed Francis drove, the scenery changed profoundly. Tract housing, interstates, strip malls, paved over Civil War battlefields and car after car, along with all the logistical flotsam each of these required, suddenly became green and brown and natural; dry if not lush, reaching up, if not building out. There were horse farms, craft wineries, clumps of trees, gorgeous valleys, sloping hills. Little of which Francis noticed.

As he turned into the long, crooked road that would lead him to the Barr family estate, however, he gradually became more acutely aware of his surroundings. The road wound down the valley, past a large white house, a barn, a tall, unabashed silo. That was his cue to turn right at the crossing, over the river and through the wooded patch until he came upon Glockenspiel; stately manor of the Nutt Barr clan.

Glockenspiel was a two hundred and four acre Virginia country manor, beckoning all to pay their respects. The home was built in the early 1850s, in the Greek Revival style, and was listed on the Virginia Department of Historic Places. According to family legend, the house was raided by Union troops near the end of the Civil War, though they left it mostly undamaged.

The house itself was 9,800 square feet and included six restored fireplaces, fourteen rooms, six private bathrooms, a media room (newly added), and a dining room which afforded memorable vistas of traditional Virginia horse country. There was a sun room, a converted workers quarters that now served as a bathroom that no one ever used, and a expansive L-shaped porch that extended beyond the front of the house and part way along the eastern side. On a clear day, a visitor could spy a nearby equestrian farm, the old courthouse and now, a Dairy Queen. To the right side of the house was a small garden that one of the workers tended to, at the behest of the Mrs. There were four small outbuildings, including an original smokehouse and a tiny brick building once used, Francis was told, for keeping milk cool.

For most, Glockenspiel was impressive. For Francis, he dare not allow his focus stray from the task at hand. Should the congressman somehow get scared, which was easy enough, and back out at the last moment, which was not uncommon, Francis' hopes of being a central part of the Empty Spaces investment, and his designs to use the service for far more than either its founder or his boss ever intended -- or imagined -- might degrade as fully and as rapidly as the wireless signal he supposed was transmitted between two phones. The congressman's mother, Geraldine Nutt Barr, as feisty as she was frail and as fearless as the congressman feared her, still, would make sure her son was pushed in the right direction.

"Mother! It's so wonderful to see you again! You look positively radiant!"

"Francis, dear. Please sit down. And do turn your phone off."

Francis smiled, gently hugged Mrs. Nutt Barr, turned his phone off, completely, and placed it on the end table.

"Sit, Francis. Honah! Our tea service."

Geraldine (nee Nutt) Barr was fourteen months shy of her 90th birthday. She was a flaming mixture of Scotch-Irish and German ancestry, born less than ten miles from her current home. It was her looks, that and her fame in Hollywood, three thousand miles away and more than sixty years ago, that brought her back to this place.

A stern, passionate beauty, so much so that even with little money, and from rural Virginia, no one doubted that she could be a star. Which she became, quickly. From school plays to regional theater in Richmond, then to Hollywood before she turned twenty.

Geraldine would appear in several popular film adaptations of classic American books, working alongside some of cinema's immortals. She studied under the great Micheál MacLiammóir and was under contract with RKO Pictures. In her very first role, playing the young wife of an elderly, wounded Civil War soldier in his final years, the young Geraldine Nutt garnered critical acclaim, along with her first and only Oscar nomination. She did not win.

She followed that role with several others, mostly supporting, though alongside many of the leading women and men of that golden age of cinema. By her early 30s, she was an established character actress, one of the few that filmgoers knew by name. All of which ended abruptly when she married, much to Hollywood's surprise, Mendips Barr.

Mendips, the congressman's late father, was a far better playboy than businessman; not that he was much of either. His father, Luscious, originally from West Virginia, which remained a family secret, had founded a small chocolate shop at the turn of the century, just as the industry was changing from local to regional in scope, and as nouveau candy barons were amassing fortunes. Luscious was among them.

Luscious Barr, who moved to Richmond, Virginia after a series of failed business ventures, was one of the first to package and distribute his 'milk chocolates' throughout the South. He died, however, at the young age of 52, with only one son, Mendips, then in his middle twenties and with no interest in the candy business, other than in how it might support his untroubled lifestyle.

Following a whirlwind romance, Mendips Barr and Geraldine Nutt were wed in Hollywood. Unbeknownst to her new husband, and to most of the public, the new Mrs. Barr proved a shrewd, calculating and driving business woman. The day after their brief honeymoon ended, she had her husband ascend to his rightful place as President of Barr Chocolates. Less than two years later, the company introduced the Nutt Barr, a milk chocolate and Virginia peanut confection that was believed by the public, thanks to a good deal of good marketing, to be the husband's love letter to his beautiful ex-movie star.

In fact, the Nutt Barr was Geraldine's creation. She oversaw its development, its manufacturing, which at the time was difficult given the scale she planned for, and its marketing. It was her husband, ironically, who fancied himself as creative as his wife, that wrote the famous Nutt Barr jingle; the jingle that guaranteed the Nutt Barr brand never truly left the public's consciousness. Till only recently. The Nutt Barr not only restored the flagging fortunes of the company, but helped turn the business into a powerful regional brand. To this day, the Nutt Barr remains among the top selling candies in America.

Despite her advanced years, her frailty, her faded beauty, the tangled history of the Barr family, and her incessant passing of gas, Francis Mustard keenly understood that the elderly woman seated next to him held the key to his triumph. Likewise, he knew her mind remained, if now soft around the edges, as shattering as a rocket.

"I am so happy to see you again, mother."

Honah Lee, the pale sturdily-built German nursing aide counterpart to the plump, dark skinned Ganja Patois, entered the sitting room with the tea service. It was served, per the Mrs. orders, in crystal glassware, accompanied by fine china and old, elegant silver flatware. The tea, ice cold and exceptionally sweet, was accompanied with buttery biscuits, well cured thick slices of ham and a glass bowl of peanuts. The view, on this bright and gorgeous mid-morning in the heart of Virginia horse country was remarked upon by all parties even if casually.

"Such a pleasure to have your company, Francis. Tell me, have you made an honest woman of Pamela yet?"

"You know that I am now engaged to her, mother."

"I know. Still, a long wait until the wedding. Perhaps I'll be dead by then."

"Nonsense. You will outlive us all."

Mrs. Barr drank in the sweet tea, which she loved dearly. "Unlikely. I do think you should wed sooner than later, of course. Put honey on this for me, dear." She did not need to motion to Honah for service. "I may never see Francis wed, considering. And my hand to God I retain hope that he will give me a true grandchild. I try. Lord knows I try. I still have big plans for him, you know that. I always get my way. Still..."

Francis nodded, sipped the tea, and reached for a handful of peanuts, grown not far from Glockenspiel. "Delicious," he noted. "Can't understand why Nutt Barr sales have been doing so poorly recently."

"Those damn busybodies," Geraldine shrieked, or would have if she could. "Got people afraid of peanuts! That's what it is. Good, healthy Virginia peanuts. God damn them. All of them. I mean that. We lived on those things! Now we have these lazy mothers and their fat children suing schools if they dare serve anything with peanuts on the menu."

"Damn shame. One of the healthiest foods there is, we know that. That's a fact. Delicious, too." Francis took another handful.

"I've told Reginald he needs to take action on this. One percent of the population has an allergy to peanuts. If you can even believe that. One percent. Suddenly, a crisis."

"I think Francis doesn't want to appear that he's doing something for the benefit of his business, you know, over other constituent needs."

"The family business is what got him that seat in Washington. That's what keeps these people employed." She feebly waved her hand, though she meant far more than just her nurses. Along with the old factory, tourism and long-time agreements with nearby farmers, Nutt Barr was indeed responsible for a substantial portion of the dollars that flowed through the region.

"That is part of what I would like to talk about, Mother Barr. Not the politics, as usual. What Francis and I have been working on for some time now is a new business service, one that would work on everyone's phone." He picked his up and waved it in front of her. "It's a means of advertising. It's especially good at spreading advertising even to people who never listen to ads. All the people that now never have a chance to hear that grand old Nutt Barr jingle...With this new service, not only can we more effectively advertise, but it helps spread the message. Any message. Like a virus, going from person to person. Especially at places where large crowds gather. Malls. Stadiums. Suddenly, everyone is whistling the Nutt Barr jingle and running for the vending machines."

"Dollars?"

"We're in early. Very early. I would expect huge returns. And this service -- it's called Empty Spaces, I know, we will change the name -- allows us to essentially personalize a message for each user. Webscale personalization, they call it. A uniquely individual message, but sent to millions. The Congressman is actually very interested, eager to get his hands dirty on something all his own. I know it would be something that would help the family business. Certainly look good in the midst of a re-election. Him a tech leader and all. Angel investor. And with the polls showing the race this year could be tight."

"Reginald getting scared to pull the trigger?"

"I won't say that." Francis took another drink of tea. Sweet, cold, perfect. "Maybe a touch."

"And this can obviously be used for other messages as well, I'm guessing. Not just that silly old jingle?"

"It can."

"Honah. You and Ganja take a leave for a few moments. Thank you, dears."

You Really Got a Hold On Me

"Love. Something important I want to talk about. About the wedding. It's great news. I'm back on the road. Call me."

"Theo. I should be there in an hour or so. I made a slight change on this afternoon's agenda. You should have it. Print it out and distribute."

"Yes, I have it."

"Good. Have to run."

"Sickspack. Francis again. We need to get Jackie out here soon. I got the congressman's approval. We want to pull the trigger on this fast."

"Very good. Both founders."

"If necessary. I want this taken care of quickly."

"Excellent. Our initial agreement remains in place."

"No changes. Just moving faster. This is the technology I've been looking out for for some time. You brought it to me. That I will not forget."

"Mr. Hawtrey. Francis Mustard here again. Chief of staff for Congressman Barr."

"Mr. Mustard. Yes. We have not had time to adequately consider your offer."

"There is no offer, sir. Rather, a partnership, long-term at that. There are many avenues where your company's interests and the congressman's position intersect. Understand, Sky Saxon has no claim on Empty Spaces. None that will stick. I've already had this examined."

"So you say."

"I already had this checked. You encouraged staff to work on their own projects if they like. Mr. Paper included."

"For select employees, those we wanted to retain, we did permit them to spend up to 20% of their time at the office on outside projects."

"We intend to move forward. And as you now know, the Congressman chairs the Telecommunications Oversight subcommittee. A Canadian company involved in mobile phone security could not have better friends."

"I understand. It's very tempting. I will call you back by the end of the week. I may need to speak with the congressman on this first."

"I may let that happen. No promises. Anything done will be above board."

I've Just Seen a Face

The staff meeting could wait. Ganja would have no doubt already called the congressman to let him know how long Francis spent with mother, and what they discussed. But, she wouldn't know everything. She couldn't know, for instance, that the canny old lady had little trouble understanding the potential of Empty Spaces. Or how it might help fulfill her sad dreams for her son, Francis thought. The congressman doubtless had to know, Francis thought, that his very demanding mother still harbored rather deep doubts about her son; his talents, his abilities, his nerve. Yet she coveted the grand prize; and only the last remaining Barr could see her dream realized. Not possible, Francis knew, but the old woman was as sentimental as she was misguided. In her mind, just as she had molded the old man into a chocolate baron, so too could she transform Reginald, even still.

"Congressman. May I sit?"

"Of course, Francis. You never need to ask. Tell me, how was mother? I've not been to the house in nearly a week, I'm ashamed to say."

"Feisty as always. Ate and drank well."

"What did you two talk about?"

"She talked, I mostly listened. Some family business though. Got a bit upset when I mentioned peanut allergies. I must say, congressman, I realize with all your commitments that it's hard to get down there as often as you would like. And when you first asked me to meet with her, I naturally assumed it was to keep her out of your hair, and away from the staff, of course. But, honestly, she's such a delight. Besides, the long drive helps clear my head."

"I appreciate you spending time with her. You two discuss anything else?"

"Project L. Empty Spaces."

Francis watched for any signs of a response, then proceeded.

"Congressman, now is the time to pull the trigger. Even your mother understands its value. There can be no more hesitation. This is our shot, congressman. If we do not move – right now -- there are other investors lining up to put money into project. We lose our one chance forever. I've got our man in Vancouver getting everything in order."

"Sickspack? The Indian fellow?" Barr tried his best not to appear so easily swayed.

"Yes. He's Indian. Canadian immigrant. Would like to come to the US, I'm sure. Very sharp. Vancouver's a bit of an incubator for young talent, but they're not set up to grow the businesses they start. No capital. Small market. Not enough hunger. As I've said, there's the potential to snag this jewel before anyone else is aware of its full potential. But that time is now."

"I understand that. You've been quite forceful on this. Still..."

"Congressman. Everyone's lined up on this. Tell you what. I would like to bring out the founders of Empty Spaces. Soon as possible. Let you get comfortable with them. They are American, by the way. From Michigan, originally."

"Oh. Same as Pam. Nice coincidence."

"Yes. Same as Pam."

"That might work, Francis. I'm not sure when's the best time, but I like the idea."

The congressman had long grown used to his mother's doubts, his colleagues sneers, the public's whispers. Francis calculated that such thoughts were swirling inside the congressman's head even as he spoke. He could play him, Francis knew, though it required practice.

"Congressman?"

Francis spun around as Theo Preston entered. "Theo. Not a good time, lad. Hold it for the staff meeting."

"No. That's all right. I'd quite like a unbiased opinion," offered the congressman.

"I think we're done here, congressman."

"No, no. Theo, please. Come around to this side of my desk."

The congressman sat back in his chair. Regardless of Francis' hidden, no doubt grandiose schemes, which the congressman was certain he reserved for no one but himself, the truth of what his chief of staff was saying was evident. Still, he enjoyed this game; withholding his consent till the very last possible moment. Besides, with someone else there, Theo especially, there was less a chance for Francis to bully him.

"Francis. I need a sounding board. I want you to go over Empty Spaces again. With Theo here. Theo, please pay attention."

Francis expressed no outward signs of dismay or anger. He methodically explained the inner workings of Empty Spaces, the market potential for what he dubbed a smartphone "relevance engine," how the algorithms captured and understood a user's mood and even the process by where one user's mood and identity were shared with a match, even if a complete stranger, within the user's general proximity.

When Theo responded to a rather pedestrian question from the Congressman, Francis was legitimately impressed with the staffer's quick insight. "It understands how the user feels, can share that feeling with another person -- or possibly another device -- in real-time, based on the user's location? If it works, congressman, the potential for integrating messages with a user's mood, one that's connected to their surroundings is huge. Pretty impressive. If it works, of course."

"It works, Theo. Trust me, it works. Isn't that right, Congressman?"

Francis was now certain, given Theo's response, that everything he had envisioned, that his plans for the congressman, for his own career, for taking Empty Spaces...all of it was now clearly under the guise of divine intervention. There could be no other explanation. And, in His way, confirmation arrived in the form of a single affirmative response from a simple aide gunning for a promotion.

"You like this idea than, Theo?"

"I do, congressman. Obviously, I can't speak to whether this service will work or not --"

"It does."

"Yes, though what I find interesting is how cleverly this technology integrates standard message types."

Francis became more alert.

"I'm not sure I follow," said the Congressman.

"Well, congressman, it's sort of a marketing holy grail, if you will. How do people make choices? Everything from political candidate to what television shows they watch or what brand of dish soap they buy."

"Or chocolate."

"Yes. Or, chocolate. There are two meta processes involved in choice. Foremost, of course, is that people need to validate their own choices. We've all done this. We continue to research a product long after we've made our purchase. We survey the choices made by those that are physically close to us, such as in an office, like here, or those close to us personally. This technology appears to facilitate that need within the brain to feel comfortable with the choices we make. Only, it does so on a exponential scale."

"Interesting. And the other process? You said two, correct, son?"

"This technology appears to collapse the full spectrum of social cognition as it relates to choice. I understand that's a technical term, congressman. Something I studied in school. Think of it this way: timing, location, environment, needs of the moment. Each of these are critical factors in the choices we make. People take in thousands of bits of data from a range of inputs every single day. All this information is distilled by a personal algorithm if you will for even the most mundane of choices. What to have for lunch? Why choose this grocery store over the next? Individuals want to believe that not only did they choose correctly, obviously, but they also want to believe that the way they chose, the inputs they focused on, or the messages they ignored, say, were ultimately directed by themselves, not by external forces. They want to believe their personal algorithm is in charge, as it were, leading their choices, and not some silly jingle or pushy salesperson. How does a person become a Republican or Democrat? The individual believes the decision is quite rational. Most of the time it is not. Rarely, in fact. Even more importantly, once they choose it becomes nearly impossible to sway them, to get them to alter their choice. As if they've taken up a side in some larger battle. To change means they originally chose wrong. Thought wrong. People do not want to admit this. Empty Spaces seems to fool people on a fundamental level. It takes all the inputs, without priority, without acknowledging that the user is filled with biases, and repeats back, through music, what the user believes is the way they are supposed to feel. Pretty clever, actually."

The congressman beamed. "See, Francis. Aren't you glad I asked him to join us?" He patted Theo on the shoulder. "I've made my decision."

TRACK FIVE
Sentimental Journey

Nowhere Man

The Congressman, for one of the few times, felt truly comfortable in his trappings. The torn expression on Francis' face after Theo was asked to sit in on their meeting was priceless. As well it should, he thought. After all, it was he, US Congressman and President of Nutt Barr Co. that made the decisions.

Flush with his victory, Barr was determined to contribute still more. Theo, who Barr only just came to realize was quite insightful, talked about the ways consumers and voters accept or reject messages. Why should Francis have complete control over campaign messaging, Barr thought? He had a say, after all. Indeed, now more than ever, perhaps, his say was essential. There was, for once, a strong challenge to his normally safe congressional seat. A young Hispanic man was running a surprisingly effective ground campaign. The messages were few, but stark and maddeningly repetitive; political earworms, Barr feared, ready to take hold inside the brains of all who heard them. Worst of all, each contained a kernel of truth; certainly enough to sway easily swayed voters:

- Young vs Old
- New Virginia (read: minority) vs Old Virginia (read: white)
- Self made vs Silver spoon
- Vigorous male vs Question mark, which, true or not, the challenger's campaign clearly embraced this distasteful wedge issue

The congressman needed his own defining issue. Something more than Francis intended, which was, truth be told, little more than a message of resignation. 'Don't allow the voters to believe there is any real choice, Congressman, nothing more', is what he said. Bunk. Barr longed for something affirmative, bold, even.

Nothing presented itself to him, unfortunately. He decided instead to shift his focus to his ailing chocolate business. In fact, it was a cruel twist of fate, Barr felt, that just as he was having to fight for his political livelihood, so too was the family business in retreat. Sales of the fabled Nutt Barr were plummeting. Worse, it was suggested that Barr, not mother, take the lead in what was sure to be a series of painful decisions, including layoffs, firings, debt restructuring. None of these were tasks he was well suited for, Barr knew. He was a man of ideas, if not action; of understanding what decisions to make or not, and when. Most badly undervalued the process. He would need to divine messages that would lead consumers back into the fold. This he was certain he could do.

He just wasn't sure how. How to create, how to refine, how to begin. Inspired, Barr reached for his phone. Theo introduced him to a website that quickly became one of his favorites. Bitter Water wasn't the most professional of sites. The facts were not, Barr knew, always one hundred percent accurate. The blogger, a woman with a silly name who worked at the FCC, truly loved chocolate, however. That much was clear. She understood its purpose, its value; beyond mere dollars. If Barr was to be uncover something to take back for others to behold, to reverse his company's descent, he was as likely to find it there, he understood, inside the welcoming ingress of a joyful, passionate blog, as in the tables and columns prepared by those who instead cared only about the numbers.

This was not merely playing to his strengths. Despite the authority of the numbers and tables carefully positioned within the spreadsheets sent to him, Barr simply refused to believe that sales of chocolate, of all things, and of the Nutt Barr in particular, would continue their downward trend. Chocolate would not die. Why cut when there was sure to be a turnaround? There had to be; chocolate never stopped. It was a matter, he knew, of advertising; of combining the right message and the right carrier of that message. Barr was sure of this. Both Theo and Francis agreed.

Soon, he would have Empty Spaces; his carrier. Now, he needed a message; exactly the right message. One as clever and inventive and memorable as his father's original jingle. How hard could that be, he thought? All he required was the right information, the right inspiration, and focus.

Blog: Bitter Water
A Brief History of the Spread of Chocolate

Cacao originated in the Amazon at least 4,000 years ago. The near global spread of cacao, or more specifically, of chocolate, which is derived from the seed of the cacao tree, can be directly traced to Mayan peoples, who have been making chocolate as early as the 6th century AD. The Maya culture spread from Central America to South America, from the Yucatan peninsula to the Pacific. Cacao was cultivated throughout the Mayan territory.

"Theo has some Mayan blood. I thought they all died out. That young man continues to surprise."

The Aztecs (circa 1200 AD) subjugated the Mayans although they, too, helped maintain and spread cacao (or cocoa) throughout the Americas. The Aztecs, like the Mayan, used cacao to make a thick, typically cold drink called xocolatl. The cacao was mixed with peppers, local spices and corn meal. The drink was quite healthful and it was thought to possess aphrodisiac qualities.

"I hate how she says cacao. The word is cocoa."

In 1502, Columbus landed in Central America; his fourth and final visit to the Americas. He was the first European to discover cacao beans being used – as both a currency and as the primary ingredient in an important and ceremonial drink.

In 1520, the Spanish explorer Cortez, who conquered parts of Mexico, presented cacao beans to Spain's King Charles V, along with the tools used for making the popular chocolate drink. The Spaniards replaced the corn meal and chilis with sugar and other spices, such as vanilla, nutmeg and cinnamon. The popularity of this drink in Spain created a surging demand for chocolate. Soon, many Spanish plantations were constructed in the Americas. In less than a hundred years, chocolate (as a drink) became popular throughout western Europe.

"One hundred years," thought the Congressman. "Can people today even think that long anymore? Is there anything any of us can create, today," he thought, "that could reliably last for one hundred years?" Sadly, the congressman realized that of the few things Americans created that had in fact lasted one hundred years or more, water systems, the New York subway, for example, the nation probably no longer had the wherewithal to replicate. "Christ, I bet the collective knowledge just to repeat those things is probably gone as well," he thought. There was a very real chance that the Nutt Barr might not make it to 100 years. Unless, of course, he unlocked some magic. The congressman redoubled his focus.

By the early 1700s, chocolate houses and coffee houses that prominently feature chocolate are popular throughout London, France, Germany, Spain and Switzerland.

The advent of the steam engine, which spurred very low-cost, mechanized grinding of cacao, led to significant price drops in chocolate. By 1730, chocolate was transitioning from luxury item to popular treat.

"Chocolate." The word alone, Barr knew, was treat enough. Rich, tantalizing, accessible; just this side of decadent. A forgivable sin. He felt as if he were getting closer now. Something that mentioned the price, low-cost, was overly indulgent, but tasteful; expressive. Market research, he thought, always starts backwards. He reached for his tablet. Coffee houses are everywhere, but not chocolate houses. Should the company create a new business, he wondered?

Ideas:
1.   Chocolate houses

Barr quickly thought better of this. The capital required would certainly put the family business deeper in debt. He didn't care for that idea. Mother would care for it even less, no doubt. Plus, he wondered, could he convince people to drink chocolate several times a day, like they did with coffee? Was there something that could be added, he wondered, to make this more plausible? More caffeine? More sugar? Advertising, no matter how effective, he thought, could make people return again and again. He kept reading.

In 1765, America's first ever chocolate factory is started. This was one of the most productive factories in the world for its time.

In 1828, the cocoa press is invented. This innovation again leads to reduced prices, increased usage and for most, improves the overall quality of drinking chocolate. This is achieved primarily by means of using the press to easily squeeze out the cacao butter which helps control the amount of fat in the drink.

The congressman paused. He recalled the sheltie the family had when he was a boy; a Christmas present to him from his father. Her name was Coco Butter. Mother never cared much for dogs. His father, however, enjoyed her company, as long as she was not barking, which was rarely. For the younger Barr, set apart from others by his parents' fortune, not built for farming, nor horse riding, and, as his mother reminded him, not diligent about the business side of Nutt Barr, or his studies in general, Coco Butter was a beacon; a call from God that he was loved, that his presence was known, and that the pattern of his days and his nights and all in-between would be made bearable.

At eleven years old, not terribly old for a sheltie, and Barr himself only 16, he returned from school to find the dog had been put down. Which, because his parents told him together, he knew that he dare not cry, dare not question. Which he did not. Ever. This did not ease the pain.

Britain was critical in the spread of chocolate. An English company developed fondant chocolate in 1847, replacing the coarse, grainy texture of solid chocolate with something much more smooth and velvety, similar to how we know it today.

The Cadbury Brothers, also of England, initiated mass production of chocolate. Prince Albert, husband of Queen Victoria, helped oversee The Exposition in 1851. It was here where a number of prominent Americans are first introduced to chocolate creams and other solid chocolates. These recipes and methods for preparation are brought back to the States.

In 1923, the Chocolate Manufacturers Association of the United States is formed.

Two years later, in 1925, a Cocoa Exchange is founded in New York.

In 1927, Luscious Barr founds Barr Chocolates, later Nutt Barr Co., a popular regional chocolate company that later introduces the cult favorite, Nutt Barr.

The congressman stopped there. He knew the rest. About Nutt Barr, about the rising popularity of chocolate after the War, and how mass produced, low-cost chocolate bars became a staple treat in the 1950s, with scores of different chocolate bars, literally, available for sale in every region of the country. He knew the industry was changing. As it always had, he reminded himself. Even if he wished it were not so.

There was no inspiration. No message. No new jingle, as it were. He shuddered to think what might happen should the company fail. He shuddered to think what his mother's final thoughts of him might be. It was safer, he decided, if he went back online. "I'll skim just a few more posts," he told himself.

Barr, in fact, truly did love reading about chocolate, even if the grinding task of operating a chocolate business was not his ken.

Blog: Bitter Water

Medicinal properties of chocolate

The medicinal use of chocolate, both as a primary remedy and as a vehicle to deliver other medicines originated with the Olmec, Maya and then Aztec peoples.

"That word I like. 'Peoples'. I suppose if I lose in November, I can always travel. Mother has her nurses."

The early Florentine Codex (1590) offered a prescription of cacao beans, maize and the herb tlacoxochitl to alleviate fever and shortness of breath. In addition, manuscripts produced in Europe from 1600 – 1900 revealed over one hundred medicinal uses for chocolate. These included tonics to improve digestion, bowel function and to overcome fatigue. Chocolate paste was used as a preferred delivery medium for a variety of pharmacological additives, in fact

"Christ. I'm over 50. About grandpop's age when he died. Need to take better care of myself. What do I do? Forty five minutes on the treadmill every morning. That's probably not enough. Although, I do favor mother. Probably have her genes."

Cacao butter has long been used to treat burns, wounds and skin irritations, and as a laxative.

Laxatives reminded Barr of his mother, which once again made him sympathize with her nurses, Ganja and Honah. Mother did not know that Barr paid them both significantly more that she believed.

Studies confirm: women who eat chocolate regularly have a better sex life than those who do not. According to Dr. Salonia [link], chocolate is less like a food and more like a drug. For women, chocolate enhances libido, overall sexual satisfaction and minimizes mood swings as a result of their menstrual cycle.

Barr was now starting to feel pessimistic. Empty Spaces, he thought, even if it could help spread the Nutt Barr jingle, or some other song, to millions of people, may be for naught, at least as far as the chocolate business was concerned. "Ours is no longer a world about joy," he considered. "Numbers. Algorithms. Charts." Instead of pleasures like an affordable chocolate bar, Barr feared, clinical gratification, self improvement, denial were now all the rage. Could chocolate, with the best of messaging, thrive in such a world?

The beloved Nutt Barr jingle, when deconstructed, was nothing more than information, a message transposed upon a signal. Like a human voice, broken into 1s and 0s, aggregated into standardized packets, and transmitted, along with thousands of others, over a single telephone wire; one of millions. In such a world, Barr feared, jingles of any sort could not survive, could not spread, could not evolve into living objects that resided comfortably within a collective, shared memory. Ads, like consumers, were now driven by clicks or views or touches or engagements; quantified and calibrated in real-time for a variety of ever-changing, highly specific audience targets. Exactly the wrong solution for today's world, Barr thought; when people needed jingles, joy, magic. Chocolate, he feared, was similarly being deconstructed.

Yes it's true, chocolate can prove toxic to dogs and other domestic animals. That is because of the way these animals metabolize theobromine. Early signs of theobromine poisoning in dogs include nausea and vomiting, restlessness, diarrhea, muscle tremors, and incontinence.

"This may be true, technically," Barr thought. Though he recalled more than one happy occasion when he gave a bite of his Nutt Barr to a very grateful Coco Butter.

Medical marijuana? How about 'medical chocolate'? A substance in chocolate called anandamide binds to cannabinoid receptors and literally mimics the effects of marijuana!

An American politician, Barr reflexively recoiled at the mere mention of the word marijuana. No good could ever come of it, he knew. Still, a chocolate high, he wondered? Was that what the author was suggesting? He skipped to other posts.

The following word cloud represents the most common words I have used this past year when describing chocolate:
Luxurious. Mouthfeel. Intensity. Dark. Rich. Butterfat. Dense. Nib. Sweet. Premium. Coating. Smooth. Crystals. Hot. Infuse. Swiss. English. French. Flavor. Tasting. Raw. Percentage. Blend. Notes. Origin. Morsel. Pure. Velvety. Creamy. Melted. Texture. Aroma.

Wait. Perhaps, Barr wondered, his focus on music, on recreating a jingle, was all wrong. Yes, when done right, a song or jingle seemed to penetrate inside a person's head. Implanting itself within their long-term memory, forever; laying dormant, but waiting to spring to life. What of words, Barr thought? Words, too, had power. Had everyone forgotten that? Might Empty Spaces put a single word inside a user's brain, and that spur them to action? Barr spoke a few words out loud, hoping to test his theory: "Raw". "Hot." "Melted." "Mouthfeel." Barr quickly felt self-aware and continued reading. He was certain, however, that he was getting warmer.

Blog: Bitter Water
Chocolate and the Industrial Revolution

Chocolate began as a cold, grainy drink, filled with spices, available only to the few. But, over its long history,   innovations in the growing, distributing and making of chocolate led to significant price reductions, the creation of a smoother texture, solid chocolates, milk chocolates, filled chocolates and, ultimately, to the amazing variety of chocolates and chocolate bars we enjoy today.

The benefits of the industrial revolution on chocolate included low-cost manufacturing, high-volume production, wide-scale distribution, as well as innovation in candy types, flavors and mixtures. Industrial-scale packaging and advertising complemented these innovations.

As much as many of us true lovers of chocolate prize expensive, handmade chocolates, molded in elegant designs, for example, the true joy and pleasure of chocolate is that it is plainly wonderful and available to everyone.

That was it!

Barr realized that his company, the entire industry, in fact, had trod the wrong path; for years now. Only, now the results were finally becoming evident. Luxury products, specialty chocolates, chocolates to promote health, all in the name of conquering new markets, increasing profit margins, diversifying. Wrong! The past several years, for example, Nutt Barr Co., admittedly with his blessing, had poured significant resources into a 'luxury' line of chocolates. These premium chocolates had never sold to expectations and, Barr now thought, distracted the company from its true mission: chocolates for everyone.

Chocolates were an indulgence, true, but not a luxury. Rather, something for everyone, just as the blogger implied. That would be his message. Something for everyone. People wanted, Barr knew. This would shape the cornerstone of his message. "Something for everyone" he repeated to himself. Plus, owing to his most recent decision, to invest in Empty Spaces, Barr would soon possess the means of spreading this message. His cleverness, along with Empty Spaces, would save the family business. "Something for everyone. Good enough if not great". Indeed, that was a message, Barr realized, that could extend far beyond chocolate. Mother and Theo would both be impressed with this, he thought. He didn't care what Francis might say.

Irony is not a trait afforded a man who inherited his wealth. Nor involved in politics. Still, this must be, the congressman thought, what people describe as ironic. His favorite site about chocolate is by a woman who lives in Washington, DC, and who is apparently a ardent fan of Empty Spaces. Which he will soon own. Even if it means working alongside, as nearly equals, with that prick, Francis. Barr leaned back in his chair, smiled. He wondered when the next lobbyist or constituent group was scheduled to stop in and seek his approval. Life was good, once more.

Getting better all the time, in fact. Because Francis, who still needed Barr's money and Barr's access, was finishing a plan, about to be sprung, that would allow them to take complete ownership of Empty Spaces, cut the two founders out of the picture, and take legal and physical possession of the code, all in one fell swoop. Everything was nearly set. All that remained, essentially, was to bring the founders to them. Barr, of course, would not dare get his small hands dirty on such a scheme, but, ultimately, he knew what Francis proposed was the right thing to do. Mother, herself, said as much. Empty Spaces was simply too important to share.

Really, it wasn't even about the money.

Flying

"For those about to rock. Fire!"

"Inside voice. Not everyone wants to hear the same music, remember?" JaDe had his large headphones on and was singing, loudly. Since he exclusively relied on Empty Spaces, that likely meant something, Jackie knew. It had taken all Jackie's powers to force JaDe to join him on a flight, all expenses paid, to Washington, DC, for a meeting with Reginald Barr, congressman, businessman, and, per Sickspack's confirmation, the lead investor for Empty Spaces.

This was not easy. Despite earlier promises. Despite the big check that awaited them. JaDe rarely left the apartment. Getting him to leave the country, fly 3,000 plus miles, dress appropriately, do something with his braids, still undetermined, and sit for a business meeting was no small feat. Both harbored nagging, if minor ill feelings over the brief series of arguments that ultimately led to the two men seated next to one another in a large plane, on the tarmac at Vancouver's YVR airport, preparing for takeoff.

Jackie still wondered, nervously, if part of JaDe's hesitance had anything to do with his use and/or promotion and/or selling and/or distributing of marijuana; an activity that, yes, in the 21st century was greeted with much more than disdain, particularly by the government of the United States of America. There had been no problems, thankfully, during their long wait at the gate in Vancouver. Jackie promised himself to not worry about this concern again until they landed, a few hours from now, and made their way through US Customs.

JaDe, meanwhile, clearly nervous at leaving home, if not flying, pulled out his phone and began typing his latest blog entry. Jackie watched for a minute, before losing interest.

Blog: Daytripper
Names for Marijuana

I'm leaving on a jet plane. But I hate writing on my phone and considering the circumstances can't dictate, so I have instead chosen a topic that's easy for me to type: my favorite colloquial names for marijuana:

- ganja
- weed
- grass
- dope

- pot
- reefer
- mary jane
- chillums
- funk
- Marley
- burrito
- jolly green
- Kronic
- herb
- smoke

Jackie glanced at his phone. "Looks like we'll be leaving almost on time. Nice. Still surprised it's Washington, not San Francisco. Seattle, even. Or Boston. Who knew people in Washington, DC knew anything about technology?"

"It's America. Government's got all the money," JaDe responded. "Still not happy about this. You do understand that, correct? These people never heard of video calls?"

"Yes. I understand. Yes, they have heard of video calls. We've done those. I have, at least. But we won't seal any deal on a video call. Besides, apparently this is a fairly conservative investor. He wants to meet us in person. Sickspack assures me this is a formality."

"Meet us in person? We are scheduled for a 90 minute meeting. How the hell are they supposed to learn anything about us in 90 minutes they can't on the phone?"

"If you were about to give a stranger several million dollars, wouldn't you like to meet them first? Doesn't seem that unreasonable."

"Fine. Don't need me. This is your baby."

"No. You helped. We're an American band, remember. This thing hits bit, and I know it will, we'll be rich. Seriously rich. We. Plus, think of it like this. With two of us, that's two on any board, two on any contract, two members of any executive team. We have more leverage that way."

"I own a home in Vancouver. Don't need the money."

"True. But how are you gonna use that money? It's all tied up in the house. Selling dope to our neighbors hasn't been going so well lately."

"That's true. Business sucks for everybody. Maybe something the government is putting out. You think? I mean, my shit's not even that great anymore. Plus, stuff I buy, all garbage. I honestly would not be surprised if government is attacking us at the source. I mean literally, like seeds, like the DNA of seeds, even."

"Or, you're maturing. Doesn't have the same effect as it once did. You're getting older. All that yoga having the detoxifying effect you hoped it would. Oh, and maybe the flight attendants don't need to hear you mention marijuana in every sentence."

"Mention it? You think what we do online isn't monitored? Worse than speech, cause that can all be archived. Of course, voice will soon enough." JaDe held up his phone for effect.

"You can hide your tracks. Make yourself lost."

"You maybe. You know how that shit works. Not most people. It's all there. Everything. Say, let me borrow your computer. Think I'll post something about the illegalization of marijuana. Should know this by heart."

Jackie passed his laptop to JaDe. "Why not? I live with you. If The Man is after you, I'm already doomed." JaDe didn't hear. He was already thinking of what to type, even as the pilot was announcing the reason for a slight delay.

Blog: Daytripper
A brief history of the illegalization of marijuana in the United States of America

Cannabis -- marijuana -- was criminalized in several Western countries beginning in the early 20th century. In 1937, under FDR, the United States passed the Marijuana Transfer Tax Act. This was the first national law making cannabis possession illegal. The Act criminalized not only the production of marijuana but also hemp! Likely because hemp was a cheap substitute for papers and the paper barons of the time, including Randolph Hearst and the Mellons, hoped to destroy this fledgling industry. Nearly a century later it remains illegal to consume, possess, grow and sell (or trade) marijuana in the people's republic of America.

Even in countries such as Canada, marijuana is only tolerated but still not technically legal. Fortunately, Canada and some states in the US now make possession of small amounts of marijuana punishable by only a fine. Still, many courts in the US continue to send users, particularly young users, to "treatment" programs to "cure" them of their addiction to "narcotics".

"Have to shut it down. We're getting ready to take off," Jackie told him.

"I'll finish it once we're up. Don't want to bring the plane down."

"Not funny. Shit, I hate flying."

"You hate flying!"

"Yes. Hate it. Take offs are the worse. And turbulence."

"Well, we will have both of those, I can pretty much guarantee you that."

"Thanks. Not helpful."

"I need to assure you, now? Listen. When I was in the CFL, I flew dozens of times. Hundreds. Try flying out of fucking Winnipeg during a blizzard in a plane the CFL can afford. Trust me, you have nothing to worry about. Except maybe those two dime bags I put in your suitcase."

Jackie nearly twisted his neck. "Tell me that's a joke."

"Relax. I got nothing on me. You're clean. Look, we're already leveling off."

"Okay. I'm good. For now. Last time I flew was about two years ago. Christmas. To visit my parents. Few months after Pam and I split up. My mother liked Pam. Not sure why, exactly."

"Pam know you're going to DC?"

"No."

Planning on seeing her? Lots of time, I suspect. I bet our big investor won't spend more than 5 minutes with us."

"No, ninety minutes scheduled, I bet it goes two hours at least. Assuming they like us."

"They're flying us. They like us. So...gonna see Pam or not? I mean, she's getting married. Wish her a nice life?

"I don't know. Maybe I'll surprise her at work."

"That should go well. I know how much women love when their ex-boyfriends stop by their place of employment."

"The air up here's making you real funny."

"Fine. I'll drop it. You know, we're flying into Washington National Airport, right? George Washington. Washington grew pot. You know that? Give me your laptop again."

"It's called Reagan National Airport. For a long time now, I think. Whole different world."

"How can Washington, the capital, for all the money that flows through that place not allow for a cost benefit analysis of drug laws? Nearly half of the entire cost of law enforcement in America is related to drug offenses. Did you know that?"

JaDe reboots Jackie's computer.

"I did not."

"Did you know that America -- the United fucking states of America -- has 1 million plus people in jail. Jail, fuck that, prison, not jail. For nonviolent drug offenses. Non violent. Do you know that one million people are arrested every year for marijuana. Marijuana!"

"I read your blog. I live with you. I know this."

"And we're going to ask these people for money? You sure you want to do this? We don't need their money. Have you seen the number of downloads?"

"Yes. We are going to ask them for money."

Blog: Daytripper
A brief history of the illegalization of marijuana in the United States of America (cont.)

In the late 1800s, in both the United States and England, it was common for doctors and pharmacists to use marijuana to help alleviate a variety of ailments,. This was typically delivered via a tincture (an extract of marijuana with alcohol). One of the earliest articles in the medical journal The Lancet featured Sir John Russell Reynolds, the personal physician to Queen Victoria. He prescribed marijuana for the Queen's various pains. Marijuana was an accepted part of life.

In seeking to illegalize marijuana, authorities repeatedly attempted to associate the word itself, marihuana, derived from Mexican Spanish, with Mexicans, thus conjuring negative attitudes of the poor and brown. The term cannabis, or more specifically, the term used by pharmacists, cannabis indica, which had long conveyed notions of safety and medicine, began to fade. Start using only the word cannabis and watch how quickly perceptions change. Words have power!

JaDe looked up from the computer. Jackie was reading a book on his smartphone. "Speaking of Washington, you ever read polls? Who will be elected? How Americans feel about this issue or that?"

"Sure." Jackie knew this was a leading question.

"Have you any idea why marijuana is still essentially illegal, throughout the United States, even though a significant majority favors legalization? That's true. An overwhelming majority of Americans believe medical marijuana should be legal, plus, believe that adults should be able to smoke it if they like -- or at least not be punished for possession. Been that way at least a decade or more. And, yet, what has changed? Tell me there's not big money behind keeping it illegal."

"I'm on your side, remember?"

JaDe, uncomfortable in his small seat, fidgeted, looked about the cabin. He was hoping for a discussion. Jackie was not forthcoming. Both returned to their screens. Briefly.

"Remember those 1 million marijuana arrests every year that I mentioned?"

"I do."

"Political prisoners. That's what they are. Pot laws are the new Jim Crow. Because powers that be don't want us to have this stuff. Only, no one mentions that. And that's not everything. Consider the prison costs, the courts, law enforcement. California alone says if they could tax marijuana it would bring in billions annually. Billions. That's one state."

"Yes, the biggest state."

"Come on. The government refuses to let states decide their own policies and tax rules on marijuana? Don't even get me started on chemtrails."

"Chemtrails? What's that?"

"I thought you said you read my blog!"

Jackie shrugged, returned to his book.

Blog: Daytripper
A brief history of the illegalization of marijuana in the United States of America (cont.)

The Controlled Substances Act of 1970 classified marijuana as a Schedule I drug. It is considered to have a high potential for abuse and no legitimate medical purpose. The Act prohibits the possession, usage, purchase, sale and cultivation of marijuana.

"Have you any idea of how much more harmful -- and non-natural -- cigarettes are than marijuana? One is illegal, the other you can buy at the party store."

"My parents live near a small party store. I sometimes walk there when I need to escape the house for a bit. Which is every time I visit." Jackie set his smartphone aside. "Here's a story for you, since you won't let me read. It's true. The phone at my parents' house rings something like 20 times a day, minimum. And each time it's like some momentous event in the Paper household. Like, my dad is in his chair, watching the local news, okay? I remember local news being on only rarely but I think now it's always playing. My mom is also in the living room. Sitting on the couch, her glasses on, reading the Bible. She started reading it like 30 years ago, but she can't focus. She reads one passage then looks up and asks my dad something, like what they should have for dinner.

"Anyway, I think she's up to Deuteronomy.

"And this scene plays out repeatedly throughout the day. Every day. Have I set the scene?"

"Yes," JaDe nods, pleased Jackie is now comfortable enough to speak.

"Their phone rings. Loudly.

"Nothing. No response from either of them.

"It rings a second time. My dad turns to my mom and says, 'what the heck. Is that the phone?' Like, this is some shock, a complete surprise. The phone ringing.

"Third ring.

"My mom takes her glasses off, which are hanging down her nose. I have her nose. Bad for wearing glasses."

"I know. I didn't want to say anything."

"Funny. Anyway, my mom sets her glasses down on the end table by the couch. Sets the Bible down on the couch.

"Fourth ring. It's a cordless phone, obviously, but they never seem to keep it nearby. I cannot understand why. I've given up trying to teach them.

"Fifth ring. My mom gets up to retrieve the phone. It's in the spare bedroom. Also no idea why. It works just as well when she keeps it right next to her I tell her. Even better, in fact.

"She yells from the spare bedroom.

"'I can't read the number.'

"Sixth ring. My dad mutes the local news. 'What?' Hearing not so good.

"'I can't read the number,' my mom yells.

"'I bet you left your glasses in here.' She carries the phone into the living room, handing it to my dad.

"Seventh ring. 'Can you see the number,' she asks.

"Eighth ring.

"Then, silence.

"'They must have hung up,' one of them will say.

"'Well, they'll call back if it's important, I guess.'

"Mom sits down on the couch and picks up her Bible. Dad un-mutes the news. Mom glances around, eyeing her glasses. Walks the phone back to the spare bedroom, where the base is kept. God knows why. Returns to the living room, opens her book. 'What do you think we should have for dinner? she asks.

""I don't know. What'd we have yesterday?"

JaDe nods. "When they get old, and the kids move out, all parents become stoners."

The flight attendant interrupts, asks what they would like to drink. She is not that attractive, not terribly friendly, probably overworked. Both men choose from the options given, take their drinks, and return to their individual screens. JaDe chooses to finish a blog post he began working on earlier in the week; one that he hoped would garner him more readers than the site typically attracts, which, after nearly two years of effort, remained stuck in the low ten thousands.

Blog: Daytripper
Effects of cannabis

Cannabis has both psychological and physiological effects on the body, which are primarily triggered by tetrahydrocannabinol (THC), a cannabinoid. The psychoactive effects of cannabis, what most people term the high, are highly subjective and dependent upon the kind and amount of cannabis consumed and the method of consumption. When smoked, for example, the effects, which include euphoria, giggling, relaxation and possibly an altered state of consciousness, are evident within minutes, and typically last for several hours. For some, a feeling of sexual arousal, sensuality, libido, and, paradoxically, feelings of introspection occur. For many others, brief periods of paranoia and forgetfulness are not uncommon. When taken orally, the effects usually take significantly longer to manifest, though again last no more than about 4-8 hours.

Popular culture tends to focus on those effects that reflect altered states of perception and understanding. Memories are distorted, or flood the brain, and short term thoughts become difficult to sustain. Time and distance are out of place here. A reduction of alpha waves and basic motor activities is also common, as is an increase in heart rate – along with bloodshot eyes. In scientific studies, each of these pronounced effects of cannabis are absent by the following day. Yes, you can smoke a marijuana cigarette on a Saturday night and be perfectly ready for work come bright and early Monday morning.

Cannabis effects several areas of the brain, most notably the cerebellum, which controls movement and coordination; the hippocampus, which manages memory, learning and stress; and the cerebral cortex, which oversees higher cognitive functions. These areas of the brain have the highest concentration of cannabinoid receptors.

There is no credible link of long-term cannabis use and an increase in heart attack of other cardiovascular events. A number of studies, however, have found an increased risk for depression and bipolar disorder in long-term consumption

Fact: The cannabis that is available for such research studies in the United States is grown at the University of Mississippi and controlled exclusively by the National Institute on Drug Abuse (NIDA). They, alone, define who may use the cannabis, for what study, with what expected outcomes, and using only (their) scientific protocols. The potency of their cannabis remains unknown.

JaDe paused, looked about the cabin, stretched his frame. He wondered how much distance they had flown. Jackie was staring out the window, periodically taking pictures of the landscape below. Jackie could feel JaDe's presence. He turned to face him. "How's the post going?"

"Fine, I suppose. Haven't found the hook yet. Do you know that the primary source of medical training after medical school, and this is a fact, is paid for by drug companies? Drug companies."

"Explains a lot. I gotta piss. You mind?" Jackie and JaDe each unbuckled and stood up. Jackie walked back to the lavatory.

One common effect of cannabis that everyone knows about, even non-users, is the "munchies". Overwhelming personal evidence, knowledge gleaned by practitioners of alternative medicine and, yes, clinical studies, all confirm: consumption of cannabis increases appetite.

"Back."

JaDe looked up at Jackie. "Let me get up. Need to stretch."

"Finished?" Jackie pointed to the laptop.

"No. Still needs work. I'll let it sit. Did you know that at high doses, cannabis is an effective treatment against Alzheimer's?"

"I did not. I would have thought exactly the opposite."

"People don't know. Don't want to know, more like it. Damn. I need another soda. Is it really such a burden to provide customers with one entire fucking can of soda?"

"I brought a couple waters."

"Don't want water."

Jackie was seated, dutifully buckled in, staring out the window. "You ever wonder, what would happen if aliens visited us? How people would react? I mean really react?"

"Sure," JaDe responded. "Ever see those videos of tribes, like in Papua New Guinea, where a tribe meets a white person for the first time? Or some tribe in the rainforest in Brazil encounters new technology? I think people would be like that. Fearful. Curious. Surprised. Joyful."

Jackie stared at JaDe. "That's exactly what I think. We would be scared, hesitant to approach. Maybe even have a weapon at the ready, friends at our back. But, some of us at least, would approach. Slowly. Reaching out. Still fearful, but curious. Hopeful, even. What magic might they possess?"

"Hope to live long enough to find out. Say, did you know that chocolate has some of the same effects on the brain as marijuana"?

"Really? I think that's just myth. Like more crime when there's a full moon."

"No. I've been researching the effects of cannabis; some fairly scientific studies. It is no myth. Chocolate, or chemicals inside it I should say, mimics THC."

"Wonder why I prefer one and not the other?"

"Maybe I should switch to chocolate. Haven't had a good high in a while. Not just my stuff, either. Anything I've bought. I'm certain the government is getting to our seeds. Or maybe putting something into the growth material? That can be the only explanation. Say, got any chocolate to go with that water? Worth a try."

"Doubtful. Maybe the trail mix has some chocolate in it. Let me check."

"Please do. Long fucking flight."

Tell Me What You See

The jet airliner began its descent into Washington, DC. The city was overcast, and not till moments before landing could they see below. Nearest the window, Jackie spied the Capitol Building, shining stark and bright against the evening sky. He scanned the surface, quickly spotted the Pentagon, what he presumed was a body of water -- the Potomac River, he guessed -- and then the wheels hit the ground.

The men, on cue with the rest of the passengers, stood up, stretched, reached for their bags. Each had only a single carry-on, expecting this to suffice. "Not so bad. Little over five hours." Jackie spoke out loud, partly because he felt that lent proof to the notion they were no longer eight miles high, and partly owing to his renewed concern that JaDe might have issues with the authorities now that they were physically inside the United States. The pair slowly exited the plane with the hundred or so others.

"Glad we went through US Customs back at YVR airport. Let's grab something to eat."

Fuck, Jackie thought. We did go through US Customs back in Canada. "Oh, that's right. Food sounds good to me."

The airport was reasonably clean, bright, filled with brightly lit signs, large windows hinting at the outside world, hotel-like carpeting running into corporate-like tile, suggesting an entitled professionalism. Jackie was pleasantly surprised by the interior, though. Its yellow metal columns, high ceiling, helpful signage, and wide corridors offered an austere comfort. Unlike YVR, however, there was nothing about the place that hinted at its actual physical location, or of the history of the region. Still, it was nice, he decided.

Reagan National was only about a quarter-filled, people either moving too quickly or taking too long, which both men found frustrating. Though much warmer than Vancouver, Jackie remained in his blue Michigan hoodie, t-shirt underneath, denims, and sneakers. JaDe wore a white athletic t-shirt, form fitting, and grey cotton slacks, similar in design to standard canvas pants. His dreadlocks, shiny black skin, noticeably thick arms and eager smile all made him stand out, not merely alongside Jackie but nearly everyone else in the building. The two men made their way uneventfully through the airport;

Unfortunately, the selection of food, at least compared to the abundance of options they had grown used to in Vancouver, was sorely lacking. Worse, anything that might have proven acceptable was closed. The pair took the first door they could find leading to the outside world. Before the noise of jets taking off, the throngs of aimless and aggressive people, the semi-anarchic taxi queue, or even the heat, which was a shock to them both, could resonate, Jackie's phone notified him of a message. "It's from Sickspack," he said.

"Better not have cancelled. I'll grab us a cab."

From Sickspack:

Your meeting with RKO Barr and Francis Mustard is scheduled for 90 minutes. The Congressman is very conservative. I mean that personally. Consider again that it may be best -- for all of us -- should JaDe not attend. I can tell him this if you prefer.

Go to bed early. Sleep. Wake up very early. Shower, shave, look the part. Jacket, tie, black leather shoes are all mandatory. White shirt strongly recommended. Remember, this is your first time. It may all seem overwhelming, not very pleasant. Not to worry, however it turns out. I expect you have more than one magic trick in your bag, whether you believe that or not.

I wish you the best of luck, Jackie.

"Get in." JaDe motioned Jackie into the taxi.

"The Vandellas. Crystal City," Jackie told the driver.

"Damn. I'm hungry. What time is it?"

"Local time is one after 9:09."

"9:10. Got it."

"Get some food and get a good night sleep."

"I hope. All this traveling. I do need to calm down."

"Ever been to DC before?"

"No. You?"

"No. We played Maryland once, that's not far from here."

"Really? At Maryland?"

"No. Home. We only played teams like Maryland at home."

"So again, that's a no."

"Where the fuck is Crystal City?"

"Not sure. Near Arlington, I think. Not far. Tall glass buildings, nothing else."

"What'd your message say?"

"Good luck."

"That's it, good luck?"

"Mostly that, and details for our meeting."

"8:00am. Fuck. That's just cruel and unusual."

"Agreed. I much prefer working late than early. I never trust people that get up really early. Like they're trying to cheat the rest of us, somehow. They'll get more than their fair share while we're all still in bed."

Despite the hour, Francis was still at the office, busy at work on the congressman's various re-election press statements, legislative schedule and campaign strategy. Many on the Hill wondered why Francis remained with Barr. Francis knew the whispers and would pay back those with loose lips, in time. He knew the truth of the matter, and it was as simple as it was obvious: Barr was weak. Which, in Washington, weakness always created an opening for someone prepared to wield power. Francis long ago jumped in. For as ineffectual a congressman Barr was, Francis was powerful. Well connected with other offices, with the news media, the Capitol fundraising cabal and K Street lobbies. None of which the Congressman had the stomach for. Francis chose the issues to focus on, made it clear which way the congressman was to vote, and why; and, not least of all, ran the office virtually as his own.

Empty Spaces would change the 'virtually' to reality, and, Francis knew, take him much higher. The financial potential of Empty Spaces was great, certainly. There were obvious reasons why the congressman, who needed Francis as much as Francis needed Barr's money, should want to invest in the technology. Only, there was more, much more. Francis, from the start, singularly understood the potential for Empty Spaces. It was far greater than even Sickspack, who was clever enough, dare imagine. As for Barr, his unquestioning ignorance prevented him from viewing Empty Spaces as anything more than an investment; one that might also complement his existing – inherited – business. Weak and stupid, Francis thought.

Empty Spaces, Francis knew, was a wormhole, a magical path into a person's mind, capable of unlocking and understanding all that made a person feel exactly how they felt at any particular moment. Their joy, anger, sadness, aspirations; all exposed. More still, and Francis was shocked how few understood this, Empty Spaces provided a delivery mechanism that carried in its payload a message designed to snatch that feeling; connect with it, own it. With those two components, Francis knew, he could, if not control the person, certainly direct them. That was the true potential of Empty Spaces. Direct millions and millions of people, only freely, with their consent, with a technology that he would soon control. His excitement was palpable. No way would he ever allow Barr to truly take even partial possession.

Politics was power. And all politics was local. Empty Spaces was a means of directing hyperlocal, real-time individualized messaging – of the kind that stuck inside a person's head – but on a hyperglobal scale. Think local. Scale global. That is what Empty Spaces offered its holder. And he, Francis Howerd Mustard, of Fitchburg, Wisconsin, son of simple, hardworking working class parents, would soon take ownership of it. Then the whispers would cease.

"Just passed Arlington Cemetery."

"Can't see much at this hour. Still lots of traffic, though."

"For as powerful as America is, isn't it remarkable it's only 200, 300 years old?"

"Know what you mean. I read not long ago that chocolate, it's been around a good 3,000 or more years. Back then, it was ground up, mixed with these spices and made into a drink."

"Really? Alcoholic drink?"

"I think so. There were two types, actually. The fruit drink was definitely alcoholic."

"Reminding me how hungry I am. Speaking of old -- "

"And food --"

"Right. Cannabis seeds --"

"Naturally."

"Cannabis seeds were used in food. In China. Nine thousand years ago. 6,000 BC. Three hundred years versus 9,000 years. Remarkable, don't you think?"

"I suppose. I bet music's been around just as long."

"Possibly. Cannabis is mentioned in the Talmud. Did you know that?"

"Is that true?"

"Fuck. I don't actually know. Something I read once. I do know that when Napoleon arrived in Egypt he discovered a huge hashish trade."

Jackie moved to the center of the seat. "That one. Our hotel." The driver nodded. He looked Egyptian, Jackie thought. Jackie glanced in the rearview mirror. "Fuck. I probably should have cut my hair."

"Relax. Damn. They want Empty Spaces. They want us to take their money. That's why we are here. Besides, no one's gonna be looking at that moptop of yours. Not when they can stare at my beautiful braids. Everyone loves a handsome black man."

"Theo? Still here at this hour?"

Francis walked out of his office, assuming, as always, that he was the last one to leave. False. Theo was still there. At his desk, in the center of the staff office, positioned between a bare wall and the desk of a young legislative aide.

Francis never tired of looking at himself in the mirror. He admired his hard jaw, his piercing eyes. Despite the dash of extra flesh around the jowls, the sallow complexion, it took no leap of imagination to view himself in the mold of a great American hero. Strong. Chiseled. Well dressed. Well equipped. Everything about him, he thought, the Average American Male that had, inexplicably, gone perfect. Still, there was no doubting that Theo was outright handsome. A handsome, young, smart black man, Francis thought. Powerful combination in this town. How could that never have occurred to me before?

"Still here, Mr. Mustard. Nothing else to do. Going over some polling data. Also going through some of the constituent mail."

"Hard work is its own reward." Francis grabbed the chair at the nearby desk, sat down and pulled himself close to Theo. "The congressman and I know you are doing an excellent job. That does not go unnoticed."

"I appreciate that, sir."

"Good. From now on, never interrupt a meeting I'm in. Understood? And if you need to see the Congressman, and it is extremely unlikely you should ever need to see him, you go through me. Only. Are we clear?"

"The thing I hate most about Washington, DC? Probably that no one ever will give you a straight answer. Ever. About anything. Ever watch a politician? See them on a news shows? Not a one is clear about anything. That is no life for an adult."

The two men had checked into their hotel and taken the elevator to their room on the fourth floor. Within seconds their bags were open and clothes and toiletries were strewn about. Jackie was first into the bathroom. JaDe scanned the room service menu. "Shit. After ten. Late night menu is all they have available. Still looks good, though" he called out. "Glad this Barr is paying for everything."

The room was nice, large, though still a hotel. As far as JaDe was concerned, having spent months of the year in hotels during his playing days, unless the hotel room was adequate for a pasha, he would always rather sleep in his own bed.

Their suite encompassed two connected rooms. The bedroom half contained two large beds, each with too many pillows and a covering patterned in black and purple that served no actual purpose. Black walls across from bright white walls was meant to symbolize something, though JaDe had no idea. The new working class motif, he suspected. There was a narrow table designed to serve as a second desk, a large, thin black plasma screen, and a window that looked out into what JaDe assumed was Crystal City. If he crooked his neck he could make out the Washington Monument, which, for him, was the first reassuring sign he was in Washington.

Jackie emerged from the bathroom, walked over to JaDe and grabbed the hotel menu. "Burgers? Four beers?"

"Suppose. Wish I didn't love red meat so much. How about we also get dessert? Not my dime."

"Fine. You pick. You know I'm not big on sweets."

Jackie called down the order. He decided he was too tired to focus on re-reviewing the slides he put together for tomorrow's meeting. He promised himself to review them first thing in the morning. And again in the cab ride over. These were not requested, he merely wanted no stone left unturned.

The two men chose up beds, turned on the television and waited for their food to arrive. Neither were much interested in the news, weather, stock market, nor in baseball, though the Spanish language soap opera held brief appeal. Within a few minutes, both pulled out their phones and read until their food arrived.

"Did you know that the Saturn V rocket, that was used to send men to the moon -- in the 1960s -- was the most powerful rocket, the most powerful vehicle, actually, ever made? It's launching capacity was five times greater than the space shuttle's. I realize it was for going to the moon, but still. Imagine if America had continued its focus on propulsion? On building rockets that could take people far beyond the moon? Where could we go by now? In 10 years? 100?"

"We'll never know."

This was an unsatisfactory response. Jackie turned away. His bed was closest to the window. As he lay there he could see lights from the surrounding city but none in the sky. "Imagine how far another race, one smarter than us, luckier than us, perhaps, with a much much bigger head start in propulsion could travel."

"You won't be talking about this shit at the meeting, will you?"

"Don't you worry. It's just that, we -- America, all of Earth, possibly -- seem to have given up on reaching out to the stars. Literally. What if others are out there? We need a way to call them is all I'm saying."

"If aliens were to call us, it would probably get routed to your parents. And they'd miss the call."

"I've thought of that. Seriously. Since we are determined not to go to them – "

"Go to who? Aliens?"

"Yes, aliens. Since we are determined not to go to them, seek them out, then we need to make sure they come to us, somehow. And, yes, if they do call, instead of it being routed to someone's crazy parents, we all get the call, say. Just in case."

JaDe was unresponsive. Jackie leaned over to his bed, and grabbed the remote. "Gotta be something to watch."

"Room service." The words were reinforced with a sharp knock at the door.

"Fuck me," said JaDe. "About time." He jumped out of the bed and walked towards the door. "Got a few bucks? For a tip?"

The food was gone within ten minutes. The beers were gone within thirty. Before the hour was up, both men were fast asleep.

Jackie could not know that he would never again speak with JaDe.

Norwegian Wood

Pam was asleep in her bed, wearing only her oversized blue Michigan tee; the sheet wrapped around her. Francis put his boxers back on and sat up against the headboard, laptop across his legs. His work beckoned. Only a few hours earlier he released a boilerplate press announcement which plainly stated Congressman Barr's intention to run for re-election to Congress. The objective being, he told all, that a perfunctory statement would not-so-subtly convey the message that the congressman had, despite many rumors to the contrary, absolutely no fears of his opponent. Victory was assured. The campaign was a distraction, one that needed to be dealt with as speedily as possible so that the congressman may quickly return to his real work: serving the people.

FOR IMMEDIATE RELEASE
CONGRESSMAN RKO BARR COMMITTED TO EIGHTH TERM
WASHINGTON, DC, June 22 -- Congressman RKO Barr of Glockenspiel, Virginia, is proud to announce his re-election for Congressman of the United States, representing the people of the 42nd District of the Commonwealth of Virginia. This will be the Congressman's eighth term of office.
A citizen legislator, Congressman Barr is also the President of Nutt Barr Co., the largest employer within his district and one of America's most successful, longest-running makers of fine chocolates at affordable prices.
"I look forward to continuing my role serving the people of Virginia in Washington, DC," noted Congressman Barr. "I consider myself blessed to be uniquely qualified to aid the people of my district. Know that I am unmovable in my efforts in restoring America's greatness through a commitment to tradition, private enterprise, family values and honorable public service."
###

Barr, of course, fretted that the announcement was palpably inadequate. That perhaps his re-election campaign messaging should focus on something big, maybe a law and order issue. Francis laughed at the thought, even now. Who could possibly believe such nonsense from such a weak man? He placated the congressman by reminding him that his formal campaign kickoff, with press in tow, was scheduled for this weekend at the friendly confines of the Barr estate. Barr could stand above the media, the lobbyists, the constituents, all the ring kissers, and deliver any message he wished.

Weak, stupid man.

Francis already knew what Barr was planning to say. Barr would tell the world, or at least those in attendance, that he was seeking far greater than just re-election. He was launching his own exploratory committee for President. Francis Barr would remain his right hand man, of course.

The election for President was barely more than two years away and the long process of increasing his visibility, of introducing himself to those beyond Virginia, of showcasing his talents, his patriotism, his accomplishments, would begin at the site of his birth, the founding of his family business, which employed so many in the private sector.

Weak and stupid, Francis knew. No matter. For Francis, his end game was clear. The years of gathering favors, courting big-money donors, building relationships with the media; all invaluable. All would soon be put to good use. They were still not enough. Francis required more. Even Empty Spaces, exactly as he envisioned, was not enough. At least, not from the start, not until he fully understood exactly how to make it work best for him.

Francis knew he possessed all the qualities of a great President. He also knew, and delighted in the fact, that he was at his brutal, determined best when fighting in the trenches. This could not be hidden. Owing to voter weakness, both in what they fixated upon and how they declared their choices, Francis long knew that his very best simply did not translate effectively on camera, or while standing in front of the public. Both still necessary to succeed. Empty Spaces would finally shift that balance in his favor. But first, he needed to understand how to maximize its effect. He required a test case. Barr. And even Barr's mother, that foolish old woman, would play a part.

Mother Barr, that foolish old woman with her foolish old dreams had her end game, just like Francis. She believed her son, her actual son, the feckless RKO Barr, could become President. She had, in fact, long convinced herself of this grand illusion. You're fooling yourself, thought Francis. Still, the old woman was nonetheless shrewd enough to know that for her boy to have a chance, he needed Francis at his side, to fight his battles, to guide him through the darkness. Through the years she ensured that he remained her son's chief. He was duly rewarded. Francis, she knew, could always do what her son could not. Now, as she so astutely picked up on the messaging potential of Empty Spaces, the time to strike was nigh. The family would possess a tool capable of spreading the noble word about her son to every voter, every skeptic, just as in the past she helped spread the good word about the Nutt Barr.

Weak, stupid man and his fool mother, Francis thought.

No message, no matter how powerful, no matter how viral, could overcome Barr's evident failings. When the time was right, Francis would jettison the impotent Barr and his impotent office and his deliberately minimized campaign and his feeble mother's pathetic dream and launch his own run.

First, he needed to learn everything he possibly could about the process of a presidential run if he were to succeed. This would require, he knew, understanding exactly how people made their choices, and when, and if they could be moved from those choices, and how much of their choice was based on personality, on fear, intellect, history, closeted biases, what friends and family might say, and at what point does the individual voter believe they have gathered enough information to finalize their choice, or abandon their first choice, and how much of their choice is based on their view of themselves, their needs, or their ideals for the country, and what leads them to a indeterminate yet visceral dislike of their chosen candidate's opponents? So many questions.

With Empty Spaces, Francis would unlock the minds of voters. Each of them. Of this he was certain. But the risk was simply far too great to use himself as test case. No, Barr would serve the role of guinea pig. The process, the timing, the legal requirements, the messaging; all were essential. Pushing the hapless Barr through that proverbial grinder would teach Francis everything he needed to know. Only then, with Empty Spaces in hand, literally, Francis would have the power to liberate each voter's hopes, fears, concerns – emotions – and imprint upon them an inexplicable desire to choose Brand X. Only, in this case, Brand X was not a product, but a politician; one seeking votes. Francis saw himself, and this he told no one, not yet, not even Pam, as Brand X. He would be President, he vowed.

For now, only hours away from having Empty Spaces in his grasp, Francis sated himself by reviewing the rules concerning presidential campaign committees:

A Presidential exploratory committee is an organization established to help determine whether a potential candidate should run for an elected office. The exploratory committee creates a legal entity for a candidate and a legal means for seeking funds and spending funds for the purpose of contemplating a run for office. The transparency rules pertaining to contributions, expenditures and disclosure do not apply to an exploratory committee.

The exploratory committee offers multiple opportunities for a candidate to promote themselves and their message. They may announce, for example, the consideration of a run for President. Then, they may announce the formal registration of such a committee (with the Federal Election Commission). Next, they may test messaging and fundraising appeals by announcing the intent to transition from exploratory committee to formal campaign. Then, the campaign committee itself, with all the rules, registrations and disclosure required by law.

Pamela stirred. Francis turned. He was spent but her ass was still playing tricks with his man brain. He ran his hand across her thigh. She made a soft noise and rolled over. She was not a girl who misses much, he thought. Still, much as she obviously valued ambition in her man, Francis suspected Pam had no idea exactly how highly he thought of himself, or the extent of his aspirations. If there was any fault he found with her, aside from her too-thin legs, or how she spent far too much time on that dog, that was it. He returned to the task at hand. "You gotta be cruel to be kind," he thought.

TRACK SIX
Blast From Your Past

Got to Get You Into My Life

Zero hour eight a.m. comes much too early. Jackie consoled himself with a singular thought: soon, a few hours from now, he would have investors -- fucking investors – with millions of dollars. Invested in him, in his idea; his dream. Within a few hours, he would be a rich man. Life would change, profoundly, perhaps. Little surprise that he had difficulty staying asleep. Plus, JaDe snored, loudly.

Mercifully, he fell asleep for good, just after 3am, midnight in Vancouver. Only to be shocked awake by his phone's deliberately loud alarm a mere three and a quarter hours later. Instead of waking JaDe, he decided to head into the shower first. This way, Jackie assumed, while JaDe was showering, he could get dressed, play with his tie, which was sure to unnerve him, review the slides he created and have answers fully rehearsed for any probable questions his angels might present. Breakfast was scheduled to arrive in 45 minutes.

At that moment his phone notified him: MEETING MOVED TO 5PM

"Mother fucker."

JaDe stirred.

Short of cancelling the meeting outright, this was the worst outcome possible, Jackie thought. He was awake, cleaned, nearly fully dressed, ready to go. Now, what? Go back to sleep? That was simply not going to happen.

"Fuck. Fuck. Fuck."

JaDe rose. Mumbled incoherently.

"Meeting pushed back. Now at five fucking pm."

JaDe grumbled cheerfully, rolled over and went back to sleep, depriving Jackie of the opportunity to vent his anger on a live human being.

"That should cool their jets," Francis thought. Last minute time changes were a favored trick of his, always sure to wobble the best of adversaries. These men, he knew, were amateurs.

"What's that, love," Pam asked. She came by, placed herself in front of him and kissed him on the mouth. Last night he called her 'baby's breath', which she loved. Francis was fit and confident and a rising star and they were engaged and she had had more than two glasses of wine during the evening and her hormones were demanding that a man, any man, lay on top of her, make her feel good. Francis had obliged, pounding her thin, soft, pale body with a firm affectionate abandon while being driven wild, beastlike, when she placed her narrow feet on his calves while underneath him. Pam was still glowing.

"Your ex. Afraid I had to push back my meeting with him. From 8:00 to 5pm."

"Ex? Besides, you do that with everyone. Old trick."

Francis turned towards her. "You never did tell me if you two actually slept together?"

Pam was momentarily taken aback. "Of course we slept together."

Francis, though disappointed, expected as much. He recovered just as quickly. "Remember. This is important. Do not meet with him, please, until we've finalized our agreement. Let me speak with him first. I don't want any distractions."

"Distractions? Him or me?" Pam couldn't resist the chance to tease. "If him, wouldn't that get you a better deal? Isn't that what you're after?"

"You had a touch too much wine last night, baby love."

"Don't say that. Just because you never drink."

Francis ignored this. "I have to go. With yesterday's re-election announcement, I'll have more visitors than normal. Press, mostly, but also the supplicants who will want to stop by and kiss the ring. How anyone can get on bended knee to that man, I'll never know."

"Fine. I might as well go into work early myself. Wait. What if Jackie stops by, wanting to take me to lunch? That's something he would probably do."

The coffee and breakfast was quite good, at least. Jackie, despite having eaten late the night before, was famished; unusual, since he was not much of a breakfast eater. JaDe, to Jackie's amazement, bounded out of bed the moment the food arrived, devoured everything Jackie had ordered for him, had more than his fair share of the coffee, then went back to bed and immediately fell asleep. He never said a word. With the possible exception, Jackie wasn't certain, of "jelly".

"What the fuck am I gonna do?" Jackie said it out loud, hoping to stir JaDe. He was not successful. He deliberately turned on the television. Nothing. Lost, Jackie flipped open his computer, ignored the slides, as he knew he would, because he was so pissed about the meeting being postponed, and, just as he feared he would, pulled up Pam's work information.

At the FCC website, he quickly found her profile page. The picture was one he remembered well. He took it, in Vancouver. Staring straight ahead, strand of hair just down her face, a pretend forced smile, a faux look of surprise. Utterly beautiful. Despite everything, he did miss her.

He missed her blonde hair and its smell, and her blue eyes and sharply pretty face and killer ass and soft flat stomach and her little feet. At times, he missed her company, and her advice, and her brain, which, he knew, was as fast, sharp, and deadly as a ninja star.

Wedding announcement or no, for the most part Jackie accepted that it could never work between them. Not long term, at least. That was past. He was resigned to this. Still, he had several hours to kill, he was in Washington, and he ought to stop in, despite her never having called him in a year and even despite any likely knowledge she had of Empty Spaces. Now, at the edge of his triumph, was the time for magnanimity.

Truth was, Jackie genuinely wanted to share his big news with her. With everyone, of course, but most especially those he was – or once was – closest to. Besides, she would probably enjoy his surprise visit.

Only, despite the looming presence of Pam on his brain, he sought a possible back-up plan. Though he would never admit this to her, Jackie remembered that Prudence Skiffle, the woman he communicated with online, more than once, had more than once mentioned she worked at the FCC. He scanned his correspondence. Correct. FCC. Same address. Same floor. Her messages were often quite flirty. Might something happen? After all, Jackie reminded himself, he was here till Sunday.

Everybody's Got Something to Hide Except for Me and My Monkey

Pam seemed in a rather good mood, Prudence thought. During the morning meeting she even stopped one of her minions from making what Prudence was sure to be a remark about the small box of chocolate truffles that sat open on her desk. Probably got laid, she said, only to herself, then felt terribly guilty for it. Maybe, Prudence thought, Pam was merely being nice because she wanted that final report on Empty Spaces sooner than later. She wasn't terribly pleased with the draft. Of course, she was rarely terribly pleased about anything. Prudence decided it best to re-review her most recent edits:

Empty Spaces creates an ad-hoc peer-to-peer network between two, and potentially multiple mobile devices using a 'viral' means of hopping from one device to the next based upon proximity and personalizable user settings. In this manner, Empty Spaces potentially spreads rapidly across users. Unlike a virus, once embedded within a device, Empty Spaces does not seek to mask its behavior. Users may erase the service from their device or, should they continue to use the software, configure what data and resources Empty Spaces may access and/or transmit. Though Empty Spaces 'accesses' a client device without prior explicit permission, it does not appear to cause any harm to the recipient user's device or data in any known manner. The exception to this are short electromagnetic bursts that theoretically limit the client device's available microprocessing resources. There is also a minor negative impact on the user's battery.

Prudence was distracted, as at that moment, Francis Mustard appeared, walked past her desk, speaking loudly and assuredly on his phone, and headed straight towards Pam's office.

"Theo. Yes. Press conference went well. I'll be back in a few. Here's what I need you to do. I am working with a man named Sickspack...Shit."

"Theo. Francis, again. I'd like you to...Fuck."

Accepting that his call wasn't going to make it through, Francis casually typed a message then placed his phone back into his pocket. A few minutes later, both he and Pam left the office. An early lunch? Prudence thought that odd. Probably back to her place for a quickie. Once again, she sought forgiveness for her unkind thoughts.

The moment Pam exited the floor, her minions converged; stunned, bewildered. Prudence strained to hear what they were saying. Clearly, they were baffled. Prudence checked her phone for any information. Francis held a press conference this morning, apparently, just before lunch, where he announced the launch of the campaign for the re-election of Congressman Barr. Nothing unexpected, no other relevant information presented itself.

"Yes. Must be off to have a quickie," she decided, which, rather than feeling guilty this time only made her realize just how long she had gone without. Prudence reached for another truffle. As was so often the case lately, it did little to satisfy any deeper cravings. A waste of good money. Then she wondered if perhaps everyone but her was in on some secret, having a good time, off having sex during work hours, and eating good chocolates, and spending time, even during the middle of the day, with people not their mothers. She reached for another truffle, despite already confirming that it wasn't terribly gratifying.

"Jackie, I see here on my smartphone that you have left the hotel, yes? You did hear the meeting is moved to 5pm, obviously. I suggest you remain at your hotel. Do text me if you have any questions. Sickspack."

Jackie removed Sickspack's access on his location, then forwarded the message to JaDe. Probably still asleep, he thought. Jackie watched the streets pass as his taxi made its way to Pam's place of work. He had a large breakfast, and was not at all hungry for lunch. Perhaps, she wouldn't mind just hanging out in her office for a while, he thought. Or her place, possibly.

Outside the FCC headquarters Jackie waited semi-patiently. There was a good chance he could simply set his mobile phone to de-activate the rudimentary security device on the large glass doors, allowing him to safely pass through. However, it was much safer for all if he simply waited until someone else entered, someone with an official FCC identification embedded in their phone. He could then piggyback onto their access code without harm. This was correct, though it consumed nearly ten minutes of waiting.

It was only while walking across the atrium of the FCC building and into the elevators that would take him up to Pam's office that he was suddenly struck with two thoughts:

1)   Should I text her first? Let her know I'm coming?
2)   What if she doesn't want to see me?

Having foolishly thought of neither of these when he hastily left his hotel room, while JaDe slept, or during the taxi ride over, or while waiting to pass through the ground floor doors of the FCC building, Jackie decided now was no time to entertain such thoughts. Instead, having downloaded a map of the building onto his phone, directing him straight to Pam's office, he pretended that he both belonged inside and had a meeting already scheduled with Ms. Drogeny. He also decided to step up the pace and walk more purposefully.

Probably why he did not at all notice the PRUDENCE SKIFFLE nameplate on Prudence's cubicle, positioned only a few steps from Pam's office. Also why he felt stupid when he arrived at his destination and Pam's door was closed. The light was off. He stopped short. "Should I knock?" He pondered this. "Is she out? In a meeting? Should I grab a chair somewhere and wait? Will someone ask me my name, my business, why the fuck am I sitting outside Pam Drogeny's office?"

Confused, he walked to the nearest cubicle. "Excuse me, I wanted to see Ms. Drogeny."

"Do you have an appointment with her?" Prudence asked.

"Yes. Well. Yes, but I'm early."

"I'm sorry. She left a short while ago. I'll pull up her calendar. No, it's blank. I don't know when she will return. See here, empty spaces the rest of the day."

"Oh. Do you happen to know if she will be here this evening? Say, after about 7pm or so?"

Prudence grew plainly suspicious. "No, I'm sorry. That I don't know. Would you like me to leave her a message?"

"Never mind. I have her number. If she does return by, say, 3 o'clock or so, could you please let her know that Jackie Paper stopped by?"

"I will. Wait. Jackie Paper? From Empty Spaces? It's Prudence. Prudence Skiffle. We've chatted."

Prudence stood up, pulled away from her chair and for only a fraction of a second wondered if the minions were watching. Or if this was some set-up. Thoughts ricocheted inside her head. Didn't Pam once say she knew him? Slept with him, in fact? Was he the one? I think there's at least two involved with Empty Spaces.

"Tell me, how do you know Pam?"

"Oh. We used to work together. Couple years ago. I'm here on a business meeting. Thought I would just drop by. You know, say hello."

"Nice. But I don't know when she will return." Prudence wasn't sure what else to say. She surprised herself by asking, "would you like to go for lunch?"

Before Jackie could respond, Prudence's brain made some quick calculations.

1) It had been a really long time.
2) He knows Pam.
3) Pam, the devil boss, might not be back all day. She had time for a long lunch.
4) The minions, who would no doubt love to report on her, were currently in a state of shock, what with Pam leaving abruptly without letting them know why. Any stories they tell will be immediately suspect.
5) She had already called her mother.

"I know a nice place. We can walk from here."

"I'd like that," Jackie responded.

He reminded himself to keep his jacket, shirt and tie free from any stains. He also couldn't stop himself from thinking that this Prudence was a more than adequate replacement for Pam.

For her part, Prudence was acutely aware that something inside that was always denied for too long was now awakened.

If I Needed Someone

"Like the moon and the stars and the sun" Jackie said, speaking over the din of the lunch crowd. Zapp & Roger's, a local dining institution, was typically crowded, noisy, old and perfectly suited for its task: providing an affordable safe haven for the government lifers needing a quick, comforting meal. Along the wall of the well worn restaurant was a row of booths able to fit no more than four persons each, and that snugly. A long bar offered food and beverages to those preferring to eat alone. A quick takeaway service was available to those chained to their desks.

The emphasis, clearly, was on portion size, guilty pleasures, speed and volume. In this case, volume meant the number of patrons they could serve at one time, as well as the noise from all the movement, the conversations, staff barking out orders, kitchen help working manically.

If not terribly attractive, the place certainly had character, all of it earned the hard way. The floor was a dark brown, almost red tinted wood, worn down by years and people. Booths were upholstered in a green fabric of a kind Jackie assumed was popular, briefly, decades earlier. The ceiling was high and dotted with lights and fans. On the wall on the booth side were large wood and glass frame mounts each bearing memorabilia celebrating local icons or sports victories. Jackie loved the place, instantly. For all that Vancouver offered, they had nothing like this grand old diner.

"That's fascinating, really. So, you say you had a meeting with Pam? About Empty Spaces? She's engaged, I understand. Good for her. I've met her fiancé. He was here earlier today, in fact. Left together. Just before you arrived, I'm afraid."

Prudence seemed to be talking awfully fast, Jackie noticed. This set him at ease. "We're friends. I've not seen her in some time. My partner filed the FCC paperwork for spectrum use. Seemed too trivial to ask her for her help on it. Maybe I should have. I'm just in town for a couple days, thought I would stop by."

"Lovely. How do you two know each other, then?" Prudence had ordered a half sandwich and soup special and was being careful to take her time eating her food.

"Oh, we met at university. University of Michigan."

"University of Michigan? Interesting. I recently read that researchers there were studying whether chocolate triggers the production of opioids. Opioids are chemicals, like those in opium, that produce a feeling of euphoria. Probably corporate funded."

"Funny. My partner, JaDe, was telling me recently about how marijuana and chocolate are related. Something about how the brain is effected similarly."

"Yes. I think that was in one of the articles I sent you. It's called anandamide. It means bliss. It creates a pleasurable sensation in the brain. Not as strong as marijuana, obviously, but similar. Both latch onto the same receptors in the brain, oddly enough. So, yes, chocolate and marijuana are related."

Jackie failed at stifling a yawn, owing to poor sleep. Prudence became acutely mindful that she must not talk only about chocolate. She attempted to recall her email chats with Jackie.

"Tired. Not much sleep. Plus I'm on Pacific time," Jackie confessed, hoping that would assure Prudence that he was not yawning because of her. She was attractive, he thought. Cute. Heavier than Pam, though not in a bad way. Nice. Pleasant conversation.

"A refill on that sweet tea, sir?"

"Thank you," Jackie responded to the waitress, a thin, though not frail white woman, possibly in her 70s. Jackie would not have been at all surprised to learn that she worked here since before his parents bought their first house.

"For you, miss? More chocolate milk?"

"Oh, no thank you," said Prudence, cursing herself for having ordered the first one before thinking.

She smiled at Jackie. "People have been drinking chocolate for more than 2,000 years. Though not chocolate milk, obviously. The Mayans would grind up chocolate, mix it with spices and peppers and water and froth it by pouring it from a cup to a pot, back and forth, till it became the desired consistency. It was called xocolatl, a fun word, don't you think? Probably better than this. I've had some surprisingly poor chocolate lately; these past several months, in fact."

"That's another thing you and JaDe have in common. He's been complaining about how bad his marijuana has been lately." Which, to Jackie's credit, he realized immediately after about the fourth word that what he was about to say was not something that needed to be said, at all, because it would obviously make him sound like a drug addict and/or that he was trying to pawn Prudence onto a friend.

"Er. Well..." Prudence paused, her brain buzzing. Was he the one Pam slept with? Or the partner? The one that smokes marijuana. Pam's toadies have mentioned she has a thing for black men. Was that a joke? Jade sounds more like the name of a black man.

Realizing there was a lull, Prudence decided to fill it with chocolate.

"Actually, for a good part of chocolate's history, when people said the word chocolate they meant a drink. Not now, of course. Chocolate is primarily a solid. Did you know that in Europe, hot chocolate is different from hot cocoa. Hot cocoa is from a powder, like your mother probably made for you, with no cocoa butter. Hot chocolate, however, is a drink made from a bar of chocolate, which is frothed in warm milk."

"Interesting. Maybe there should be chocolate shops for drinking, just like coffee and tea shops?"

"I know. Those did exist, actually. In England, a few hundred years ago. Quite popular. A few still exist. I think they must be quite nice. Another example, it's common to order a chocolat chaud, as it's called, in Belgium, which is steamed milk served with a bowl of chocolate chips. You dissolve the chips in the milk."

"Sounds comforting," said Jackie, partly lying, partly realizing that he was forcing Prudence fill the void. He needed to carry his weight. The lunch crowd they came in with was slowly turning over to another group; reasonably well dressed men and women, aged about 30-60, near as he could tell. Tables were being wiped down, and the place became a bit noisier even than before.

Prudence took advantage of the lull in their conversation to consume a few spoonfuls of her soup, now only just warm. Jackie glanced at his phone, as inconspicuously as he could muster. No new messages of note. Plenty of time, though. Plus, this was going well.

"When I was working on Empty Spaces, I was captivated by the fact that radio waves, which are used to send information from one nearby phone to another, can travel, well, forever."

"Forever? Really? I sometimes can't even tune in a radio station that I know is less than 50 miles away."

Jackie couldn't recall the last time he spoke with someone, not his parents, that listened to radio. This made him like Prudence even more.

"It's true. For example, Voyager 1 and Voyager 2, spacecrafts sent out during the 1970s, primarily to photograph Jupiter and Saturn. They are the most travelled human-made objects in the universe, in fact. Billions of miles from Earth."

"Billions?"

"Yes, billions. They travel at about 35,000 miles per hour. They have these thermal electric generators to create electricity. Both continue to collect data. And both send information back to Earth via their on-board radio transmitters."

"Fascinating."

Actually, there was supposed to be four Voyagers launched, but NASA's budget got cut."

"I understand about budget cuts."

"Oh, yes. Obviously." This was not, in fact, terribly obvious to Jackie.

There was another silence, one that Prudence was determined not to prove too eager to fill.

"Anyway, both still send information back to Earth -- it takes about 10 hours or so for the signal to arrive. Of course, Voyager has a 25-watt radio, compared to your smartphone, with its 3-watt radio transmitter. Still, considering the distance, not terribly powerful. But the signals can be heard, even billions of miles away, because, well, primarily because of really big antennas, which we have here on Earth."

Jackie was determined not to contemplate, not now, what size antenna or how large the antenna arrays might be, if such exist, on some unknown distant planet. "The antenna on Voyager is 14 feet in diameter while the antennas on Earth that pick up the signals are over 100 feet in diameter."

"That is big."

"Yes. Whereas on our smartphones..." Jackie held his up, "...have extremely small antenna, obviously. And they are omni-directional, so the signal is scattered. Although, having multiple smartphones sending out the same signal at once, even if omni-directional, mitigates the issue somewhat."

"So you're saying our phone calls are able to travel into outer space? The signals could get picked up, somehow?"

Jackie held in a blush as best he could. A first date, he now considered this a date, and he was talking about smartphones and radio propagation and coming damn close to mentioning aliens. He was pretty sure that at some point he mentioned marijuana. JaDe would never stop laughing, he thought. Which made him wonder why he had not yet heard from his roommate. He took a quick glance at the time. Still plenty of time. Damn. How do people manage from 8-5 every single day? Jackie could not comprehend. This, despite having been amongst their kind up until only a few months ago.

"Well, in theory, yes. The radio waves can go on forever, technically. Though naturally they spread out, ultimately become unrecognizable from their original form. However, if you had multiple smartphones connected, working in concert, all at the same location, sending out the exact same information, combining signal strength..."

"Then they're strong enough to make it into space?"

"Again, technically, yes. Although, it's best, of course, if there's not a lot of interference. The Voyager satellites transmit in the 8 GHz range, where this is not much interference."

"I had a three day class on radio signals, interference and electromagnetic waves when I started at the FCC. I retained some of it. Funny. Radio waves travel at the speed of light, I remember that."

Jackie recalled a critical property of electromagnetic waves, the inverse-square law, which pertained to the power density of a wave, and the distance to or from the source, which was partly relevant to this part of their conversation. He forced himself not to mention it.

"Yes. The combination of all these factors, the size of the antennas, the direction, lack of interference, power of the signal, are all important factors. Certain frequencies we use on Earth, such as what we use for Empty Spaces, use new allocated spectrum that's still reasonably free from interference."

"We could call another planet then, theoretically. Is that what you're saying? Maybe some alien world?"

Jackie assumed Prudence was teasing him though her expression betrayed nothing. She was more perceptive than he realized.

"Sure. Why not? If there is someone out there, I mean, who can say, I think it worth making the call."

"Call them, literally?"

"Why not try? I mean, we have all these signals, all this information generated constantly, much of which escapes the Earth. But, most of it, for obvious reasons, is directed back at ourselves, at people like you and me. Millions and millions of calls, every day. Why not at least try and put in a call to space?"

Jackie noted the slight smile from Prudence when he said 'you and me'.

"Is that possible, what you're saying? Would we know what to say? How, even?" Prudence was mildly interested, and still more happy to have an attractive man seated across from her, talking.

"I'd like to think that any message we send out could be received and understood by anyone capable of picking up the signal. If it's a form of advanced life, capable of detecting radio signals, electromagnetic waves --" Jackie was sure he was losing her. He decided to retreat.

"It probably doesn't matter what the message itself is, exactly. Because we can assume that if they cannot understand everything we say – or anything we say – than it's probably the case that they do not have the ability to reach out to us, regardless of what we do say. If that makes sense. I think just sending a deliberate message itself is the important thing."

Prudence noted that her soup was gone, there were only a couple bites left of her sandwich, which she had deliberately tried not to finish. According to her status, Pam was still out of the office, and she was having a nice lunch with a nice, decent looking, smart man, who was about her age...and who apparently had a job and meetings and dressed in suits. Even if extra long time for lunch.
"Anything else?"
The old waitress saved him. "Another tea, please? Prudence?"
Prudence had already promised herself that she would not order another chocolate milk, though she wasn't much for water. "Tea. Earl Grey. Hot." Jackie smiled.

"So, you work at the FCC? How long? What's that like?" As much as Jackie did not really care how long Prudence worked at the FCC, or why, or what it was like, Prudence had less desire to actually talk about that part of her life. Fortunately for them both, she muddled through it quickly. College. NIH. FCC. As if all planned, even if not. The waitress returned with their drinks. This was followed by a mildly awkward pause, a few sips of their drinks, a few bites of their remaining food. Jackie was not terribly hungry but wisely picked up that Prudence was waiting for him to eat more before she could eat more. He complied.
"I read a lot of your work on chocolate. On your site. Pretty interesting. Especially the recent article about advertising and chocolate."
Prudence feigned a smile. "Oh, yes, how advertisers repeatedly attempt to link women's emotional needs with chocolate. They use coded words, even in the product names, like 'Delight' and 'Bliss'. And they talk about cocoa butter and melting and mouth feel. Really, it's a way for the advertisers to tell women that they should find some time to be alone, with their chocolate."
"Funny."
"I know. Contrast that with ads for men that focus on energy, protein, caffeine." Prudence became more animated.
"But never focus on how it makes you fat, right?"
She stopped. This stung more than it probably should have. Prudence accepted that Jackie simply couldn't know everything about chocolate the way she did. About it's actual chemical properties that foster a calm, happy mood. Or the flavonoids in cacao beans that are powerful antioxidants. Or how chocolate helps fight high blood

pressure. And how it, unlike so many other sweets, does little damage to a person's teeth.

"Well, chocolate is fine. In moderation, of course. It's got quite a few healthful properties, actually."

Jackie retreated. "You discussed older ads as well, correct? In a follow-up post?"

"I did. Chocolate has long been advertised to women as a meal replacement; a fast, happy method to get their nutrition as they do their household chores. Now, of course, a lot of chocolate products are advertised directly at women but to make them feel that it is okay to buy it for their family."

At which point, Empty Spaces found the perfect song for Prudence, for the moment, for talking about what she loved, for escaping from work and talking with someone she thought she might really like. She reached for her phone as it lay before them on the table, both barely able to hear the music over the noise of the diner. "Honestly, I love it, really. That song is exactly how I feel. How did you ever get the idea?"

Despite all the hours spent building Empty Spaces, fixing it, promoting it and now, with someone about to invest a great deal of money for it, Jackie still would rather talk about the idea of Empty Spaces more so than just about anything else. He was visibly pleased that Prudence asked.

"I wasn't bored with my music. That wasn't it. My music collection was one of the possessions that I most prized. But I wanted to be surprised again. I had lost that. I wanted to have those moments where my mood or circumstance or thoughts were captured by some favorite song, one I had long forgotten, or perhaps something I'd never heard before, and have that wash over me."

"Serendipity," Prudence added. "That's how I feel when it plays the exact right song to match what I'm feeling."

"Yes, serendipity. A sort of instant, unplanned, but very real moment. A new memory; gifted. Without knowing it, exactly, in those words, that's what I wanted to create."

"Just because we have everything at our disposal doesn't mean we want to have everything pre-determined," Prudence added.

"That's right. Plus, music is universal. It's everywhere. Familiar. Recognizable. The perfect vehicle, I suppose, for serendipity. To unlock our mood. For sharing something about powerful ourselves."

"It really does know me. I can sense that."

"Well, thank you, I'm always happy to hear that. People almost never listen to music, willingly, that does not fully and accurately reflect their mood."

"That's what's so remarkable, really. How it understands my mood so perfectly. Without that, I wouldn't trust it. Certainly not to share my feelings with some stranger."

"Interesting. Pam asked me to put together a report on Empty Spaces."

"Oh, really? That is interesting. I guess I'm surprised. Why wouldn't she tell me that?"

Jackie was convinced that lunch was more than a serendipitous meeting. Fuck. Why would Pam ask for a report? Did she want to know what he was doing? Was she doing grunt work for her fiancé? That did not seem like her. Whatever the reason, Prudence could tell that Jackie's tone had suddenly changed. He clearly pulled back.

"Our registration was fairly standard. The fee was paid. I know that. Was there a problem?"

"No, nothing like that." Prudence sought to reassure her lunch date." She placed her hand on his, felt nothing in return, then pulled back. Bad timing. "I think, well, I'm not sure why, exactly, though I suspect Congress is reviewing the effectiveness of opening up unlicensed spectrum for services like Empty Spaces. It was part of a larger report, that I know. Typically Congress asks the FCC to provide an annual review of various programs and regulations. Empty Spaces was one example of that, is all. A good one, obviously."

"Nice coincidence. How long did you work on it?"

"Oh, off and on, a few weeks, but it wasn't a priority, just part of other research. I started using Empty Spaces long before I got the assignment. Interesting, don't you think, how you mentioned that western music has certain patterns that computers understand and how we have all this data available for nearly every song? But it's less so with eastern music. I know that eastern cultures are not terribly fond of chocolate. Not like we are, certainly."

"Nor for marijuana, considering the penalties for those caught with it."

Jackie suspected that Prudence was trying to move the conversation away from her report. Less rightly, he suspected that Pam deliberately left her office knowing he would seek her out. He was certainly the type to just drop in, she would know that. Researching Empty Spaces, and possibly even him, but never calling? Prudence must know more that she's not sharing, he thought.

"So...you say chocolate is a health food?"

"Yes. It really is. Dark chocolate, especially." Prudence knew she was talking too fast. Could she not have mentioned having worked on

Empty Spaces? Or, perhaps mentioned it another time, a more appropriate time, she thought. "Obviously, we eat chocolate for pleasure, but the beneficial effects have been well documented. Chocolate's anti-inflammatory properties helps in the fight against things like cancer, heart disease."

"Yes, I think you mentioned that. What about as an aphrodisiac?" Jackie asked the question, more to steer Prudence back toward him and less to send any signals. Prudence, for her part, assumed the question was a poorly coded message.

"Possibly. Every culture says that about one food or another."

"I prefer savory foods myself. I've never been much of a sweets eater; chocolate especially."

Prudence wasn't sure how to respond. Was he lying to her? What would be the point? She took a moment to rethink her lunch date. She decided not. He was merely uneasy over her report remark. She wondered if there might be any repercussions if she forwarded him a copy.

"Here, try this." Prudence took a small elegant bar of chocolate from her bag, unwrapped it carefully. She broke off a piece for Jackie. Neither was sure if he should put his tongue out, though both soon became hyperaware that each was contemplating just that. Prudence placed the chocolate in his hand, leaving it there a fraction of a second longer than necessary. "I just purchased this. Haven't had this brand in over a year. Very expensive. Very good."

Jackie wanted to like it.

"Good." Obviously, she expected more. "It's good," he repeated.

"Just good? It's a bit stronger than most people are used to, I know. Give it a few seconds, let it coat your whole mouth."

Jackie tried to hide his swallow.

"Very good."

Prudence knew he was lying.

"I haven't had a piece of real chocolate in some time, actually. I'm just not a big fan is all."

Prudence believed him, even if this was tough to comprehend. "This is actually one of my favorites. I wish I could afford it all the time." She took a piece herself.

"What?"

"I think they must have changed the recipe."

"No good?"

"No. It's not bad. It's just not great. It's…fair, I suppose. Just like all the other chocolates I've had lately."

Getting Better

Prudence was needlessly upset, he thought. Jackie attempted to re-boot the conversation. "I never realized there was so much to the history of chocolate."

"Well, it's just a hobby. Something fun to talk about."

"Like what? Off the top of your head."

"That's easy. For example, there are many competing explanations for the etymology of the word chocolate. The word chocolate is Spanish, technically. The controversy is over how the word entered the Spanish language. Most have long assumed that chocolate, the word, derives from the Aztec. Their language was called Nahuatl. The word, chocolatl, is said to have evolved from the Nahuatl words xococ meaning bitter and atl meaning water -- or drink. However, the word chocolatl, itself, cannot be verified, calling this view into question. There is a Mayan word, chokol, I believe their language is called Yucatec, which means hot, and this word was eventually linked with the Nahuatl word atl for water. Thus, cho-kol-at-l, if you will."

"Interesting. Which do you trust?"

"Neither." Prudence laughed, playfully. Another word from the Aztecs, chicoli, meant frothing stick; the stick used to prepare ceremonial chocolate drinks. From this came the Aztec word chicolatl, and from that, ultimately, chocolate. Don't get me started. I have plenty I could talk about. History, health benefits. Tastings."

"I understand, believe me. JaDe, my roommate --"

"Oh, he's your roommate? And your business partner?"

"Yes. Roommates first. Then, partners. He's actually kept me grounded through this whole process.

"I see."

"He grows a lot. Indoors. He blogs about hydroponics and things like yield and what kind of ventilation and lighting is optimal. That's his passion. I think maybe some people have brains that demand they channel their passion somehow, and can't stop, no matter what else life demands, till eventually it just squeezes everything else out."

Prudence was not sure if this was a put down.

There was no more food. No more drinks. His meeting was still a few hours away. Jackie liked Prudence, more than anyone he had met in some time, but unlike that little saltine with butter he met on the Seabus several weeks back, Prudence volunteered little evidence that she would hop into bed with him. He wasn't sure what to do next.

His phone vibrated. He was thankful for the interruption:

"One toke over the line."

"Excuse me. It's a message from JaDe. My partner. I should probably respond to this."

Jackie dialed JaDe as he stood up, walked towards the diner entrance. No answer. Tried again. No answer. Returning to the booth he sent a text: "Congressman Barr's office. 5pm. Call me."

"So, what about you, Jackie? Do you have a passion that squeezes everything else out?"

Jackie was a smart, decent looking man just shy of 30. His career was spotty, true, but he was bright, could focus for long stretches of time and, most importantly of all, had created a program that had now been downloaded -- and used -- by millions. And, he suspected, should all go well, should Empty Spaces rocket into some mythical massive mainstream market, as he hoped and prayed, despite being a non-religious, barely spiritual person, he would wind up, almost certainly, with a great deal of money in the bank. What's more, he had friends. No weird sex hang-ups, far as he knew. He had a degree from a university, a future, a decent enough sense of humor. Obviously, a reasonably attractive woman in Washington, DC, thirty-ish, with a job in a cubicle in a big government office who clearly had OCD about chocolate, could do a lot worse than he, Jackie thought. Probably had done a lot worse. He was quite a catch, he told himself.

Yet, despite all this, Jackie wasn't sure if he should bias Prudence's view of him, possibly forever, by talking about what he really, truly was passionate about; the thing no one else knew about him, save JaDe, maybe Pam, probably his parents: the possibility of reaching out, calling, literally, beings from another world, another planet, another galaxy. Just to say hello, even. Hopefully, to hear back. Especially to hear back. This was no passion. This was his mission. One he knew from experience that was best left unspoken.

For all the plusses that might go on any ledger that any woman, Prudence included, might come up with to score him, such a list would probably be thrown out, he knew, once he started talking about creatures from another planet. Thus, he chose not to mention it at all.

Lunch was over. Prudence was gone, the restaurant was nearly empty, and Jackie still had far too much time to kill. He didn't want to go back to the hotel and wait. JaDe wasn't answering his phone. He nursed his tea. Prudence insisted she enjoyed lunch. She even gave him her number. Still, Jackie wasn't fully convinced. A report for Pam. The abrupt departure. Was this a set up, he wondered? He suddenly felt hyper superstitious; everything was suddenly a sign, everywhere, and none that he could read clearly. Nor control. It was easier just to keep his focus on lunch, and what might have gone right. Or wrong.

Jackie could point to the exact date -- 15 August 1977 -- that Dr. Jerry Ehman, while working on behalf of SETI, discovered the Wow! Signal. He did not mention this. Wow!, always written with the exclamation point, that's how relevant it was, lasted for 72 seconds. Seventy two seconds! The signal frequency was 1420MHz. He could not have expected Prudence to know these things, just like probably almost no one knew where the word chocolate originated from. Nor did he mention any of this.

Jackie could have discussed, but did not, the many theories, the varied evidence, over whether Wow! was real or not, an error, or not, a singular, inexplicable burst of electromagnetic energy or little green men desperately sending out an SOS to anyone, any planet within digital ear shot. He did not.

Nor did he, he did not believe, complain about the abandonment of SETI and projects like it not only by the US government, still his government, but the scientific community as well. Because even he knew made him sound, well, at very least conspiratorial. After years of scanning the night sky from a massive telescope array in northern California, with nothing more than the evocative Wow! signal, funds were cut off, once faithful users ignored the project, no longer did strangers offer up use of their idle microprocessors to help analyze the near-infinite amount of data the telescopes picked up. None of this was mentioned.

Astronomers, just in Jackie's lifetime, had discovered thousands of celestial bodies likely to be planets, with a good hundred of these -- 100 -- with the size and temperature and possibly the atmosphere to sustain life in ways all humans might readily perceive the term. This was confirmed. He never discussed this. At all.

Jackie had long since fully accepted that such thoughts, which he had entertained since childhood, were now, in adulthood, with everyone working, or looking for work, everyone busy, everyone uncertain of their jobs, their pocketbooks, their futures, all that, was the equivalent of asking for a civil conversation on the possibility that Santa Claus actually exists. And so he never revealed any of this. Ever. The once or twice with JaDe was when he had smoked too much, but that was it.

Details may indeed make up the totality of the person, but they are rarely appealing qualities on a first date. Start talking about signals from space and aliens and seeking ways to reach out to them, and, well, attractive, smart women with jobs…His mind trailed off. His thoughts, he knew, should be laser focused on Empty Spaces, on his big investor meeting. Or, perhaps even Pam. They were not. They were on failure. His. America's. Everyone's, he decided. Are we not explorers? When did the future, with all its uncertainty, scare us more than embolden us? What do we seek? What calls us?

When Jackie's parents were still young, a man, Frank Drake, developed an equation that estimated the number of advanced civilizations likely to exist in the galaxy. It was Drake, in fact, who, using his assumptions about advanced life in the Milky Way, helped to pioneer the SETI project, and its search for extraterrestrial life. The man's efforts led directly to construction of various telescopes, antennas, the necessary R&D that could enable scientists, astronomers and others to work together in determining where in the vast emptiness of space to look, where to listen, how to listen, how to determine if what was heard, if that was the correct word, was relevant -- and how so. Not surprisingly, perhaps, given what little, if anything was discovered, funding, other governmental priorities, the passage of time, a dismissive, scornful public, all had let this project and those like it collapse and die. Too busy, too fearful, too self-aware, too self-limiting, Jackie thought.

Though disappointing, this was acceptable. At least now it was, now that Empty Spaces was big and about to get much bigger. Because Jackie long ago realized that projects like SETI were fundamentally flawed. Doomed to failure. At least in this current iteration of human development. More than flawed in fact, they were backwards. We should not be listening for signs of life beyond our planet, our solar system, our galaxy, Jackie thought. If by some miracle we hear them, what then?

Instead, we should be the ones placing the call.

Which was, at its most basic, and its most secret, exactly what Empty Spaces did. Which was another thing he vowed never to tell anyone. Ever. Especially not his investors. He was certain, of course, that they would never find out.

Don't Pass Me By

The sun was up. The sky was blue. Jackie came to several decision upon exiting the restaurant. Firstly, that his initial doubts regarding Prudence were misplaced. Lunch had indeed gone well. She asked him out, not he, her. She gave him her contact information. If Pam was playing at anything, Prudence was not involved. Considering that, he decided to ask her out for dinner. Tomorrow, Saturday. Tonight, almost certainly, the Congressman, his chief of staff, Francis, and others, Pam, perhaps, would take him and JaDe out to celebrate. Jackie decided he would call Prudence later this evening. Considering the circumstances, he assumed that would not be awkward.

He texted JaDe once again. Again, no response. Jackie decided that if JaDe smelt of weed, didn't look or behave professionally, and he hated to even think this, he would not allow him to participate in their meeting. This was simply too important.

He also decided, and he was increasingly certain of this, that Pam was deliberately avoiding him. He had never received anything directly about her engagement. Upsetting, but probably understandable, he thought. However, she must have known that the Congressman was going to invest in Empty Spaces. She assigned an underling, Prudence, to conduct research on the service. Why? Nothing Prudence suggested was satisfactory. Pam was keeping tabs on him, Jackie thought, somehow, by keeping tabs on Empty Spaces. He was not sure, exactly, how to process this information, however.

He decided that at today's meeting he would not mention his relationship with Pam, or even acknowledge that he knew her, unless directly asked by Francis Howerd Mustard himself. So what if he knew that Jackie and Pam were ex-lovers. Let him stew on that.

Lastly, Jackie realized that he had had way too much tea at lunch. He made a mental note to completely empty his bladder well before his appointment. Then once more, just to be safe.

These decisions were each finalized on the taxi ride from the diner to the Longworth House Office Building where he was scheduled to meet Barr and Mustard in less than two hours. Despite the inviting weather, and though the walk from the restaurant to Longworth was not terribly far, Jackie decided under no circumstances would he allow himself to sweat or get his nicely shined shoes dirty. As the taxi circled the Capitol Building, Jackie pointed his phone towards a series of official looking buildings to find out which one was Longworth. The screen responded quickly, then displayed the most popular pertinent information, which he read rather than having his phone dictate to him:

Completed in the spring of 1933, the Longworth House Office Building is the second of three office buildings constructed for the United States House of Representatives. Longworth is designed in the Neo-Classical Revival style popular in the second quarter of the twentieth century.

Severe overcrowding in the Cannon House Office Building (completed in 1908) led to the construction of the Longworth Building.

In January 1929 Congress authorized $8,400,000 for acquiring and clearing the site and for constructing the new office. The foundations were completed in December 1930, and the building was accepted for occupancy in April 1933.

Because of its position on a sloping site, the rusticated base of the Longworth Building varies in height from two to four stories. Above this granite base stand the three principal floors, which are faced with white marble. Iconic columns supporting a well-proportioned entablature are used for the building's five porticoes, the principal one of which is topped by a pediment. Two additional stories are partially hidden by a marble balustrade.

Jackie paused the scrolling data to find out what balustrade meant, then continued.

Longworth presents a somewhat more restrained appearance than the neighboring Cannon Building, which was designed in the more theatrical Beaux Arts style.

The building was named in honor of Nicholas Longworth of Ohio, who served as Speaker of the House of Representatives (1925-1931).

Jackie texted JaDe: "At Longworth. Where you?" After staring blankly at his phone for at least thirty seconds with no response, Jackie concluded reluctantly that JaDe, who had let it be known in more ways than one that he was not comfortable in this setting, had abandoned him. Jackie, honestly, did not know how he felt about this, nor how he would feel about it after the meeting. Nor was he sure what this meant for their relationship, for any contract, for anything he might sign or might want JaDe to sign; or not.

At some point, Jackie understood, everyone becomes acutely, consciously aware that they cannot be exactly like someone else, with the same values, priorities, feelings; no matter how close, no matter how much they share, no matter what else they may have in common.

Jackie would not come this close to his dream to not punch it through; JaDe or no.

He paid the cabbie and walked into a side entrance of Longworth, as instructed. He checked his phone. Still over an hour before the meeting. He felt exhausted. Rather than find a bench to sit down he decided to first locate the Congressman's office, exactly, then find a men's room, clean up, call JaDe one last time, and prep himself for the meeting. He noted the irony that perhaps for the first time in his professional life, on the eve of his biggest meeting ever, he badly wished that the meeting had taken place at 8am rather than 5pm.

The inside of Longworth conjured thoughts in Jackie's mind of some grand old elementary school. The floors were marble, with marble baseboards bordering the walls, each of which appeared to be painted various shades of white or beige. Long hallways were dotted with old, albeit modest light fixtures. Jackie noted the fold-out windows atop each of the old wooden office doorways. He made a mental note to learn what those were called.

Entering the correct hallway, he became self-aware of his footsteps clicking on the marble floor. There was little activity in the hall, with the exception of one office, about 75 feet away. A man stood outside its entryway, suited, tied and stoic. He was obviously waiting for someone to arrive or possibly for someone to come out and allow him in, even though the door was open. Another group, two women, two men, all smartly dressed, coming from the other end of the hallway, were walking quickly toward the same office. One of the women, Jackie noted, was older, probably in her early 50s, blonde, but, from his vantage point at least, looked hyperfit, attractive and, in his mind, thunder in the sack. Like Pam in 20 or so years, he considered. Jackie discovered that the office with all this activity belonged to Barr.

He turned around, pretending as if he had just realized he forgot something, and ventured down a connecting passageway. Better to use a men's room further away, he decided; not wanting to meet anyone from Barr's office before the actual meeting. He was not sure why he felt this way. He also became aware that there seemed to be no place he could go inside Longworth that would allow him to make a phone call. At least, none discreetly. He texted JaDe once more. "Meeting still at 5. Be here early. If not early, DO NOT come late."

Almost instantly he second guessed his message. Also almost instantly, his phone buzzed. Unfortunately in this case, it was from Sickspack.

"Hello?"

"Sickspack? I don't have a good connection."
"Jackie? Oh, sorry. Wrong number."
"Oh."
"Good luck."

The call dropped. Jackie suddenly felt very alone. He took the elevator down to the entrance he came in at, stepped outside hoping for better reception and a sense of privacy, and called JaDe one last time.
No answer.
"Fuck." Jackie checked for JaDe on his phone's map. Nothing. "Fuck fuck fuck." Next, he checked JaDe's most recent public updates.

- "I'm waitin for my man. $26 in my hand."
- Landed in Washington, DC. Flying sucks for a big man. Flying sucks period.
- Jackie and I headed to Washington, DC. Big news for Empty Spaces project? Possibly. Housemate having his period? Stay tuned!
- Found this article [link] that says chocolate contains a substance -- anandamide -- which attaches itself to the same brain receptors as THC. Similar effects as marijuana. What next? Outlaw chocolate?
- This weed sucks! BC putting something in the seeds? US government? This smoke aint what it used to be. I know.

Jackie breathed in the warm, pleasant air. JaDe had not wanted to be part of this; not this meeting, not flying to Washington, DC, leaving Vancouver, upsetting his oddly conservative lifestyle. Jackie understood that now, better than when he strong-armed JaDe, figuratively, into coming out here. JaDe, clearly, knew how important this was to Jackie. That's why he came. This far. For all that, Jackie was grateful. Though right now, all he could think of was JaDe had left the hotel, most likely for some weed, and if he made it here on time, or at all, there was the very real possibility he could be fucking stoned. And if that killed the deal, Jackie wasn't sure if he could ever forgive him. He banged out a quick text to his friend: "I'm going into meeting *alone*. Will call as soon as it's over. See you back at the hotel. Wish me luck!"
Jackie silenced his phone, placed it in his pocket, walked back inside the building, found another men's room, just to force a piss out. He washed, made sure he was not sweating, had no nose hairs poking out, rinsed his mouth. Then parked himself on a marble bench at the

intersection of two hallways, not far from Barr's office, and waited for the next 35 minutes to be over so the meeting could finally begin. And also his new life.

The wait may have seemed interminable, but the first 120 seconds of the actual meeting were, despite Jackie's best efforts, a blur. He walked into the congressman's office a respectable but not needy four minutes prior to his appointment. The interior of the office was larger than anticipated. A small desk with an attractive woman, young enough to still be in college, Jackie thought, was positioned near the door. There was a series of cubicles, possibly five, just beyond her. Though the meeting was for 5pm, there was at least one person at each cube and at least two persons at two. There were two interior offices, each with its door closed and light on. One belonged to Francis Mustard, Chief of Staff. The other belonged to Congressman RKO Barr.

In rapid succession, Jackie was led by the attractive college aged woman to a black male, Jackie's age or a bit younger, and a good deal more handsome, named Theo Something, Jackie couldn't recall. Then, a quick knock on the door and he was taken straight into the Congressman's office where he had already said hello and was surprised by the clamminess of the congressman's weak grip and been requested to take a seat, which he quickly obliged, and sat there, waiting, unsure of what to say or do.

Theo left, apparently to fetch Francis. Jackie realized the Congressman had said something, a pleasantry, asked him about his flight, made some joke about rain in Vancouver, and with a quick motion of his left arm beckoned Jackie to take a look around the office.

Barr's office was, to Jackie's mind, exactly as expected. Large wooden desk. Tall American flag in the corner. A bookshelf filled with exactly the right books, on history and business, along with pictures and other trappings designed to reveal, no doubt, that the Congressman was the kind of person the visitor should expect. On the walls resided all manner of framed letters, certificates, awards and memorabilia that similarly reminded visitors that this was an important place, one where respect and decorum, possibly mixed with a touch of awe, was warranted.

Barr was thinner, paler, shorter than he appeared on his website. His jacket was off, though his white shirt appeared crisp, new, and tailored to fit. He wore a red tie, bit thin for Jackie's taste, and what Jackie suspected were, despite having zero knowledge of the subject, very expensive cufflinks.

Jackie was seated about three feet beyond the desk. An empty chair, positioned closer to the congressman was for Mr. Mustard, he assumed. Indeed, Francis walked into the room rather aggressively, then placed a tablet on the left edge of the Congressman's desk so that all could view the screen.

"Busy day. This should not take long."

Jackie could not help sizing the man up. Seemed a bit bland for Pam's tastes, he thought. Though he did carry himself well. She probably liked that.

"Anything else, Congressman?" Theo stood in the office doorway.

"Theo, please join us."

"Congressman, I do not think that wise."

"Not to worry, Francis," offered the congressman, motioning for Theo to take a chair.

"Sir, I'm going to put Maxwell on, he may divulge privileged information provided to us --"

"Francis, I know we can trust Theo. Come. Sit down, young man. Right here."

None of this had anything to do with Empty Spaces, Jackie sensed. Indeed, for a few brief seconds, they appeared to forget he was seated amongst them. Francis stared at Theo before speaking. "Congressman, you and I have had a number of discussions regarding Empty Spaces these past few days. This remains a delicate matter. After our meeting, I would like to discuss rules regarding office procedures. There can be zero tolerance for distractions, congressman. Let's not forget, we are in election mode."

"We're always in election mode, Francis. But, fair enough," said the congressman. "Bring Maxwell online."

"And Sickspack, correct" Jackie spoke up.

"Not necessary," said Francis. "The Congressman and I spoke with Mr. Shankar no more than an hour ago."

"Didn't you say that there were two founders, Theo?" questioned the congressman.

"JaDe Shockwatel will not be able to make it, I'm afraid," Jackie offered quickly, before Theo could respond. "I will be able to answer any questions, sir."

Francis shot him a look. "He hasn't returned to Vancouver, has he? You both flew here. On the congressman's personal dime, I might add. You both checked into the hotel room we booked for you." It was not till several minutes later that Jackie realized this was a level of detail that a chief of staff -- or anyone -- should not have possessed.

"Maxwell here."

"Good day, Maxwell," Francis and the congressman spoke at the same time.

"Jackie," offered Francis, "we asked Maxwell, whom I know you've spoken with already, to explore some of the strategic and technical issues surrounding Empty Spaces."

Jackie nodded.

"Late last year, the Congressman," Francis motioned to the congressman, "sought to diversify his assets. Given his existing commitments, this office, obviously, we decided that the best role for him was that of an angel investor. Targeted investments that could benefit from his background, experience, connections. Yet which would not require a commitment of time or exposure that might otherwise interfere with his many duties. Are we clear so far."

"Yes," Jackie responded, not certain if everything was clear, in fact.

"And, per the congressman's subcommittee work in particular, where he is involved closely with the FCC, we began exploring opportunities in the high tech sector; wireless, especially. Of course, the congressman's work with the FCC is experiential. Nothing about his role or investment with Empty Spaces, for example, will even be allowed as a perceived breach of his duties" Francis waved his arm, suggesting Barr's office, the Longworth Building, the US House of Representatives, America, freedom. He paused, waiting for Jackie to respond.

To what, exactly, Jackie wasn't sure. "Okay."

"Empty Spaces aligns fully with the larger strategic goals the congressman and I have established. We understand it's potential, we appreciate the ability to get in early, obviously we have a very good idea of what it will take to ensure the continued growth and success of the service. Based on my discussions with Mr. Shankar, certainly we can do a far better job of monetizing the platform." Francis again paused. This time Jackie said nothing. He glanced at Theo without moving his neck. Expressionless. The congressman was similarly mute.

"Before I have Maxwell outline exactly why, I wanted to be the one to tell you personally Jackie. We have some concerns with Empty Spaces. With mine and Maxwell's help, we are confident these can be remedied."

"Concerns?"

"We fully intend to proceed with our investment. However, you will not be a part of it."

Jackie was shaken but quickly recovered. "What. You're wanting to buy it outright? Not invest? I'm not sure if I can agree to that. Not here."

"Jackie. We believe, and have compiled evidence to back this up, that you do not, in fact, possess the legal ownership rights to Empty Spaces. Maxwell."

Francis held up a hand. Before Jackie could respond, the attention of everyone else in the room quickly turned to the screen.

"Thank you, Francis. Congressman. There are several issues with Empty Spaces."

"Wait. What are you talking about? Issues?" Jackie was furious, if unfocused. Sickspack had bailed, JaDe never showed up. Now these fucks were looking to, what, get better terms? Because some fat fuck on a video call who looked like he lived on diet coke and jagged little pills had a report to present?

"Mr. Paper, please let Maxwell finish," Francis urged, dismissively.

"Several problems, in fact. I have correspondence from a Gong Shwo, a researcher in China, who has discovered technical issues with Empty Spaces that suggest a potential security breakdown. Quite possibly a violation of FCC rules regarding the legal use of unlicensed spectrum."

"There is not a security concern with Empty Spaces. I've responded already to Mr. Shwo. His analysis -- ."

"Maxwell, continue."

"A bigger problem, of course, is legal ownership. Mr. Paper conceived of and developed Empty Spaces while in the employ of Sky Saxon, a Canadian company, headquartered in Richmond, British Columbia. The technology, algorithms, user data and all related materials are, in fact, their legal property. They intend to file an injunction against Mr. Paper, if necessary. I expect a declaratory judgment on ownership in their favor. They have a solid case, including numerous files, emails, texts and other information from their servers to support these claims."

"False. Empty Spaces is solely mine, and JaDe Shockwatel's. Sky Saxon had --"

"Congressman, the Mr. Shockwatel he is referring to is a drug dealer."

"Oh, bullshit. JaDe smokes marijuana. He even has a prescription for it. We live in Canada."

"If I can continue. There are significant privacy concerns with Empty Spaces that will also have to be addressed before the service can be properly monetized. New rules pending before Congress, which the congressman himself recently introduced, may outright preclude services such as this, unless specific action is taken. I believe Francis and Congressman Barr have already taken the lead on those."

Maxwell continued to bludgeon Jackie with false, if damaging accusations.

The sum time of the meeting, including walking into the Congressman's office, introductions, that weird shit with letting Theo join, getting Maxwell Edison's video optimized and everything else, took less than 15 minutes. Jackie now stood outside the Longworth building. He race walked about 50 paces down the block, trying to get away, leaned against a young tree, and puked. When he had finished, he dry heaved. He felt ill, scared; humiliated. Throwing up made it all much worse. Empty Spaces was going to be taken from him, somehow. There would be no investment, no angel, no millions. His one great idea, his one big chance. He stood erect, breathed in the warm air, too fast, shielded his eyes from the bright sun. He searched his pockets for gum. He called Sickspack.

Voice mail. Tried again. Voice mail. He left a message. More fear than rage in his voice.

He started to text JaDe. Stopped. What could he say? How could he convey that none of this was his fault, and yet everything was lost, out of his control? Truthfully, he wanted to cry.

He called Pam.

Voice mail. Called again. Voice mail. He left no message.

How could this have happened? Somebody spoke and he went into a nightmare, was all he could recollect. This was a set-up. It had to be. Sky Saxon, for as much as Jackie hated working there was not the kind of company to pull something like this. Not unless promised – or threatened, with something. Other employees created entire businesses while under contract with them. No, it was all a set-up. They never were going to fund Empty Spaces. Just try and take it away, he thought. That had to be it. And Francis and the congressman and probably that Theo fellow; all were part of it. And that fat fuck, Maxwell. And Sickspack, most likely. Pam and her report. Was she part of this? A pawn? He had to ask.

JaDe?

Jackie hated to even think it. Hated to allow his mind to even ask the question. Only, where was he? He hadn't shown up, hadn't returned any of his calls or texts. Now, this...

Jackie stood there, alone, for as long as the meeting itself had lasted, as well dressed men and women, all appearing as if they had important things to do, walked past, ignoring him.

It felt as if someone had knocked him right in the face. Cars and busses drove by, filled with people going somewhere. Laughing at a fool like me, he thought. As his dream transformed into a nightmare, as the worst possible outcome he had previously imagined was now the best he could hope for...Jackie realized he had no answers, no reply at all. He feared Empty Spaces, and everything it represented, was gone, forever. Taken from him. His body shook. He thought of crying.

A few blocks away, Prudence Skiffle was having an early dinner out. The first time in nearly a year when she had both lunch and dinner out on the same day. As with lunch, dinner also came as an unexpected surprise. More surprising still, much more, in fact, was that her dinner was of far greater consequence to Empty Spaces and even to Jackie than the nightmare meeting he just lived through.

Misery

Prudence knew she was early but didn't care. Better here, at Yaz, an 80s themed restaurant that Michelle Maybelle invited her to last minute than staying late at work. Barely 6pm, and the place was already starting to fill up. Yaz was at once dark and bright. This feat being attained by the fact that the club was, technically, cavernous and not well lit, and much of the walls and furniture were a deep purple. By contrast, the dark tables each held a small bowl with its own bright LED light inside, and multiple thin screens were placed along the walls, which temporarily lit up the space in moody blues.

Prudence felt out of place at once. Not solely because she always went straight home after work, but because it was clear that Yaz's patrons were much younger than her; most, at least. On a purely mathematical level, she was slightly below the mean age, this owing to the handful of significantly older patrons that occupied two booths at the far corner of the main floor, where two large purpley lit screens hummed and flashed. This did not make her feel any more comfortable.

Prudence scanned the menu. A number of drinks to choose from, but little food. Yaz mostly offered tapas, appetizers and the like. Prudence ordered a milk coffee, with extra chocolate syrup, no alcohol. This was made, for all to see, by an attractive man at a small cylindrical bar, one of at least three such stations on the floor, all bathed in purple light, each with a large pale blue light directly above. A group of Hill staffers, shockingly young to Prudence, who was only in her early 30s, walked into the club. The screens on the wall, sensing new entrants, switched tracks, increased the volume, and added red to the purple colors blasts.

Today was a good day, Prudence told herself, sipping her drink, opening herself up to the loud music and the strange people and all the colors. It was Friday. Pam was out most of the day. She met a nice man. True, he lived thousands of miles away. Still, it was nice to noticed, she supposed, while wondering if he would call, or if she should call him. It had been a long time since she was with a man, she thought, then thought that she had thought this quite a lot recently.

Indeed, she alternately hoped and feared she would meet a nice man at Yaz. What would mother say? Meet a man at a bar and spend the night at his place? Shocking, if nonetheless a thought worth clutching She took a sip of her milk coffee and decided to update her blog while she waited for Michelle to arrive.

Blog: Bitter Water

My name is Prudence, and I am a chocoholic.

"Hello, Prudence."

I am also a chocolate snob. And yet, I love milk chocolate. Until very recently you could not convince other chocolate snobs that such snobbery and an open, passionate love for milk chocolate -- quality milk chocolate -- were compatible. For them, only the darkest, most intense, blackest, bittersweetest chocolate qualified you as a true lover of our most blessed food.

Milk chocolate, one of the great affordable luxuries of the western world, has long been dismissed as a food for children -- or commoners. Fortunately, the days of the false idolatry of the dark have come to an end. No more must we turn away from the richness of cacao butter, of a touch extra sugar, of milk, of -- heaven forbid -- fillings.

Taste and see!

Some of our great chocolatiers, schooled in all things dark, have at last begun incorporating their experience and handling of the finest cacao and are now, as I write, crafting superb milk chocolates, reinventing the entire product category, and upending our notions of what can be achieved with the humble milk chocolate bar. Milk chocolates transformed through the inclusion of more and better cacao, expert care, resulting in a less sweet, slightly harder rich milk chocolate. For adults! Think of the delicious, velvety mouth feel of milk chocolate, only now tilted towards the slightly bitter yet deliciously aromatic notes found in dark chocolate.

Prudence had more to add but noticed Michelle entering the restaurant. She stopped typing on her phone and placed it in her bag. Michelle, as always, looked beautiful; expertly kept, from head to toe. Prudence, as always, found it difficult to not compare herself to other women. Michelle was clearly more successful, more poised, probably more capable. Although, Prudence liked to remind herself, she had a steady job, guaranteed pension -- in about 20 years -- and was taking care of her mother. Physically, Prudence was certain that her face was the more attractive and that she had a more pleasing figure. That said, Michelle clearly kept herself in peak condition. Michelle's jet black hair was obviously the result of regular, very professional care. She was impeccably dressed, as always. The tight-fitting yet conservative dress, cerulean in color, likely cost the equivalent of a week's pay, Prudence guessed. A necklace comprised of a series of concentric silver rings accentuated the outfit. Not to mention, of course, heels that complimented all she had, all she wore. Prudence quickly estimated the cost of the outfit and just as quickly wondered if any of Michelle's ensemble could be worn with anything else. Ever.

"Red wine, please," Michelle asked of the waiter as she took her seat. "Prudence, you look especially happy this evening. Meet someone special? Very special, perhaps?"

Prudence blushed. "Michelle! No."

"Really?"

"Well, I did have a lunch date today."

"Always nice. Someone from work? Met online?"

"Actually, he came to the office today. To see Pam. She was out."

"And you swooped in? Bitch eat bitch world."

"No. Nothing like that. Pam wasn't in so I asked him out. It was the polite thing to do."

"Are you going to be polite with him later?"

"You're terrible. Not likely. He lives in Vancouver. I think he's flying out on Sunday."

"Two whole days from now. Your bird can sing."

Prudence had no response. Michelle suddenly turned deadly serious.

"I don't have much time but I needed to talk to you about that NIH report."

"More details? Have they opened the study up again? My report is finished, though I'm happy to hear more. Pam edited out most of what I put in, just so you know."

"The study was halted. Long before the original planned end date."

"Does that matter? Nothing was found."

"Nothing was found. Correct. The study was one of many at NIH to look at smartphone radiation, the impact of electromagnetic waves on the brain. The kind of stuff that's straight out of the NIH playbook."

"Yes."

"I received a call regarding the report. This person, no, I can't tell you who, told me there had been pressure for the study to be halted. Immediately. Everyone on the team, there were between 5 and 9 at different points, have all been re-assigned to separate projects."

Prudence wasn't quite sure what Michelle was suggesting. "Any idea why? It seemed rather innocuous. And the conclusions -- initial conclusions, at least -- weren't alarming or anything."

"After the call I received, which came this morning, probably I shouldn't tell you that, I was then immediately forwarded additional information on the study. Unreleased. Off the record. No, don't ask.

Again, I can't tell you from whom. I can't forward it to you, either. Understand? So, don't ask. Only, I think you should read it. I think you will want to know."

"What? I'm not sure I follow."

"I will order a second glass of wine. You may scroll through the attachment while I imbibe. Do you understand?"

Prudence realized she was meant to take Michelle's phone. And do…something. Which, truthfully, made her excited. This was Washington insider stuff, she knew, the likes of which she had never once been privy to, despite her lifelong physical proximity to such insiders.

She reached for Michelle's phone. It lay on the small purple table. Michelle picked up her drink. As if on cue, a song escaped from the restaurant speakers, and bursts of red flashed from the wall screens.

"Like a virgin..."

Prudence brought the phone nearer to her face. The screen adjusted for her eyes.

"I do like my wine," Michelle noted. "Though I have a tendency to drink it too quickly."

Prudence glanced at Michelle. Her glass was about two thirds full. The first part of the screen was full of information about the study, the date of the study, the particular office within the NIH that authorized the study.

Michelle took another sip.

"Is there something I should be looking for?"

No response.

Prudence decided to quickly scroll down the screen, taking in what she could. Her hands were visibly shaking. She did her best to try and focus in on any particular words, findings, links; anything that stood out. And desperately sought to commit all to memory:

- Impact upon receptors in the brain associated with pleasure; calming.
- Causal relationship.
- Statistically significant correlation with occurrence of repeated electromagnetic bursts.
- No observed relationship based on long-term accepted-level exposure.
- Significant reduction in effects of THC upon relevant brain receptors.

- Presumed subsequent reduction in usage and enjoyment of cannabis.

Prudence glanced at Michelle. Two, maybe three small sips of wine left. Michelle reached for her glass, looked about the room. "The bartender's a looker."
Prudence continued.

- Lasting harm to the brain otherwise unknown.

"What does that mean? Lasting harm to the brain? That explains nothing." Michelle ignored her.

- Electromagnetic bursts diminished effects of cannabinoids. Subjects (n=164) reported significant drop in feeling of being "high". Similar effects noted with select lipids, including anandamide.
- Rapid, repeated electromagnetic bursts appear to pose greatest disruption to specified brain receptors.
- Reduction in dopamine levels was documented (more tests warranted).

Prudence looked up at Michelle. "Have you read this? That's at least twice it mentions electromagnetic bursts. Bursts obviously means something. That's what's most important, correct? Bursts, not long-term exposure?"
Again, no response.
"I eat chocolate everyday. You know that. Everyone knows. It's my favorite food. I thought lately that maybe I had some sort of, I don't know, like a long-term cold, or allergy. Something. Or that all the stuff I was eating was just bad. Tell me, please. Is this saying our smartphones are making us not like chocolate as much? Is that it? I know about anandamide. It's like marijuana in a way."
"Honestly, I can't say. Everyone has a smartphone, right?" Michelle reached for her glass, no more than a sip or two remained. She glanced at the two tables filled with the older patrons. "Perhaps only some people are impacted."
"Some people?"
Prudence realized she was talking too loud, despite the music.
She leaned in to Michelle. "This seems to connect marijuana and chocolate. It doesn't say it but mentions things in chocolate. And why only some people?"

"I expect it has to do with those electromagnetic radio bursts it mentions more than once. Ongoing exposure was not the issue. Bursts. You read that."

"So bursts, that's the key? Not other types of exposure"

"The report was rather specific." Michelle fingered her glass. Prudence read as fast and as much as she could.

- Additional studies required to isolate possibility of other impacted brain receptors.
- Broad active pharmacological connections between chocolate and anandamide and marijuana and THC.
- Potential for diminishment of feelings of relaxation and bliss.
- Clear physical evidence of structural transformations on cell receptors. Appears to inhibit bonding of receptor proteins and select compounds.
- Our focus was on THC.

"I'll ask for the check, Prudence. I need to be going." Michelle waved for the waiter.

"No, a few more minutes. Please."

"Check, please. Yes, thank you. Take your time."

Prudence looked up. "I meant him, not you," Michelle said.

"Leave your phone with me."

"I can't do that."

[Click here for links to team members.]
[Click here for links to study participants.]

Prudence clicked on one of the links. The screen remained on the report. No signal in Yaz, she assumed. Or perhaps the link was broken. She wasted time checking. Broken link.

"I think this is saying, somehow, that people, maybe just certain people, their test subjects, at least, are losing their ability to, what, to enjoy, get enjoyment out of marijuana, obviously, but also chocolate. Right? Because it contains anandamide. I happen to know that. Is that what it's saying? It can't really, can it? Because of frequent electromagnetic bursts. What is – Oh, shit. Empty Spaces. That's what this is looking at. Typically, it has minimal impact on the device. But when it hops, there's a burst. A noticeable one. And it's always hopping. Hop, hop, hop. That's, what was it, something like 30 or 40 bursts a second? My report included that. Wait. Was there a reason why

I was asked to write the report? Am I involved? Who knows about this?"

"Prudence. I'll need to authorize my smartphone to pay the bill." Prudence looked up. "Just one more minute. Here, use mine. I'm buying." She passed her smartphone to Michelle. "The code is 1234."

Michelle gave an admonishing look.

"I don't keep much money stored on the thing."

"I'll need my phone, Prudence."

"Wait. Let me take pictures of your screens. That's not forwarding."

"No. I don't think I can do that. Sorry."

A call rang out from Prudence's phone. "It's your mother," offered Michelle. She took her phone, stood up, and left. "Call me. You're always welcome to sit in with us at Party Line. Still."

"Prudence, dear. Why does my phone show you at some bar? Are you staying there for dinner? Are you seeing that boy again? Is he there with you?"

Despite the light and the noise and the people and especially despite what she had just read, which she knew she only partly understood, but was terribly important, Prudence decided to have a long conversation with her mother. About her lunch date. About her meeting with Michelle. About eating almost an entire expensive DARS chocolate bar, from Japan, in one sitting, late last night, because it seemed the only way to extract the pleasure from it; pleasure that never came. About a lot of things, in fact. Just to talk. Because mom was always there.

For No One

"Sickspack? No reply? Fine. Call me later. It had to be done. We're all agreed. You get what you want. Everybody wins. Besides, you know those two built Empty Spaces while under contract. Fuck, I'm still not convinced that Shockwatel fellow ever had anything to do with it. Dumb jock hoping to cash in, you ask me. Remember. Do not take any calls from him or Jackie Paper until Monday morning, earliest. None. We'll have everything concluded by then. This is much more than just holding hands. These are the big leagues, Sickspack. Somebody's gonna get fucked. Don't let it be you."

"Pam, love. Finally realized your phone ringer was off?"

"Sorry. I think it's been off since your press conference this afternoon. Guess I was just so excited."

"Went well, don't you think?"

"For who? Me? You? The congressman?"

"You, of course."

"Really?"

"Really. I asked if I could be the one to tell you. Savage Media liked what they saw today. They want to bring you into the studio for testing."

"Mother fucker. Fucking mother fucker! You're not making this up, right?"

"Of course not. I knew they would love you, babe. Why else would I pull you out of work today? Certainly not to have you sit through some boring Barr press conference?"

"That's...I don't know. It's great. It's fucking totally amazing is what it is."

"Job's not yours yet, love. But I did have separate meetings after the main event and I can tell you they think you are exactly the type they want. The two you met today will be at the fundraiser at Glockenspiel tomorrow."

"Francis, that would be...I still don't know, hon. Like a dream come true that I didn't even know I had."

"The meeting with your ex, however..."

"What? You're not going to tell me he showed up in a hoodie or something like that?"

"Worse. Total shitstorm. He's out."

"Out. What do you mean he's out?"

"While we were examining the technology, which there are issues, several in fact, I'll tell you the details later, turns out that the company he worked for, Sky Saxon, actually owns Empty Spaces. He made it while under contract. Apparently, they weren't too keen with his work so, near as I can tell, he quit, took everything with him and started looking for investors as if it were his. We'll have to make our deal with them."

"Son of a bitch. Jackie's smart. Really, he is. But --"

"But, what?"

"But, well, he always let stuff slide. I bet you he did all the work on his time but was stupid or lazy and used work email or his work phone to, I don't know, to check the status or something. Enough for those assholes to claim it's theirs."

"Maybe. Claim seem pretty strong. Wait, going through the tunnel."

"You there?"

"Here."

"Looks like we're going to cut a deal with them. Pretty quickly, I'd say. They're happy to sell it outright. All clean."

"Nothing for Jackie? He built it."

"He built it for them, Candi Darling."

"Don't do that. No Candi Darlings. You could figure out a way to keep him involved, somehow."

"I don't think so, love. Deal's pretty much signed and sealed. Sky Saxon won't share, that's for sure. Congressman wants this done."

"You could change it. Barr listens to you. Hell, he's afraid of you. Jackie deserves to be part of it."

"Still have feelings?"

"That's got nothing to do with it. He fucked up. So, what? He shouldn't get cut out completely. This is probably his one big shot."

"Listen. We can talk about this another time. I need you to get those press statements out. Can't do anything until those are put to rest."

"Look. He's left three calls on my phone."

"You're not listening."

"I am too listening. But he called three times."

"Get our press out and that pushes us closer to the deal. Closer to the deal means we might be able to figure out a way to get him back in. Okay?"

"I suppose. Two of his calls were recent, Francis. Probably right after you told him he was cut out of the deal."

"The other one?"

"No message. Earlier today, around the time we were going to your office to meet with the Savage Media people."

"Probably just before he went out to lunch with that cute assistant of yours. What's her name, Prudence?"

"What are you talking about? Jackie and Prudence? Not likely."

"It's true."

"How could you know that?"

"There's a picture of the two of them. At Zapp & Rogers. From today. She posted it to her wall. Don't you keep tabs on your staff?"

"Mother Barr! Wonderful to hear your voice. Yes, it went exactly as we discussed. The Congressman will help that Canadian company out with the government contract. The Barr Family will get 81% of Empty Spaces. I'll get 19%. Yes, ma'am. I really do believe it will help your boy become President. Yes, I do believe that. Imagine it. A Barr in the White House. He won't forget me, I hope. Yes, of course. I'll be there early tomorrow. Big day for us all."

"Maxwell, you bitch. That shit from China. Epic. Sealed the deal with the congressman. You know he's got no spine. I swear up until a day or two ago I still thought the cowardly son of a bitch might cut and run. How did you discover that shit?"

"Francis, this is what I do. Simple, really. I put out a few posts on some message boards for security geeks. Asking about Empty Spaces. This guy from China sends me a message. Tell him I'm a professor. Big US University. Probably thinks I'm gonna help him get out of fucking China. Forwards me the data. Appears to me to be sloppy coding, is all. Still, a hole's a hole."

"Our boy, Jackie, is sloppy at everything, you ask me. Fuck him. Helped us get a better deal with them Sky Saxon cocksuckers, though. They try and ask for more and we'll force them to admit there's a potential backdoor in what they claim now is their product. It will kill their reputation."

"It's a theoretical hole, near as I can tell. More like sloppy coding, like I said."

"It's how it plays, my friend. Besides, they'll now have a seat at the table when Big Government contracts are handed out. Not that small Canadian shit. Gotta run. Taking Pam out for a nice celebratory dinner."

"Nice ass on that one."

"Careful, my friend."

"Sorry. Thinking out loud."

"It is damn fine, though, isn't it? I'll send you a new picture. Remember, make sure you take out those servers before Sunday night.

That's when our two lonely boys will be heading back to Vancouver. I want no loose ends."

I Me Mine

It was getting late. Pam was the only one left on her floor. She reviewed the draft press announcements the FCC, her office, would release late tonight, Friday. Minor releases about a minor concerns, and thus tailor made for the Friday news cycle dumping ground. They said little, despite Francis' insistence they helped support Empty Spaces.

The first release reiterated that services using FCC sanctioned unlicensed spectrum did not cause interference. Ordinary, unimportant; of mildly political consequence. The second release was of equally little value. A recently concluded, albeit inconclusive NIH study, noted that long-term exposure to smartphone radiation did not appear to cause cancer.

Pam feared, however, that the release of this information somehow would put an end to any negotiations or outstanding concerns regarding Empty Spaces. And that, despite his assurances, Francis would then be free to work solely with Sky Saxon, cutting Jackie out permanently. Only, despite her taut brain, she couldn't fathom how. She promised Francis she would post them both. She informed staff that these were going out, tonight. Everything was done by the rules. Both drafts looked fine. Only, her heart wasn't in it.

[Empty Spaces downloads: 19,155, xxx]

She knew Jackie well enough, knew he would have poured his heart and soul into Empty Spaces, knew what it symbolized to him, thought she knew how losing it would hurt, deep. Imagined how losing his one big idea, that single big ticket idea he searched for so long, would haunt him, probably forever.

Pam also knew that he very likely did work on the product, his product, while on somebody else's dime. "Fuck up," she thought.

"Is it any wonder I reject you first?"

But her heart wasn't in that, either.

Yesterday

Pam was ignoring him. That was the second call this evening and nothing. Straight to voicemail. JaDe, likewise, wherever the fuck he was. Sickspack? He had to be a part of all this. Jackie was certain. Had to be. There was no other explanation.

No one was answering his calls.

He remembered that JaDe's sister lived in Baltimore, about an hour or so away. Or at least she once did. Jackie wasn't completely sure. And he needed to be sure because the nice Capitol Police Officer who held him in custody felt it best that Jackie not leave here on his own. Here being a small white room, even the floor was white, deep below the Longworth office building, in one of the underground corridors that apparently, for real, connected all the congressional offices with the Capitol Building. Twenty years of schoolin' and they put you in a white room, with black curtains, he told himself.

There had been no formal charges brought against him. At least, none so far. The police officer, a white male, pale, bad case of rosacea, barrel chested, several inches over six feet and at least 40-50 pounds over 200, had easily subdued Jackie. No brutality necessary.

As the minutes passed, and as Jackie stood outside the congressman's office building, the rage and anger and hopelessness boiling in his brain, just as the utter sense of the loss of Empty Spaces and everything with it left an inexplicable pang of unholy emptiness inside his stomach, Jackie, literally, did not know what to do. Mocking himself wasn't helping. Hating the world was likewise having no effect.

He picked up a rock and threw it. Threw it right at the window he was sure belonged to Congressman Barr. Or Mustard's office, one or the other. He missed. But it felt good. He searched for another rock, which was less easy than he expected. Found one, several steps away, threw it, connected. Only, instead of the sound of shattering glass there was a sort of metallic ping noise. Not at all satisfying. The rock hit the metal grate protecting the window. Manically, he searched for another rock, and another; a spare. He threw the first, connected. Again, a ping sound. The windows must not be real glass he realized.

"Fuck!"

No matter. He had one more rock and he promised himself to make it count. Which is when the police officer, whom Jackie never saw coming, grabbed him, forced him to the ground, handcuffed him, causing a small tear in his new jacket, put him inside a car, which did not look like a police car from the outside, drove him around to the other side of Longworth, pulled him out of the car, walked him into the building, down a flight of stairs, to an elevator, down an unknown number of feet, and into a brightly lit hallway. The entire time, the nice officer explained where he was taking Jackie and why.

The entire time, Jackie attempted to explain why he was alone, why he threw the rocks and why Congressman Barr was the biggest dick on the planet, with the possible exception of his dick chief of staff. The nice officer told him to "cheer down" inside the small white room while he checked out his story. Jackie gave him JaDe's contact information and the name of the hotel.

He had no data access. His texts were not getting through, though he did have a faint, but workable, call signal. Only, no one was answering. He refused to call his parents. Not yet. To punish himself while he waited, Jackie read several recent articles he had saved offline for when he had time to read them, which was clearly now. Articles about start-ups, recent investment rounds, valuations, breakthroughs; the dream. His dream.

Karma Tech raises $50 million at $600 million valuation. Spector Voorman led the round.
Money will go toward building out the developer platform
Founder and newly minted CEO Mal Evans posted the news on the company's blog:

Karma Tech is about magic, serendipity, about finding people and making relationships, without searching. With Karma Tech, users who avail themselves to digital nexus points placed by other users in various locations can, with the swipe of their smartphone, learn about who was there before them, and why, and for what reasons. Years ago or only moments before. In this way, connections are made to people and places and points in time that would not have existed before. By layering Karma Tech technology overtop the real world, we help people to connect with one another, forge new relationships, shift time and collapse space.

Each of us at Karma Tech strongly believes in the power of unplanned discovery, and we provide the tools to make it happen. We are all committed to this vision and incredibly lucky to have investors to help make our vision a reality, virtual or otherwise.

Today, we are pleased to announce that we have raised $50 million in funding to help us build the tools, infrastructure and developer community that will allow us to achieve our goals. This funding round, led by Spector Voorman, will provide not only capital but also the experience and relationships vital for our continued success. We are also announcing today that Karma Tech will be opening offices in New York and Vancouver, BC, to complement our efforts in San Mateo, CA.

Our user base has grown from myself and a few friends, to over *10 million*. The opportunity to create lasting relationships, to build a service that allows everyone to offload information they have about themselves and their location and to mash-up this data to create serendipitous connections is truly meaningful -- and a HUGE business opportunity. Thanks to this investment, no one is better positioned to capitalize on the future of random personal relationships.

Thank you and keep checking back for more revolutions!

That should be me, Jackie thought. Investment rounds. Valuations. Making big announcements on the company blog. "Fuck." Expecting something similar, a big investment, a giant valuation, a backslapping corporate blog post, Jackie, himself already drafted such a message about Empty Spaces on the plane. "Check back for more fucking revolutions…." He found the draft on his phone and deleted it before he could re-read it; no more punishment, he thought. Not tonight.

After nearly one hour, the nice officer opened the door. He politely explained there was indeed a hotel reservation under his name at the aforementioned hotel in Crystal City, lasting until Sunday afternoon. He verified Jackie's identification; a British Columbia driver's license. And, per a Theo Preston, who was still at the office this Friday evening, Mr. Paper was indeed at a meeting in Congressman Barr's office earlier in the day. No damage had been sustained. There was no prior record. Jackie appeared to have cooled down since the arrest. The officer politely re-confirmed that if Jackie could get someone to come pick him up, his friend perhaps, and if he promised to behave, he could go.

Jackie suspected that, seeing as no one had yet returned his calls, the officer probably was going to release him at some point during the evening, regardless. He hoped so, at least.

Which is when his phone rang. It was Prudence. From lunch.

"Jackie Paper, here."

"Jackie. It's Prudence. From lunch. We need to talk. Listen, I read a report that --"

The connection died.

Jackie pressed his phone, called her back.

Busy signal. "Dammit."

He waited. She would call back, certainly.

The call came through seconds later, as expected. "Hello, Jackie. Are you busy? I need to talk to you."

Call died.

"Dammit."

Jackie stood up, opened the door of the little white room, told the police officer if he could text from this spot, it should go through and someone would come and get him. He texted Prudence his whereabouts, thanks to the police officer's help. Jackie did not at that moment explain to Prudence why he was in a small room in a sub-basement hallway somewhere underneath Capitol Hill. He said nothing about police or rocks nor spoke of betrayals. Best to save that till after she arrives, he thought.

The police officer promised that when Prudence arrived at the designated door, above ground, that someone would escort her down to the little white room. Which was the truth. Prudence arrived less than 20 minutes later.

"Jackie. Why are you down here? Why the guards? Actually, never mind that. I have to tell you something. It involves Empty Spaces. Where can we talk?" Prudence looked about. She recognized that having a police officer standing nearby was certainly not a good sign, whatever the reason.

"Why don't we just go back to that place you took me to for lunch," Jackie offered.

"That should work. I suppose. I've never actually been there at night. I assume it's open." And with that the pair walked toward the elevator, close, though careful enough not to touch hands.

As the elevator door opened, the nice, fleshy police officer came running after them. Jackie immediately stepped inside, pulled Prudence in, and pressed the close door button. The door held. He pressed it again. Nothing.. Prudence slapped away his hand and pressed down on the open button.

"Mr. Paper!" The officer placed him arm on the elevator door, held it from closing upon him. He put his face down, took a couple seconds to catch his breath.

"Mr. Paper. I'm sorry. I'm so sorry. The news just came across my computer. From the local DC police." He paused again to take in oxygen. "Your friend. Mr. Shockwatel. Earlier today, sometime around noon, apparently. He was shot and killed."

Jackie stepped all the way to the back of the elevator. Leaned against the hard metal bar. And wept.

TRACK SEVEN
Band on the Run

A Hard Day's Night

Two inconsequential press releases, at least by government standards, primed and ready to go, on a Friday evening when no one would read them, no one would care. All she had to do was press send. The FCC.GOV website handles the rest.

Pam still couldn't help but think that the sooner she clicked the send button, the sooner their information would be unleashed upon the world, or lost within it, the sooner, she suspected, without knowing how, Francis would get his hands onto Empty Spaces. Completely. And Jackie would be cut out, forever. Francis was, after all, pushing for these announcements to be made official; announcements that, truthfully, had been fully and duly vetted by the FCC and, frankly, were remarkably innocuous, even by government standards.

She had not seen Jackie in over a year. Much had changed. Her life was here now, as was her future. "I'm older than that now."

She pressed send.

FOR IMMEDIATE RELEASE:
FCC REVIEW OF UNLICENSED RADIO SPECTRUM APPLICATIONS AND DEVICES
Washington, D.C. The Federal Communications Commission today released a Final Review Order concerning unlicensed so-called "white spaces" services. According to Pamela Drogeny, Associate Director with the FCC's Wireless Telecommunications Bureau, "the FCC finds that new unlicensed wireless services are spurring novel applications, more empowered users, and advancing marketplace competition and innovation that supports private sector jobs growth."

After careful study, the FCC concludes that these new services are causing no interference with GPS equipment, commercial radio, broadband infrastructure, existing mobile services or other radiofrequency (RF) devices. No existing services have been negatively impacted by last year's decision to allocate spectrum for unlicensed use.

As part of its ongoing effort to ensure compliance, the FCC will continue to require all services and applicable devices under the White Spectrum program to file designated paperwork and submit any applicable fees. The Commission will continue to balance its mission of fostering new and innovative services while protecting the interests of incumbent commercial entities. [See attachment for a complete list of reviewed 'white space' applications and services.]

Federal Communications Commission
445 12th Street, S.W.   Washington, D. C. 20554
This is an official announcement of the Federal Communications Commission
Internet: http://www.fcc.gov

FOR IMMEDIATE RELEASE:
FCC CONCURS WITH NIH STUDY.
Washington, D.C. The Federal Communications Commission has accepted a recently concluded National Institutes of Health (NIH) study initiated at the Commission's request and in collaboration with the nation's wireless industry, which found no conclusive evidence of a link between long-term electromagnetic radiation exposure, such as found through common smartphone usage, and cancer.

According to Pamela Drogeny, Associate Director with the FCC's Wireless Telecommunications Bureau "we hope this study, vetted by America's leading clinical research organization, allays user's fear over any potential harm from using a smartphone."

Based on an NIH panel review, the study was halted following clear evidence of a lack of supporting data that long-term exposure to low-energy smartphone radiation posed a threat to the populace. Based upon its recommendations, the FCC will not require handset manufacturers, carriers or distributors of smartphone related services to include a health warning with their materials.

"Americans engage in over 3.25 trillion minutes annually on their smartphones, just for voice calls," said Ms. Drogeny. "We also collectively listen to over 6 trillion minutes worth of music and participate in nearly 5 trillion cumulative minutes of texting every year. Smartphones are among the most popular, productive -- and now acceptably healthy -- activities that Americans engage in. The science is clear." The FCC will post a link to the NIH study once its results have been finalized for public review.

Federal Communications Commission
445 12th Street, S.W.   Washington, D. C. 20554
This is an official announcement of the Federal Communications Commission
Internet: http://www.fcc.gov

"Hello, my love."
"Evening, babe. Still at work?"

"Yes, you know I am. Can you take me out tonight? Somewhere nice? I need to get out of here."

"Of course, babe. Not too late. Tomorrow is our big day at the Barr place."

"I know. God I hate that mean old woman."

"Pick you up in 20 minutes. You need to change first?"

"Yes."

If I Fell

"Momma told me not to come."

Prudence lay there, in the quiet of Jackie's hotel room, trying to feel regretful. She did not.

"Tell me I'm the only one," she wanted to ask.

She couldn't sleep, her mind refused to go quiet. Jackie, beside her, thankfully, had fallen asleep. He was wonderful. This night was wonderful. For her. For him, tragic as well. And, though she was here, which helped, she assumed, his pain remained. And this thought only intensified all the other thoughts shuffling inside her head; thoughts, even now, past midnight, mere hours till morning, that refused to be silenced, refused to stop flashing in her brain like some torturous voice mail light on her phone, insisting she acknowledge it over all else.

Prudence did what she always did in situations where she couldn't sleep. She thought of chocolate. Not of eating it, nor buying it nor preparing it, nor even writing about it. Rather, on how it was defined. Literally.

"Give you everything I've got for a little piece of mind." By now, she had practically memorized the entire chocolate industry definitions manual.

Chocolate is the term given to products that are derived from cocoa and which are mixed with fat, typically cocoa butter, sweeteners, spices, nuts and other ingredients to produce a solid edible product. Dark chocolate, milk chocolate, white chocolate and related terms are designations that are subject to government regulation and are determined by the inclusion, exclusion and proportions of certain ingredients. Common flavor additives in chocolates include mint, orange, vanilla, coffee, cinnamon, raspberry and chilis. Other ingredients added to a chocolate bar or confection are most often nuts, peanuts, caramel, crisped rice, and fruit.

"I fooled around and fell in love. Is that how this is supposed to work?" Prudence snuck a glance at Jackie, sleeping soundly, which surprised her. "Trying to touch and reach you..." Not once had he mentioned Pam. Not once had he compared her to Pam, in any way. She must have slept with the other guy, Prudence decided, angry at herself for letting such a small thought leak out.

Chocolate liquor is the ground or melted form of the pod (or nib) of the cocoa bean. Cocoa butter is the fat component of the ground or melted bean. Cocoa powder is the nonfat component of the cocoa bean which is ground into a powder.

"Strange how seeing his friend's clothes put away and the bed made so neatly seemed to have more an impact on him than even talking about it."

Unsweetened chocolate, typically used in baking, is chocolate liquor mixed with fat, typically cocoa butter, which the maker can adjust in quantity, to produce a solid substance. It is pure and bitter, imparting a strong chocolate flavor which is highly dependent upon the prior fermentation and roasting of the nibs.

"Although, he never was totally clear on why the Capitol Police arrested him. Was it even an actual arrest?"

Dark chocolate is made by mixing chocolate liquor with fat and sugar, in varying quantities and types. Milk chocolate is dark chocolate with milk added. This is typically in the form of condensed milk, milk powder or soured forms of milk solids. The US government requires a minimum 10% chocolate liquor for anything called milk chocolate.

"What if Michelle is wrong? The study could have been legitimately halted because they found no direct cancer link. A disbanded team claiming a link between bursts of radiation and brain receptors; what does that even mean? That's not proof. I'm not losing my love of chocolate. My brain is the same as it always was. Maybe it's a hormonal thing. Plus, so many chocolate companies have been cutting back. That's a fact. It's a quality issue, more than anything, I bet."

White chocolate is a confection made through the use of cocoa butter and sugar. There is no chocolate liquor and no cocoa powder in white chocolate. The government does not strictly regulate the term white chocolate. Some white chocolate manufacturers do not include actual cocoa butter but instead use other fats, such as vegetable oils.

"Oh, God. What is mother going to say? And I didn't use protection. How could I have been so stupid? He seemed so perfect. I was afraid the moment would vanish. Stupid. We take a cab from the Capitol all the way back to his hotel. There was plenty of time. I know him only from online conversations. What if I'm pregnant? What about mother? Speaking words of wisdom? More like words of shame."

This wasn't working. Jackie stirred. The hotel room fan was whirring, drowning out extraneous noise. There was a tiny light overhead, red, probably a smoke alarm Prudence thought, and the light from the clock radio, which was a shocking bright blue. Otherwise, darkness. She gently rolled over, reached for her smartphone, touched it and the device glowed awake. Jackie moved in closer though his face remained buried in his pillow. He snorted then quickly went silent again. She focused her mind on the screen.

FOOD AND DRUG ADMINISTRATION
DEPARTMENT OF HEALTH AND HUMAN SERVICES
TITLE 21--FOOD AND DRUGS CHAPTER
SUBCHAPTER B--FOOD FOR HUMAN CONSUMPTION

"Drastic measures."

PART 163 CACAO PRODUCTS
Subpart B--Requirements for Specific Standardized Cacao Products
Sec. 163.110 Cacao nibs.
(a) Description. (1) Cacao nibs is the food prepared by removing the shell from cured, cleaned, dried, and cracked cacao beans. The cacao shell content is not more than 1.75 percent by weight, calculated on an alkali free basis, as determined by the method prescribed in 163.5(a).

"Christ! The campaign event. Lord, forgive me. Pam is going. She bragged about it. Barr will be there. His whole staff. Maybe we can get in. Find out if he knows about the study. He can't possibly. It would kill his business. He won't go through with the Empty Spaces purchase. Can we get in? Will they try and have Jackie arrested? Will Pam have me fired?"

Sec. 163.111 Chocolate liquor.
Chocolate liquor is the solid or semi plastic food prepared by finely grinding cacao nibs. The fat content of the food may be adjusted by adding one or more of the optional ingredients specified in paragraph (b)(1) of this section to the cacao nibs. Chocolate liquor contains not less than 50 percent nor more than 60 percent by weight of cacao fat as determined by the method prescribed in 163.5(b).

Jackie's smartphone vibrated loudly, causing Prudence to jump. "Timer. Vancouver time. Reminds me to take a vitamin D supplement before bed. Forgot to disable it." He rolled onto his side and snored, not too loudly, and was asleep. Prudence returned her the small screen.

Sec. 163.130 Milk chocolate.

Milk chocolate contains not less than 10 percent by weight of chocolate liquor complying with the requirements of 163.111 as calculated by subtracting from the weight of the chocolate liquor used, the weight of cacao fat therein and the weights of alkali, neutralizing and seasoning ingredients, multiplying the remainder by 2.2, dividing the result by the weight of the finished milk chocolate, and multiplying the quotient by 100. The finished milk chocolate contains not less than 3.39 percent by weight of milkfat and not less than 12 percent by weight of total milk solids.

"Should I even care? So what if Empty Spaces maybe kills our taste for chocolate. Wouldn't that be freeing? I spend far too much thinking about it, eating it, shopping for it, talking about it. What could I do instead with all that time? I could probably lose a few pounds, besides. God, mother's going to kill me. Did I leave tracking on? Shit, shit, shit. Oh, God, what if she calls? Don't be silly, Prudence. You told her not to wait up. You texted her you were okay. Yes, just before having sex, you texted your mother. So, no, she won't call. Not now. She'll call bright and early in the morning."

Sec. 163.123 Sweet chocolate.

Sweet chocolate is the solid or semi plastic food prepared by intimately mixing and grinding chocolate liquor with one or more optional nutritive carbohydrate sweeteners, and may contain one or more of the other optional ingredients specified in paragraph (b) of this section.

"How old is he? Didn't he say 29? Does he know I'm older than him? Older than Pam? Not much, true. Jesus, we get together because of Empty Spaces but not from using Empty Spaces. There must some lesson in that."

Sec. 163.150 Sweet cocoa and vegetable fat coating.

In the preparation of the product, cocoa or a mixture of cocoa and chocolate liquor is used in such quantity that the finished food contains not less than 6.8 percent by weight of nonfat cacao solids, calculated on a moisture-free basis.

"What if he didn't like it? Or doesn't like me? He seemed awfully practiced. At least, he knew what he wanted. He could just leave. Dammit. This is his hotel room. He could make me leave."

Jackie sensed her movement, turned, placed his hand on her thigh. Prudence considered, decided now was not the time. She put her smartphone aside, rolled over, pretended to be asleep, and within 5 minutes actually did fall asleep.

Upon waking, Prudence had hoped for mental clarity. Her hopes were dashed. Jackie was making noise in the adjoining room. By the smell of it, brewing coffee. Prudence reached for her undergarments, then for her smartphone. She noticed two messages. She read the first:

"Prudence. It is 7am. I know you are with that boy you had lunch with. It says here you are at his hotel."

All Prudence could think of was how much the message felt like a knife in her side. Even at her age, even though she supported her mother, even though she was a good daughter, a good employee, a good person. She had made the decision to have sex, unprotected sex at that, with a man she thought was handsome and nice and smart who was clearly feeling alone, desperate, sad, and they had this amazing, circuitous connection, and he almost certainly will check out of this room tomorrow, if not today, and now she would never see him again. Prudence took in a deep breath. This was her decision, she reminded herself. She realized, even having slept on it, that she felt no regrets.

A new text from her mother arrived. She ignored it.

The other message was from Michelle. She could not ignore it: "Prudence, the tests were conclusive. Empty Spaces was explicitly used during testing. Brain receptors were impacted. The original study was not seeking to determine links with cancer. The study was halted prematurely due to political pressure. The methodology and purpose were altered after the fact. Data was destroyed. This was told to me in confidence. I am trusting you to not share this message. Use the information well."

Prudence let herself free fall onto the edge of the bed. "What do I do?" The thought ricocheted inside her head. Her face was ashen. She couldn't speak.

Jackie entered the room. He saw her face, assumed that perhaps she felt about JaDe, in some small way, just as he did. Or perhaps feared that he was about to tell her to get out. He pulled out the small desk chair, brought it in close, kissed her on the lips and sat down, facing her.

"I texted his sister. Last night, after calling JaDe's parents. I couldn't go through that again. Not another phone conversation. Pathetic, really. I never met her, but still, I should have spoken with her... JaDe's parents told her, of course. I didn't know what else to do. They're driving down. From Michigan. Maybe they don't like to fly. I don't know. Would the long car ride help? Would they just breakdown on the plane? That could be why they're driving. The police said I can't see his body. We're not related. Not married. I don't know what else to do."

"I'm so sorry. I hope you know that. There's something I need to talk to you about, though. Concerning Empty Spaces."

Jackie stood up, turned away. "Barr and that prick chief of staff of his have taken it. They want it for themselves. Maybe even Pam. I didn't want to believe it, but now I'm pretty sure she's involved. She must be. I'm not going to let them have it. Not now. Not after everything."

"You're right. We can't let them have it. We have to stop them." Prudence stood, equally emboldened.

Jackie smiled. "Empty Spaces belongs to me and to JaDe. Everything I am, everything I hope to be, is locked inside it."

"I know where they are. Today. They're all going to be at Barr's estate. There's a big campaign event being held there this afternoon."

"Good. I want them all together. This time I'm not going to get blindsided."

"But first we have to stop at my apartment."

"Okay. As long as it's quick."

"And if you care about me at all, you will be nice to my mother."

[Empty Spaces downloads: 25,338, xxx]

Baby's in Black

Despite only a few hours of sleep, Francis felt supercharged. He prided himself on requiring less sleep than most. Plus, everything was finally coming together, as expected, only sooner and faster than hoped. Better, too. He reached for his phone and took some pictures of Pam. Her blonde hair and perfect ass and thin limbs, captured forever. Francis felt as excited by her image as her flesh. Pam, still sleeping, had only traces of evidence about his picture fetish. Levon barked once, forcing him to stop after just two pictures. "Could you feed him," Pam asked as she rolled herself in the sheets and turned her body toward the light.

"Of course, babe." Least he could do. After last night, he certainly owed her, Francis thought. The memory remained vivid. When he picked her up at the office, she was obviously upset. She wanted him to let Jackie back in, somehow. She worried that posting an NIH study that was no longer being funded may have been done in haste. She suggested, rightly, that he had set up the meeting with the Savage Media people at the same time Jackie would be available, knowing he would try and see her. Their wedding was approaching much too quickly, there was too much to plan.

Francis told her that, legally, there may be nothing that could be done to get Jackie back on the project, but he would absolutely try. This was a complete lie. He promised that he would make more time, even during the campaign, for her and the wedding. Mostly a lie. The Savage Media people were naturally going to attend the congressman's press conference which just happened to be the same day Jackie and his partner were scheduled to meet with him and the congressman. Which was true, though incomplete; as he deliberately left out his calculated scheduling change with Jackie and prior arrangement with the Savage producer.

Then, for taking her out, and for reminding her how smart, how talented, how pretty she was, and for reminding her that Savage Media had the second most popular television news channel in Washington, DC, and that still more news producers were going to be at the fundraiser, and confessing his desire to spend more time with her, and for a number of other good deeds on his part, some real, some imagined, Pam did exactly what she knew Francis most craved. She got into her bed, took off her clothes, and lay there, still, seemingly frightened, and let him lay on top of her, force her legs wide, hands round her neck, and pound her till she came like a school girl. He replayed the night, shaped the memory and forgot to feed Levon. Though he did make several quick calls.

"Ganja? This is Francis. How does the old lady look? Listen, double up on her meds, understand? Do that and I make sure you are rewarded. We clear? Good. If she acts crazy during our big event your big Jamaican ass will be looking for work."

Pam entered the kitchen, hair still wet from the shower, dressed only in a soft, though unattractive salmon-colored bathrobe. "Shower's all yours. You didn't feed Levon? Bad man. Levon! Come, boy!"
"Sorry, dear, forgot. My head's all wrapped up in this afternoon's big function." Francis took his phone with him and walked through the bedroom into Pam's small but fully functional bathroom.

With Francis in the shower, Pam pulled out her phone from the left pocket in her robe. "Jackie. Hello. It's Pam. I hope you are doing well. I'm sorry I wasn't available when you stopped by. Call me. I will probably be gone today from about noon until 7pm, or so, so I may be unavailable. Bye." Not exactly sure why, she tried not to imagine Jackie having sex with Prudence. Even if they did go out for lunch Prudence was not, Pam assured herself, the type to jump into bed with a man.

"Hello, yes, this is Pam. Oh, yes, well, it was nice meeting you. An audition? Monday morning? Yes, of course I can make it. Thank you. Yes, I will be at Glockenspiel. Yes, all day." Fuck me.

Pam made coffee and sliced an apple while waiting for Francis to finish, which she ate with some peanut butter. She checked the month's To Do list on her phone. Mostly, it was wedding related. As much as she wanted to be married, to have a beautiful wedding, and as fully capable as she was, few tasks stressed her as much as those related to her own big day. It had to be special. And it would be, she knew, even as it consumed more of her time and focus and fears and doubts like some black hole where more and more of her collapsed inside of it never to escape. She was already dreading having to tell two, she had already decided which two, of her office pets would not be invited. She sent a quick text to her wedding planner. The young, female cellist at the restaurant Francis took her to last night would be perfect, she thought.

Francis entered the kitchen. He was cleaned and dressed. Levon barked, which he ignored. "We can leave from your place," Francis said. "Straight from here to Glockenspiel. No point in taking two cars."

"No, but then I'm there the entire time, even while you're making sure everything is ready."

"It will be fun. Promise. Plenty to do. Lots of people to meet. Plus the media will be there early for canned shots. That's really your best time to meet with them. Here's a thought. We could do the wedding at the Barr estate. Don't give me a look. Just keep an open mind. Some of the views really are amazing. Check out the surroundings while we are there. Think of today as a dry run."

"My mother and I already secured a location. You know that."

"I do. Just consider it. Make your assessment. Mother Barr already told me we could use the place."

"I'll assess but don't expect any change. I have to go dry my hair." Pam went to the bathroom. Francis grabbed one of Pam's large coffee mugs, filled his cup, and sat down.

"Sickspack, did I wake you?"

"No, I was awake."

"Maxwell tells me he'll have people take physical access of the servers by tomorrow evening at the latest."

"That is not my concern."

"Just tying up loose ends. We already have our own version of the code. Here's what I need you to do. I want you to help me test Empty Spaces today, at a party I'm having. At least 200 persons there. How do we make sure it's on my phone and I can get it onto everyone else's? I'll need you to make sure I'm all set up."

"That is not a problem. Two seconds."

"You misunderstand. This is our first stab at directing a message. I'll need your help with that part. Can't trust Maxwell to do it. I know exactly what I want the message to be. Rather, I know exactly how I want everyone there to feel, which for now is just as important."

"I understand."

Francis could hear the loud steady hum of Pam's blow dryer all the way out into the kitchen. He checked the time, made another call. "Theo, you at the Barr estate yet? Good. You have my list of the important media and campaign supporters attending. See their needs are taken care of, understood? Oh, Theo, one more thing. Do not forget. I take care of those who know which side to choose. We good? Excellent. I'll be down there in a couple hours."

As he finished speaking, Francis received a text from Maxwell. "Asshole. You know I don't like working with that Indian fucker. Don't let him know what I'm doing." Francis didn't have time for this. He wondered why the people who were exceptional at their jobs were so often assholes. He scanned through last night's pictures of Pam and selected the best one. He sent it to Maxwell. "That should make the fat fuck happy," he thought.

He walked to the bathroom. "How much longer, love?"

Pam opened the door. "Ten minutes. We've plenty of time."

"You're right." He kissed her. "Just wanted to let you know there's still coffee." His phone rang. It was from mother Barr. He closed the door behind him and returned to the kitchen. "Mother Barr. Yes, of course Pam and I will be there. I can't believe you would ask that. Well, I'll have a talk with Ganja and Honah both right when I get there. Though you should take your medicine. They are right about that. We want to keep you around forever. What's that? Yes, Theo will be there. Yes, he is a handsome young black man. I will see you soon. My love to you."

"Congressman. I trust all is well. Yes, sir. The releases went out last night. No, sir. Sky Saxon is more than happy to play ball. Eager, I'd say. I had Maxwell look into the CEO myself. Yes, even if Mr. Paper tries to make things nasty. Which he won't. Not the type. Besides, both him and his partner will face an expensive battle to prove ownership and they do not possess the funds."

Francis shook his head. How is it possible, he thought, that the congressman could have so much and still be so weak, so fearful?

"That is correct, congressman. Sky Saxon will be listed on the government's procurement contract. The split has not changed. 81% for you, Mother Barr, and the Mamacoco fund. 19% to me. Nothing to worry about. Yes. Also correct. Agreed. Your re-election is a great test for Empty Spaces. Perhaps we should try it out today? Just imagine, congressman, how many more will be using Empty Spaces a year from now. No. No misgivings."

Francis clenched his teeth. So close, he thought. Soon enough, he would never need to concern himself with this man's neediness.

"Congressman, you know I leaned on Pam to authenticate the non-interference results. But they are legit. Rushed, perhaps. Still, correct nonetheless. Just because a bunch of incumbent wireless companies bitch about something new like Empty Spaces won't help them. They look slow and old, afraid of change. Especially now with the FCC's okay and your backing, of course. This is a day to celebrate.

Glockenspiel. The media. Supporters. All who want to come out and kiss the ring -- that's always gratifying, right?

The signal was breaking up.

"Think of Empty Spaces this way, congressman. All these ephemeral bits of data are generated by each of us dozens, maybe hundreds of time a day, every single day. They are like little electrons. No, DNA. Each a strand of DNA. One may be meaningless. In total, however, they create the person. Empty Spaces lets us know everyone's DNA. All the strands. We know exactly how to connect with them, engage with them, where they are located. We deconstruct and recombine these DNA. There will be nowhere to hide."

Francis put his phone away.

Pam was standing there, to his side, looking perfect. "Oh, love, didn't see you there. My bad. You look amazing."

"Thanks. Was that the congressman?"

"Yes." The two began walking toward the door.

"What were you talking about?"

Francis stopped, turned to face her.

"That stupid faggot is afraid of his own shadow. And his crazy old mother actually believes her son can be President."

She's Leaving Home

"Try to understand. He's a magic man." Clearly, Prudence thought, this was not what she would say to her mother. In fact, she would say nothing. She needed to focus all her energies on reaching Barr and stopping Empty Spaces, somehow. Whatever her mother wanted to say, needed to say, would have to wait. Prudence steeled herself for a possible confrontation, nonetheless.

Jackie showered and dressed. He wore his suit, again, as instructed. Not for her mother, Prudence promised, but for the formal event at the Barr estate. This, she explained, was some sort of tour of the grounds and barbecue and political glad-handing affair with speeches and news crews and the kind of people Jackie typically would never interact with. Even with big Empty Spaces money; the thought of which re-activated the aching pit in his stomach.

Despite her assurances, Jackie nonetheless suspected, given that he was a man with no job, technically, and unkempt hair, and had just violated her daughter, that if he showed up dressed in khaki shorts and a Michigan hoodie that Prudence's mother would die on the spot.

Prudence showered, and for still more obvious reasons put on the same outfit she wore to work yesterday. This made Jackie smile, which, all things considered, he felt a rare touch of guilt.

"I'm not sure if I'm supposed to say this, but I think you look better without make-up."

"Thank you," Prudence held a blush in check.

"Just a few minutes, right?"

"Scared? Don't worry. But, yes, just a few minutes. Mother and I live only a couple miles from here. I just need to change my outfit and, yes, put on some make-up." At this, Prudence could not hold back the blushing.

"Time to go over a plan? How exactly do we get invited to this soiree? How do I get Empty Spaces?"

"I'm not prepared to go over it yet," Prudence replied.

"In other words, you don't know."

Prudence turned to him. "I will know when the time comes."

An average white band was playing from the cab driver's radio. Jackie refused to let Empty Spaces guide his choices at this moment; a hollow protest, he knew. He stared out the taxi window. A wide black road, strip malls, apartment towers; Arlington seemed to him like Vancouver gone wrong. There was no nexus point. No reason to walk anywhere. No neighborhoods, as far as he could tell. No water, no mountains. Just a place for people to live. And maybe to work. This was sad, he thought. In fact, everything was sad.

His phone rang. It was Pam.

Prudence stared at him. He stared back. It rang again. He refused to answer. A moment later, it notified him of a voice mail. He quickly deleted the message. He would not allow Pam to sway him; she was fully capable of that, he knew. Maybe even still. He would not talk to her. He would not listen to what she had to say. That was the only way to be safe, he decided.

Another notification popped up on his phone. "Shit. Empty Spaces was mentioned on the FCC website. Last night."

"What does it say?"

"One second. Mostly...It's listed along with several other services. Empty Spaces and other unlicensed services do not cause interference with existing radio frequencies and applications."

"That's it? Nothing about brain receptors? Does it mention an NIH study? One that was recently halted?"

"Checking. FCC website. Yesterday, yes, posted,. Also by Pam. An NIH study about smartphones and cancer. No linkage found. Etc etc etc."

Prudence reached for his phone. "That's bullshit. It's a fake. They weren't looking for a link for cancer. Well, maybe they were at the outset, that I don't know for sure. But they did find a link between Empty Spaces and impacts on certain brain receptors. The same brain receptors that cause people to take pleasure from things like chocolate."

"Seems unlikely. Why would Congressman Barr lie about that? His money all comes from his family's chocolate business, right? I read that myself. That's not some lie from Sickspack, at least."

"I don't know. I'm just certain that this whole cancer thing is a dodge."

"Are you? I mean, really sure? Think it through." Jackie knew this sounded dismissive, which wasn't entirely his intent. However, he was told so many lies, had experienced such duplicity surrounding Empty Spaces in the past 24 hours that he simply could not believe this latest. Prudence was not lying, he was certain of that. But she had been lied to, he suspected. That was why, he thought, she was tasked with writing up a report in the first place; a report that was never needed, he suspected. A dodge of some sort. This was all just some other way of taking – and keeping – Empty Spaces from him.

"Jackie, I promise you. I knew my taste for chocolate was diminished. That's a fact. And it's been getting worse. Ever since I started using Empty Spaces. There's something in it, I'm sorry, there is, that's causing this. And I read what was on Michelle's phone. Trust me, she's a woman that gets to the source. It's real."

Jackie stared out the window, unable to believe what he was hearing. The cab turned into a complex of condo towers, all reddish brown brick, all ten stories high, all approximately 25 years old. The driver pulled into the parking lot, stopped near the front entrance where Prudence lived. Jackie reached for his wallet to pay the driver.

The pair walked into the apartment building and took the elevator up to floor number 9. Prudence stood still. Jackie was saying something, though she could not hear him. She needed to focus all her energies, not on explaining things to her mother, not on fighting with her, which would not succeed, but merely, for now, keeping her at bay, and making her realize that this moment, at least, was absolutely not the time for a discussion; about anything.

Jackie continued speaking as they rode up the elevator, obviously nervous, defending his creation. "That was when I realized that so much of our life, our location, our circumstances, are so collective. I knew I could create something from that simple inspiration. I won't give that up. I'm sorry."

They were standing now in front of the door of her apartment. The apartment she shared with her mother. Prudence turned to him. "Empty Spaces will not be the only thing you create. I can promise you that." And then she kissed him. And knowing how she looked, and knowing where she had just come from, and knowing what she had done, last night, for the first time in a long time, and it was easily the best of the few times that she had done it, Prudence made the sign of the cross then kissed the jesus and mary chain enfolded around her neck that she was given as a teenager. She unlocked the door, ready to face her mother.

Your Mother Should Know

Jackie noticed two things right away. Prudence's mother was much older, much more frail, and significantly fiercer in appearance than he was expecting. Also, the apartment appeared to be, albeit clean and welcoming, best described as the inside of a Catholic Church garage sale, blowed up. There was, however, a very nice view of the Pentagon and even the Washington Monument from the large living room window.

"Mrs. Skiffle, a pleasure to meet you."

Jackie wasn't sure if he should have been more pleased with himself for actually remembering Prudence's last name, or more surprised at how weak and cold and small her mother's hand felt inside his.

"You may sit." she said, waving Jackie to a well worn couch composed of green cloth fabric and a brown wood frame. Jackie understood this was an instruction as much as a pleasantry.

"Nice jacket. New?"

"This is the boy that's getting you in so much trouble?"

"Mom! Listen, I'm leaving in 20 minutes. Best to get it all out now."

The two women walked down the short, narrow corridor to what Jackie assumed was a bedroom or bathroom. Which probably didn't matter much as he could hear everything.

"You told me that he knew Pam. More than know, I suspect. He was going to see her." Now he's with you?"

"It's not like that. I need to get my make-up."

"Oh, he's that special? You have lunch and later go to his hotel room? I taught you better than that." Jackie could not know how exhausting this was on the old woman.

"Yes. You taught me better than that. You did. I'm not being sarcastic. I need to change."

Jackie heard the bathroom door shut; a sort of hesitant slam.

"What about church?" Mrs. Skiffle was obviously now talking to Prudence through a door. "We go on Saturdays. You know I don't like Father Bernard. I don't want to miss church."

"You don't like Father Bernard because his service goes over an hour."

"Prudence!"

"Mother. We can go to mass tomorrow. I promise."

"Why? Where are you going now? Why are you getting so dressed up? It's not even noon. Where is this boy taking you? I did not see you all last night. I couldn't sleep."

"A fundraising event. The Barr estate."

"Barr estate? Why? You know Pam is dating someone from his office. Pam. Your boss. Whom that boy knows." Prudence suddenly regretted telling her mother everything about yesterday's lunch.

The door opened. Jackie could not know that he was moments away from seeing Prudence at her very best. Her hair was tamed and playful, her eyes sparkled, the red dress, her favorite, worn only once before, was cut to accentuate her best features, of which there was plenty. She restrained herself from applying too much make-up.

Prudence stood in the doorway, facing her mother. Her mother was welcome to judge, say what she needed to say, but Prudence was not to be swayed, not now. A moment passed, in silence.

"I need to get back into the bedroom."

Prudence's mother remained in the hallway, deciding it best to not follow her daughter. Prudence stared at herself in the long mirror behind the door. She felt rushed, uncertain, but happy; almost liberated. She looked her best, that was obvious. Maybe not perfect. Possibly not even the best she had ever looked, she thought. But certainly the best she could look right this moment. And no more than a few feet away sat the man she had given herself to, without regret.

I have to go, she thought. I have to upset my mother. I have to stop them. I don't know what to do. I am happy." She sucked in a bit of air and walked out the door.

There her mother stood, just as resolute. "You slept with him. Last night. In his hotel room. You are pregnant. I know this."

Though she was born a long, long time ago, Jackie thought, as he heard every single word, mother superior could definitely punch above her weight class. He wondered if perhaps he should just run away. From here, from everything, from everyone.

He chose to stay.

I Need You

"This is your car?"

"It runs perfectly fine."

"It's what? At least 20 years old? More, probably."

"It was my father's. Mom and I don't like to drive. You drive."

A big white Cadillac Eldorado, Jackie thought to himself. I've only heard about them. "Yes, I'll drive."

Jackie got in, using the handle to open the door, sat in front of the steering column, searched for a means to push the seat back. Was Prudence really this short? He turned toward her. Prudence handed him the keys. "Actual keys? This thing is ancient."

"I'm sure you can handle it," Prudence responded testily. Jackie suddenly wasn't so sure. He almost never drove anymore, and never in a car this big, this wide; with no camera, no connectivity.

"Damn."

"What now?"

"There's not even 50,000 miles. When was the last time this was out?"

"What does that matter? Go, already."

Jackie was driving too fast, owing less to being in a rush and more to the fact that the accelerator pedal had no feel to it. "Shit."

"What?" Prudence was stressed enough, still uncertain of what she was going to do, and how. Jackie wasn't helping.

"I just realized. I'm starving. Seriously, starving. We have to get something to eat."

Prudence quickly checked her phone. "Next exit. After this one. The Isley Brothers. Breakfast all day. Four stars."

"That will work."

Four stars did not do the place justice, Jackie thought. He thoroughly enjoyed his two cups of coffee, with cream, three pecan pancakes and a side of very salty but delicious ham. Prudence had an egg, over hard, hot tea, and a side of biscuits and gravy, which she loved, although channeling her mother she did complain the gravy contained too much sausage grease. Not everything could be perfect.

The pair had sat down, glanced at the menu, ordered, were served, ate every bite, paid, left a nice tip, and were out the door all in less than twenty five minutes. Which, given the circumstances was probably too quick. Now that his stomach pangs had been replaced by carbs and grease, Jackie realized that he was awash in emotions; stressed, angry, sad, bitter, confused. None of which he discussed at the table.

Likewise, Prudence ate much faster than normal; a woman possessed. Except, she still did not know how to conquer that which possessed her. She only vaguely understood how to even frame her mission: somehow make bad people give back control of Empty Spaces, kill it off, and somehow convince still more people, though which might include the first group of people, the bad people, to acknowledge, publicly, that Empty Spaces, probably more than any other service but not necessarily, now that she thought about it, was killing off people's taste for chocolate. Or, if not their taste, exactly, their desire for chocolate, their ability to extract the unadulterated, blessed, natural joy and, well, bliss, it so freely offered. As well as marijuana. She wasn't sure if more time would help.

What she did know, however, was that her efforts had to start with the man driving her to her destination. "Jackie. I'm not sure you fully understand. We aren't trying to just get Empty Spaces back. We have to kill it."

Jackie kept his eyes straight ahead, staring down the two-lane road for several seconds. He glanced at her. "What are you talking about? Of course we're going to get it back. And of course I'm not going to kill it off."

"No. What Michelle showed me was true. I know it. She uncovers things. There was a study."

"A study? Yes, a study. We both saw what the FCC posted -- just yesterday, remember? There was a study, two in fact. One mentioned Empty Spaces. It caused no interference. The second study..." and here Jackie emphasized the word 'study', "did not mention Empty Spaces at all. Merely services like Empty Spaces. And, surprise, no harm found. Nothing."

"It was never about cancer. That was a dodge, a cover-up, I'm not sure how. Ignore that. The people in the study, whatever their original intent, discovered that Empty Spaces, I'm not sure why, but somehow it's harming people."

"No one is being harmed. No one. No one but me. I am being harmed. I created Empty Spaces. It was stolen from me. From me and JaDe." Jackie felt hot as he choked JaDe's name out.

"It reaches our brains. Changes them. You have to understand. Things like chocolate, we no longer experience it like we once did. I was probably one of your earliest users. I have my phone set to run Empty Spaces all the time. I always have this earpiece stuck in my ear. Empty Spaces is inside it and it's continuously jumping onto other people's phone. You have to understand that what you built is always running, always jumping from one person to the next. It never stops. Chocolate isn't the same for me anymore. I knew this was happening. I didn't know how, but I did know that I wasn't enjoying it as much. Not like I used to... I just couldn't verbalize it, couldn't conceptualize it, somehow."

"Not liking chocolate? This is what you consider harm?"

"Not just chocolate. Marijuana. They reach the same place. Chocolate and marijuana, both. What about your friend? Why not --"

"JaDe was fucking killed over marijuana. Some fucker shot my friend in cold fucking blood over some fucking marijuana deal gone wrong." Jackie's rage had escaped. He couldn't put it back. "Empty Spaces kills people's desire for marijuana -- good. Fucking let it."

"You're speeding. Slow down. And what you're saying is garbage. You know that." Now was not the time, perhaps, but Prudence had her own raw emotions to unleash. "People like marijuana. There is nothing wrong with that. People like chocolate. Some of us love it. Yes, that's right, love it. Eyes on the road. Who are you to let that get taken away from us? You don't get to decide. I'm going to do everything I can to stop it."

"Is this about Pam? Because we used to sleep together. Is that it?"

Surprisingly to Prudence, this was the absolute single worst thing Jackie could have said at this very moment. Somehow, it made everything worse. Everything associated with Empty Spaces, including Jackie, had soured. And no amount of chocolate, not now, maybe not ever, could not make it better.

Next there was silence. The road became hilly. Trees were mostly replaced now with green fields. Periodically, markings of an equestrian training ground, or the homes of the Virginia gentry could be seen not far off the road. Prudence's phone indicated where they should turn. As Jackie neared the long and winding road that led to Glockenspiel, the markings of an outsized event were already evident. Several plastic white tents that could hold at least 25 people were up, or going up. There was one van, a satellite antenna on top, that obviously belonged to a television crew. In the distance, people could be spotted walking along the main front grounds of the Barr family estate.

Why Don't We Do it in the Road

"Pull over."

"Here? On the side of the road?"

"Yes. We'll need passes."

"Maybe not. There seem to be lots of people here, already. We're dressed like we belong. I bet we could just walk in."

"I want to talk with the congressman. We'll probably need passes to get inside the house." Prudence touched her phone and placed a video call to Michelle.

"Michelle. It's Prudence. I need a favor."

"I think you've used up all your favors, Prudence, dear."

"I know. I swear. Everything you did was because it was the right thing. Don't forget that. That's never bad. And no one else knows you've told me. Well, one." Prudence tilted the phone camera toward Jackie. "He's the guy I had lunch with yesterday. The one I told you about. He created Empty Spaces."

"Hello."

"I need two invitations to Congressman Barr's fundraiser. It's today. At his home. We're at Glockenspiel right now."

"What are you planning on doing?"

"Honestly. I don't know. But Jackie tells me that the congressman now owns Empty Spaces."

"Owns it? I've not heard that."

"It's complicated. But, yes, the Congressman owns it. Him and his flunky, Francis Mustard. Pam's better half. I just want to talk to the congressman. I swear I won't mention you. Maybe he doesn't know about the study. The real one. He couldn't, right? I mean, his business is chocolate."

"You know what I know."

"I'm sure you received an invitation. Or know someone that did."

There was a pause. Michelle went out of focus. "I have two. I was not planning to attend, anyway. They should be in your phone. That will get you inside."

"Thank you. Thank you so much."

"Good luck."

"Now what," asked Jackie?

"Please. Can you trust me? I'm sorry for everything that's happened to you. I am. I wish I had met your friend, JaDe. I do. I can tell how much he meant to you. You had this dream about getting rich -- and that's taken from you. I can't probably know what any of that is like. I love Empty Spaces. You know that. But what it's doing, this isn't your fault, but it needs to be shut down. We can go without it. But chocolate we've had for thousands of years. Marijuana, too, I'm guessing. Empty Spaces is not all you can do. There's always more of ourselves that we can call upon."

"I have a confession to make."

Prudence leaned back in her seat. I cannot believe he's going to talk to me about his relationship with Pam, now, after everything. With everything else going on. Prudence assumed her facial expressions conveyed each of her thoughts.

Jackie took her hand. He could not gauge how she was thinking. The big car suddenly seemed much smaller. "Yes, I wanted to build something insanely great. I wanted to make something that people would love -- and even associate it with me. My name. I wanted to get rich from it. But, that's not the only reason I created it..."

The circumstances, the seriousness of the moment; words failed him.

"How can I say the words I know that you'll understand? Do you know how much the government spends on telescopes? How many satellites we've put into space?"

"No. I don't understand. What does this have to do with anything?"

"Just listen. America spent how many billions of dollars over two generations to launch shuttles into space? Think of that. We barely understand the oceans, the environment. Human behavior, like criminal behavior, the ways children learn; think of how much better science could understand all those if we spent the same amount of money on them as we have on sending rockets into space."

"Can we please discuss this later? I think you're just avoiding --"

"All that effort, it's wasted. There's something out there, Prudence. Only, we're doing it wrong."

Prudence reached for the door handle.

This wasn't working, Jackie thought. How could he possibly explain to Prudence that, in fact, the extra burst of electromagnetic energy, sent at exactly the right time, every time, over and over, without end, connecting people, connecting phones, sending its secret extra signal drifting off into space, was put there deliberately. By him. From the start. It was built into the code, purposefully.

How could he possibly explain to her why he did it? The logical absurdity of his actions, he knew, were such that, though no longer willing to lie for his calling, he still couldn't reveal the truth. Like the impact a favorite song had upon him, his work was not rational. Any words, in isolation, like lyrics, would prove simply incapable of revealing the scope of his aspiration. Something was out there, he knew. All he wanted to do was reach out and connect with them. In this world, such talk was heretical, he well knew.

"Let me find Pam. This study you're talking about, she must know something about it. She posted the findings. I just need to speak with her first. I can convince her to help me get it back. She's my way back in."

Prudence pulled away, sat fully upright in her seat, an expression of disappointment clear on her face. "Do what you have to do. Just drive me closer to the house. I'm going to find the congressman."

If I'm going to cry, Prudence thought, that will have to come later.

You Can't Do That

Though early for the formal event at least, there was already a young man, one of the congressman's local staffers, directing traffic. He motioned for Jackie to park in a makeshift lot approximately thirty feet from the house. He and Prudence got out of the car, looked at each other, said nothing, and walked toward the large front porch. At the steps, they paused. "I'm going inside. I assume the congressman is there."

"I'll look around," Jackie said. Both knew this meant he was going to seek out Pam.

Prudence turned, walked up the well maintained old wooden porch steps. A mass of flags and patriotic bunting aligned the porch rails. There was no one at the door, no one checking her credentials. Perhaps having a big Cadillac and a form fitting red dress was sufficient. Prudence stepped inside.

One step beyond the small, tasteful foyer, a space nearly half the size of her living room, Prudence thought, a makeshift gathering space had been assembled. If the congressman were to give a speech inside, at least to a select audience, it would most definitely be here. Only, he was not here. Many others were. Some, no doubt, part of Barr's campaign staff, some volunteers, she suspected; a few apparently there simply for free food and drink. All, except for the locals, were obviously well above her pay grade.

It was unlikely she could remain inconspicuous, so Prudence did her best to pretend that she belonged. As she poked around the dining room, the kitchen, the parlor, what she assumed was an area for formal tea, she began to worry that the congressman was not in the house, not even on the grounds. Maybe he just shows up, late, Prudence feared, proffering the illusion of working tirelessly, gives a rah-rah speech, asks for everyone's support, then leaves. "Dammit. I need to talk with him in person. Preferably alone"

Prudence anxiously walked down a short hall leading to a strikingly narrow staircase. The stairs were cordoned off. With a touch of desperation, she pulled out her smartphone. A politician, she thought, especially one in the midst of a re-election campaign, at an event where cameras were present, could only be one other place: standing in front of a mirror, rehearsing. Prudence searched her phone. Perhaps the grand Glockenspiel had its floor plans posted online.

"Jackpot," she said out loud. A profile of the congressman and the estate a little more than two years old was accessible. And the article, blessedly, included a layout of the house. On the very floor where she stood, not more than twenty-five feet away, was a bathroom, fully remade nearly a decade ago, per the author, to the congressman's liking.

Prudence stood there, alone, in a narrow hallway, in front of a thick brown wooden door with a antique-looking glass doorknob. "There are things known and there are things unknown," she told herself. And, not bothering to knock, she placed her hand on the knob, reminded herself why she was doing this, and forcefully pushed the door open.

She was in.

The Congressman, however, fully dressed, rehearsing his remarks, standing right in front of a large mirror, nearly as wide as the large marble basin, underneath a series of bright, metallic lights, expecting to be alone, shrieked like a colicky baby.

Though a politician, one seemingly bred for the role, Barr was never completely comfortable being so out in the open. Even in his own home, even when everyone was either working for him or needed his support, at least as much as he needed theirs, Barr remained uncomfortable even in his own skin. Which is probably why he let out a second squeal as Prudence approached him. As with all politicians, however, he quickly regained his demeanor, forcefully as he could muster, and told her the room was occupied. Noticing only then how her red dress clung to her body, and the way her bosom suggested that at any moment it would break free, Barr incorrectly identified Prudence as just one more political groupie; albeit one about ten years older than most. He attempted to dismiss her out of hand.

Prudence was not to be dismissed. As quickly as she introduced herself, as quickly as she attempted to reassure the congressman that she was not there by accident, did not need to use the bathroom, was not some groupie, which he obviously thought, she launched into her story, doing her best to state it, all of it, succinctly, rationally, calmly, but persuasively. She did her best, she thought, to make Barr understand that if he failed to take action, everything his family had established, everything that led to his good fortune, could potentially be wiped clean. Empty Spaces meant no chocolate.

She wisely kept the part about marijuana to herself.

For many reasons, few of which Prudence could understand, and none of which he was prepared to discuss with her now, Jackie needed to speak with Pam. He cursed himself for earlier refusing to even speak with her, certain then that she would, somehow, convince him into letting everything go. No. Now, Jackie realized, she was his lifeline, his conduit to regaining Empty Spaces. And, he hoped, in proving Prudence wrong.

Call reception was spotty in Virginia horse country, apparently. No worries, Jackie thought. He hoped to see Pam in person. Prudence was certain she would be in attendance. Not sure where to begin looking, however, he walked along the side of the house, toward a small tent marked MEDIA. A much larger tent, with a view of the estate, the rolling hills, horses, was still being erected. No doubt where the congressman will give some grand speech, he thought.

Maybe Pam will show up later, he wondered. They were early, after all. He pulled out his phone, assuming their must be several streams of conversations covering the event. He had these aggregated, scanned the most recent posts, hoping to find anything relevant. There was little of value. He felt stumped. Luckily, Theo, from the congressman's office, looking as handsome and well dressed as ever, was just then walking towards the media tent.

"Mr. Paper?"

It took Jackie a moment to recognize him. "Theo, right? Congressman Barr's office?"

"Yes. What are you doing here?"

"Oh, I'm a guest. I have my pass." He held up his phone, worried that Theo might contact security. "I'm friends with Pam Drogeny."

"Pam? Mr. Mustard's fiancé? Interesting."

"Yes, that's right, Mr. Mustard, Pam's fiancé. And the Congressman." Jackie couldn't stop himself. "Listen. They tried to take Empty Spaces. Did you know? Not invest in it, take it from me." Everything came streaming out.

Theo listened patiently. When Jackie finished, Theo took hold of his arm and walked him several feet further from the main tent. It was a rather lovely day out, Jackie thought. Perfect weather.

"Mr. Mustard has a way of bringing out the worst in the Congressman. In everyone, it seems, even Pam. If he wanted to take Empty Spaces, he probably already has. If he has his own plans for it, wants to lock you out, change it, I'd guess that's already under way. He is usually thinking a few steps ahead. From the few discussions I've had, I have my doubts that he thinks of the service in the same way you do. Maybe he felt you would stop him. Please know I was not aware of any of this."

Jackie wasn't sure what to say. He wanted to be angry at Theo, at everyone. But he seemed earnest, Jackie thought. Caring. And, Jackie realized, sharp enough to know that perhaps Mustard and company may have already taken Empty Spaces, physically. No one was back in

Vancouver, guarding their place. Jackie felt stupid for not even thinking about that. Shit, he thought. The right people could make it look like he and JaDe were small-time drug hoods. Robbed. Some sort of payback. Would the police even care? Mustard and Sickspack have a copy of the code, might they prevent him from accessing any of it? There was so much he never considered, even the obvious.

"I am sorry, Mr. Paper. I hope a solution presents itself. I have to go now." Theo motioned toward the media tent, which was filling with news staff converging on the food table. "Oh, and when you see her, please tell Pam I said hello."

"Good day, sunshine!" Despite himself, despite everything he was responsible for, nothing could make Francis more joyful, more enraptured, than his time with Mother Barr. Or so he sought to make all around him believe, especially Mother Barr, herself.

The Mrs. was wheeled toward Francis by Honah, with Ganja at her side.

Francis squatted, making sure he was at eye level, then leaned in and kissed the family matriarch on her well-polished cheek. "Geraldine, you light up a room. It's a gift. Truly. Never goes away."

"And you brought this beauty, I see," she said, lifting her eyes toward Pam.

"Mrs. Barr," Pam offered, taking the elderly woman's hand, "it's always a delight."

Pam was suitably briefed on how to interact with Mother Barr. During the car ride down, Francis reminded her that more than anything, Pam must, with all she had, let it be known that she viewed the old woman exactly as the old woman viewed herself. A star. One not made; rather, the qualities were in-born. She was once a star, literally, Francis told Pam, and that means she believes she is always a star. Always. And should be treated accordingly, always. In her presence, there is nothing else you think of other than the fact that the woman is a star, lighting up all that surrounds her. She warms you, as she warms all.

"Dear, you look more beautiful each time I see you. With this strapping man," she glanced toward Francis, "I'm sure your children will be perfect. Absolutely perfect." This made Pam slightly uncomfortable, though she was gracious in accepting the compliment.

"This is a big day for Reginald, obviously," Mrs. Barr noted. Then coughed. Coughed again. Wheezed. "Isn't that right, Francis?"

"Indeed."

Pam looked surprised; only partly feigned.

"This is not just the launch of his re-election campaign, dear," the wily perceptive old woman said. "Francis didn't invite all those news trucks out here for that. Isn't that right, Francis."

"Right, as always." Francis turned toward Pam. "In about two and a half years from now, love, Reginald Barr, presently Congressman Barr, will be elected President of the United States of America. Francis spoke proudly. Today he will tell everyone of his plans. He will outline all his strengths, his vision for the future. Consider today a pre-emptive strike, if you will. I will be there to guide him through the process, of course. With help." He winked at the Mrs.

The matriarch beamed. "Pamela, love. Can you leave Francis and I, please. For just a few minutes. Thank you."

Pamela looked to Francis for confirmation. He affirmed.

"Honah. Ganja. Show the future Mrs. Mustard out. Francis, please wheel me into the tea room. No one is allowed in there. We can talk. I'll be glad when all these damnable people are finally out of my house."

As Prudence completed her tale, Barr did his best to appear nonplussed. Above all, he knew he had to find Francis. Or mother. Possibly Theo. Quickly. Someone to explain this tale and tell him what to do.

"Come with me," he offered to Prudence. "No. Wait here." Barr decided it best to not have Prudence a part of this.

Prudence insisted she follow him. Only, her phone rang. It was her mother. "Mother, I can't talk right now. I'll call you back."

"Prudence. I'm not feeling well. This morning. It upset me. My heart is still racing."

The call reception was poor. Prudence had a difficult time hearing. The congressman made his escape from the bathroom, Prudence still inside. "Mother? Are you there? Mother, I can't talk right now."

"I'm sick."

"Sick? Are you laying down?"

"Yes."

"What does it feel like?"

"My heart won't stop. It's beating too fast, I think."

"Take an aspirin. Should we call 911?"

"No."

"Speak up, please. Are you sure?"

"I'm sure. I'm upset, is all."

Prudence sensed she was talking too loudly, and attracting attention. She closed the bathroom door. "Mother, listen. Take an aspirin. Lay down. I'm going to be home today. Later. I promise."

"I will wait."

"Call me again if you feel worse, okay? Don't hesitate. I love you, mom."

The call died.

Pam was nowhere to be found. Jackie wondered what he was going to do, whether she showed or not. He believed Theo. There was a sincerity there, one not practiced. He sat down on a white painted wood bench, letting the exhaustion and emotions and tragedies of the past 24 hours wash over him and, hopefully, drift away. He let Empty Spaces once again back into his life. He placed his earbud in his ear, closed his eyes. The air felt especially nice. Theo, he suspected, was probably right. Mustard brought out the worst in everyone; the congressman. Pam, no doubt.

If Francis and the Congressman were going to use Empty Spaces for their own purposes, and not simply to get rich, or richer, as was the case, as Jackie had long assumed, the process was likely already underway. Meaning, if he failed, failed to take back control of his property, he would not be rich himself. Nor famous. Nor, he feared, would the portal to his boyhood dreams ever come around again. He would have to work; at some job he hated, no doubt. He would receive little or no credit for his invention. Possibly, if Mustard carried out his threat, he might face a lawsuit or two. He may, in fact, already have a criminal record thanks to his foolish rock throwing incident. And worst of all, if what Prudence said was true, his one lasting achievement might actually cause people real harm.

And his best friend in the world was gone. Dead. Followed me out here, to Washington, DC, at my insistence, no less, and now lies dead.

So many bright lights, Jackie thought, like stars, gone dark.

Except, he realized, sitting there, tired, confused perhaps, with the sun washing over him, the smell of grass filling his senses, people milling about, full of life, that for inexplicable reasons, he did not feel as bad about all this as he should have. True, things had not worked out as he expected. True, despite what Prudence said, Empty Spaces was probably his only shot at something big, something grand. JaDe was gone. Yet despite the utter tragedy of his death, a part of Jackie, even if just a small part, knew that there was a better place for his dear friend. Plus, he met Prudence. There was something potentially lasting about her, Jackie knew.

Whether he regained control of Empty Spaces or not, he was happy just in knowing that he built it. He was happy; or reasonably close. Boyhood dreams and secret hopes for changing the world were idols, preventing him from accepting the present and embracing the future. Things were good. Not great, but good. He was like everyone else. There were ups and downs. Life goes on. Day after day. "The world is round. The wind is high. It turns me on," he told himself.

He then leapt from the bench.

"Oh, fuck. What have I done?"

I'm not happy. I'm not settled. These thoughts are not mine. They are what I'm supposed to think, this is what supposed to feel.

Shivers ran down Jackie's spine. He started to run. "Oh, fuck. That's what they're doing. That's why they want Empty Spaces."

Jackie realized that the music playing softly in his ear, the music Empty Spaces, his creation, offered up to him, burrowing its way into his soul this very moment, with people all around, was, and this should not be, not exactly what he needed. It was not exactly how he felt. Empty Spaces was not working, not how it was designed to work, even though he knew it should be working perfectly. These were not his feelings. Instead, Jackie realized, bounding for the front of the house, Empty Spaces was not embracing his feelings, not liberating them, but manipulating them.

"This is how they want me to feel."

You're Going to Lose that Girl

Jackie sprang up the steps of the big front porch and burst through the front door. Prudence must be here, he thought. I have to tell her. We have to stop this.

"Jackie?"

Pam was standing just beyond the door, engaged in conversation with a man at least ten years her senior. The tag on his jacket made it clear he was with some news organization. Seeing her now, so close to him physically, yet part of a different world, Jackie finally realized in that single moment, this time for good, that anything they once had together was now over. Finally.

Pam, as effortlessly as she carried herself in all situations belonged among these people, this life. That was obvious to everyone, Jackie now included. He felt neither vengeful nor grief stricken, nor indifferent. Rather, accepting. All was forgiven, he thought. Whatever role she played in all this could be reversed. Pam was not, Jackie knew, a bad person.

This did not change the fact, however, that there was still much to say.

"Pam." Jackie walked to her. Hugged her. He had almost forgotten how pretty she was. "I have to speak with you. Now." Pam excused herself from her conversation. He took her hand and they walked toward a corner of a large formal room hoping they might speak more freely. Jackie positioned Pam at the edge of a couch and took a seat beside her. "You look great," he said. He quickly added, fearing she mistook the comment, "I need your help. This is important."

He wasn't sure where to begin.

"JaDe is dead. Murdered. Yesterday afternoon. In Washington."

She could not stop crying. She worried that someone important might see her; Francis, especially, or that old witch, or some TV news producer. As supportive and helpful as JaDe was to Jackie when he and Pam were splitting, in so many ways, just by being there, he was at least as good to Pam. To everyone, really.

After a minute of crying on his shoulder, Jackie gently took Pam's face in his hands. "There's more."

Pam stared back at him. "Do you have a tissue, please?"

He did not but there was a cloth napkin on a nearby table stand which he retrieved. He wanted to move her past this.

"Thank you."

"Pam, listen. The congressman, and your fiancé, stole Empty Spaces from me. Please tell me you had nothing to do with that, correct?"

She stared at him. "No. Of course not." That she did not deny Jackie's interpretation of what happened to Empty Spaces was, however, in that brief moment, telling for them both.

"You seem different."

"What? Gained some weight? Hair's still the same?"

"I don't know. Things matter to you now."

"It was always there. Just had to look for it."

She clearly misunderstood. "Jackie, I never cared that you weren't sure what you wanted to do. Only that you were never prepared to do what it took to find out what that was, exactly. I never called because I knew I had to make my life her, that if I stayed in contact I would just use you as a sort of safety valve, a way back if I failed. Does that make any sense?"

"I don't know." He paused. "Honestly, I can't talk about this stuff right now. Empty Spaces was stolen. I want it back. I have to get it back. Really. As in have to."

"And you want my help?"

"Well, yes. I suppose. In a way. But not for selfish reasons. Though, it's mine." It took mere fractions of a second for Jackie to realize that to get Pam's help, right now, he couldn't mention anything about trying to call aliens or boyhood fantasies, nor about how he was now certain that Barr and Francis, somehow, had turned Empty Spaces upside down, were using it not to allow people to share feelings, but to direct their feelings. He decided, at that moment, though he hated more than ever not being fully honest with her, that it best to focus on what was in fact, to him, the most pedestrian of issues. Empty Spaces was killing off people's desire for chocolate.

"Listen, I can't tell you how I know this but the report you linked to on the FCC website last night? The NIH one? That was false. Not false, per se, misleading. It was never about cancer. Empty Spaces, the way I designed it, as it seeks out other users, just before it jumps to another device, there's a burst of energy. That burst is deliberate. It repeats the process over and over, radiating out from a user's phone, or worse, their earbuds. It doesn't cause cancer. Jesus, far as I know. But what it does is it effects receptors in the brain. Sort of sterilizes them, is the best way to describe it. Which diminishes people's ability to enjoy certain things. Chocolate, in fact. That's the main thing, at least." Jackie paused, took in a breath, allowed himself a brief moment to reassess. "Shit. Maybe I shouldn't do anything. Barr steals Empty

Spaces, let it destroy his candy business. Fuck if I care. No. That would just harm him. Too many others will be harmed. Or worse, manipulated somehow. I can't let that happen."

Pam was always fast. Always able to focus on the issue at hand, even when Jackie missed it entirely. "If you got it back, couldn't you just fix it? No energy bursts?"

"Honestly, I don't know. First, I'm not completely sure of the extent of the damage already. I've not actually seen this actual report, even still. Don't make a face. Trust me. I know what I'm talking about. As for changing it, cutting out the bursts, I built those in deliberately; it's part of the code. Take that out, the program dies. Partly, it's necessary to hop from phone to phone. Partly, well, it's something I never told anyone."

Jackie always kept secrets. Even when it was completely unnecessary. She made a face this time.

"I know. I know. Look, there's already millions of users. Literally. And even if I fixed the part that shouldn't be there, which I'm not sure I can, it wouldn't solve everything. What's already out there can just continue to hop from user to user. Forever. It works. Pretty damn well, I might add. I can't make millions of people just turn it off. It's self propagating."

"What do you want me to do?"

Again, he wasn't sure. "I'm not sure. If we could publicize the harm, maybe. Somehow get the NIH to re-start their investigation. Get people to turn Empty Spaces off. I know this will sound like I'm jealous or something, it's not that. I think your fiancé might have been the one that got the study aborted, somehow. I think I know him well enough that my instinct here is correct."

Pam feared that everything Jackie was telling her was true.

"I have my own confession to make. Francis got the congressman, or most likely his mother, to sign off on everything he did to get Empty Spaces. I know this now. I told him to make you a part of it, Jackie. He told me that it was stuff you did with Sky Saxon so you had no legal right to it. He's not bad, so much, just driven. I know that's something you don't want to hear. He told me something else. Just as we were driving out here. He doesn't much care about Empty Spaces for the money. That's not the first reason, at least. He thinks it can be used to make people feel a certain way; a way he wants them to feel. And if he can manipulate how they feel, without them knowing it, well, it's basically like controlling them."

Jackie stood up. It was true. Just as he had experienced out on the lawn. It took him a few seconds to gather his thoughts. "That's...I don't know. It's fucking brilliant, actually. Audacious. But terrible. That was never what Empty Spaces was supposed to be about. I swear. Not at all. That never even dawned on me. I'm gonna go bust his fucking nose."

"No, wait. We'll talk. Besides, trust me, he's a lot fitter than you are." Pam stood up. The two hugged. "I'm glad you're here. I'm glad I got a chance to see you again, even like this."

"Excuse me?"

Prudence, like magic, was suddenly standing there, beside them, eyeing their embrace. Her words, without meaning, was more like a yelp.

Jackie had no idea what to say. Never a good sign, he thought.

"We're looking for the congressman."

"He's not in here. Obviously."

"We needed to talk, that's all."

"Prudence," Pam offered, "we needed to talk. That's all. If there's something between you two, well, I'm happy for you."

That was not expected, Prudence thought.

"I need to find the congressman also. He only just left, headed toward there." She pointed toward the tea room. "I think he said he needed to find his mother."

"I'll take you," said Pam. "Francis is there with her."

Jackie mistook this for an all-clear. A step behind the two women, he asked Pam: "how is Levon?"

Prudence stopped cold. Stared daggers. "Levon? Who is Levon?"

Pam turned, facing them both. Jackie never could master the art of knowing when to not speak, she thought.

"Levon was our dog," Jackie offered feebly. "Pam took him when she moved to DC." Pam nodded.

Prudence stared at Jackie for a few more seconds. "Oh." She started walking again. "Mom's allergic."

Barr was in the tea room, slouched, looking more obedient than defeated. Francis stood next to him. The old woman, in her wheelchair, stooped, frail, encircled, as if a prize the two men were fighting over.

"Mother. But what if this is true? That could explain the weak sales. Think of what it could do to the family business."

"God damn the family business, boy." The old woman wheezed, Her body was thin, brittle. But the sense of entitlement, of royalty, never faded. "Don't be a fool." The congressman was already turning pink.

Francis said nothing. He enjoyed this.

"Do you understand what I am saying? President. I am trying to make you the President of the United States. I turned this silly little chocolate business around. I made the Nutt Barr famous. Everything you see here, everything you have is because of me, Reginald. And I tell you it is not enough. This family could have a President. President!" She hacked again and expelled some spittle. "Look at you. You are my son. I love you. But despite everything I've done, you are not, dear boy, nor have you ever been, presidential material. I finally have a means to change that."

"No, you do not." Once again, Prudence was surprised by her tone. Neither Barr, Francis, nor the old woman had noticed the three interlopers approach.

"Who are these people, Pamela. Explain," commanded the old woman.

"I created Empty Spaces," Jackie interrupted. " Is that why you are manipulating how people feel?" No one spoke. "The thing you think will make your son President. It belongs to me."

"Mrs. Barr," offered Francis. "This is Jackie Paper. He worked on Empty Spaces. But I can assure you that it is now all ours."

"I have a copy of the source code. The notes. I compiled it. I know where every hook in the software resides."

"We have enough of it, Mr. Paper. Everything we need, in fact. Between Sickspack, his team, and Maxwell, it's ours. Already put to good use, obviously. Lawyers will do the rest should you try something foolish." Francis emphasized his smugness. He stepped in towards Jackie. "Besides, I know you. Fight to get it back? You don't have the guts. That's why Pam left you."

"But we can take the report public," Prudence spluttered. "The NIH study. What then? That would stop Empty Spaces dead in its tracks."

"What report," Francis responded? He looked about the room, happy to take charge. "An aborted NIH study? That was inconclusive? About cancer? Trust me. Everything's dead and buried. Go public and you will lose your job. Your benefits. Health coverage. No one will believe you, anyway. Besides, who would stop using Empty Spaces, even if you succeeded? It kills off the desire for marijuana? That's a small group on your side. Trust me. And as for chocolate --"

"Francis? You knew," asked the congressman? "You knew, from the very beginning what this could do to the family business. And you did nothing?"

Francis turned to the old woman, then back to the congressman. "Congressman. You continue to think small. If I hadn't pushed you, if your mother hadn't pushed you, where would you be? A minor congressman in a minor district with a regional candy company that you inherited? Running for president is about messaging, about making people see in you the desires and dreams and feelings they have for themselves. And making them viscerally dislike your opponents. They don't have to know why, they merely have to feel it. Empty Spaces is the means to that end, congressman. How can you still not understand that?"

"How come I was never told of any of this, Francis?" Pam began to calculate the scope of Francis's betrayal. "You pushed me to run a report you knew was a fake. What of my career?"

"Pam, love, if marijuana does anything, it makes it harder for messages to get through. We can't have that. You must know that."

"If Empty Spaces works so well," the congressman responded, "and you have your hands on it, Francis, then you can take it to anyone. Correct? You say you have the code, the technology. Forget the financial percentages, you possess what you want. It's not about the money."

Francis had honestly never expected the congressman to pick up on that. "What are your options, Congressman? Besides, you don't even like running the family business."

"Reginald?" The old woman edged her chair closer to her son. "I do not have much time on this earth. You were not the son I wanted. We both know this. You can redeem yourself. There is time. We will find someone for you. You will get married. You will have a child. You will act your part. And with this one's work," she pointed a bony finger toward Jackie, though she meant Francis, her arms were weak, "we can make you President. I believe. I am prepared to do whatever is necessary."

Theo entered the room.

"All together now? This day continues to surprise. Excuse me, Congressman, guests are seated, the press is outside waiting. It's show time. Ms. Drogeny, I can show you to your seat if you like."

TRACK EIGHT
All Things Must Pass

Come Together

"Come." Jackie pulled Prudence into a small room, where help was once kept out of sight. Everyone else had left, either to watch the congressman's speech, or, Jackie assumed, work through their own issues.

"Why in here? Are you going to stop this or not?"

"There is a reason I do not want to kill it off."

"Then how are you any different than that asshole out there?"

"Listen to me. Just let me speak. It's not what you think. Empty Spaces was a program. Ones and zeros. I should have left it at that. But I tried to do something else; bolt a dream on top of a piece of software. I never imagined that anything to do with Empty Spaces would harm anyone. I swear."

"But it does do harm. I don't understand why you resist this. Because you want to be rich?"

"No. I mean, I do want to be rich, obviously."

"What? Is it the marijuana?"

Jackie walked close to the window. Twisted the blinds fully open. Looked across the estate. A man with no home, no job, no children. Still with so much to lose, he realized. Empty Spaces. His big payday. JaDe. Prudence, maybe? "Tomorrow never knows." Time, he thought, to reveal his true self. He hoped words could suffice.

"Jackie?"

"Do you know that there is silicon on Mars? One planet, near Earth, with water and minerals, in our own completely average solar system. And it's one of what? Millions? Billions? There has to be life out there, Prudence. That's what this is all about. Seeking out life and making contact."

'Jackie --"

He raised his hand. "And if -- if – life exists beyond us, then it must have a way to communicate. Right? I mean, all life communicates. With itself. With those around it. This was my way, Prudence. That's all. Empty Spaces was my way of sending out a small harmless signal. Or so I thought. One that could escape Earth. One filled with our voices."

Jackie paused, stared back outside again. "Did you know that Earth actually makes noise? Solar winds colliding with the planet's magnetic core. There's a name for it. It's called Auroral Kilometric Radiation. That noise is a signal. Communicated into outer space. Meaning someone could pick it up. Like a radio signal."

"Oh my God. I understand."

Prudence wasn't sure to feel angry at Jackie, or sorry for him.

"Is that what this is about? Messages to outer space? Aliens? I had sex with a man who fucking believes in aliens. Lord, forgive me. No. Not believes in them. Tries to call them. Call fucking aliens!"

Jackie turned toward Prudence, grinned. His hair covered his eyes.

"I wanted to add our message, that's all. A message in a bottle, from all of us, in concert. Empty Spaces, when it hops, links people together – literally – and sends out their combined message."

"Jesus Christ. Lord, forgive me. So what's the message?"

Jackie paused. Gave an embarrassed smile.

"Well?"

"It's a song. A favorite song."

Prudence waited.

"From me to you."

"From me to you. That's the song?"

"From me to you. Clever, don't you think?"

"That's your message to aliens? Not even, like, coordinates or something?

"It had to be simple. Replicable from everywhere. The program takes a slice of power from each device. It then –"

Prudence looked sick, though her voice was piercing. "In the emptiness of space, a message that will ricochet throughout the heavens, for eternity, landing only God knows where, and that's your message? A pop song?"

"That's it. 'From me to you'. Music is my poetry. I was filling up the space between us all with music."

Prudence remained flummoxed.

Jackie wasn't sure if she needed comforting. "I included JaDe's favorite song, for, you know, if they ever want to respond."

"Respond? Jesus Christ. Lord, forgive me. Respond? Jackie…And what was his favorite song? For this return call from aliens? No. Don't tell me. I don't want to know. We don't have time for this. This is crazy, Jackie. Listen, I think… I think you are trying to convince yourself of something. Trying to hold onto something, even still. Let all that go. If it helps, Empty Spaces is popular. You did succeed. So what if you're not rich. If you have to work, just like everyone else. Trust me. It really isn't that bad. Maybe your dreams were naive or silly. Or maybe they were amazing. I don't know. Those are your dreams. That I understand. But this dream of yours, this particular one, as you realized it, is causing harm to people." She paused to breathe in. "There are new dreams."

"Despite everything, I'm proud of it. Really. It was quite the trick."

"Whatever you do after this, even if it's never as well-known as Empty Spaces, will still be just as much a reflection of you. Maybe even a greater one."

"Maybe. I'm not so sure. For most of us we're lucky to just be that one hit wonder."

Prudence brought herself closer to Jackie. "You need to kill it. Right now. Please. Will you? For me."

Jackie was prepared for exactly this question. He took in a breath, hoping to calm Prudence as much as himself.

"Thing is, I'm not sure I can."

Prudence completely surprised him with her response. She kissed him. Then spoke. "Yes you can. I know you can. I know I'm right about you. I've known it from the very first. Soon, we'll both probably have no job and no money. Mom will have a lifetime of I told you so's. But, I promise you, you can do this."

Jackie smiled. He wanted to believe her, madly. He wanted to succeed, even if only to thank Prudence for the faith she had in him. Though, truthfully, he could not. He simply had no idea how he could kill it off or shut it down.

His phone buzzed.

His knees went weak.

"What's wrong?"

Jackie turned a whiter shade of pale. He stared up toward the ceiling. Then back at Prudence. The phone buzzed again. He forced a smile.

"Jackie, what's wrong? Are you going to answer it?"

"No."

"Why?"

"It's not a call. It's a command."

"What do you mean?"

"A hack. Something I built in, you know, for my own purposes. Don't make a face. For if ever I need to go for broke."

"I don't understand."

Jackie pressed the speaker icon on his phone.

Prudence strained to hear.

"Live and let die."

[Empty Spaces downloads: 37,489, xxx]

Something

"Why can't you just shut it off!"

Prudence was growing increasingly frustrated. Jackie sat under a large tree, a tulip poplar, in full bloom, one of several on the grounds, attempting to piece his wayward thoughts together.

"What?" He was doing his best to bring his mind into focus. The fresh air, he thought, might help. That everything had fallen apart so quickly did not.

"Kill it. Make it stop. You created it. Turn it off!"

"It doesn't work that way. There's no such thing. Millions of people have downloaded it.

"Nonsense. The web can be shut down. It's been done."

"Not really."

"What about a pulse? An electromagnetic pulse? I've heard people talk about those."

"Science fiction bullshit."

"You have to do this, Jackie. Kill it."

"There is no kill switch to Empty Spaces, Prudence. It simply never occurred to me to consider building such a thing."

Kill Switch

A "kill switch" is a security device, physical or virtual, accessible remotely or on the device itself, that is used to shut down a machine or device or program should an emergency arise. Unlike a normal shut down, which follows a series of protocols in a manner that does not harm the device, for example, a kill switch is designed for an immediate abort.

Empty Spaces had no kill switch. In fact, Empty Spaces had no means of powering itself down or shutting itself off, under any circumstances. Even if all its servers were unplugged, literally, the program would continue to hop from phone to phone, possibly forever, as people sought to share their music and their feelings.

"I can't. Our only hope is to make people stop using it by telling them about the study."

"You have to! We'll never get our hands on that study. They'll have NIH scientists lined up against us."

"Are you not hearing me? Literally. I cannot shut it down. There is no means of shutting Empty Spaces down. I never thought of that, I don't know how to do that. I'm not sure it's even possible."

"But –"

"Unless..."

"Unless what? Whatever it is, do it."

"No. I mean, maybe if we were to shut down everyone's phone. Forget it. I was just trying to think of how it would even be possible. It's not. There is no Empty Spaces off switch. Period."

"Fuck!" Prudence looked around, as if someone would not only discover their plans, but admonish her for such foul language. "Then do the phone shut down thing. Do it. This is spreading."

"Yes, I know." He appeared to look through her.

For the first time, Prudence noticed something in Jackie. Love. For her. It was unmistakable. No music was necessary. Ignoring its ill effects on her killer dress, she sat down under the tree, on the grass, next to Jackie, smiled, and stared piercingly into his eyes. She leaned in close and kissed him. "Thank you. This isn't just about chocolate. I'm prepared to lose that. But if this can take chocolate from me, than what else from others? There must be a kill switch idea you overlooked. That's the source. I have faith."

Kill Switch (examples)

Kill switches are used in everything from large industrial machines, home gym equipment, computing software and communications networks. Examples:

- In a automobile engine, a kill switch interrupts the circuit delivering electrical power to the spark plugs, which, when shut down, means the engine's pistons stop functioning and the engine instantly stops.
- Various machinery that requires human oversight typically has a kill switch whereby if the operator becomes incapacitated, which can be determined by periodic responses, check-ins and/or physical connection with the machine itself, the machine shuts down automatically. Think lawnmowers, jet skis, trains, cranes, freight elevators.
- Gasoline pumps are designed to shut off at once should the pump be physically removed.
- Saws, lathes and the sort of large equipment one might find in a high school shop class is equipped with a kill switch.
- Some people believe, incorrectly, that some instruments, such as electric guitars, have a kill switch. False. And when Prudence mentioned that she had read something about this to

Jackie, and how it was somehow related, because it's music, he quickly, though gently, shot the idea down.

- Home treadmills have a kill switch. If the runner falls off, the device powers down.
- Computer software often includes a type of kill switch. That is, an algorithm embedded within the program that, should the user attempt to operate pirated software, the program either won't run, won't run all features or infects the user's entire computer.

Jackie wasted a good deal of time trying to dream up a possible Empty Spaces kill switch by thinking of all the ways computer software incorporates them. Prudence looked up, wondered what was happening at the main tent. The voice she heard did not sound like Barr's.

Jackie heard nothing, as he focused his energies on concocting a plan. The fact was, he had never considered a kill switch for Empty Spaces. Not once. Nor had he envisioned a scenario where such a thing might ever be desirable. Probably worse, at this moment, was that had he considered a kill switch, one that could shut Empty Spaces down inside every user's phone, he was reasonably certain, and he did not wish to admit this to Prudence, that he would have no idea how to create it. JaDe, God rest his soul, would not have been able to help, either.

Jackie considered his options:

- The last time he checked the numbers, and that was on the morning of his flight to DC, 27% of users had downloaded Empty Spaces directly via a server. While the majority of users, which numbered in the tens of millions, received the service as it hopped from one user to the next, Jackie felt that the server download path offered his best shot at shutting Empty Spaces down. No server access, and a crucial path for millions of new users is wiped clean. This would at least slow down its spread.
- No one knew the insides of Empty Spaces as well as he did. Including those hot shot engineers that Sickspack hired to go through it. They missed several important functions within the code. Even that Maxwell fucker assumed the additional energy burst was just sloppy coding.
- Most of the users, if server downloads were a reliable analog, were in Western countries. Possibly this was a bias in how the

software understood Western music, he thought. Some clue must be culled from this fact, he told himself.

"Well? Anything?
"A moment!" "Please."
Jackie stood up, stretched his legs. His back was sore. He only then noticed that another tree, merely a few feet away, held a bench swing. He walked to that, sat down, and rocked. Prudence followed. "I'm close. I just need to think this through."

- Despite issues related to servers or Western biases, anyone could be using Empty Spaces, at any location, this very moment. There were no boundaries, no gateway, no access point.
- Shutting down the servers would help. He could not do that from his smartphone, however, at least not without difficulty, but he could shut them down from his hotel, or possibly from inside the Barr house.
- The problem remained with the hop. It worked. Very well. How could that be stopped?
- And what if I do succeed? What, then? Does any solution harm the user? Their device? Someone's network? Data? Files they've saved? Their own music collection? If he shut it down, somehow, would that also shut down some user's phone right as they were calling their mother? Or an ambulance? Any solution might prove worse, he feared. At least, for some people.
- "Fuck." Jackie suddenly realized, amongst all the papers he signed with Sickspack, and with Rep Barr -- wait, did I sign anything with Rep Barr, he asked himself -- there was probably something in one of them where really really bad things, legal things, lawsuit things, prison things possibly, would happen to him should he do anything that might harm the service. Screw them, he decided.
- What would JaDe do?

He stopped the swing.
"I think I know what to do," Jackie said. Prudence stared back, not sure if she could believe him.
"Just like that?"
"It's crude. But it just might work."
"With a little help from your friends?"

Jackie winked. "I know a guy. A professor, I believe. In China. Well, not know him, exactly, but he knows me. And Empty Spaces."

"And he can kill it?"

"I think we can together. He probably knows this shit better than I do. "

"How are you going to make this happen?"

"Something JaDe told me. He thought my plan for Empty Spaces to hop from phone to phone would never work. Not because of technical reasons, but personal ones. Most people, he said, have crappy taste in music. His view, not mine. Which, at the time, I told him didn't matter, at least for my plans, because people with crappy tastes can hook up just the same. The song reflects the person. Only, JaDe said that people have such horrible taste in music that even they are embarrassed by it. Not just people with crappy taste, but everyone. They would never want to share that one favorite song, say, like the one they listen to only in the car, when they're all alone. The song they can't even let their spouse know they love."

"Not following. What's the plan, exactly?"

"I'm not going to shut down the program. I'm going to make it work even better."

"I thought --"

"Let me explain. I can access the servers. I already checked. Sickspack and Francis haven't completely shut off all my access points. With Gong Shwo's help, we quickly make Empty Spaces even better. Simply by making it even more personal. Much more personal than it ever was before. So that one song the user listens to when nobody is around, the song they would never share, the one that fully expresses who they are, at their most vulnerable, most private, will now be exposed to all."

Prudence looked as if she still did not follow.

"The users will kill the service off on their own. Because it's become too honest, too personal. Don't you understand? Empty Spaces learns. Tell it to not play a particular song, say, not share it, the program understands. It knows, if you will, that there are some things the user simply doesn't want revealed. The program learns that and doesn't play the song, even if it perfectly expresses who they are. People, as much as they share, as much as they share seemingly everything about themselves, do not truly share everything. It's too painful. Or embarrassing. Probably exhausting.

"We infect Empty Spaces by making it work even better. Those deep, dark truthful feelings, and the songs to match, are unleashed. If I'm right, users will shut it down voluntarily."

Prudence grabbed Jackie. Kissed him. "That's because I love you. I honestly love you." She released him. "Except. I do not see how this actually does anything. You and some Chinese guy, what's his name, are going to make one of the most popular new services on mobile devices work even better? This is your plan?"

"His name is Gong. He understands how I developed the service. He picked it apart. He knows how to get to any hidden code -- don't look at me like that – as well as anyone. Probably can do it faster and better than I could, I'm guessing. Certainly faster than Sickspack and Mustard."

"You can trust him?"

"I think so. He views it as a vulnerability. Plus, he's eager to learn how I built it."

"And he will he agree to this?"

"I won't give him a choice. I'm not totally convinced I can do this alone. And even if I can it will take much longer than I want. Possibly too long. I imagine once there are a certain number of users, maybe we've already reached that tipping point, there may be no going back. Only, let's not focus on that now. The plan is, the first time Empty Spaces, the new and improved Empty Spaces, shares the user's dirty little secret, they will voluntarily wipe it off their device. Or at least, never again use the service – meaning, no hop. It's like a denial of service in reverse. I'm not breaking any laws. I'm not harming the service. I'm making it better. There is nothing malicious occurring. It shouldn't harm anything else on the user's device. No data. Nothing. Except possibly very brief embarrassment."

Jackie pulled out his phone. "First, I start by being completely honest with Mr. Shwo. Except for the whole alien bit since in this instance, I think honesty will just slow things down."

"Fine. Just, do it now. Do it fast. I want this stopped. And I'm sure that fucker Francis, forgive me, dear Lord, already has people trying to remove your access. Wait. Did you hear that?"

Prudence wondered if someone was spying on them. The pair looked around, saw no one. They were, however, suddenly aware they had spent the past thirty minutes on the grounds of the Barr Estate, literally, during a very public, highly visible social function. Anyone could have spotted them, reported on them.

"We should probably leave now."

"Agreed. One more thing." Jackie again looked through her. "This doesn't reverse anything that's already happened, you understand, right?"

"You mean any calls to little green men?"

"No, silly. I mean, if there has been any damage to our brains, to certain receptors, say, the ones that help people like you enjoy chocolate, I don't know if this can reverse it. Or maybe it can reverse it for some people and not for others. Or just a bit for some and a lot for others. Whatever has already happened, I can't change."

"I don't have to love chocolate. I don't even have to like it. I can still live my life. But I know how wonderful it was for me. It would be nice if other people can feel the same."

"Isn't it ironic, don't you think? Killing it off by making it better."

"Right now, all irony is lost --"

"Wait! Before we leave. Let me tousle your hair."

Prudence pulled just out of reach. "Why, exactly? I'm having a perfect hair day."

"We have to walk past a lot of people to get back inside the house. We don't want them to think we were plotting something. If I mess your hair, they'll just think we were off somewhere doing it."

"Mess my hair and we may never do it again."

Jackie smiled. "But if I shut it down?"

"Shut it down and you can take me into that horse barn at the bottom of that hill and tear off my one really nice dress and have your way with me."

Maxwell's Silver Hammer

Jackie did not have sex with Prudence in the horse barn at the bottom of the hill on the grounds of Glockenspiel. Not because he failed. The motivation to put her nice dress back on, drive back out there and sneak inside the barn and find an actual spot to commingle had long since passed.

Owing to the skillful coding of Mr. Shwo and Mr. Paper, however, both of whom Prudence decided deserved her gratitude, albeit tendered very differently, Empty Spaces was brought down. Completely. In a matter of weeks. As the hostile, prickly Mustard and the yielding, befuddled Sickspack responded impotently, the last user abandoned the service forever; many not even sure why, exactly, they were no longer enamored with its serendipitous sharing of their feelings.

If Jackie and Prudence ever did have sex in Barr's horse barn, though, it quite possibly could be revealed to all in the digital pages of "Must Go Free," the popular new Beltway gossip rag started by Maxwell Edison. Despite his work for the turncoat Francis Mustard, mostly because of it, no one on the Hill would ever hire Maxwell again. Notwithstanding his obvious talents.

This turned out to be a blessing. For the raging, effectual Maxwell, at least. For he had plenty of dirt on most of the players in Washington, both the professionals and amateurs, and plenty of sources happy to provide dirt on all newcomers. Maxwell also, very quickly, had plenty of readers. In fact, millions of them, almost overnight, thanks to his luminous, if obvious, idea. Though a savvy programmer in his own right, it was the dirt, the salacious minutiae, the wild accusations, the audacious titillating rumors that Maxwell posted, rather than the look of his uncomplicated website that drew in the eyeballs. Day after day, several times a day.

Maxwell, in fact, not necessarily for the right reasons, became quite the Beltway celebrity.

"Must Go Free"
The Maxwell Report for August 16

BREAKING: YOUR NEXT CONGRESSMAN? WITH HIS PANTS DOWN!

MEET YOUR NEWEST HOTTEST NEWS BABE. CLICK HERE FOR SLIDESHOW.

CONGRESSIONAL STAFF SHAKEUP FOLLOWING INVESTMENT SCANDAL. THE STORY BEHIND THE STORY!

WHY WAS THIS NIH STUDY HALTED?

WHAT IS THE FIRST LADY WEARING?

BUSTED! CONGRESSIONAL STAFFER TAKES PICTURES OF HIS LOVER AS SHE SLEEPS!

SMELL THAT SMELL! THE RAPID RISE AND RAPID FALL OF A POPULAR MOBILE SHARING PLATFORM.

Oh! Darling

You can't always get what you want. However, you quite often do get what you need, even when not looking, even when not sharing. Empty Spaces, in its original incarnation, sought to provide a means of communicating with others; strangers, even. A means of sharing the true selves of its users; or, at least, an idealized version of such. Through music.

What was missing, however, was a means not of tuning in, but of turning off. A way to make everything stop, a way to shut everything down. With or without Empty Spaces, with or without phones and social media and status updates, whether true or false, and anonymous longings, and virtual chats, and flash mobs and long distance dedications, love will find a way.

That which people want to share most, it turns out, is, as it ever was, that moment when everything else fades away, and the happy collapse of time and space and circumstance, across the vast emptiness of space, changes them forever.

The beat goes on.

Octopus's Garden

For some, such as Michelle Maybelle, despite their critical role, evident if nonetheless in the background, not much has changed.

"I am a smart, capable, attractive and highly successful woman," Michelle reminded herself. "I have two degrees, a precious cat, a brand new husband who loves me. Friendships. Money. Influence. Why do I read this shit every morning?"

Michelle put her smartphone away vowing once again to better resist the easy lure of Beltway gossip that the Maxwell Report giddily supplied every morning.

"Beltway porn," she mumbled.

She would not keep her vow.

Far worse than this minor transgression, however, yesterday and today, and tomorrow never knows, she would choose to ignore the fact, despite her new husband's growing suspicions, that at every lunch, at every dinner, at each of her sister power mashups, and sometimes at other times, Michelle Maybelle required at least two full glasses of wine to make it through the day. Every day.

I Want You (She's So Heavy)
[38 Likes]

Yes, I am pregnant.

No, it was most definitely not planned.

Had you told me a year ago that I would meet someone, that I would have sex with that someone, that I would get pregnant by that someone, and that someone would be the kind of person to convince me to announce my pregnancy to my dearest friends, and the entire world, all at once, with the touch of a button, well, I would say you were rambling as much as I am now.

But, it's true. I am pregnant. "We" are pregnant.

Yes, it changes everything.

Yes, that is a good thing.

All things must pass. This is the start of a new life, truly. A new beginning. Yes, for both of us. It's like a double fantasy, really. Even if it is a touch overwhelming at times.

I honestly had no idea how many groups – people – were out there that catered to someone like me. First time pregnant, early in the pregnancy, not sure how to cope, wanting to learn everything that being a mother requires.

Knowing there's always someone out there, maybe they live down the hall or thousands of miles away, someone I don't even know, someone not trying to sell me something, just trying to help me, answer my questions, reach out and offer support, share their knowledge, makes me think that those who say things like now is the worst time to bring a child into this world are just so sad and wrong.

As for me, most of the time the only thing I can feel, that are not aches and pains, or a craving for a juicy well-cooked hamburger with exactly catsup, mustard and one onion slice, is...bliss. Strangely enough, no chocolate cravings. None at all.

Yes, the attachment is a picture of my stomach. No, you do not need to look away. This will be the first and only picture of my belly you will see until long after the birth.

And, yes, mother is happy. Mother is truly, deeply, without reservations happy.

And I love her.

P.S. A big hug for the always amazing Michelle Maybelle. She recently started her own business and has asked me to join her! It's a mobile banking start-up to be run by women for women. Of course, I will have to give up my steady government paycheck and benefits, but

Michelle is very persuasive. Besides, what has playing by the rules ever gotten me?

Oh, yes. Everything I could ever ask for!

Here Comes the Sun

Jackie woke up, got out of bed. Clicked on his to do list, which, just by having one he counted as a deep, personal failing.

- Finalize resume.
- Get haircut.
- Interview at 3pm.
- Company focus: Global digital security packet API enhancements for mobile government field workers in temporary non-secure environments over public metered channels.

Question: What do you see yourself doing in five years, Mr. Paper?
Answer: Killing all of you.

Prudence probably had fairly low expectations on the job front, for now at least. But Jackie knew she was going to hold firm on the hair. The fact that she had written, very specifically, in pen, on her nice stationery, what to wear for his job interview was, he took it, further proof that her recent demand for a husband who at least looked professional when going into a job interview was unwavering. Plus, she texted him once more: HAIRCUT!

Which was fine with Jackie. If everything is going to change, and it is, than a new look might help. No point in living in the past.

The sun streamed through the blinds. Jackie was sure he could pull all of this off. Forever, if necessary.

Because

Blog: Daytripper
While my guitar gently weeps. The final post of Daytripper.

A very wise man once said, "and those are the memories that make me a wealthy soul." I am rich because I have so many memories of JaDe Shockwatel. I remember JaDe and I going to the Asian supermarket not far from the apartment, back in Vancouver. JaDe, who rarely liked venturing too far from home, loved the Asian market. This black man from western Michigan, chosen at an early age to play football, had, somehow, by magic, wound up thousands of miles away, in British Columbia. And at a grocery store surrounded by what he viewed as positively enchanting foods; of a kind he had never seen before, never heard of, never imagined. Things like lotus root, daikon, hairy melon. That always made him laugh. Plus, all the fish, the amazing assortment of seafood, from all over the world, and the old Chinese women always complaining, always talking too loud. "The farther one travels," he told me, "the less one knows."

JaDe is Dead

I know I'll often stop and think about him. Never again, though, will I speak with him, spend time with him, share with him. Each time I think of this I feel ready to cry.

Not that long ago, though it seems to me an eternity now, JaDe was murdered. I did not see JaDe die. I was not with him. Near him, yes, but not with him. A man described as a black male, late 20s or early 30s, 5'6", 140 pounds, light skin, wearing a gray Georgetown Hoyas t-shirt and dark blue or black cotton jogging pants shot JaDe as he entered a residence on the Southeast section of Washington, DC.

Yes, JaDe was there to buy marijuana. Yes, I made him go to Washington. No, this cannot be changed.

I met JaDe many years ago. I had my own radio show at the Vancouver co-op station. It was about manifestations of God and spirit in popular music, called I Am and So Are You. Once at week, 11pm - 2am. JaDe called in regularly, made surprisingly astute requests; songs I had never heard. Then he started texting me. Then we met. Then we became friends. Then I moved in.

Now he's dead.

I attended JaDe's funeral. This was not easy to do. His parents were devastated, obviously. I can think of nothing worse than having your son dead, murdered. The funeral took place at St Bernard's near Muskegon, Michigan. On the shore of Lake Michigan. The sky was bright, a cool wind was blowing off the lake. The service was nice. The people were nice. The memorial was nice. The cemetery. The plot. The headstone. All of it. Hauntingly, depressingly nice.

And no one's music matched my own.

Perhaps one day, I will post pictures of the service. Not today.

JaDe's parents asked me to ship out some of his belongings. We hugged. I tried to tell them about his life in Vancouver. About the business we were hoping to build. How much he liked it out there.

JaDe always said he never wanted to play in the NFL. This was not completely true, apparently. His dad told me that JaDe once confessed to him that he was unlikely to be drafted. His father, who had been so proud of his son, coached him when he was young, helped get him a scholarship at Michigan, came to believe that JaDe could never let his old man down. Knowing he wasn't going to make it in the NFL, JaDe simply never tried, and therefore never failed. He left for Canada, for Vancouver, thousands of miles away. Making a new life for himself there; escaping what he thought were expectations he could never reach. JaDe was wrong.

"JaDe never could let me down," his father said. "I loved him so much. Not making it into the NFL was never a disappointment to me. I was always so proud of him. If JaDe made it or not or had some other dream, I was okay with that. I only wanted what made him happy."

This did not make me either of us feel any better. Not that his father was trying to, I suppose.

Another wise man once said, "there is no dark side of the moon really. Matter of fact, it's all dark."

Indeed.

JaDe is dead. Dust in the wind. There's nothing you can do that can't be done. Sucks, I know.

Out.

TRACK NINE
Cloud Nine

You Never Give Me Your Money

Jackie rolled over in bed. Prudence was gone. He was alone. His last remaining days of freedom, he thought. Months of sporadic contract work, over. Monday, three short days from now, he would begin a new job. A regular job, finally, with hours and a desk and a boss and an actual water cooler in the actual break room.

"Can't have a child and not have a job," he reminded himself.

He reached for his phone. Despite the ungodly early hour, which would soon prove much later even than his new wake time, there was already a series of messages.

"Balls." He was attempting to sanitize his language, with spotty results.

First message
Dear Graduate,

Our congratulations on your success with EMPTY SPACES. We hope you always remember the special influence that your university had on your career. At the U-M, philanthropy is about more than dollars or cents. It's about you – improving life for people here and around the globe through your support for a great public university.

We invite you to read about your fellow U-M donors and how they've made great things happen in arts, education, health and the student experience. Then share your own giving story and inspire others to join you in making the world a better place. You can give cash, securities or other assets to an endowment you create.

"Out of college, money spent," Jackie thought.

Was that a cry? Jackie lifted his head up. No. The baby was still asleep. Sweet, merciful father.

Second message
Dear Mr. Paper:

Newby & Best are intellectual property counsel for Koschmider Corp. It has come to our attention that your EMPTY SPACES product incorporates several features that are claimed by our client's patent (see attached). Pursuant to the attached, Koschmider Corp claims exclusive ownership to the name EMPTY SPACES, all related names, registrations, licenses, licensees, worldwide trademarks, code, algorithms and any user data associated with the use of the EMPTY SPACES product and other services, data and applications used in connection with the service, manufacture and distribution of EMPTY SPACES.

Koschmider Corp has advised us to litigate this matter in accordance with their property rights and the fullest extent of the law. Please feel free to contact us at your convenience. We look forward to hearing from you.

Very truly yours,
Johnny Gentle
From the Law Firm of Newby & Best

United States Federal Trademark Registrations:
Mark Reg. No. Reg. Date
KOSCHMIDER CORP 0J,023,573L

Third message
Going to see mother. Back soon.
Much love.

Jackie set his smartphone back on the nightstand. Turn and face the strange changes my ass, he thought. And quickly fell back asleep.

Sun King

MOONBEAM SANCTUARY
Dearest You,
As the light of the moon is a reflection of the sun's rays, so too must you be a reflection of your truest self. At Moonbeam Sanctuary we offer a holistic healing environment designed to collapse your stresses and complexities and liberate your inner light.

WELCOME

Morning had broken. Sickspack Shankar passed what was now a make-shift chiropractic room, a steam room, a massage and acupuncture room. He walked past the men's quarters, the women's quarters. He entered the sunlit meeting space, with its new welcome sign. Once a place for business meetings and deals and greed and duplicity and now a place for discovery.

His skin appeared a richer brown than before and he now sported a short beard, mostly gray. The radiant smile, as always, remained. He was greeted by a familiar marble Buddha statue.

Potential investor-participants in his latest venture had gathered here at the break of dawn to hear his pitch. Moonbeam would combine a holistic facility, healing institute, sanctuary, and serve as the leading intellectual voice in unleashing the fullest potential of those wealthy individuals who sought to optimize their true self.

Three men and two women greeted Sickspack as he entered. The room was brightly lit, far too hot, with a lush spread of vegan food laid out on small table against the back wall. The room was filled with plants, an electric-powered waterfall that ran over a series of brown stones, Tibetan bowls, shaman drums and mostly pleasant odors. There was also a very large gong which was placed there in a past life. And gentle, calming music. None of that electronic music which always made Sickspack feel quite ill.

"Loving regards," said Sickspack, who wore a loose-fitting white pullover shirt and matching pants of fine Egyptian cotton. He also sported comfortable sneakers with no laces. "I know you. You know me. I am proposing, with your participation, that we break down the borders of consciousness, the limitations of expression, and the very notions of value and self-worth."

He gently raised his left arm as the female yoga master motioned to speak. "Moonbeam Sanctuary will offer personalized, holistic and ongoing treatments for an elite clientele. We will facilitate their transition from the present, which ends, as it always must, to a more eternal and communal realm. Only through a spiritual-bodily interaction, to be accelerated by each of you, can this be achieved. All I require is for you to seize upon this vision. And $100,000 each in seed money. Now, please. Your questions."

Sickspack leaned over for a bite of hummus.

Mean Mr. Mustard

Rep. Barr Appoints Theo Preston as Chief of Staff

Washington, D.C. U.S. Representative RKO Barr has appointed Theo Preston as his Chief of Staff. Theo was born in Baltimore, Maryland to Billy J. and Cilla Black Preston and raised in Rappahannock, VA. Theo is the oldest of two. His mother is on the

Rappahannock city council. His father sings the blues for The Handbags and the Gladrags.

Theo attended University of Virginia on scholarship and graduated suma cum laude with a BA in Speech and Communication. He has a JD from George Washington University.

Theo specializes in American manufacturing policy, and the use of tax credits to spur technology innovation. "With the continued loss of millions of domestic manufacturing jobs, Virginia and America must create new incentives to ensure American companies keep and create good-paying jobs here at home," said Mr. Preston. "That is the primary mission of Representative Barr and I am proud to serve him in this role."

Francis Howerd Mustard has accepted a position with the RIAA, a lobbying organization representing the music industry. The Office of Congressman Barr wishes Mr. Mustard continued success in his future endeavors.

###

It was early. Theo drained the last of his coffee, and scanned the release one last time. He verified the distribution list. No, you watch your back, Mustard, he thought.

[Send]

In an instant, the press release was available to the world.

Theo leaned back in his chair, a chair that once belonged to Francis Mustard. He briefly considered how he might re-furnish the office. Next, he reached for a tablet and switched on the local morning news. It was a commercial. Theo pulled out his phone and texted Pam: "good luck babe!"

Barely a mile away, in a posh office on nearby K Street, where resided numerous well-heeled lobbying groups, though which for him might as well have been located on some distant planet, Francis Mustard could not free his mind from a single recurring thought, one that spun round and round like an old record: I should have killed that queer when I had the chance.

Francis now earned quadruple his old salary, had an expense account with minimal oversight, and a driver on call. All of which, he knew, which he felt, was a posh prison cell, nothing more. His path to power, his manifest destiny, had been cut down and taken from him. His future, stolen.

"I should have killed that queer when I had the chance."

Polythene Pam

"Good morning, ladies and gentlemen, and welcome back to Breakfast with Hawk & Dove, the number one breakfast news show for the nation's capital. Joining Hawk & Dove this morning, on her very first assignment, our new Lifestyle Features correspondent, Pamela Ann Drogeny."

Pam took a seat at the couch, joining the two hosts, both white, both pushing 60 though pretending they were pushing 50, and each wearing dark suits and bright power ties. The form fitting blue dress and matching high heels revealed Pam's well-constructed figure, tapered calves, thin ankles. Her skin was just tanned, her teeth a bright white, lips, full and red, her blonde hair hung down past her shoulders, the bangs covering her forehead -- a last minute change by the stylist Pam wasn't completely on board with. She wore a silver necklace and no other jewelry.

"Welcome, Pam."

"Thank you, Hawk. Thank you, Dove."

"Tell us, what do you have in store for us this beautiful morning," Hawk asked, reaching for the mug on the small round coffee table set before them.

Pam made a quick mental note to have the producer either ditch the table or get a glass one. No one could see her legs.

"Well, lads, for my first assignment, I visited the original Nutt Barr Co. factory near Rappahannock. This historic building houses one of the oldest continuously operational chocolate factories in America. The company was recently sold to Brazil's Cachaca conglomerate. I'll have that coming up right after this commercial."

"And...we'll also be bringing you more on breaking political news, the weather, and wait until you see what this mother of three tried to do at her local car wash. Back in 2."

As the producer signaled 'cut', he winked at Pam. It had gone even better than she dared expect. She knew, instinctively, that this is exactly where she belonged. And neither the bright lights, the sizable crew or the two long-time news anchors touching her as they moved in close for a still shot, the pricks, rattled her in the least. She did, however, feel a touch sick in her stomach. And wondered if anyone could possibly notice the imperceptibly slight bulge in her tiny belly. And, for only the first time in her life, she craved fish.

"God, I hate that mother fucking Norski asshole," she thought. And steeled herself to keep the bile down.

She Came in Through the Bathroom Window

"Oh, look out!"

Ganja yelled from the bathroom.

Honah poked her head inside. As always, both women were wearing the pale blue partly cotton uniform that the Mrs. felt fully befitted their station.

"What?"

"She dead. Dead as fuck."

"Not just asleep? You sure?"

"Dead. And stank like dead."

"Call Dr. Robert. Come take this mean old bitch away."

Ganja stepped out of the bathroom and walked to the parlor. She plopped herself down onto the white couch she, like all staff, were expressly forbidden to sit on. She twisted her body, put her feet up on the couch, kicked off her dirty shoes. "I'm done cleaning the shit off that witch." She lit herself a joint. "Kill that smell."

Honah followed her into the room. She draped herself on the white chair across from Ganja. Ganja reached across, handed Honah the cigarette.

"It's Friday. Let that gay son of hers find her."

"If he ever comes to visit."

Honah took another drag, passed the joint back to Ganja. A haze of smoke was already beginning to overpower the venerable elegance of the room.

"It's such a nice day, outside. I'll open a window." "Good day, sunshine."

"There's gotta be something of that bitch's we can steal." "Bedroom first," Honah replied.

Golden Slumbers

Prudence walked alone through the gates of The Family Stone, yellow daisies, her mother's favorite, clutched at her breast. Her mother's death, she knew, was not a shock, no matter how sorrowful. A new baby, a husband, a new life had all hastened acceptance upon her. The pain, she realized, stemmed less from her mother's actual passing, which was painful enough, and more from her mother never having a chance to see her beautiful grandchild.

Prudence walked past a number of headstones. A few had fresh cut flowers. Some had small flags placed in front. All were well tended. As she turned, walking on grass now toward her mother's gravesite, a car drove past the nearby access road, slowly; searching. Prudence came upon her mother.

CYNTHIA SKIFFLE
Bittersweet

"Everyone of us has all we need." That's what mother used to say, Prudence reminded herself.

"More flowers for you, mother. I know you like them."

She paused, alone but self-aware. Prudence then knelt onto the ground, absentmindedly removed some of the grass from around the headstone. "I am glad you saw how great Jackie is for me, mother. He really is a wonderful husband, a wonderful father. The baby, of course, your grandchild, is perfect. And, yes, looks just like you."

"I'm not sure what else to tell you. Everyday was just like the last for so long and then, suddenly, I was in a whole new world. And without you. But with people now who love me even as much as you always did, mother. Which helps."

Prudence made the sign of the cross, said a brief prayer, and raised herself up.

"Oh. Guess what? Pam sent me a very nice card yesterday. And a beautiful silk blanket for the baby. I think she's happy for me. For all of us. Honestly. I heard there's a young man who has her old job at the FCC. Apparently, he's quite handsome, and single. Pam's minions now fight over him. Isn't that funny?"

"I want you to know mother, that I am happy. I don't have any regrets, certainly not of all the time we spent together. Even when it was hard, when I felt, only sometimes, that I was being cheated out of something greater. Not true. Still…"

Prudence looked up.

"It's time for me to fly."

Carry that Weight

A NEW LEADER FOR A NEW VIRGINIA

Congressman Barr had to chuckle at the headline in the OUT Magazine spread on him. He was neither new and had been a part of Virginia, still old, all his life. He did, however, fancy himself a leader. Plus, his new striped suit and wide purple tie and new black leather shoes made him feel almost visible.

To be fair to the magazine, Barr was just as wrong about everything, he knew, as the writer was about him. Not so long ago, Barr thought, he would have been utterly terrified if:

- Mother died
- Anyone even suspected he was homosexual
- The family business was gone

Yet, in the span of a few weeks, all three had happened, in rapid succession. Each time, shockingly, rather than terror, it was as if a weight had been lifted from him.

Barr's homosexuality, for many reasons, most wrong, had now become a shining public beacon of Southern blue blood meets contemporary Virginia. He was now something of a minor folk hero. Plus, his party was now in power, meaning even more would come to kiss the ring.

Naming Theo his Chief of Staff, and ensuring the young, highly photogenic man had a prominent role in his office, if well-earned, brought out an entire new cadre of supporters. The money from selling the Nutt Barr business could now be used exactly as he wanted, and without requiring any real decisions on his part. Life was good, he thought. Getting better all the time.

The End

Jackie cupped the boy, his dear baby son, Lonnie Donegan Skiffle Paper, in his arms. He was so small, soft; smelled so fresh, truly. The portly, pale infant was comfortable in his cotton diaper and small white tee, joyfully oblivious to the drool pooling down the front. In Jackie's hands, the little boy sprang to life, giggling, even at a mere three months old, in a manner that consumed his entire body.

Jackie lifted the boy high over his head, and brought him back down. Then again. And again. Cocoa, their chocolate brown poodle, instinctively protective of the child, barked out a reprimand.

After Cyn's death, Jackie and Prudence culled many old belongings, converted the second bedroom into theirs, and turned Prudence's old room into a nursery. Much was tossed out, given away, or sold off. Though not all. At Prudence's insistence, many of the mother Mary paintings and all the crosses now hung liberally from the bedroom walls, despite Jackie's minor protestations. The nursery also housed the dog's food, spare toiletries, and served as a storage space for sheets, blankets and other items. Including, Jackie knew, many of Cyn's belongings that Prudence would probably never let him throw out.

Jackie rubbed noses with his boy. Both laughed. Cocoa barked. Prudence entered.

"Treats! Yeah!" Jackie spoke up for both him and his new son.

"Your favorite," said Prudence, holding out a tray of her specially prepared double stuffed brownies. "Just the way you like them."

Jackie took one, ate it, leaned over to kiss his wife.

"You woke him," she said. "We agreed on a schedule."

"You agreed. Besides, I did not wake him. He was already awake."

Jackie held Lonnie high again. "And I will raise you up," he said in a rising voice.

"Be careful."

"He likes it."

"He may like it but it upsets his stomach."

Jackie brought the boy down and pulled him in close. He kissed the child a bit too vigorously then placed him gently back in the crib. Jackie took a second brownie, smiled at Prudence. They both looked down at their child.

"He's so small."

"Of the angels come."

"Quiet. He's falling asleep. On his own."

The couple softened their voices. Jackie stroked the boy's cheek, unable to stop himself. He stared into Lonnie's eyes, which were now no longer fighting sleep.

Prudence sang out, softly. "One two three four five six seven, All good children go to Heaven..."

Jackie whispered. "I sure do pray that all the world is right with you, little one. Always. If I could only make it so."

"And they have built a home sweet home," Jackie sang, barely above a whisper.

The quiet of the moment was abruptly pierced by the discordant ring of a phone. Both his and Prudence's phone, in fact. Cocoa barked.

Again, the phones rang out, louder and harsher than Jackie had ever recalled. Followed quickly by a song; a song he knew well, if one he never expected to hear.

Prudence stared at him, reached for the nearest phone. He stopped her.

"Let it be."

For Jackie, nothing outside their tiny happy home mattered. His little boy smiled, eyes wide open once more, every part of his tiny happy self joyful and light, fully in the moment.

"Obla di obla da…"

Outside their apartment, and all over the world, millions of other phones refused to stop ringing.

Each was playing the same song.

JaDe's favorite.

"What a long strange trip it's been."

[EMPTY SPACE]

Her Majesty

I would be remiss
if, in closing,
I failed to
thank my dear
wonderful wife,
who's truly only
gotten better
with time.
None of this
would be possible
without her.

[EMPTY SPACE]

Coming Soon!
It's All Too Much
Book 2 in The Empty Spaces trilogy

Excerpt:

Call me Bob. I am the Zimmer Man.
And this is The Madonna.

Coming Later!
You Won't See Me
Book 3 in The Empty Spaces trilogy

Excerpt:

God is a black man with no sight.
God is a black man with no sight.
God is a black man with no sight.

Endless Nameless

This is a work of fiction. That should be obvious. But those and that which helped me are, indeed, quite real. I wish to thank the people, works and things that inspired and sustained me throughout the surprisingly arduous process of writing a book. These include but are certainly not limited to:

- The Beatles
- Mystery Science Theater, particularly Soul Taker, Atomic Brain, and Space Mutiny
- Better Made Hot Chips
- Again, my wife
- Driving in the car, alone, or with my boys, or with college buddies, on long road trips
- West End Blues, by Louis Armstrong
- Scrivener
- iPhone, MacBook Pro and the products of Steve Jobs
- Chocolate
- A rare, live recording of The Velvet Underground from March 15, 1969

You may reach me at brianshall@gmail.com or at www.brianshall.com.

First Edition: November 2011
ISBN: 978-0615551333